Caffeine Nights Publishing

Night Is Watching

Lucy Cameron

Fiction aimed at the heart
and the head...

Published by Caffeine Nights Publishing 2017

Published in Great Britain by
Caffeine Nights Publishing
4 Eton Close
Walderslade
Chatham
Kent
ME5 9AT

www.caffeinenights.com

British Library Cataloguing in Publication Data.
A CIP catalogue record for this book is available from the British Library

ISBN: 978-1-910720-43-1

Also available as an eBook

Cover design by
Mark (Wills) Williams

Everything else by
Default, Luck and Accident

Acknowledgements

Where to even begin to thank all of the people who have made this book possible? The first thanks goes to my family and friends who listened to me talk about this idea for years before finally sitting down to write. A huge thank you to Graham Smith and the Crime and Publishment gang for their ongoing belief and support. Thank you to Kelly and Stewart Rae, Bob and Carol Bridgestock, Karen Campbell-Ace, Tom Branney and Mike Craven for procedural hints and tips, and Matt Hilton and Ron Butlin for the kick start support I needed to get this show on the road. Thank you to everyone at Dumfries Writers for helping me improve my writing tenfold, to the Theatre Royal gang for sending me home when I needed to write and all my friends and family who have read various drafts of this book and given me their thoughts. Thank you to Darren and Caffeine Nights for taking a risk and believing in me.

And last, but by no means least, thank you to my dad, Jim, for reading every draft of the book with support and encouragement and letting me live in his shed for years to make this dream a reality.

For Mum and Dad.

Thank you for teaching me to believe anything is possible.

Night Is Watching

1.

The woman is still alive as her blood drains, her face contorts in a twisted, silent scream. He has hung her upside down for ease and pleasure and her soft, naked flesh still goosebumps to his touch. Her hands hang inches from the carpet, suspended in a macabre pirouette. He never did ask her if she liked to dance. Her long brown hair twists like a rope to the floor, appearing to anchor her in place. Her lips part then press soundlessly back together, her eyelids flicker.

He steps slowly from the corner. He tilts his head to inspect her, but finds nothing, so blows her a tender kiss, turns off the light and leaves her alone in the dark.

Detective Sergeant Rhys Morgan arrives at the scene at one-fifteen a.m. on a bleak Monday in late October. He's not the first to arrive and won't be the last. He watches from inside a standard-issue car. The air hangs heavy with the promise of rain. The street is lit up with flashing blue lights and overspill from nosy neighbours' front doors, their dressing gowns pulled tight, necks straining to get a glimpse of what is happening at number fourteen. Blue and white police tape is strung wide, gripping onto slippery lamp-posts, sagging where it has been lifted to allow those unlucky enough through.

A tall man appears at the front door. His skin, normally rich and dark, seems pale. He runs his hands over his shaved head and inhales deeply. The street audience hold their breath. He murmurs to the young female Constable who stands guard. Her fingers tremor slightly against the dark clipboard. Rhys knows this man. They worked together in what feels like another life, used to be friends. Used to be close.

Detective Constable Dan Davies.

Davies squints, shields his eyes from the glare of the lights then heads slowly over. He speaks as he climbs into the car,

'Alright?' Rhys stares straight ahead. 'Long time, no see.' Davies taps his fingers on the dashboard, rubs the stubble on his chin. 'Look, Rhys—'

'Tell me about them.' Rhys nods towards the house, eyes blinking in time with the flash of blue lights. Davies taps his fingers on the dashboard again.

Tap. Tap. Tap. Then he stops, his shoulders drop and he starts talking, staring the whole time through the slowly misting windshield.

The call came in to the front desk from a concerned neighbour at around midnight. She was walking her dog and thought she saw movement in the otherwise still house. She knew the residents and was under the impression they had gone up north to visit their only son, Tony.

Rhys turns and looks at Detective Constable Dan Davies, his profile dark against an even blacker night.

The neighbour said they made the trip north often, but usually asked her to look after their cat. She didn't find it odd that this time they had not. The neighbour was vague, unsure. She hadn't seen them for a day, possibly two, perhaps three. The line of Davies's jaw tightens. Two Constables had been dispatched...

Davies's words trail off, his head bows. Rhys turns his face away, looks back towards the house.

Shadows grow and shrink in the front hall of number fourteen. In the silence another man is spat out. He is short with pale, doughy skin, at home here, but this is not his house. He marches over; the icy blast of night air as he wrenches open the door is a physical assault.

'About bloody time.' His accent is not local. He nods to the car. 'If you two have finished your little chat in here...' A fat finger pokes into Rhys's space. '...there's some actual work to be done in there.' He strides away, the car door bouncing against its hinges.

Rhys joins him on the front step.

'I assume you are...' The short man holds Rhys's eye as he removes his notebook. 'Detective Sergeant Rhys Morgan?' He doesn't offer his hand. 'Detective Inspector Pat Quinn.' Quinn tilts the notebook just enough for Rhys to see the page is blank. 'Hope we didn't wake you?' Quinn smiles, a movement at odds with the rest of his face. He snaps shut the notebook. 'You best follow me.' Quinn nods to the side of the house, replaces the notebook and pulls out a packet of nicotine-replacement gum. 'There's access to the kitchen through the back porch.' His lips smack open and shut. There's a glint of something in his eye. 'Hope you've fully digested your dinner.'

They squeeze their way around the edge of the house into the back garden. Tacked onto the back of the property is a small porch crammed with coats, wellington boots, umbrellas, plant pots and numerous other items with no place else to go. Another Constable stands guard. He's young and clings to his clipboard like a life raft. He takes Rhys's details, doesn't quite manage to hide the tremor in his pen. Rhys and Quinn climb into their white paper boiler suits, struggle to balance, tie everything tight. Crime Scene Investigators are in place, their lights positioned, bathing the home in stark yellow light. Doubtful this is how the inhabitants would have imagined it would end.

The heat from the house hits Rhys as soon as he steps into the porch. The carpet tiles are worn and dirty and covered in a light shower of broken glass. Quinn stops and turns, silhouetted against the light from the kitchen like a giant cartoon.

'Through there, in the kitchen, we have one white female who appears to be in her late fifties.' Quinn's voice is loud in the confined glass box. 'Looks like she lives here with her hubby. Neighbours have said the son lives up north. Why the hell anyone would want to do that? Your guess is as good as mine.' Over Quinn's shoulder Rhys sees an array of smiling faces in picture frames on the yellow kitchen wall. On a cruise, on a beach, at a wedding. Moments of happiness captured behind glass. The one nearest the door is crooked. Quinn's clammy face smiles. 'After you.' He steps back allowing Rhys to inch past.

Detective Sergeant Rhys Morgan worked missing persons, not murder, missing persons. Everyone knew that. He didn't work for promotion or glory, or luckily as it turned out, money, he needed to find all the missing and lost and make sure they got home. He needed them to know someone cared for them when they no longer cared for themselves.

'Rhys,' Divisional Superintendent Wallace had said a few days earlier, his tone as flat and smooth as a lake. 'They need a hand over at King's Mill and I know you're the man for the job.'

'King's Mill, but that's murder, sir?'

'Oh come on, Rhys. It's not that bad.' Wallace smiled at his own joke. 'I prefer to look at it more like a temporary move, broaden your horizons, "mix it up a bit" as they say. They need some support.' He held Rhys's gaze 'You, are that support.' Wallace ran bony fingers down his lapel.

'But, sir, what about–'

'Your current caseload will be covered.'

'That's not what I was.... Murder... You know why I'd rather not, sir, I mean come on–' The Divisional Superintendent held up a silencing hand.

'Life is littered with things we don't want to do, Detective Sergeant.' Rhys's superior's tone dropped a degree colder. 'I have given them your contact details. You're to check in with Detective Inspector Pat Quinn first thing Monday morning.' He pushed a brown A4 envelope across the desk. 'Here's a brief outline of the current case.'

And here he was, simple as that.

Rhys's mouth dries as he steps into the room, something sticks at the back of his throat. The kitchen is small and claustrophobic. The woman's body hangs right in front of him, dominating the space, an elaborate sculpture in a poorly hung exhibition. Quinn's hand is on his shoulder. He points to the floor. Rhys takes his steps with care.

'We're pretty certain it's Cathy Reynolds,' says a voice that could be Quinn's. Everything tilts, slightly off-balance. The rest of the room seems suddenly far way, like Rhys and Cathy are the only two people in the world.

A butcher's hook is screwed into the ceiling, slightly off-centre. The rope that hangs her by the ankles is rough, bloodied where she twisted and struggled. Her naked body sags in all the right places, but in the wrong direction.

Her skin would be soft to his touch.

Rhys tilts his head, his mouth too dry to swallow. The sound of his heart throbs in his ears.

The cut to her throat is deep and black, the skin puckered right to left. Not quite a smile, but not sad. It had been done as she hung there full of life. Her face is streaked from a black red, to a pale pink where the blood has turned from a gush to a trickle, blocking her nose and filming her eyes. The wrinkles and creases like scabs, drying in the overheated kitchen.

It's her facial expression that stops Rhys's heart.

A twisted, unrecognisable scream. Frozen mid-movement in a way Rhys can't quite understand. A pure terror has stretched and pulled at her flesh. Is it this fear that has bulged her eyeballs?

Rhys kneels down and holds his face close to Cathy Reynolds, half expecting her to move, to feel her icy fingers grab his arm, hear a scream from her contorted mouth. There's no way to tell if the cold rush against his face is from her, or his imagination. A sudden movement at the edge of his vision causes Rhys to turn. There's nothing there, just a breeze creeping through the house, or possibly the cat making a break for freedom now the doors are open.

Rhys rises. Eyes held by Cathy Reynolds' blood-red stare. The twist to her face tugs at the base of his stomach.

The kitchen floor is covered with more cheap carpet tiles, the same garish yellow as the walls. Tiles that should be soaked deep crimson, not splashed and sprayed. Not drips and pools. Not an expanding spectrum of red to orange. There is blood, plenty of blood, a twisting spray across the kick boards, up the dated laminate doors, but… A nod to the floor.

'There's not enough blood.' Rhys's words are loud, straining to be heard over the deafening silence of death.

Quinn does a slow clap. 'They must've sent you for your brains.'

'You done in here?' A weary voice sounds from the hallway.

Quinn twists towards the huge bearded man who fills the doorway.

'For now.' The huge man steps into the kitchen, his body deflating with a loud sigh. Offering no introduction, Quinn pushes past into the hallway.

'Detective Sergeant Rhys Morgan.' A massive hand shakes his. Rhys's glove twists, slick with sweat.

The huge man doesn't notice.

'Winters,' is all he says. They stare at Cathy Reynolds in silence. 'Welcome to King's Mill eh? A nice warm welcome from the "Couples Killer".' The smile Winters gives him is small and sad.

The front pages of local papers, national papers, television news stations and radio sound bites hammer through Rhys's mind. Couples slaughtered in their own homes. The women drained of blood, the men beaten. Hysterical people outside King's Mill station as he drives past morning after morning. Weary colleagues fading into nothing, viewed across a crowded bar. Rhys sits alone, the people he is looking for absent. His colleagues sit in blood and filth, high five and crack inappropriate jokes to keep themselves sane.

'Morgan,' Quinn's voice bellows from the hallway, 'I don't remember inviting you here to socialise.' The two men squash around the corpse in the ever-decreasing kitchen space. Rhys nods a goodbye as he steps slowly into the hallway.

A bead of sweat runs down the side of Quinn's face.

Together they stare at the cupboard under the stairs. There are several yellow tent markers used by the Crime Scene Investigators on the carpet next to pools of blood.

'Constables Johnstone and Bayne were first on the scene. That's her there, Bayne, at the door,' says Quinn pointing at the pale female Constable who still stands ramrod straight. 'Johnstone goes round the back to see if he can gain access. When he sees our first victim through the window, he breaks the glass in the porch door to get in.' Quinn pauses, smiles. 'I'm sure Winters will have a moan about that.

Bayne calls it in while Johnstone checks the rest of the house bringing him to this spot.' He gestures to a spray of blood across the light floral wallpaper. 'Johnstone knows what he might find when he opens this door,' Quinn points at the cupboard, 'and he's right. When he opens the door, Eddie Reynolds's, the husband's, body falls out.'

Rhys imagines a man lying there, the top half of his body slumped onto the carpet, his legs being sucked into the cupboard's dark mouth. 'What the poor bugger doesn't anticipate is for Eddie Reynolds to open his eyes and scream. Johnstone nearly died by all accounts, proper shat himself.' Quinn makes a sound that could be a laugh. 'Bet he'll never watch a horror movie in the same way again. Lucky we had an ambulance on the way and Johnstone's a skinny bastard so they could both fit in.'

'He was still alive?'

'Johnstone? As near as Constables get these days. No offence.' At the front door Bayne doesn't move a muscle. 'Yes. Eddie Reynolds was still alive. Since when did a corpse ever open its eyes and scream?' Quinn shakes his head. 'We assume he's been in there the same amount of time as...' A nod towards the kitchen. 'He'll probably wish he was dead, even if he does make it.'

'Eddie Reynolds was conscious. Did he say anything?'

Quinn shakes his head. Rhys detects pity. 'The initial attack seems to have happened here,' a point to the blood spray, 'but we won't be sure until *he's* finished.' 'As for Mr Rey–'

A crash of thunder sounds so close the house shakes. 'Bloody hell.' A car alarm goes off. Dogs bark. A baby cries. Rain starts to pour from the sky.

Illuminated by a streak of lightning, Bayne turns fast, her face an even paler shade of white.

'Sir.' She hurries towards them.

'Bayne.' Quinn swivels to stare at her. 'What part of "Do not leave your post under any circumstance" are you failing to understand?' She drops her eyes.

'It's just, outside.' Her thumb jerks weakly towards the door. 'It's Detective Inspector Andrews, sir. I thought you should know, sir.'

'Andrews?' Quinn's venom hits her as if it's her fault. She doesn't flinch as he barges past; she tweaks a smile at Rhys so small it may have not been there at all. 'Just what I don't fucking need.' Quinn's voice echoes in Rhys's head. He racks through the mental files. Andrews. The name is there somewhere, a breath away.

The commotion on the street is framed by the front entrance, a private television screen showing reruns of a black and white freak show. Each step Rhys takes towards the wooden frame enlarges the image before him.

The man outside is screaming. The man is Andrews, but his appearance sheds no light. His skin's so pale it glows, stretched over the pointed contours of his face. The downpour plasters his long, dark hair into his eyes and around his neck. From the already gathered crowd, press bulbs flash, mobile phone videos whirl to life. Quinn and two uniformed Constables start a strange dance, splashing and sliding in the gutter, fingers gripping then slipping on Andrews's coat as they first try to persuade, then force, him into the standard-issue car. Rhys steps towards them, the rain instantly soaks through his heavy wool coat. Cries from the crowd are unclear background noise, a soundtrack that doesn't quite fit. Constables rush to hold them at bay.

Up close, through the rain-soaked car window, Andrews's skin is translucently thin; his veins pump thick and blue and make his face look cracked. His tiny bead eyes shine and dance. His upper lip curls, part smile, part snarl. Rhys doesn't flinch as Andrews slams his hand against the glass. Inside, one of the Constables pulls him back.

Rhys stares at the glass. The rain running down the window makes the image look like a child's painting.

The image of a fresh bloody handprint.

2.

Elsie dreams of her dead cat. She watches him skit back and forth in the shadows, his skin no longer saggy with dehydration, his fur jet black and soft. He springs onto her knee and nuzzles her neck, purring, warm and comforting, alive. Her fingers move to touch him and he fades. Her eyes open, her stomach drops. His remaining sibling and Elsie look each other in the eye. Does she miss him too? The real cat turns its head in dissatisfaction and leaves the room. It's taken Elsie exactly one month to dream her cat back from the dead. It took far longer with her husband.

Elsie blinks the room into focus. It's dark. She's nodded off in the armchair again. The heating is on expensively high yet she still can't get warm. From nowhere, the cool breeze tickles across her face, tender as a lover's fingers. She shivers. No amount of looking will reveal where the breeze comes from, or where it's going. No amount of asking will help.

'Leave me alone,' she mutters, knowing it will make little difference.

Something outside clatters. Is that what's awoken her?

She pulls the blanket tighter around her bony shoulders, lifts the edges high around her neck, covers her sagging flesh. She knows it's a feeble defence for when the breeze comes, which it always does.

The clatter again – this time becoming a deep scraping sound.

Across the room, the pitch-black window goads her.

It takes too long to do anything these days, simple things youth took for granted, so Elsie sits, unmoving. She often thinks spitefully of her young, beautiful self, of her lack of appreciation. Her crooked fingers reach out, touch her face, skin soft, sore and sad. She's glad there are no mirrors in the room. Vanity is a fickle, yet long-serving companion.

Upstairs something creaks. Her eyes turn slowly towards the ceiling.

This sound she knows. The sound of the old house retracting in the cold night air. Do old bones make the same creaking sound? Is *that* the noise that's awoken her? She knows every sound this house makes, the same as she knows every crack in the plaster and cobweb just out of reach. It's been her home for years, and now? It closes in on her and she's afraid she will suffocate and be found one day, a pile of bones and cloth in this very room. At least the remaining cat won't starve. A small smile tugs at her mouth.

What does it look like these days, the upstairs of her home? How much shame should she feel that this is a question she can't answer? Long ago the stairs became too much, a mountain she could no longer conquer. The nice young man from Home Help offers to take pictures on his mobile phone. Pictures on a phone, indeed. Does he think she came down in the last shower? The rooms are clean enough for the sparse guests and sparse enough for the guests not to interfere. What more is needed?

The clatter and scraping sound again.

It's outside, isn't it? Pain and frustration of equal measures pulse through her body. She pushes herself upright, sways and struggles to catch her breath. Shuffle by shuffle she edges to the window and pushes back the fine net curtain with a near-useless arthritic fist.

The cul-de-sac is tranquil, as one would expect for the hour. The pavements glisten wet, the gutters run full. The houses are dark, only the occasional security light flashes. A child's nightlight throbs. Elsie spends many hours looking through this window, watching the world go by. She sees family rows and reconciliations, births and deaths, generations come and go. She sees couples watching television, children crying at having to go to bed, and late-returning husbands eating dinner alone. It is the grand and the mundane, all as interesting as each other, all part of her own private show.

She wonders if anyone ever watches her? A shiver runs across her skin.

It's a sound at the top end of the cul-de-sac that has roused her. Movement outside what the local children refer to as the 'old witch's house'.

The house is set well back from the road edge. It was the first house to be built and with its slightly elevated status, appears to have spawned the rest of the houses around it. The garden is dense and green, shielding the house from the world's eye. A gravel path cuts a line to the heavy front door. The windows that can be seen on the upper level blink down like bright little eyes.

The house has stood empty for years, ever since the owner was found dead. Local children's imaginations ran wild as their parents protected them from the killing truth of alcohol abuse. Without her 'rock', some said drinking partner, the remaining lady of the house quickly became both reclusive and volatile, hurling abuse at anyone who tried to help until they gave up trying. Chasing children with a broom and a couple of large toads taking up habitat in the lush, neglected garden led to the inevitable. Eventually a distant and unsuspecting relative took pity on her and carried her away like the wet rag she was, to dry out in some distant town. They would finally be getting their hands on the cash pay out that drove them to help the old soak. Or perhaps the local children were right and she had been a crazy witch who killed her husband to make potions. Elsie smiles to herself, anything is possible.

The sound scrapes again. It's the tail lift of a large, non-descript removal van. Two burly men in dirty overalls begin to manoeuvre a sideboard up the gravel path. It's a surprise the whole street isn't awake. What time is it? Elsie rubs her eyes and focuses on the large mantelpiece clock. Three in the morning?

Two different men come out of the house and talk in mime at the tail lift. Both are tall but one is significantly younger than the other. The younger is blond, with broad shoulders and lean physique. He holds himself with an elegance she has not seen for decades.

An exact elegance. Elsie blinks. The younger man is slightly out of focus, like she has forgotten to put on her glasses even thought she only needs them for reading. Didn't she just look at the clock? She rubs a fist against her eyes once more. The younger man remains blurred around the edges.

The smell of freshly cut orchids fills her nostrils. Her brow furrows. There is an underlying smell, one she cannot place. It turns into the taste of rust along the back of her tongue.

A slow sense of unease prickles up her spine.

The young man turns his face towards her house. The prickles scatter all over her body. The pressure in her head is instant, a claw clamped around her brain. She gasps. Her vision pulsates, a shade darker. Door after door slams in the tunnel of her mind. Locking her out. She cannot breathe. A deep pain starts to throb somewhere inside. Her eyes drop from the window and focus on an imaginary spot on the carpet.

When she looks back, the younger man is gone, leaving the older gentleman alone.

Everything changes.

The gentleman is a silhouette that pulls into full colour and clear crisp focus. Elsie can't move from the spot and doesn't want to. The older gentleman is mesmerising.

Has he always been out there alone or was there someone with him? Elsie can't remember and doesn't care.

She can see now the gentleman is around eighty but no jealously flashes through her as he strides around. He has a thick head of white hair and posture as good as a man half his age. His dress is smart, a full three-piece suit and tie, a heavy overcoat to protect him from the elements. As the tail lift lands softly, he looks around the cul-de-sac and for a moment and their eyes catch.

It is so different, yet exactly the same.

Elsie is a rabbit caught in headlights; embarrassment flushes her cheeks. Then he smiles and there is something more, something so unusual she's forgotten it even exists. Her stomach flips. Her heart misses a beat and for once, not in a medical way. The dashing stranger is smiling the warmest smile she has felt in a long time. He is smiling it for her. Before the edges of her mouth can respond, he turns and is swallowed back into the house.

Elsie continues to stare out of the window for a long time. Staring at the front door's rectangle of light. Staring through the removal men as they ferry the furniture in. She sees nothing other than the soft edge of the gentleman's smile.

The headlights of a car entering the cul-de-sac snap her back to reality. She blinks rapidly to clear her vision. How long has she been stood here? Doubt creeps into her mind. Does the dashing gentleman even exist or is he just part of another elaborate daydream created to make it all worthwhile? Her slowing heartbeat is answer enough.

She shivers, acutely aware that every part of her body aches. The room smells musty.

The car pulls onto her neighbours' drive.

Somewhere in the back of her mind, Elsie notes that it takes longer than it should for Rhys Morgan to haul himself out. Physically, he is on the street but his mind is elsewhere. He doesn't register the goings-on at the top of the cul-de-sac. Thankfully, he doesn't catch Elsie as she peaks through the window. The soft net slowly drops.

The armchair embraces Elsie as she collapses back into it. She is more exhausted, yet alive, than she remembers ever being.

'Stop being so stupid,' she says. 'You're not sixteen for goodness sake.'

The room starts to slip out of focus. A soft smile plays on her lips. Well maybe she could pretend she's sixteen, for a little while. And then he is here with her, her dead cat, jumping to her knees from the floor of her dreams.

Upstairs something creaks.

The sound of the house retracting in the cold night air?

Or is it more of a scrape?

3.

'Naughty boy. Naughty. Little. Vile boy,' the shrill voice spits. 'Always in trouble. Never learning. You remember what this means for the naughty little boy? No? You are so stupid you've probably forgotten. Thick little boy. Thick, little, vile boy.'

He lets his body go floppy and drop to the floor. It's harder for them to lift him this way. Harder to shift and form his limp limbs. She shrieks more inaudible, high-pitched words. She laughs, a loud sound full of spite. The little boy closes his eyes and waits to feel the impact of violence, but it does not come.

Not yet.

Light and dark play on his eyelids as she moves around him. He screws his eyeballs tight. The metal on metal sound of the bolt doesn't escape him. She has made it louder to ensure he hears. The door scrapes across the stone floor.

The cupboard is open.

Liquid forms in the back of his throat. Not the cupboard. Please not the cupboard. Not again. Anything but the cupboard.

All he wanted was a glass of water. How was he to know he wasn't allowed to use the glasses anymore; that he now has to use the bowl? Why does she always change the rules? How is he supposed to learn if she keeps changing things?

Too much time is passing.

He peeks out through soft eyelashes. She towers over him, all skin and bones, like a giant stick insect. Her hair is pulled back in a tight plait, stretching the skin across her narrow face. Her arms jerk around her body and she screeches for him, for her ally. Screech, screech, the sound whistles through the hole where her tooth should be.

The man is already in the room, just out of sight. His footsteps are so soft they could be missed unless you know what you're listening for. The man is small but he's strong. He's the strongest man the boy has ever known. The boy doesn't know his name so calls him Strong Hands.

Strong Hands smiles down at the little boy. A big, rotten-toothed smile. His big, strong hands loom out and the boy wants to scream. Strong Hands grabs him by the shoulders, far too hard. Her voice in the background taunts and gives Strong Hands orders, orders the hands do not disobey although the boy is sure they could. Strong Hands is so strong he could easily win against her but he doesn't even try. The boy is too afraid of her, too small to fight back, but Strong Hands isn't. He must do her bidding because he wants to, because the little boy really is naughty and vile.

Pain spasms as Strong Hands digs into the muscle. The little boy stays limp but Strong Hands lifts him by the tendons, flesh on flesh, stretching in pain.

The little boy screams and all they do is laugh.

The steps are few but last a lifetime. The boy screams again, claws his fingers at the cupboard edge, its dark mouth ready to swallow him whole. A splinter sears like hot metal down his nail bed. Screams a pitch higher rise with bile, warm and bitter in his mouth. The shrill voice laughs hard, and spits instructions at Strong Hands.

'Screaming like a girl. Pathetic. Listen to him, screaming like a girl at a little splinter. Poor pathetic little boy needs helpie welpie from proper grown-ups.' They both laugh. The little boy sees only patches of colour pulsate through his tears.

Strong Hands gets the pliers.

No! The splinter, not the nail! The pliers are cold against his fingertip. The world throbs red. A tearing sound and the nail is gone.

The little boy can get no air into his lungs. Every muscle in his body contracts, every millimetre full of pain.

'Cry baby. Crying like a baby. Not such a big boy now, eh? Naughty little baby.' Fingers jab in the light, then nothing in the dark.

Little boy all alone. Left to learn in the dark. Vile little boy left alone to learn.

He can feel every heartbeat pulse in his aching flesh. He sucks his finger to stop the throb of pain, warm and bitter in his mouth, comfort in the dark. His eyes squeeze tight to prevent more tears escaping. The blanket of dust wraps around him and his bones quake with fear of what's to come. This is never the end; the cupboard is always the beginning. Endless time passing locked up in the dark.

In the dark, the naughty little boy imagines. He imagines what it would be like if Strong Hands went away. Things were better before Strong Hands arrived, weren't they? Strong Hands only came along because of everything else that happened. If Strong Hands wasn't here maybe the shrieking would stop, maybe she would be different? If the naughty little boy was good, if he tried harder, maybe it could be like it was before?

'Are you hungry vile little boy?' The screech wakes him. 'Remember, don't look at me or I'll be sick. You want food? Who provides the food for dirty little boys? That's right, I do. I provided the food to eat, the heat to cook and the plate you eat off. You are lucky, you vile little thing, lucky I am so kind-hearted that even after you misbehave so much, I still provide for you. I provide the food.'

A crack of blinding light. The door opens.

'Remember the rule: don't look at me or I'll be sick. You stink. You disgust me. Get him out. I said, get him out!'

Soiled and stiff, he is lifted, light as a leaf from the dark. He sits on the floor in the corner. The floor is flagstone and although he tries, he can't stop the shivers as the cold numbs his naked legs. After all, naughty boys never get to sit at the table however good they are. Good is never good enough. The bowl is put in front of him. She screeches and jabs until he eats all the meat, even though it's raw, wet and slippery in his hands, tough and chewy in his mouth.

'Bet you want to be sick, vile little boy.' She dances in her glee. 'Sick, sick, sick, be sick like the baby you are.' But he isn't sick and he eats it all.

Thrown back into the hole, the naughty boy cries. He hears them laugh, laugh at the vile little boy. The smell of the raw meat fills his nostrils, the taste metallic on his tongue. His throat churns. His stomach churns, but he won't be sick no matter what.

No, he won't be sick.

He won't ever be sick.

4.

The grass is as green as the last time he walked through the summer field. The field of dreams. Overhead, sun shines, fractured on occasion like old cine film whirling through a cheap projector. Trees and flowers are huge and wondrous as if seen for the first time through a child's eye. Colours are primary and intense, leaves vibrant and waxy.

A section of this endless field is fenced off, a pure white fence made of no describable substance. Inside the fence grow the most beautiful of the trees and flowers, tall and luscious. Plants bloom and birds sing. This fenced section far outshines the rest of creation, a paradise within paradise. Two figures, one male, one female, run naked between these sunlit perfections laughing and chasing each other. Inside the garden, they are happy, at peace. They are too distant; this little garden is too distant for him to see their faces, yet he knows they are happy, in love. There is something about the female, something he recognises but cannot place.

Slowly from the large apple tree in the centre of the garden comes the serpent. Laughing, it slithers under the fence towards him. The laugh is evil, out of place for this paradise. The serpent's rotting black skin emanates a stench that turns to bile in the man's throat.

Fear grips the man as he looks into the serpent's vivid blue eyes. Breath tight in his chest, he turns to run. It is as if he is trying to run through water.

As he staggers forward, an amazing bright light flashes electric in the sky. It makes the landscape around him black then white then black. Negative to colour. Over and over, he stumbles and falls as the invisible water tries to pull him down.

The serpent slithers closer and closer at a speed faster than the man can comprehend until he feels the fork of its tongue like icy fingers on the back of his neck.

Paradise falters. His very core turns cold.

5.

The coffee is cold and bitter. Anna would laugh at the comparison, except it isn't funny. She pulls her dressing gown tighter, swills the cold liquid in the bottom of the stained mug, she really must get round to buying some new ones. She stares at the kitchen window. It is dark outside, all she can see is the reflection of the lights inside, same as she has done all night, all night while she's sat and waited for Rhys to come home.

Rhys left not long after they went to bed. Anna's stomach lurched as his mobile rang loud in the silent bedroom, the same lurch it always does. Nothing good ever came of that ring. She wanted to wish him luck, but she didn't, instead she rolled further into the duvet, listened to him stumble around in the dark trying not to wake her. She wanted to get up and make him a coffee, or tea, something to take with him, a piece of toast in case he didn't get a chance to eat. But she didn't, instead she slowed her breathing so he wouldn't know she was awake. She waited for the pressure on the bed, of him leaning in to kiss her cheek before leaving, but it never came, nor did the whisper of 'I love you'. She shouldn't be surprised, or disappointed, but by the time Rhys closed the bedroom door behind him her head hurt from clenching her teeth so tight. She sat up and listened for the clink of his keys as he picked them out of the bowl beside the front door. There was still time, she could get up and make him coffee. The keys clink. The front door closes.

Anna stands now and pads to the kettle. Flicks the switch. Watches the steam build and pour out of the spout. She could've got up, laid out a fresh shirt and underwear ready for when he rushed back in. But she didn't. She rattles the spoon in the mug.

Above her the floorboards creak.

Anna goes back to the table.

Rhys came home about four. She was sitting as she is now. She'd risen ready to greet him. Whatever it was he'd been called to see would be bad; she'd been married to him long enough to know that.

'Rhys?' But she can't have said it loud enough. He didn't head to her, he headed straight upstairs. She'd drawn breath to call again but didn't want to wake the children. 'Rhys?' Another loud whisper. But he was already in the bathroom, the pipes clunking as he turned on the shower. So she'd sat and waited. Made him the coffee she should've made hours earlier. Risen once again as he'd left the bathroom. But he hadn't come to her. She'd listened as he'd gone to that room, the one they don't talk about anymore as all the words have been used. He'd gone to that room and softly closed the door.

Anna's teeth grind. She could've gone back to bed, but knew she'd never sleep, so instead she's sat all night like some pathetic impersonation of herself getting more and more pissed off while Rhys moved around above her in that room. That godforsaken room.

'Mum?' Hot coffee splashes on her hand as she jumps in surprise.

'Ouch. Jesus. Harry, why are you up, it's the middle of the night?' Her hand feels like it's on fire. Water. Run it under water.

'It's not the middle of the night, it's six-o-eight, and you're up, and so is Dad.'

'What have I told you about sneaking up on people?' Anna turns on the cold tap, holds her hand under the flow.

'Thought you saw me.'

'How could I see you with my back to the door, Harry?' Anna takes a deep breath. Counts to ten in time with the throb in her hand. It's not Harry's fault. It's Rhys's, as per usual.

'Mum?' Anna looks at Harry over her shoulder. 'Are the baddies back?' The frown is etched across his brow.

'What makes you ask that?'

'Because Dad's in there.' Harry's eyes gesture up. Rhys and that bloody room. Anna turns off the tap, wraps her hand in a tea towel and crosses to crouch in front of her son.

'I don't think so, but if they are, it's okay because Dad's going to catch them before they do any more bad things.' Harry's brow is still furrowed. 'Remember what I told you?'

'That... ' his eyes gesture up, 'that is Dad's special room where only he can go as it's where he plans how to catch the baddies.' Anna smiles, even though she doesn't mean it.

'Exactly, so there's nothing for you to worry about, is there?' Harry shakes his head, but he's fooling no one. 'Why are you up so early?'

'Someone's moved into the old witch's house.' New subject. New conversation.

'Don't call it that. We talked about that, remember? Witches don't exist.'

'Dad says they do.' Anna rises. Why would Rhys say that? Bloody typical.

'Dad's a silly billy.'

'Mum, I'm not a baby. I'm nearly nine.'

'I know. You're my big helper and I'd be lost without you. I need to have a shower, then you can help me make breakfast?'

'Can I have eggs? Please?' Harry adjusts the strap of the toy sword he's taken to wearing. A current obsession with swords and knives. It's her father's fault. He bought round his knife collection to show Harry, even though Anna said he was too young, stored them away for when Harry's older.

'Yes, you may.' Do they even have any eggs? God, her hand hurts.

'For your information, witches do exist. I looked it up, and werewolves and goblins and vampires, or Nosferatu, that's what some people call them.'

'No, Harry, they don't.'

'Yes, they do. Google says so, and Dad says so, and Dad's a policeman and policemen don't lie, remember?' What the hell can she say to that?

On the kitchen table Anna's mobile phone vibrates.

'Your phone's ringing,' says Harry, casually turning the screen to read it. 'It's... Daisy.' Except it isn't Daisy, that's the name Anna typed in when she thought she was being big and clever.

'I'll phone her back.'

'What if it's important?'

'It won't be,' is all she can reply as she heads for the shower.

6.

Rhys pours an extra large coffee. Milk. Plenty of sugar. He sits at the kitchen table. Harry seems tiny as he stands next to him talking about witches. At the counter, Anna violently scrambles eggs. Her cardigan is a deep blood red.

Blood splatters up kitchen kick-boards. Faces grin out of family photographs. A bead of sweat travels down the side of Detective Inspector Pat Quinn's fat face. Cathy Reynolds face twists; her eyes snap open and she screams, a sound so loud it makes Rhys's ears ring. Rhys blinks. Rubs his eyes.

'Dad?' The chair leg screeches on the tiled floor. Harry climbs up beside him. 'Are you listening, Dad?' A small round face with dimpled cheeks peers up at Rhys, distorted through the coffee steam.

'Sorry, son. What was that?' Harry sighs, shakes his head.

'I said, someone's moved into the old witch's house.'

'And I said, he wasn't to keep calling it that.' Anna places a plate of scrambled eggs and toast on the table. The hard sound of ceramic on wood.

'And I said, you said, witches do exist and you're a policeman and you're not allowed to lie.' The scrambled egg wobbles on the plate. Its creamy liquid soaks onto the edge of the toast. The coffee is bitter in spite of all the sugar. Rhys pulls the sugar bowl towards him. Anna's scowl deepens. She shakes her head. She's mad and Rhys has no idea why. He was so quiet when he came home from the crime scene, tiptoed up the stairs, used the family bathroom rather than the en suite so as not to disturb her. He didn't even bother to make a coffee so the kettle wouldn't wake her. May as well not have bothered it would appear.

'Dad.' Harry pulls his focus.

'What?'

'Witches?' Harry upturns his hands copying a gesture of adult frustration. It makes him look like a tiny man. What are they talking about? Witches?

'I said the existence of witches can't be proven either way. Lots of the things it is claimed they can do can be explained.' Anna bangs another plate of scrambled egg onto the table.

'Like through science?' asks Harry.

'Yes.'

'But some of the things can't be explained?' Harry glances at Anna as he speaks, 'like through science?'

'Indeed. But then people believe in many things that science can't explain. Gods, miracles, so why not witches?'

Louise comes into the room. Anna's scowl is razor sharp.

'Oh, god, he's not still going on about witches, is he?' asks Louise. She shakes her head. Sits down. Plays with her mobile phone.

'Not at the table,' says Anna, pushing the egg towards her.

'Dad says they're real,' says Harry.

'No, he doesn't,' says Anna.

'Yeah right, and so are werewolves and vampires and Bigfoot,' says Louise without looking up from the mobile's screen. Rhys studies her. She is fourteen, caught between being a little girl and a woman. His sister had been the same at that age.

'What's Bigfoot?' Harry's face creases.

'You're such a baby,' says Louise. The headache starts across Rhys's forehead. He rubs his temples, pushes thoughts of his sister from his mind.

'Children, please,' says Anna. Louise's face twists.

'Your mum is right about one thing: no more calling it the old witch's house,' says Rhys. He rises, rustles Harry's hair. 'They were definitely not witches, just people who were stupid and drank too much.' Rhys pours the rest of the coffee down the sink. A light stain on the cream enamel.

'Like that man you worked with?' asks Harry.

'Like lots of men I work with.' Harry shrugs and folds back the crinkled corner of his comic.

'Do you have to go already?' asks Anna. Her eyes flick sideways towards Harry. Rhys looks at his watch even though he knows the time.

'I don't want to be late.'

'They didn't mind calling you in the middle of the night.'

'You know how it works. I was lucky to be able to get home for a few hours, I don't want to take the piss on my first day.'

'Dad!' says Louise. Harry giggles. Anna stands with her hands on her hips and glares.

'It's my job, Anna.'

'A job you don't even want.'

'It's a temporary move.' Stalemate. Anna shakes her head, piles more egg onto Harry's plate.

'Mum, stop. I've got enough already.'

'You're the one that said you wanted eggs.'

Rhys looks at Anna's back, the curve of her spine rises like little clots.

'I was thinking, as we have new neighbours,' Anna shoots a silencing look at Harry, 'we could be neighbourly and invite them over for drinks?' What? Why is she saying this now?

'Yeah,' says Harry, 'then *we* can cast a spell on *them* and get rid of their witchy badness!' His face beams.

'Harry! Please!' Anna's voice is loud. 'Then we can all see what nice normal people they are.' She holds Rhys's eye. He will not admit to the pleading look he sees.

'Okay, fine, whatever.' Anna shakes her head and starts clattering things into the sink. Does this head shake mean something different from the last? He hasn't time for this.

Rhys picks up a piece of toast. It's like sandpaper in his mouth. He kisses Harry on the cheek. He kisses Louise on the cheek. She doesn't even try and hide the rubbing off with her sleeve.

'Be good for your mum.' He kisses Anna on the ear. Did she turn her cheek away? 'Have a good day.'

The front door closes behind him to silence.

The press are out in force. Rhys swears he hears someone shout his name as he takes the front steps to King's Mill Station. The facade of the building is dark grey and covered in pigeon shit. It looks like the type of place adulterers would come to be stoned, liars to have their tongues cut out.

A Constable is on guard at the entrance. He's to ensure no camera crews gain access. He demands to see Rhys's identification even though Rhys has been here many times before. It takes a moment for Rhys to find it in the small box of things he's moving in. The Constable stands and stares. He taps his foot as if he has a hundred more important things to do. Rhys finds his identification. The Constable scrutinises it, grumbles something inaudible about the incompetence of management, and allows Rhys access to the small reception area.

King's Mill is the poor relation to Quarry Road, the two main stations that make up the area's Division. Quarry Road knows it has had all of the funds spent on it and doesn't give a shit. It sits in warmth and comfort while King's Mill sinks back into the squalor it came from. The teams based at King's Mill have an underdog status. This makes them proud, like the poor who fight all the harder to achieve. It always makes Rhys smile to see this disappear instantly if they are given the chance to work at Quarry Road, their glee, like rats deserting a sinking ship. Refurbishment lead to expansion, departments were split between the two sites. No one has ever bothered to stick them back together.

A short, silent Constable leads Rhys down an equally short, turquoise corridor, past a row of vending machines dispensing fizzy drinks and chocolate bars. Then they are there. At the heart of the case. The 'Couples Killer' operation room. There is no drum roll or fanfare just a bland middle-sized room with a small back office. Through the window that looks into the back office Detective Inspector Pat Quinn and a short, fat man are in deep, heated conversation. The short, fat man thrusts a newspaper inches from Quinn's face. Quinn's head bows. Expletives are the only words that can be clearly heard.

A line of desks runs along the left hand wall. Each has a computer and telephone. In the centre of the room several tables are pushed together, an area for briefings. At the very back of the room, central to the window, is an empty desk. Next to it, a coffee machine and a wire-thin man waiting for a drink to dispense.

'Detective Sergeant Morgan?' asks the wire-thin man. Rhys nods. 'We thought you might like this desk, sir.' The man points to the window seat.

'Thank you,' says Rhys outstretching his hand.

'Detective Constable Spenser,' says the thin man. His handshake is warm and damp. Spenser flinches every time a new expletive punches through the thin wall. It makes him look like he has a tick.

The right-hand wall of the operations room holds a timeline to the case that stretches from its birth to its latest victims. Dozens of arrows link image after image. Some of people, some of places, some of medical equipment. There is a large map with fluorescent pins in it and strings stretching off to small cards of information. It's a giant combined mind map. A cobweb with a spider poised just out of sight. Rhys hasn't seen anything like it before, thought things like this only existed in the movies.

The handle of the door to the small back office cracks against the wall as the short man exits.

'Get it sorted, Quinn,' the short man shoots back over his shoulder. 'Don't make me regret my decision.' The man stops in front of Rhys.

'Detective Chief Inspector Alec Jenkins.' He extends a hand.

'Rhys Morgan.'

'Glad to have you on board.'

'Sir.'

'I'm sure DI Quinn here will make you more than welcome, get you brought up to speed.' Jenkins pivots towards Quinn. 'Won't you, Detective Inspector?'

'Yes, sir.' Jenkins holds Quinn's eye. On the back wall a clock ticks.

'Excellent. Then there shouldn't be any more problems.' The DCI turns and heads to the door. He stops, his fingers on the doorframe. 'Eight months and we are no nearer catching whoever this is.' A gesture to the timeline on the right-hand wall, a damp mark on the doorframe where his fingers have been. 'I don't need to tell you gentlemen how imperative it is we get results, fast.' Jenkins turns, holds Quinn's eye once more. 'There is no room for error, Quinn, not an inch.'

'Sir.' The DCI nods and is gone from the room. Behind them a cup drops out of the coffee machine, hot water hisses. Rhys turns to Quinn. Quinn stares at his shoes, draws a deep, ragged breath. As he exhales he rubs hard at his eyes, the kind of rub that will make him see stars.

'Fuck,' is all Quinn says. He runs his hands through his greasy hair, his face even paler than Rhys remembers. Quinn takes another deep breath, strides across the room to the back office and slams the door. The vibration knocks a hole-punch off the top of a filing cabinet. Rhys holds his breath, waits for a scream from Quinn that never comes. Spenser laughs nervously.

'He's under a lot of pressure.' Spenser flutters to the fallen hole-punch; starts to pinch up the small, round bits of paper. He makes Rhys think of a bird. 'The DCI is right, eight months we've been at this and nothing, but I guess you know that already.' Spenser laughs again. 'Eight months and nothing. We all know what that means,' Spenser stops pinching at the paper, uses his fingers to make speech marks as he speaks, 'one DI out, that's Andrews, another in,' Spenser nods to the back office. 'Although in this case there are other, you know, factors, what with Andrews being... Anyway, full review of the case, that's a lot of pres–'

The door to the back office opens. Quinn strides out, slaps a newspaper onto the desk.

'Okay,' says Quinn. The front page of the newspaper is dominated by a picture of Quinn wrestling Andrews into the standard-issue car. The headline reads 'Policeman held in ongoing investigation.'

'Now before we go getting all excited, Andrews, sadly, is not our killer, otherwise we could all go home and spend time with people we actually give a shit about.' Quinn grinds his forefinger onto Andrews's grainy black and white face. The print smudges and makes Andrews look like a ghoul.

'He's the one that has spent the last eight months fucking this investigation up. Now it's our turn to make un-fucked. Whilst we have the deepest sympathy for Andrews, since it has been brought to our attention he's suffering from, how can I put it politely, being a mad bastard, we have work to get on with. We were hoping he could go away and finish looping the loop quietly. Doesn't look much like that is going to happen now. As if the shower of shit he's already turned this case into isn't enough.' Quinn sighs deeply. A phone starts to ring. Spenser grabs it from its cradle.

'Yes. Yes. I'll... someone will be right down.' Spenser hangs up the phone. 'That was the front desk, sir. Tony Reynolds, the son of last night's victims is in reception.'

'Yes, Spenser, I know who Tony Reynolds is.' Spenser stammers, looks at the handful of punched holes he still holds. 'Right.' Quinn digs through his pockets, pulls out the packet of nicotine-replacement gum. He studies it in disgust then tosses it onto the desk. 'We'll speak to Tony first, Andrews second. I'm going for a cigarette.' Quinn turns to Rhys. 'You get the coffees in. And I mean coffees from the canteen, not that pile of shit in the corner.' He nods to the coffee machine. 'And I'm referring to the coffee machine not you, Spenser, before you go calling HR.'

7.

Detective Constable Dan Davies appears to have resumed 'service as usual'. His rich black skin shines. His deep brown eyes sparkle. He is close shaven, his shirt immaculately pressed. He swaggers slowly across the room like the tosser he is. A young female Constable smiles at him. He smiles back, his teeth a perfect line of white. Even after all these years a ball knots in the base of Rhys's stomach as he watches. In his right hand Davies carries a fruit pot. In his left what looks like some kind of posh coffee from the shop across the road. He doesn't look like a man who attended an unimaginable crime scene hours earlier. He looks clean and fresh and ready to work. He looks exactly as he always has.

Rhys shakes his head, drops his eyes to the pale tabletop. As he blinks Davies's dark silhouette pulses against the plastic surface like someone has taken a photograph and his eyes can't quite recover from the flash.

Rhys is in the canteen less than two minutes after leaving the operations room. He buys two coffees. The place is bland but functional. A grumpy middle-aged woman spoons beans onto warm bread masquerading as toast. It's the kind of place you don't eat in if you know better. If you have another option.

'Morgan.' Rhys lifts his head. 'We have got to stop meeting like this.' Davies gives him a flash of those pearly whites. Why is he talking like they are still friends? 'Ten years of nothing then twice in hours.' He peels back the lid of his fruit pot and pops a grape into his mouth. 'People will start to talk.' Davies laughs nervously. Rhys does not. The coffee burns Rhys's fingers through the cheap plastic cup. Doesn't Davies remember what he did? The agreement they all came to? 'Finally come to your senses and decided to join us on the dark side?'

'I heard you needed someone to show you how it's done.' Davies laughs again, the sound feels like a grater on Rhys's bones.

'You keep telling yourself that, mate.' Did Davies put the emphasis on the final word? Rhys holds his eye.

Rhys remembers Davies clearly. All his excuses about how his wife didn't understand him, about how they had drifted apart. Rhys wonders if they're still drifting, and how many other women Davies has had to help him stay afloat.

'Look, Rhys—'

'Dan.' A tiny blonde Constable calls as she starts to weave her way across the room. She is dwarfed under the weight of her uniform and a tray laden with a full English breakfast. She smiles and tries to wave. Milky tea sloshes across the tray.

'Oh shit,' mutters Davies. 'That's my cue to leave.' And Davies is gone before the Constable reaches the table.

'Bastard,' she says, then 'hello,' followed by something else Rhys doesn't catch over the squeal of her tray as she slides it onto the table. She waits for a response, so he nods and smiles. She sits opposite him, rips open three small sugars and pours them into her tea. 'It tastes awful otherwise.' She talks to him, but her eyes don't leave the door until, Rhys supposes, Davies is long gone. 'Chantelle Watts.' Her eyes come back to him.

'Rhys Morgan.'

'Pleasure to meet you, Rhys Morgan.' They shake hands awkwardly over her cooked breakfast. She stirs her tea with the handle of her fork. 'You know Dan then?' Rhys half nods, half shrugs. Chantelle Watts stabs the fork into her sausage; the ting of metal on ceramic is loud. She lifts the sausage and inspects it with distain. 'Me too, unfortunately.' She bites off the end of the sausage aggressively. 'Me too.'

There are more cracks in the walls than Rhys remembers. The paintwork has been touched up in the wrong shade. A hum comes from the overhead light bulb. The chairs are crude and plastic. Dirt and shoe rubber stain the floor in lines. The footfall of thousands as they wait to be questioned and interrogated, detained or released. The villains and the victims all mixed into one. On the plus side, no one has been sick in the room in the last twenty-four hours. It's not ideal but it's the best they have.

Quinn welcomes Tony Reynolds into the room. Tony's face is swollen and blotchy. He looks like he has cried since the moment he took the call about his parents. A man drowning in his own tears. Right on cue Tony inhales deeply, a wet, snotty sound.

'I'm sorry for your loss,' says Quinn. Tony looks at him like he has no idea what the words mean.

'I didn't lose them.' The chair legs scrape as Tony sits.

'Can I get you anything? Tea? Coffee?' asks Quinn.

Tony half shrugs, 'I guess a large vodka is out of the question?' He tries to smile but instead spasms out a bark of laughter that morphs into a wail. The sound seems to catch him off guard. He clamps his hand to his mouth. Quinn's eyes drop. Rhys watches Tony. Tony blinks rapidly, a fat round tear escapes. Then another. This is what murder does to people. This is why Rhys would rather be anywhere but here.

Quinn uses his index finger to push a small box of tissues across the table. The box is well used. The noise as Tony starts to pull a tissue out is deafening. The tissue sticks in the box's jagged mouth. Tony pulls at it aggressively,

'For fucks sake.' Tony hurls the box across the room then crushes his hands against his face and lets the sobs break free.

Quinn and Rhys watch in silence. Quinn sits opposite Tony and sips his coffee, the thin plastic of the cup squashing beneath his fingers. Rhys stands against the back wall. Knee bent, one foot against the grubby tiles.

Tony drops his hands. A thin line of snot glistens on his top lip. Everyone pretends like there isn't a box of tissues on the floor in the far corner. Rhys pulls a white handkerchief from his pocket. A whiff of Olbas Oil penetrates the stale air. Quinn's head turns to face him.

Anna's bloody mother. Anna had told her mother that Rhys was transferring to murder. Rhys knew exactly why Anna told her, so her mother could help her build up a case for the defence. Or is that prosecution? Anna tells her mother more about their marriage than he is privy to. Last time she came to visit, she dug out his handkerchief, dowsed it in Olbas Oil, told him that Olbas Oil on a handkerchief was used to breathe through at murder scenes. It covered the smell of decay. Rhys told her she had been watching too much American television. Anna snapped not to talk to her mother that way.

36

'No, thank you. No offence, but Mum says handkerchiefs are dirty.' Rhys sees the realisation his mum will never say these words again flit across Tony's face. Tony's lip quivers. His elbows drop to the edge of the table. His face finds his hands again.

Quinn turns and sniffs disgustedly at the air, the sound almost hidden against the backdrop of Tony's crying. Quinn's eyes narrow as he slowly shakes his head. Rhys folds the handkerchief with far more care and attention than he feels. He slips the handkerchief back into his pocket and tilts his head to look at Quinn. Quinn's mouth is a firm, pressed line.

Minutes tick past.

'Tony.' Quinn eventually speaks, cuts through the sobs. 'You don't mind if I call you Tony, do you?' Tony looks up. His blotchy cheeks flame with anger.

'You can call me bloody Katie Price if you like, I don't care. I want to know what you're doing to catch the person who did... this... ' Quinn's jaw tenses.

'When was the last time you saw your parents... Tony?'

'I don't know, three weeks ago?' Tony rubs forcefully at his eyes. Is he hoping he can push the tears back in? Quinn stares at him. 'They came to visit me, see my new place.'

'Very nice. How long have you lived in this new place?'

'What? Erm, about six weeks. That's why Mum and Dad came up. Mum always likes to visualise where it is I'm living, for when we're on the phone, you know?' Quinn's nod falls somewhere between patronising and dismissive.

'And how did your parents seem when they came to visit you?'
'What?'

'How did they seem?

'Fine.' Tony's eyes dart to Rhys. 'What does this have to do with... with what's happened?'

'Mr Reynolds. Tony.' Eyes back to Quinn. 'We have to build up a picture of your parents. Who they knew, the type of people they came into contact with.'

Would anyone they know want to torture and kill them? The words snuggle thick and unsaid between them.

'Did anyone they know behave oddly around them? Had they ever felt threatened in any way?' Quinn continues, 'I know it's painful, but we need to find out how they lived their lives—'

'How they lived their lives has got nothing to do with it. Are you trying to blame them? Say it is somehow their fault?' Tony places both hands flat on the table. His shirt cuff twitches against the Formica as he shakes. 'Some bastard forces his way into their home and bleeds my mum to death, and it's somehow her fault?' Tony's eyes dart back and forth between them. 'There's no need to both look so shocked. I read the papers you know, I know what this sick bastard is doing. As for my dad. Oh god.' Tony's hand flies to his mouth as he retches. He swallows hard. Fights to compose himself. 'If you had worked harder, if you had worked faster, then you would have caught him already and this would not have happened. Would not be happening. This is your fault so don't you dare try and lay the blame on them. Oh god.' His voice cracks. He retches again.

'Perhaps we should take a break,' says Quinn.

'Is there someone I can call?' asks Rhys. Are there more members to the Reynolds family or in one brief night have they been blotted from the face of the earth? Rhys steps towards the table.

'Stay the fuck away from me,' Tony pushes back from the table as he speaks. 'I need some air.' Tony fumbles at the door handle like he has forgotten how they work. 'I need some air right now. And Dad, I need to go and see Dad.' Quinn leans to help open the door. 'Stay the fuck away from me!' Tony wrenches the door open and exits, his final, 'stay the fuck away,' echoing in the corridor.

'Doesn't he see, we're all on the same side?' says Quinn.

'Sorry?'

Quinn shakes his head in response and strides out of the room.

8.

Quinn blows cigarette smoke towards the sky. Fat drops of rain start to fall. Rhys's fingers force large buttons through tight holes.

'That was a monumental waste of time.' Quinn flicks ash into the wind.

'His mother's just been murdered.'

'Exactly, and it's our job to catch the bastard responsible, but we can't do that on our own can we? DI Andrews has proven that.'

'I'm not sure what you mean.' The wind blows the rain against Rhys's face. Quinn continues,

'We are precisely zero steps further forward than we were two and a half hours ago, two and a half hours to add to the pile of days already wasted.' That isn't what Rhys meant. Quinn lights a second cigarette off the butt of the first, shakes his head. 'We are already going to have to do a full review, a full goddamn review of every note, every breath, every fucking fart taken by every person involved in this case in the past eight months. Do you have any idea how long that's going to take? Alongside the fact the bastard is still killing, still piling shit into the storm and people are taking offence when I ask the most basic of questions.' Quinn sucks hard on his cigarette. The end crackles.

The smoking area is a tiny square of outside space, wedged between the rotting buildings. It smells like decaying vegetables. There are black outlines where the bins used to be. They perished in the bright roll out of recycling. The new bins and containers need three times as much space. This area is still deemed okay for people, though. If you like to stand close together. And don't mind the lingering smell.

Rhys raises a hand to gesture 'hello' to a smoker in the corner, except there's no one there, it's just a jacket hung up while someone smoked. Thankfully Quinn doesn't notice Rhys change the movement to a casual scratch of his head.

'Something's been missed, it has to be.' Quinn coughs. 'Something's in there somewhere, all the information we already have. Andrews may be mad but the rest of the team are good coppers.' Quinn flicks the half-smoked cigarette away as if it's the source of the disgust. It bounces off the wall opposite, lands next to the man that's actually a coat. 'Luckily next on our list is an invite to Andrews's mad hatter's tea party so we can ask him, right? Because *that* should help. *That* won't be another epic waste of time.'

The sarcasm is sucked into the wind.

Quinn takes the steps down to the holding cells two at a time. Rhys follows, slips out of his coat, brushes off the rain. The quicker they get there the quicker it will be over, whatever it is.

The scream pierces the air long before they hit basement level, a wild sound that raises the hairs on the back of Rhys's neck. Quinn's footsteps falter slightly; his fingers brush the wall to keep his balance. It takes all of Rhys's willpower not to clamp his hands over his own ears.

Quinn's pace quickens. He glances back over his shoulder to Rhys, his face a mixture of anger tinged with concern. They round the corner. Another scream tears towards them. A ragged sound of pain and anger.

The sound of Andrews.

They're running now. Quinn slides to a halt outside the only open cell door on the dark blue corridor. Rhys catches the edge of the doorframe and stops himself inches from Quinn.

The cell is tiny. Bodies cram in on either side of Andrews. Two Constables try to restrain him. Each clings to an arm. The small window backlights them like a paper puppet show. Andrews head is bowed. He is using all his strength to try and get his mouth to his right forearm. The Constable who battles to stop him is overweight and sweats heavily. He shouts to his even larger female colleague. She's having her own battle with Andrews's left arm. Neither can reach a radio or alarm. They all squash together against the wall then right themselves as Andrews lifts his head.

A meat-red mark on the wall is a mirror image of the flat bleeding patch starting to scab on Andrews's forehead. His thin papery skin crinkles around the wound's edge. The skin on the rest of his forehead looks to have slipped during impact. It reminds Rhys of trying to stick tissue paper with Copydex for one of Harry's school projects.

Andrews sees them, stops struggling. The force, or lack of, sends the female Constable staggering backwards. She swears loudly. Rhys's ears ring. There is a dirty bandage tied tightly around Andrews's left hand and wrist. The fresh bloody handprint slamming against the car window thumps into Rhys's mind. Andrews is injured? It's his blood that left the handprint?

'What the fuck is going on here?' Quinn's words break the silence as he squashes himself into the cell.

'I know you.' Andrews leans sideways, peers around Quinn.

'I doubt that very much,' says Quinn. Andrews's thin lips pull into a large grin of sharp white teeth. Quinn moves and blocks Andrews from view. 'Again. What the hell is going on here?' Quinn's words aim at the Constables, at Andrews. Rhys sidesteps to get a view into the room. To get a view of Andrews.

The large male Constable replies. His breaths are heavy.

'It was him, sir.' He points at Andrews.

'*It was him, sir.*' The mock is crystal clear. 'Where do you think we are, the school playground?' Quinn takes a step towards the male Constable. Their bodies touch, their shadows one black mass. The Constable tries to step back but there is nowhere to go. Discomfort squirms physically around them. 'Everything that happens in this room is your responsibility. Do you understand that, Constable?'

'Yes, sir.' There is a slight octave change in the Constable's voice, a hairline crack.

Andrews is stood statue still. His tiny black eyes fix on Rhys. He blinks one slow blink. Rhys anticipates the move but Andrews is a split second faster. Rhys's hand has hardly left his side as Andrews head snaps forwards and he sinks his teeth into his own forearm.

'What the...?'

Quinn's move is surprisingly quick. He grabs at Andrews's head and crams his fingers in amongst the teeth and broken flesh. It is a technique Rhys has seen used on dogs. A dog. One that refused to release a child's limb. A small sound cracks, like someone stepping on a twig. Quinn swears loudly and pulls Andrews's head back. Drops of deep red blood flick across the wall and the male Constable's sweat-soaked shirt. Andrews roars, Quinn grapples with him. Quinn's forefinger is bent back at a funny angle. The male and female Constables wrestle into the chaos of limbs. They become like a cartoon fight. A ball of confusion with arms and legs protruding. Quinn swears again and shoves hard until the two Constables are back to holding Andrews, one arm each. Rhys cannot tell if it is Andrews's blood or the combined pools of sweat that give the room a slippery sheen.

'Why are you trying to stop me?' Andrews spits the words into Quinn's face. A spray of fine blood particles land on Quinn's pale doughy flesh. 'It's not your place to stop me.'

Quinn takes deep gasps of air, pushes his right hand hard into his left. 'Sadly for both of us, it is my place. It's my job. Some of us still have some commitment, believe it or not.' He stares at Andrews. A thick line of blood and saliva runs down Andrews's chin. 'Trust me there is nothing I would like more than to step out of this room and leave you to fuck yourself into oblivion the way you've fucked this case up.' He takes another deep, pain-filled breath. 'But I don't think the local taxpayers and papers would like that very much, do you?' The blood from Andrews's right forearm runs down his fingers and drips onto the floor. The male Constable grips the arm tightly, oblivious to the blood that turns his fingers a deep pink.

'Handcuff him.' Quinn points his broken forefinger at the Constables.

'What?' The word's out before Rhys can stop it. Quinn turns on him.

'And what would you suggest, golden bollocks? That we let this circus continue until the quack arrives?'

'I....' Rhys doesn't know. 'He needs medical attention.'

'*He* needs medical attention? Look at my fucking finger!' Quinn's face is creased with pain. 'I said cuff him.' The female Constable unclips her handcuffs. 'Sit down.'

Andrews is still now. A calm acceptance or the calm before the storm? His cold stare doesn't leave Rhys as he sits.

'You.' The male Constable turns. 'Go and find out how long it's going to be before this brain quack arrives. Last time I looked there wasn't a section in my job description entitled "Look after mad ex-coppers in the cells until the station appointed shrink arrives and decides if they need to be locked up properly". I could bloody well answer that right now and I haven't got a million years of expensive training behind me.'

'She should have been here about thirty minutes ago.' The female Constable responds as the male Constable exits. Rhys steps into the vacated space. It's like stepping into an oven.

'She should have been here about three years ago, looking at the state of this.' Quinn and the Constable laugh. A release. Rhys's mouth doesn't move a muscle. Behind them an icy voice cuts through the thick, warm air.

'What on earth's going on here?' Everyone in the cell turns in unison. The woman that's spoken is tiny, but her presence is overwhelming, pushing against them through the heat. She has a short brown bob and wears a stark white medical coat. If it's for show, it works. Quinn stares down at her. 'Doctor Flynn.' She stares straight back. No handshake offered, no muscle on her face moving, bar the ones needed to talk. 'May I have a word, Detective Inspector?' Her eyes pulse momentarily. 'In private.' Quinn's head drops a fraction as he exits. The smallest of movements but enough to register on the edge of Rhys's vision. They step outside the room.

A new level of quiet fills the space. The female Constable seems to notice for the first time the blood that stains her uniform.

'I know you, Detective Sergeant Rhys Morgan.' Andrew's voice is barely a whisper.

'I don't think so.' Andrews smiles that thin-lipped smile.

'Yes, I know you.' Something tries and fails to force its way to the front of Rhys's mind. 'Let me tell you a story, Detective Sergeant.' Rhys shakes his head.

'Why would I want to hear anything you have to say?' The female Constable shuffles uncomfortably.

'Oh, please.' Andrews laughs without humour. 'Let me fill in some of the blanks from that little brown case file you were given. The one that didn't even have the decency to mention me.' Andrews pouts theatrically. Interesting. Outside, the corridor is silent.

Rhys sits on the brushed steel bench, careful to avoid the small pools of Andrews's blood that sit like oil on the surface. The cold makes his muscles contract.

'The file that doesn't even have the decency to mention me and this was my case.'

'It did mention you, actually.' Andrews head turns at Rhys's words. 'It stated that after eight months of investigation, largely lead by you, the team are no nearer catching a serial killer the press have unimaginatively titled the 'Couples Killer' and you have been replaced.'

'The file is wrong.' Andrews's words are hard. 'I was so close to catching him.' Andrews's arms flex against his restraints. The female Constable takes a step towards Andrews, Rhys holds up a hand. 'So close.' Andrews laughs again. 'So close and now you will have to start all over again.' His eyes wander in thought. 'He was right though, he was so right.' Andrews's eyes snap back to Rhys. Cold and hard and dark. 'He told me you'd come. I've been expecting you.'

9.

'Once upon a time in a far off land, there lived a girl. She was the most beautiful girl in all the land with thick brown hair and emerald green eyes. Then, one day, the big bad wolf came a knock knock knocking on her front door. Was it her beauty that attracted this ferocious beast? I doubt it, but it makes for a better story, don't you think? Especially if the first victim is young. Young and fresh and beautiful.' Rhys looks across at Andrews, lets his disdain pulse in his eyes.

Andrews tilts his head. Rhys feels like a specimen being inspected in a Petri dish. Andrews views him with contempt, like a Nobel Prize-winning cure a lab colleague has created. Rhys knows Andrews would release him on the world were he such a specimen, turn him into vapour. Rhys tilts his own head, a subtle mirror image. Andrews waits in silence then takes a small step back inside himself.

'The real story starts eight months ago.' Andrews is instantly serious, grounded. He shakes his head, tries to dispel the sudden look of disbelief that scurries across the sallow landscape of his face. 'Has it really only been eight months? Is that all it has taken to get to this?' Now his look to Rhys seems to ask a million questions. Rhys has no idea what the questions are. How many personalities are contained within what remains of this man's body, morphing to the surface when they are needed. Or when they demand attention?

Rhys keeps his face blank. When she's feeling kind, Anna tells Rhys he should take up playing poker, win enough for them to move to the sunshine and live happily ever after. When she's feeling cruel she tells him he is uncommunicative and unemotional. She stamps her feet and shouts at his lack of words. Interprets it to be lack of love. He wants to tell her she can't have it both ways. Andrews's words pull Rhys's thoughts away from Anna's stamping foot and teeth clenched so tight the tendons in her neck stand to attention. Pulls his thoughts from Anna and her blood-red cardigan.

'The real story starts two hundred and twenty-eight days ago, to be precise.' The soft film of memory slides over Andrews's

45

eyes. Rhys can almost see his mind as it tunnels into the past. He's glad not to have bumped into him on the way back from his thoughts of Anna.

'My life was different then, not just because it existed, but because it still contained the naive purity and belief that this decay has taken away.' Andrews signals around them with a jerk of his shoulders. The female Constable turns towards Andrews, arms raised ready. Andrews smiles.

'Don't worry, Constable, I promise I'm going to tell the rest of my story like a good little boy.' Rhys glances at the Constable, catches her eye, nods. Her movement has caused tiny red flakes of dried blood to dance in the air. Where they will settle? Will he breathe them deep into his lungs as they waltz around the room?

'I knew I was ready,' Andrews continues, 'ready for one last "Big case" and when her body was found, I knew this was it. Not many people can handle that, Rhys.' Andrews meets his eye at the intimate use of his name. 'One human being's excitement, gain, at another one's death. But I knew I could do one final, good thing. One good thing to help this beautiful girl with her sparkling green eyes.'

'Excitement at catching the killer, surely?' Rhys asks, even though he knows the answer. Andrews laughs, laughs the way people laugh at private jokes. He stops abruptly and shrugs.

'So she was dead, my green-eyed girl. And she was so, so beautiful in death. I can hardly imagine what she must have been like in life.' Pointless loss, no mirth. An emotion at odds with the man in front of Rhys now. Perhaps loss cancels loss in some strange way? Andrews has become a violent imprint of the man he used to be.

'It was early, five a.m. or thereabouts, but I was already up. We hadn't long had baby Victoria and I was doing the early morning feeds. How I loved the early mornings with my little princess.' Andrews's thin lips smile. 'I came late to fatherhood, Rhys, but she was well worth the wait. It was nearly spring. The sunlight was weak and newborn, full of promise.' The memory makes Andrews look almost human. It is the briefest second, a softening of the jagged edges.

'All this new life and smack in the middle of it was the dark hole of her death. It was her boyfriend who found her. He'd been out of town to visit family, not the kind of welcome home he was expecting.

'The green-eyed girl's body was still hanging when I arrived. She was naked, her smooth white skin given no decency, no respect. Her mouth was contorted into a twisted, frozen scream, the likes of which I had never seen before. Her face held terror that at the time I could not imagine. I was filled with a curiosity to discover what she had seen. Now...'

Andrews is silent for a long time.

'I was filled with an overwhelming fear.' A barked laugh. 'I used to be ashamed to admit fear.' More silence.

'They say you can smell it, you know, fear. They're right.' The smell of rust and citrus plays at the edge of Rhys's mind. Andrews's eyes turn and bore into him, a burning sensation on his already hot skin. Rhys's pupils dilate a fraction.

'It is a smell that cuts through blood and death.

'And there was plenty of blood at the scene. Plenty of blood.' Andrews's tone is almost whimsical now. Almost. 'And yet not enough.' The final words catch Rhys's attention. One small eye movement, so small it's barley noticeable. It's enough to give away his interest. It happens before he can stop it.

'Sight and smell are powerful things indeed, Rhys, but more than all of that, it's the sound that stayed with me. The sound of her body as it was lowered onto the plastic sheeting. Like the crackling of wood on an open fire. Like fingertips gently touching the back of your neck.' Andrews is lost once again in the past. Is he surrounded by the sound of crackling twigs? The scent of citrus thick in his nostrils. Rhys hopes this is the case. The furrow in Andrews's brow could mean he's wide of the mark.

'I set up teams and we worked all day and late into the night combing every square inch of her home. We bagged up everything we found from last week's newspapers to last night's chip wrappers, but none of it related to anyone but this woman.

'The main thing I remember about getting home that night was how cold I was. Chilled to the bone. My wife, Lilly, ran me a hot bath but it didn't touch the chill that worked its way under my skin. Oh, how I cried that night. Cried like I had never cried before. Lilly held me safe in her arms. All I could think was no one had been there to hold my green-eyed girl, to keep her safe.

'The following morning her parents arrived. I had to break the news to them. News that their daughter, Claudia Rose, was dead. A rose with the sap squeezed out of her. Have you ever had to do that, Rhys? Give someone that kind of news?' Rhys almost nods. 'Have you ever felt that kind of loss?' Andrews holds his gaze for a moment too long.

'So, the case file was wide open. A team of people pulled together. They all looked to me for leadership, for the right path to go down.

'We had DNA, that wasn't hers or her boyfriends, but no matches came up in the system. The same with fingerprints. She hadn't been sexually violated which was a relief – until we were told she was alive when her blood was drained.

'It didn't take long to realise we were getting nowhere. Claudia Rose was as clean living and middle class as they come. No secret lovers, no secret addictions, no family disputes out of the ordinary for an eighteen-year-old. She had no connection to gangs, dealers or religious cults. No excessive debits, feuds or angry ex-lovers. Everyone genuinely liked Claudia, not just in the news soundbite way everyone loves the dead.

'In my home-life, things weren't bad. Lilly supported my enthusiasm and drive. My passionate belief that someone somewhere knew something, that there was a vital piece of evidence waiting to be found. There was of course, indeed still is, her missing blood. That has never been found. Now I know it never will be.

'Baby Victoria became my sounding board. Please don't think less of me for that, Rhys. I never told her the gruesome details. I always made the people involved farmyard animals. Lilly still felt it was inappropriate. I shall never forget the look she gave me when she caught me telling Victoria that daddy was going to catch the big bad wolf that had grabbed the chicken round the throat.' Andrews pauses. 'In hindsight she was probably right.

'We knocked doors. We made appeals both in the papers and on television. No one had seen a thing. I still held onto the belief that the vital clue was out there, although it was getting smaller by the day.

'The thing they don't tell you about high-profile cases is the pressure. Pressure from the investigation, from the bosses, from the press. The press are everywhere, at every second. They hound the innocent and always expect answers within minutes when weeks wouldn't be long enough. At first it was fun seeing myself in the paper, all hopes hung on me. Then it became tiresome. Tiresome for Lilly when all she wanted to do was buy groceries or play with Victoria in the park. Tiresome for me when I had no answers to give.

'I never used to drink but I turned to whisky to try and dilute the image of Claudia that was burnt onto my brain. A whisky blanket to try and warm my chilled bones. I know.' Andrews laughs. 'Whisky, yet another cliché, especially for a copper. The world is full of them. I started to drink every night before bed, just to help me drift off. Then sometimes before dinner. Or just after lunch.' Rhys can almost smell cheap malt on the air, on the exhale of Andrews's breath.

'It was the height of summer by then,' Andrews continues, 'and hotter than it had been for years. They were the kind of days where you volunteer to go to the supermarket to be near the freezers. Along with the reservoirs, our case was drying up. And then she came, like a mirage in the desert.

'The second body. It was the same format so we knew instantly it was him. She was hung in the same way. Her face was twisted by the same terror. The blood was everywhere and yet there still was not enough. There was one massive difference this time and I clung to it like a limpet.

'She didn't die alone.

'Crammed into the cupboard under the stairs was the body of her husband.' Rhys blinks, sees the meaty thump of a body hitting carpet. The citrus sweat smell on the air. Blood flicked across wallpaper.

'Was there any relevance in this seeming escalation to double murder, a clue? Had Claudia Rose's boyfriend's mundane family visit saved his life?' Andrews shrugs, lets the question hang in the air.

'The second woman to die was called Jess. Her daughter assumed she was working a double shift when she didn't answer the door as planned. There was still no answer in the evening so the daughter used her emergency key to get in. That was when she noticed the blood on the internal door. The daughter had spent the afternoon cursing her mother for not calling to say she was working. I know the guilt and 'what ifs' still haunt her to this day. It would have made no difference had she let herself in that afternoon. Her parents were already dead.

'I began to wonder if the person we were looking for was a ghost.

'Killing three people or more makes you a serial killer and serial killers follow patterns, have some method in their madness. It should have been simple, what connected Claudia, our sweet youth, to a middle-aged factory worker named Jess and her husband Ron? Excluding of course the comparison in death. All obvious links were ruled out. Affairs? Prostitution? Had they met in an internet chat room? Had Claudia babysat for their grandkids? We looked down every avenue. We even went as far as looking into whether their lives could have led to them passing by chance on the street, or someone, somewhere seeing them in the same area of town. We drew blank after blank after blank.

'There was a third pair of murders two months later, another couple, same pattern. The husband wasn't the long-lost father of Claudia. Once again there were absolutely no links. Once again there wasn't enough of the wife's blood at the scene.

'Night after night, I sat up with their photos spread around me like a rug. I examined every last detail, from body measurements to skin care. I read and reread the notes from door-to-door enquiries. I searched and searched for something I now know was not there. I fell asleep every night on the sofa, alone. For some reason Lilly didn't want to hug me anymore. I smelt of death.'

Andrews stops. The silence is once more all around them. Rhys waits although he can guess how the story will end. Dirty and defeated in a cell beneath the ground. Andrews sniffs. Flexes his fingers behind his back.

'The question that intrigued me the most, Rhys, was where was all the excess blood? It disappeared, as if it never existed. Three women had been bled to death. They were killed where we, I, found them. And yet even with all the loss, all the decay, there still wasn't enough blood.

'One night when my whisky bottle and I were up late watching television one of those old black and white movies came on. *Dracula, Bram Stoker's Dracula.*'

Rhys feels his heart stop. He holds his breath.

Surely not?

'That was when it hit me, Rhys, like a bolt of lightning. My moment of epiphany if you will. We are not looking for a human killer,' Andrews leans towards Rhys, the tight muscles of his arms strain. 'But a creature of the night. A demon from the very depths of hell.

'A Nosferatu.'

10.

'What the fuck?' Rhys can't stop the words. He's misheard. The words are wrong. A grown man would not say that. A man in charge of hunting a serial killer. The female Constable's mouth hangs open. She draws breath as if to speak, then silently looks to Rhys.

'Nosferatu,' repeats Andrews. Rhys feels the word razor sharp against his skin. Rhys blinks slowly.

'I... ? What... ? Seriously?'

'Your reaction is pretty similar to the one I was expecting. Please save us all the bother and keep the "have you lost your mind?" rant to yourself. That usually comes next. I've heard it plenty of times before.'

'Have you lost your mind?'

Silence.

Rhys stands. Snaps his teeth together. Slowly shakes his head. Images of the victims' families fight into his mind. Hands clinging onto hands so tight knuckles are white. Knees giving way, collapsing in each other's arms. Internal battles and self-blame taken out on each other. They're faceless but he has known enough of their kind of grief to see every crease of skin. And all that time this, this thing in front of him, was doing what? Filling them with false hope while he chased shadows? Time wasted. Allowing a killer free, to strike again and again and again. No wonder the team have found nothing under... this. They really have been chasing ghosts.

'What's wrong with you?' Rhys stares into Andrews's beady eyes. He sees only his own reflection.

'Nothing,' Andrews sighs. 'Nothing other than having to watch all of this work go to waste. I have come so far, got so near.' The anger flames in Andrews so instantly, Rhys can almost feel its heat. 'You can't stop me, you know that, don't you? You can't take him from me. You can't stop me from getting what I want.'

'You look pretty stopped to me.' Andrews hasn't heard him.

'… The same as you can't stop him.'

'Can't stop who?'

'Him.' Andrews jerks his head back, tries to look round to the small window set high in the wall. He's not talking about the policemen who smoke their cigarettes in the bin graveyard. He shakes his head, exasperated. A child who's saying something the grown-ups can't quite understand. Something the grown-ups won't apply themselves to understand.

'Oh, you mean the big bad Nosferatu?' Rhys shivers, mocking. Laughs directly in Andrews's face. Andrews is the punchline in this appalling joke, Rhys makes it clear as crystal. Andrews swivels the conversation in another direction, a moth flitting from light to light.

'So, as I was saying, I had my moment of enlightenment, should we choose to call it that…' Rhys holds up a hand.

'I don't want to hear another word you have to say.'

'You can't stop me talking.'

'Want to bet?' Rhys steps in close.

'I have a witness.' Andrews looks to the female Constable.

'I'll be in the corridor, sir,' she says. She nods to Rhys, steps out of the room.

'It's not like you could claim self defence.' A smile plays at the corner of Andrews's mouth; he rattles the handcuffs. Rhys grinds his teeth, takes a step back.

'As I was saying, before I was so rudely interrupted, when I awoke in the morning my theory seemed no less viable. After all this time, I had the answer. I was not so foolish as to believe others would see the obvious. People are very stupid after all. I started to put my case together. At the crux, no one human would be able to remove so much blood, so completely and so without a trace.' Rhys wants to walk away. Knows he can't. Can't leave Andrews unattended. He turns his back. Stares out into the corridor. Could he stand out there with the female Constable, apologise for not asking her name, make inane conversation until Quinn returns with the doctor?

'Think about what I am saying Rhys.' Rhys snorts, shakes his head. 'Thousands of people believe in dark arts and demons.' This means nothing. Millions of people believe in God. No one is about to start hunting him down as a prime suspect for murder. Actually, bad example.

'The issue is our minds, your mind, has been narrowed,' Andrews continues. 'We are so corrupted by science that we cannot believe in anything outside our own comprehension. For centuries, people believed in witches and werewolves, Nosferatu and demons, and what they believed in must've been based on some kind of evidence and that evidence can be no different now just because we don't believe in it.' The words bounce around Rhys. Blah, blah, blah.

'Wrong.' Rhys pivots, holds his eye. 'Science makes us understand why things like that are impossible, unbelievable. Created out of the dribbling matter of minds not all that far removed from... well, yours.'

'No!' Andrews shouts, adamant. The crazy always are. 'That is what modern day society would lead you to believe. It's amazing how confined man is by his hidden agenda of right and wrong, truth and lies, mad and sane. These are not conclusions you reach yourself. This is not your freewill. This is ingrained into you from birth by the society in which you live, as it was into your parents and their parents before them. I know what everyone thinks of me, Rhys, or what they soon will. I am crazy; something somewhere in my grey matter has gone "pop". This is not the case. I have never seen so clearly or been as sure of anything in my life. It all makes sense.' Andrews stops suddenly, a far away look in his eye. His chest heaves with exertion.

Rhys steps close again. He wants to tap Andrews on the side of the head. Tap to see if his brain rattles.

'Have you heard yourself?' Andrews draws breath. Rhys places a silencing finger on Andrews's ice-cold lips. For the briefest moment, he wonders if when he removes his finger, his skin still be stuck to Andrews's lip. A fused ice burn? 'Shhhh. I mean have you really listened to what you are saying? Sever all the psychological bullshit and you are implying these people are being tortured and killed by... a vampire?'

'Of course.' Andrews's voice is soft. 'Of course.' He sighs heavily. 'There is no *implication* in what I am saying. It's television isn't it, and books? The whole teen romance thing. It makes us forget what we are actually dealing with. It makes us complacent. It makes us forget what they really are. Who was it that said the biggest trick the devil ever pulled was convincing the world he doesn't exist? Same principle.'

Andrews sniffs. Coughs.

'You've seen her face, Rhys.' The musty smell of citrus. The pinpricks of fear. 'You've seen the look on their faces. A face. You only have to see it once.' The cold rush of air. He has seen it once. Andrews has seen it countless times. 'The scream never goes, you know. The face is stuck like that. How is that possible? You think some *Twilight* teenager does that? There is no happy ending here, Rhys. Surely you, of all people, know that by now?'

The pain is there again, across his forehead. He's too hot, it's this room, it's way too warm. He feels suddenly like he's floating. Like the whole room, reality, is tunnelling far away, leaving him alone in the heavy weight of darkness. Rhys pulls at his tie. Cathy Reynolds twisted face slams suddenly close. Her eyes open and she screams, blood showers Rhys's face. Rhys jerks back from Andrews, who rises – a knowing smile on his lips. The taste of rust on the back of Rhys's tongue.

'Are you okay, Sergeant?' Rhys takes another step back. Shakes his head. Shakes his head again to clear his vision. Behind him he senses someone in the doorway.

'It's easier to believe in these fantasies, isn't it? Easier than accepting the things that human beings can do to each other?' Rhys's voice feels like it's not his own. 'This terrible evil? Evil that drains women of blood, takes it with them for some reason we don't want to think about, it's human, Andrews, and... ' And that's all? And nothing more? Those words would be nowhere near enough.

'No.'

'After everything you must have seen.' Rhys shakes his head, slowly this time. The room becomes a solid reality around him.

'No!'

Enough time wasted. Rhys turns towards the door. He needs fresh air. To feel the cool rain against his skin. The female Constable whose name he hasn't asked stands there, the front of her uniform stiff with Andrews's blood.

'Hi,' says Rhys. 'I'm Rhys Morgan.'

'Hi,' Rhys shakes her bloodstained hand. 'Constable Robertson. Are you okay?'

'Nice to meet you.' Rhys turns back to Andrews, 'I'm sorry, sorry for you and the families whose time you've wasted.'

'No!' Andrews shouts. 'You must listen to me. He will come to you. He has told me.'

'You've met this "creature" you talk about?' Rhys finger quotes the words, why is he even continuing this conversation?

'No.'

'Then how has he told you anything? Do you know what the first signs of madness are? Hearing voices. Seeing things.' Rhys raises his palms.

'I don't need to meet him for him to tell me, for me to know. Why won't you listen? Why is it so hard to understand? I need to see him. When he finds you, I need you to bring him to me. You must listen to me. You must, I must, just… ' Andrews starts to pace in the small space. 'You will all see. You will know I am right and by then it will be too late. I know the things he will do!' He shouts now, shouts to those down the corridor, those who cannot hear. 'The things he will do to your family.' His eyes swivel to Rhys. 'Oh, you will believe me as he violates your wife, as he flays your children, as… '

Rhys is on Andrews before he is even fully aware of it, hands pushing against Andrews's ribs, sending him back hard against the wall.

'What did you say?' Andrews lets out a snort. It tries to become a laugh but seems to catch somewhere deep in his chest. Rhys can feel the vibration under his palms. Andrews pulls for air. The wheezing sound is full of pain. Panic flares across Andrews's face. Air can't get back in. Andrews tries to move his hands to his chest but can't. There is a deafening moment of silence broken by a wet, bubbling sound. Black blood seeps to the corners of Andrews's mouth. His eyes bulge in terror. The edges of his lips start to turn blue.

Then the coughing starts. Deep and soul shaking.

Large globules of blood project across Rhys's face.

'I need some help in here!' Rhys shouts over his shoulder. His words bounce along the corridor as Andrews's feet slip from under him.

11.

The sky is dark. The clouds hang low and heavy. They never tire of raining. They just pause to give false hope.

Quinn has given Rhys little instruction. This is how things are set to be. In the aftermath of Andrews's collapse in the cells, Rhys is instructed to 'collect anything that looks like it may be relevant to the case that the mad bastard has squirrelled away at his house'.

Quinn's loud words echoed along the celled corridor.

Andrews had recovered enough to try and laugh as he overheard, it was a wet, rattling sound. Quinn swore a lot, shouted about proper procedure, pushed his face close to Andrews. Quinn had no care for this deranged lunatic. What he cared about was the mess the case was in. The mess the cell was in. The mess his goddamn finger was in. He didn't care about Andrews's mental or physical well-being. Care was not the word he used.

Paramedics pushed Quinn aside with disgust. They didn't care for his tone. They saw a sick man, who had been handcuffed and looked to be covered in self-inflicted bites and cuts, bites and cuts inflicted while in police care. They saw stories of police incompetency. They didn't understand, didn't want to. They fed Andrews pure oxygen. All the while, Andrews kept trying to laugh, laugh at that private joke. A joke that was anything but funny.

Sweat stuck Rhys's shirt to his back. He used his shirtsleeve to wipe Andrews's bloody saliva from his face. He pulled on his coat. It was still wet. He didn't care. He was happy to be free of the chaos.

Rhys looks up at Andrews's house. The clouds release a second wave of rain. The grass of the small front garden is overgrown. Crisp packets and chip wrappers gather at the edges, dropped off by the drunks and the wind, collected by no one. The street is the kind of street where no one rises much before the pubs open. Andrews was a Detective Inspector, he could have moved. He should have moved.

Andrews is only fifty-eight as his world implodes. As Rhys steps into the house, he realises the event has been a long time in coming.

The entrance hall is half the size it should be due to the towering stacks of newspapers and magazines packed floor to ceiling. The magazines are largely factual: nature, science and geography. They are grouped together by title. Some are in date order; others grouped by subject. They span in some instances decades, depending on whether they are a weekly or monthly release. As the dates near the present they become more jumbled, less loved. Editions are missing and upside down. Rhys runs his hand down a stack. They're damp. As is the next stack. And the next. The dozens of newspaper stacks that tunnel off into the house are dry, but the magazines are ruined. They slowly turn to pulp as the ceiling extends its dark, wet fingers down the wall and through their heart.

Constable Robertson follows Rhys into the entrance hall. Momentarily, all natural light is gone. Panic grabs at Rhys's throat. He's drowning. The air is thick and wet. Constable Robertson moves and Rhys is released. He lets out a gasp. Robertson raises an eyebrow, squeezes past. The rain on her uniform makes her smell like a wet dog. Robertson turns and speaks.

'Shame eh?' She looks at the jumbled stacks. 'Bathtub overflowed. He left it running when he was called out on a case lead.' It could almost be sad.

Rhys follows Robertson further into the gloom.

A twisted, upside down face greets Rhys as he steps into the room. Under all the blood she may have green eyes, Rhys cannot be sure. One thing he is sure of is she is young. And dead. His eyes travel quickly right but the next image offers little consolation.

The victim's photos line the wall where the fireplace would have been. Large A4 prints staring blankly into nowhere. Crime scene photos, not holiday snaps. The line starts with Claudia

Rose and ends with a large black question mark drawn on the wall.

Rhys stands in a space most people would describe as a room that would better suit being a skip. A threadbare sofa faces the prints. Either side of the sofa are stacks of brown manila files. Hundreds of handwritten and typed documents mingling with hundreds of books. They spill like a cancerous growth out into the room.

'Bloody hell,' is all Rhys can think of to say.

The sofa and coffee table are the only visible furniture. There must be other items as the books, magazines and paper bulge up and down. The room is dark. The strong smell of damp prevails. It is a cave. A cave inhabited by a strange, book-stealing creature. A creature that lives in both its own filth and mind.

The curtains across the large window are drawn. Drawn and nailed down all the way round. Crude six-inch nails hammered into place. Small lamps bathe the room in dark rather than light. Stacked and piled together in random order, the books seem themselves to be made out of a dark matter that greedily sucks up what little light there is.

Rhys picks up a book, an encyclopaedia of dark arts. The next is a history of the Nosferatu in England. Then historical figures and dark magic. The next, lords and wealthy estates hiding Nosferatu for generations. Popular demon misconceptions follow and so the list goes on, getting more and more ridiculous. Watching him from the wall are the photographs. The photographs of the dead. Those who have been tortured and bled to death in their own homes to end up here.

The ball of rage and ridiculousness catches Rhys unawares. It explodes from his stomach. He clenches his teeth to prevent its escape. He grips the encyclopaedia in his hand until his knuckles grow white. It's better than hurling it across the room.

From the doorway Constable Robertson coughs. She's not clearing her throat. Rhys looks to her. Her eyes show him she thinks the same. How do they know what within this room is real? What is already in the system? What could be a lead and what a monumental waste of time?

'Fingers crossed it should be easy to tell.' Robertson's words are barely audible.

Rhys's words are blunt. He doesn't care.

'Get all of this boxed up and back to the station. What a bloody waste of time.' He throws the book hard against the wall and is gone before it thumps onto the carpet.

12.

In the darkness, the vile little boy is all alone. His body is broken and tears run lines across his skin. Their laughter, her laughter, rings in his ears even when there is silence. The cold and the dark soak into his core.

Initially the raw, bloody food makes him want to be sick. It claws at his stomach that fights to reject it. Over time, however, it becomes the norm. A point of stability. Calm and soothing in the chaos. It replaces the love she is unwilling to give. Now it is soft and comforting in his belly. A blanket to keep him warm in the cold and dark. He feels whole. This is strange at first but soon he grows to understand and accept. To anticipate and wait. He is very good at waiting.

The thing with little boys is they grow into big boys. In the darkness one day they are not so small. They don't need light to grow, or even love. Just time. Time to think and change and develop. They develop into what they have been made, or what they deserve to be. They don't even have to be that old before this change, as the naughty, vile boy discovers. He is barely a teenager when he is big enough for the world he lives in to start to look and feel very small indeed.

The vile young man sharpens the knife one last time. He holds its razor edge up to the bathroom window and watches it glint in the moonlight. On the old dairy stool beside the bath is the shrieking voice. A grey tingle to her mottled skin, a thin sheen of grease to her dirty underwear. The cord he has bound her ankles and wrists with is nearly as sharp as the knife. The angry red grooves start to weep and bleed.

How she tries to shriek as he marks the line on her throat with a biro. He doesn't really need to but does it all the same. The shriek must have caused her lips to bleed beneath the tape. At one point it seems she is being sick. He isn't sure until it comes out of her nose. He tears off the tape to be sure she stays alive, watches as she gasps and gulps at the stale oxygen.

She looks up at him now, her crow eyes pleading. Can those be tears that pour from her stony heart?

'It was all him. Honestly. It was all him, boy.' Even now she can't bring herself to say his name. 'Why would I ever want to hurt you?' she lies. The bile affects her vocal chords. 'If I didn't do it he would have left us and then where would we have been?' On and on she rattles, deaf ears her only receptor. Blame, blame, blame. Not once does she say sorry. Not once does she say she was wrong. Not once does she say he is enough, that he is the only one she has ever wanted, that she should have put him first. Not that it would have made a difference. Not now. He expects to feel anger, pure rage at this moment. Instead he feels a strange sense of calm as he inspects her.

She really starts to try and fight as he strings her up above the bath. He has to hit her a lot to make her still.

The cut he makes across her throat opens up in slow motion. It takes his breath away. It is warm and wet as he sticks his finger in. Poor gnarled finger. Even after all these years the nail has never properly grown back.

'That will teach you for chewing it.' The shrill voice had spat. Or was it the fault of Strong Hands for pulling it off every time it grew back?

Strong Hands's time will come. Those strong hands not so strong now. The hammer has seen to that. No, not so strong now, Strong Hands.

Oh! She's wake. She opens her mouth and tries to speak. All that comes out is a bubble of crimson saliva. Her face says she is full of fury. He smiles. There she is. The old bitch he is so used to. Cursing him right up to the end.

'Shhhhhh.' He soothes, pursing her lips back together. He cocks his head and holds her gaze. 'What more do you expect from such a vile and naughty boy?' He giggles then, in spite of himself.

The blood is flowing from her exactly as he anticipated. Pumping but not spurting. It mesmerises him. Within seconds the blood flows like a silky sheet, or a veil, covering her contorting face. She should be grateful. The moonlight floods through the window and catches her body. He has listened hard within his cupboard and knows she is as afraid of the dark as he used to be.

Her blood runs the same track down the bathtub as the water always did. Invisible grooves forming a pattern to be followed in the dirty white porcelain. He lowers his finger into one of the branching flows then raises it to his lips. Sweet copper and calm. Comfort and known. Him. Her. And the blood provided by her. As always.

He looks into his mother's bleary eyes and for the first time feels she loves him. Crouching, he leans towards her and licks the side of her face. The flow is warm and fresh. He tastes her truly for the first time. Tastes her love.

Downstairs, the moonlight streams inside. It casts long shadows across the hallway, across the cupboard under the stairs. The young man passes the cupboard, kicks the door hard. Something inside groans and gurgles. No hurry. He will keep. Keep there in the dark. Let him think about what he has done for a while.

The taste of blood is strong in his mouth. He runs his tongue along his lips. Inhales the lingering aroma. It appears shrieking Mother has finally had some use. Nourishing him as never before. He giggles.

Leaving shrieking Mother to finish draining in the bath and Strong Hands to tremble in the dark, the vile young man pulls his cap down low and steps out into the beautiful new night.

13.

The dream starts the same as always but this time he knows the serpent will come. Treacle thick, the invisible force prevents him from running. Strain as he might, he cannot escape. Nor can he awake. Behind him the serpent begins its journey once more.

He can see the male and female in their paradise within paradise. They run to the white fence and call out to him. They reach out their arms, stretch towards him. Could it be her? As she should have been? She shouts. Her face is blurred. Her dimples. Her ringlet hair. Her face twists with concern and anguish. She shouts harder now but he cannot hear the words.

The serpent is a black line on the landscape that wiggles towards him. Electric lightning illuminates the sky. Its fingers fork out and bleach the colour from everything. Vision after a camera flash. He turns again and tries to run.

There is something ahead of him now. It pulsates. Black, white, black, white then colour. It is a rip in the landscape. A massive tear in the beauty. It's rolling towards him, swallowing up everything in its wake. He turns back in panic but there is nowhere to run.

Screeching, the serpent passes and disappears into the tear. It emanates an icy coldness that raises goosebumps on every pore on his body.

Then the ground beneath his feet is gone and he too is falling. The darkness swallows him up. It's as black as anything he has ever known. He tries to scream but there's no sound.

Then here, in the darkness, is the creature. His golden hair glows like fire. His blue eyes stare, penetrating the dark.

The eyes of the serpent.

The man knows he will die when he impacts the ground. The creature with the fire blond hair catches him in its arms. Now they are both falling but the man is no longer afraid. His heart beats so fast he fears it may tear free and be lost in the dark. He looks up at the creature who parts its blood-red lips and smiles.

'Ask,' the creature whispers, but the man has no idea what to ask for. 'Ask.' Its brow furrows. 'Or be prepared to die.'

Jesus Christ.

Rhys shoots bolt upright in bed, slams on the light. He's trapped in the bedclothes. The creature's arms. The bedclothes.

He's drenched in sweat and fear, still drowning in the dream. He uses panic to fight free. His gasps are loud in the cool reality. The bed is reassuringly solid beneath him. His stomach rejoins him from somewhere far above. Hands clamp to his chest to hold his heart in place.

Breathe.

Just breathe.

Until two months ago, Rhys had never had a dream. No one believes him, but it's true. He's asleep the minute his head hits the pillow and remains that way until dawn. The only things that come to him in his sleep are phone calls. Markers signifying someone else had too much and walked away. Or worse.

Then the dreams start. Novel at first. He becomes the boring person describing the indescribable over breakfast. At work. Over dinner.

At first, the garden is wondrous. Larger than life. Secure. A fun place to while away the time as his brain flicks through the files of the day. Storing the relevant. Destroying the used. That is what dreams are, right? A place to sort out the day's events? Nothing more. The garden is magic. Seen through the eyes of a child. His birth into dreaming and it takes his breath away.

Initially he is an observer of the garden. Then he is in it. Touching the lush flowers, smelling the pollens with a smile on his lips. Night after night, he awakes fresh and calm. Then it starts to change.

To rot.

Anna tells him it is because of his job. The things he sees. It's his brain's way of dealing with it. If he's struggling, there are people who can help. His response is hard, more than needed. He asks what she's insinuating by 'people who can help'. She doesn't answer. He can't tell if her face is pink through anger or shame.

Rhys rubs hard at his eyes. He rubs hard at his arms. The goosebumps have travelled with him from the garden, no not the garden but what came after.

'Get a grip.' His voice seems loud. The temperature in the bedroom must have dropped, that's all.

Next to him Anna murmurs, rolls tighter into her side of the duvet. He knows she's awake; she's fooling no one. After all this time together does she really think he believes she could sleep through the light coming on, the movement on the bed? Rhys is happy for her to pretend, no, not happy, indifferent. It will save him having to listen to her sympathies, her suggestions, having to try and explain what he doesn't really understand.

The carpet is thick and comforting beneath his toes as he goes to fetch a blanket. He has to look in several places. Why is Anna always moving things? Rearranging, changing, hinting. Hints that she wouldn't need to keep doing this if they moved. She no longer says the words. Actions speak far louder. She fails to understand, they will never move. Rhys will never leave this house.

The curtains billow slightly although the window is not open.

The blanket, when he finds it, is rough. Sandpaper on skin that's extra sensitive in the still of the night. Rhys wraps it round his shoulders, sits on the edge of the bed. The dream clings onto the edges of his mind. A shiver runs through his body. He rubs his finger and thumb together, not able to shift the solid feeling of the creature from his fingertips.

'Rhys?' Anna murmurs.

His fingers dig into the blanket.

'It's nothing.'

Rhys rises, turns off the light and leaves her alone in the dark.

14.

A thin layer of dust on the bookshelf catches in the early morning light. Teenage paperbacks next to children's classics. Rhys opens his eyes. The room pulls into focus. Polaroid photographs around the mirror smile down at him, tacked up in haste, to be completed later. In one of the photos she smiles, the biggest smile Rhys has ever seen, sandwiched between boys at a local gig. Rhys remembers that night, her happiness. Then again, it is possible he doesn't remember the night at all. The photograph is the memory. In the other photos she is with various girlfriends. A new tribe, association with family became 'totally uncool'.

Next to the bed are a variety of soft toys. Some sentimental, some part of a collection. A big pink teddy bear takes pride of place, centre stage. This one is from Rhys. He won it in the arcades on a family holiday. Then they ate fish and chips, laughed in the sunshine.

There was a family holiday, but it didn't end like that.

Suspended in a glass clip frame next to the bed is a black and white poster of a man with his shirt off, holding a baby. It is juxtaposed with a cartoon-style poster of *The Hobbit*. The walls are an inoffensive white. Polystyrene alcove. Off-white skirting. Has the skirting always been off-white or has time yellowed it like human skin?

Rhys knows every detail of this room. The angles of the furniture. The wear on the carpet. The way a magazine has been left open next to the bed. The cushion he hugs to his chest is as good as new, but dated. The Coca-Cola emblem as white against the red as the day he gave it to her.

To Jenny.

His breathing slows. He moves a fraction, the blanket still rough against his skin.

'Rhys?' Her voice is light and playful. A voice as real to him as he drifts off as it was all those years ago.

'Oh go on, Rhys. Surely you don't need two?' Rhys peers up at her through his thick eyebrows. Alert. On edge. Since she has turned fourteen, Jenny is, what he can only describe as odd. Odd and mean. She doesn't want to play what she refers to as 'childish games', games she loved and begged to play the summer before. In general she ignores him, laughs and points at him and his friends with her newfound ones. She doesn't speak to Mum or Dad anymore either. Apparently they didn't understand. Rhys thinks they understand loads. That's what being a grown up is all about: understanding and knowing loads. Oh, and not having to go to school.

One of Dad's friends from work has come to visit. Work is where you go when you finish school. He is a massive man with a huge moustache and loud American accent. The American gives them both presents, special things wrapped in brown paper and string. Special things all the way from America.

Jenny's present is a bright pink tracksuit with a sequined image of New York skyscrapers on it. Rhys can tell she hates it but she smiles politely. It's odd, Rhys is sure she loves pink and glitter. Mind you, that was probably yesterday not today. Rhys is pleased she pretends to like her gift as the American man is so excited to give it to her, and Dad would have been so mad if she'd cried.

Then it's Rhys's turn. He doesn't want to open the package. It's so exciting to look at and feel, and try and guess what it is. Plus he's frightened. He doesn't know how well he'll be able to pretend to like a pink tracksuit with sequins on the front. String pulled and paper strewn aside, he finds two amazing, bright, shiny Coca-Cola emblem cushions. They're exactly the ones everyone at school wants and dreams of one day having. If he had known at the time what a Fabergé egg was, this would have been as good. No. Better.

Everyone exclaims that the American man shouldn't have, apart from Rhys who thinks he really should, and Jenny who accidently agrees too wholeheartedly. The American man replies it's no bother and gets all teary about some kids he's never had, which is odd. He squeezes Jenny and Rhys as tight as a bear then dismisses them to play. Darting upstairs, Rhys is in the middle of deciding where to display his new gifts in his red, white and black room when Jenny appears.

'Rhys.' Her voice is light and playful. 'Oh go on, Rhys. Surely you don't need two?' The dimples in her cheeks show more when she smiles.

'What's it worth?' Rhys responds, knowing instantly she meant his new prize.

'Hmmm… Let me see.' Jenny pouts and thinks. Rhys is always impressed by how quickly Jenny can think, even if sometimes it's how to be mean. 'How about I eat all your greens at tea time?' That's a really good one.

'For a week?' asks Rhys, happy at his own fast thinking.

'A whole week?' She places her hands on her hips. 'Deal.'

'Shake on it.' Rhys stretches out his hand. Jenny goes to take it but instead grabs him and blows a big raspberry kiss on his forehead. She pushes him lightly onto the bed and picks up one of the cushions. Rhys laughs and for what seems like the longest time, Jenny laughs too. Her dark ringlets bounce as she jumps up and down with joy. For a moment, she forgets her new adult persona, and is the child he knows so well. She is back, if only for that moment. She is his big sister and he beams with joy.

15.

Anna stands with her nose inches from the closed door; she doesn't need to open it to know he's inside. So much for pretending to be asleep, hoping he'd snuggle back beside her, cuddle up and allow her to make everything okay. She stares hard at the glossed wood, stares until her vision goes blurry and her eyes start to water. What is she hoping? That somehow he will know she's here? Why should this time be any different to all the others? She inhales slowly, closes her eyes, leans her forehead against the cool wood. Silly cow. Perhaps some people never learn?

Jenny Morgan, Rhys's big sister, was only fourteen when she disappeared, decades ago, now frozen in time.

One day Jenny was there, happy, smiling, if a little irritable. The next she was gone, vanished off the face of the planet, tearing in her wake a giant rip in the fabric of the world as the Morgans knew it. Had she run away? If she had, she hadn't taken one solitary item with her. Had she been abducted? If she had, not one speck of evidence was left to call for help. Rhys has silently covered every angle over the past twenty-two years.

Rhys refuses to leave this house. He stayed long after his parents abandoned all hope. He doesn't voice the thought, but Anna knows he needs to be here in case she comes back. In case she sends a sign.

To be with him, Anna moved in. Amongst the shards of Rhys's family home they slowly constructed their own.

At first Jenny's room was the beating heart of the house. Anna wondered if she could bear it, the oddness of it all, if she could live within the memory of someone she'd never known. Why couldn't the room be tucked away in a box somewhere? Moved out of sight? Rhys would heal faster if there wasn't a constant reminder of his loss staring at him daily.

It was, is, not up for discussion. The room will not be packed away. It will not be touched.

The door to the room is rarely open. It's a secret place Rhys wants to protect from the world's eye, even if the eye belongs to those who love him most. The door is shut tight and over time,

Anna has come to all but ignore it. Like a pattern, no, stain on the wallpaper you become so accustomed to, you almost forget it's there.

Almost.

Over the years, Rhys gradually stopped talking about her, his big sister, but her shadow is always cast. Like a piece of fruit left in the bowl for too long, her memory is rotten.

Rhys couldn't stay in this room forever with his sister. He couldn't keep her safe. Now it has become his safe place. An irony that makes Anna feel physically sick.

Rhys has transferred to Murder. Something they discussed, then argued about for hours, realising through tears, they were both arguing the same point. Anna can't understand why he's doing it if he doesn't want to. Rhys says what she fails to understand is that he cannot say no. They both know his implication. She's not worked for too many years, is too out of touch to know 'how these things work'. She shouldn't comment on what she doesn't understand. It hangs in the air between them for days. Niggles like a splinter too far under the skin.

This case isn't going to be about someone who's missing, someone Rhys can save and bring home. It's about someone who's dead.

Dead.

Something inside Anna starts to sink. She has been treading water for weeks now and is tired. She doesn't want to drown, but like a kitten tied in a sack, is unsure how to prevent it.

Anna exhales slowly through her nose. In through her mouth, out through her nose. Her breath condenses on the wood of the door. She stands and watches it for a very long time.

16.

The car horn blares in the morning air. On the front step Rhys jumps, drops his house keys. It's early. Quinn can clearly see him. The rest of the cul-de-sac will have no desire to be disturbed at this hour. What the hell is he playing at? Rhys turns towards the car, through the window he sees Quinn light a cigarette.

'Hope I didn't wake you there.' Quinn takes a long swig of a fizzy energy drink then burps almost as loudly as his horn. Rhys closes the car door softly, slides the window all the way down. Quinn pulls away from the curb. Quinn's right hand is strapped. He sees Rhys looking.

'Bastard's only gone and broken it.' Quinn waves the hand in case there is any confusion. Rhys nods. Turns to look out of the window. Dawn is trying, and failing, to break.

Rhys stretches his neck, runs his hands over his face. He feels the creature from the dream's solid body ghost against his fingertips. Sees the eyes that pierce deep inside him.

Rhys stretches his eyes wide, blinks. He must know this being, this man, from somewhere. That's how it works isn't it, that's how he's ended up in the dreams. Part of the filing away process.

Night after night after night.

Rhys yawns. Things always seem better in the morning, more rational, right? But his heartbeat quickens as he thinks of the dream, everything about it so real, as if it happened, as if he is recalling actual events, events that keep on happening.

Night after night after night.

Rhys needs to be able to think clearly, that's all. Hard to do when he can't sleep properly, when he's so goddamn tired all the time. He needs to work out where he's seen this man, why he keeps appearing in the dream. Simple really. Goosebumps scatter down Rhys's arms. All he needs a good night's sleep.

'You keep telling yourself that,' says the little voice inside. He pushes it away. A few hours of peace. He rubs at his arms, focuses on the road ahead.

They're heading to St James' Hospital. Quinn has decided it's the best plan of action while they wait for the Constables to finish boxing up Andrews's front room. Eddie Reynolds is in the hospital. They're the ones that need to make their presence known. PR and policing all wrapped up in one.

'Who knows what kind of shit they'll bring from Andrews's place.' Quinn talks out loud, but requires no response. 'We'll probably find Andrews's sofa and picture of his mother in the office when we get back. Like we need more work to do.' The arrival of a sofa at the station would be a blessing compared to what they will receive.

'You've never been to Andrews's house?'

'Why would I? We weren't mates.'

'No one had any concerns about his health prior to... this?'

'Why would they? You may all sit about in circles discussing your innermost feelings over at Quarry Road; here we do things a little differently.'

'How's that working out for you?' Quinn looks at Rhys out of the corner of his eye, chews something around in his mouth.

'See you're still living in your folks old house.' Rhys turns his face away.

'And that's your business why?'

'How's that working out for *you*?'

They drive the rest of the way in silence.

St James' Hospital looms over the horizon.

Quinn spots a space in the quickly filling car park. He swerves in ahead of a four-by-four full of women and children.

'Too slow,' he mutters under his breath. He sticks his police badge out of the window and shouts, 'Police business' at their angry faces. 'Who needs a four-by-four in the city anyway?' His head still shakes as he climbs out. The slam of the car door is loud. Quinn pulls out his notebook as he strides towards the hospital entrance. He scribbles notes Rhys can't see.

The automatic door slides open and the hospital swallows them whole.

A Constable sits at the door to Eddie Reynolds's room. What percentage of him secretly hopes the killer will return to finish Eddie off, allow him to be the hero his mother always wanted?

Down the corridor, sits Eddie's son, Tony.

'Tony,' Quinn speaks, heads away from Rhys.

'Please, not now.' Tony stands.

Rhys turns and enters Eddie Reynolds' room. The room is small but alive with the hum and click of stark white machines. They run multicoloured tubes and wires to Eddie's body. He's framed in the middle like an electronic god.

Rhys steps inside.

The light inside the room flickers.

Rhys holds his breath, stares at the overhead strip lighting. Waits. The rhythmic beep of machinery does not falter. Seconds pass.

Footsteps sound in the corridor. Outside Quinn introduces himself. He enters the room with a small, bald man whose features are sharp like an eagle.

'Doctor Curtis, this is my colleague Detective Sergeant Rhys Morgan.' The doctor extends a slim hand.

'Hello. I would like to say it's a pleasure, however,' the doctor waves at the machinery.

'Perhaps under different circumstances.'

'Jesus.' Quinn's eyes are wide as he looks at Eddie. The doctor doesn't flinch. He takes the clipboard from the end of Eddie's bed. He makes illegible notes based on the monitors around them. He gives Quinn a moment to compose himself. Quinn's mouth still hangs open as the doctor begins his address.

'As I said to your colleague on the phone, Eddie will be of little assistance to you. He lost consciousness in the ambulance and has yet to regain it. If indeed he ever will.' Quinn's lips move to speak. No sound comes out. The doctor waits. 'I will tell you what little I can, although I am not sure if it will be of much help.' The doctor slots the clipboard back into its holder. He speaks, never taking his eyes off Eddie.

'As you are both aware, Eddie arrived with us in the early hours of Monday morning. As I have mentioned, he lost consciousness, was barely alive.' The doctor shakes his head in bewilderment. 'The level of pain he has endured... ' The doctor pauses for a moment, allows his human emotion to surface for air. Deep breath. He swallows it back down. Gives himself an internal shake.

'Eddie appears to have been, what I can only describe as, tortured prior to incarceration.' Rhys keeps his eyes on the doctor. Quinn's eyes do not move from Eddie.

'Eddie has been beaten, severely and with extreme malice. The initial blow to the head would have rendered him helpless.' The crimson stain on the floral wallpaper. 'The marks on his skin show this beating was done both by fists and an object, so I guess you are looking for someone strong. Strong and angry. The skin has not been deliberately broken, unlike the bones that most certainly have. Broken jaw, cheekbone and nose, collarbone and multiple ribs. The pelvis in several places. Right radius and ulna, the left femur and knee... ' The doctor stops. He is not reading from a chart. These are the things he knows.

'You get the idea. The list goes on. Heinous as this is, I'm afraid it's not the worst part.' The doctor's eyes drop from Eddie. 'The worst part is the hands.' Rhys looks the end of Eddie's arms.

'Every single bone in both his hands has been broken. No, broken is the wrong word, crushed suits better. I can only imagine the killer, is that the right term...?' Quinn nods. 'The killer used some kind of hammer to inflict such, such mutilation. Such pain.' Their heads all bow in unison. Mourners at a funeral paying last respects. But Eddie is not dead. Not quite. Chemical signals still fizz somewhere deep inside, fed by the machines.

'There really was nothing we could do, you understand. If there was we would have.' The doctor's voice is fast but speed will not detract from the horror. 'There is nowhere in the country that could repair that kind of damage. Nowhere.

'We had to amputate both his hands.'

If a pin dropped they would all have heard it. The mechanics of the life-giving machines that beep around them drop an octave. The doctor clears his throat.

'One of your people has already been for his clothes, taken what I assume are the relevant pictures and samples. I can show you the paperwork if needed?'

'No need,' says Quinn. 'It's standard procedure.'

'Standard procedure?' The doctor stares up at Quinn. 'How can this,' a gesture to Eddie, 'be anything near standard procedure?'

'You'd be surprised.' The doctor shakes his head.

The lights inside the room flicker. There is a flash. Blindingly bright in the clean white room. Rhys blinks rapidly. Shadows in his eyes.

'What's that?' A power cut? A power surge? That can't be safe where people rely on electric machines to keep them alive. His heart beats slightly faster. Is there a backup generator?

'What's what?' Quinn and the doctor look at him blankly.

'That flash. The lights?' Rhys nods his head upwards.

Everything slows right down. The doctor and Quinn melt away. The lights flash again. They turn the room into a series of silhouettes. Black. Then white. Then black again. The smell of must and orchids fills his nostrils.

His stomach drops and he is falling.

Pitch black rushes at him from all directions. He wants to scream. He opens his mouth but no sound comes out. Then the creature is there. It catches him. It makes him safe. The creature's fingers brush the back of his neck. Every hair on his body stands on end. He turns his head to the creature. The vivid blue eyes hook his.

The eyes in his dream.

The eyes holding his from the door.

17.

'What the fuck?' The words are out before Rhys can stop them. The eyes holding his from the door? The doctor's voice twists back up to full volume. The room pulls sharply back into focus.

'Detective, are you okay?' The doctor reaches out to Rhys. He turns before the fingers touch him.

'I can only apologise for that, sir.' Quinn scowls. 'As I am sure you are aware we in no way promote or tolerate that kind of language…'

'The door.' Rhys is already moving. No time to wait for affirmation. 'Then. There was a man at the door.'

'What?' Quinn's voice is sharp. A deep red colour starts to creep up his neck.

'I don't think so, Detective.' The doctor glances to Quinn. 'Look, it is rather warm in here and what I've just been telling you, are you sure...?'

'A man. There was a man at the door.' Rhys says the words for himself. His hand touches the doorframe inches from where the creature's face had been.

'I'm sorry.' The doctor's voice is behind him now. 'I really don't understand... '

Rhys is already out of the door. His knees like jelly. His fingertips on the wall to steady himself. The corridor is ice cold.

There he is.

The creature, the man from his dreams, his nightmares. Rhys only just sees him as he disappears around the corner. His golden hair perfectly cut to the nape of his neck.

Rhys starts to run. His shoes echo in the eerie silence. His knees don't betray him.

'What the... ?' Quinn and the doctor must have reached the doorway.

'He really can't go running off around the hospital like that, Detective. He will cause alarm in the… '

Rhys rounds the corner as the man disappears. He should have caught up with him by now. He's running full pelt. Around the next corner and the next. Always the man rounds the corner up ahead. Surely there can't be this much corridor, this many corners in one hospital? Rhys's shoes skid on the polished floor. He rounds the next bend.

Should he stop? Stop and take a serious look at himself? This isn't quite right is it? But then again, it isn't so wrong either. He probably knows this man, must do. An old case? One of the kids' schools? All he needs to do is speak to him, get some clarity. Do what he needs to get rid of the feelings of dread darkness brings. He can then dream of the garden in peace.

That makes perfect sense.

The corridor straightens out. The man disappears through a set of double doors. Rhys reaches them, hears the click of the locking sensor.

'Fuck.' Rhys thumps the door. The keypad. Nothing budges. Behind the glass panel in the door, something moves. Rhys presses his face against the glass. There he is. The creature. The man? Rhys cannot breathe. The man picks up a file and turns to the door. His vivid blue eyes lock with Rhys's. The wind roars in Rhys's ears. And then the creature behind the glass smiles. A smile that slowly stretches its face like someone's hands are beneath its skin. The head tilts. The ground beneath Rhys's feet gives way and he drops into darkness.

A sharp, desperate pull of breath. A blink. The floor is once more solid beneath his feet.

Rhys stands, breathes deeply. A fine sweat has broken out all over his body. He looks through at the glass panel.

Nothing.

He steps away, runs his fingers through his hair. His head spins. What the bloody hell is going on?

Suddenly the doors swing open. Rhys's heart stops.

Two young nurses step towards him. They chat and laugh. Rhys tries to push past. For a small woman, the female nurse is surprisingly strong. She stops him dead.

'I'm sorry, sir. You can't go through there. Not without authorisation.'

'I'm a police officer.' Rhys reaches for his identification. It's not there. Where the hell is it? Harry best not be playing with it again. The door's locking device clicks back into place. Shit.

'Please, I really need to go through there. I'm here on police business, with Doctor...' Shit. What was the doctor's name? Carter? Campbell? 'Doctor Campbell.'

'We don't have a doctor here by that name, sir.' The male nurse speaks this time.

'Yes! Yes you do, he's back there with my colleague.'

'I'm sorry, sir.' The female nurse. 'We really can't let anyone through without prior permission.'

'I have that.'

'I don't mean to be rude, but I don't think you do. Do you, sir?'

'Okay, fine.' Rhys stands his ground. 'Can you tell me, did a man go through there. Tall. Blond hair?' Why is the male nurse smiling? Has he seen him?

'No, sir.' The female nurse speaks. 'I've been on the desk all morning. It's been quiet, definitely no tall, blond men passed my way. I would remember that.' Why are they smirking?

'Why are you laughing?' That stops them. 'Why is that funny? It's a serious police question. I don't see any reason to laugh.' With perfect timing a walkie-talkie crackles down the corridor. Two security guards fill the far end. Head towards them. Head towards him.

'Yeah we've found him, Guv, outside the chemo suites.' There's a crackle of response. 'Yeah, he looks fine. We'll bring him up.'

'Hi guys.' The friendly approach. 'Sorry about all this, I don't really know how to explain...'

'There's no need, sir.' The tall one gestures for Rhys to move between them. Away from the doors. Away from the nurses who don't giggle anymore. Away from the man.

'Not to us at least.' The second slightly smaller guard retorts. His face is long and thin with small teeth, like a weasel.

'Could you do me a favour before we go?' Why is no one listening? Why won't they help? It's not a lot to ask. 'Nip in there,' a gesture to the secure doors, 'and see if there's a tall man, with blue eyes and blond hair?'

'There's no one in there with hair.'

The weasel realises too late he's spoken out loud and pointed to the chemotherapy sign above the doors. If they were in a cartoon, the tall guard would slap him around the back of the head.

'What the fuck, Dave?'

The male nurses gasps.

The words crash around Rhys. Along with some sense of reality. What on earth is he doing?

'Shit, sorry, I didn't....'

Get a grip.

Right now.

Rhys's head pounds. He needs fresh air. They are all looking at him like he's crazy. Why would they think otherwise? He is only upstaged by the weasel and his runaway mouth. Rhys doesn't want confrontation. He knows how it will end. The tall guard cracks his knuckles, speaks,

'Let's not have any fuss here.'

There's nothing more to say. Rhys follows the guards quietly back along the corridor, without glancing back at the doors once.

The doctor waits for him in a small room to the right of reception. He rises as they enter.

'Detective, are you okay?' The doctor's arm twitches. He stops himself reaching for Rhys.

'Yes. I'm fine. Sorry. I thought I saw someone I knew. From my son's school. Someone important that I need to catch up with. You know how it is.' The doctor's lying head nods.

'You really can't go running off around the hospital like that, I'm afraid.'

'Again, I really am sorry. I don't know what came over me. It's been a long week, you know how it is.' Rhys laughs. Too loud. Too forced. It's only Tuesday. Rhys looks around the room. Needs a distraction. An out.

'Where's Inspector Quinn?' The doctor visibly perks up at the change of subject.

'He said he would wait for you at the car.' Rhys is sure those are not the words Quinn used. The doctor gestures to the door. Dave the Weasel offers to show Rhys the way out.

'There's really no need.'

Dave the Weasel follows him anyway, until he is clear of the building.

Quinn stands by the car, leans against the no smoking sign and lights a cigarette. The gathering wind tugs at his hair.

'What the fuck's up with you?' Quinn's stare is cold.

'Nothing.' Rhys opens the car door. 'The flashing light in there made me think I saw someone I knew.'

'The lights weren't flashing.' Quinn takes a long drag of his cigarette. 'And it was some *guy* you knew.'

'Sorry?'

'You asked if there was a man at the door. Before you set off on your little chase. You're not, you know...?' Is he for real? Rhys stares at him.

'I'm married.'

'So what?'

'I'm tired. I got it wrong. Let's forget about it. Jesus.' Quinn flicks his cigarette away as if it has somehow offended him. Somewhere deep inside his leather coat, his phone rings. Loud. The National Anthem.

'Hello... yeah... go ahead. Okay we won't be long.' Quinn flips the phone shut, stares at Rhys across the roof of the car. 'Much as I'd love to watch you chase men, sorry, "people", round here all day, they've finished unloading. Time to reassemble crazy Andrews's front room. By the look of things, you're the perfect man for the job.'

18.

Will is late. It is ten-thirty in the morning and still he manages to be late. Pam shouldn't allow herself to be surprised. She's been married to him for long enough.

Pam collapsed three days ago, and due to her age, has been confined to the overcrowded hospital ward ever since. Due to her age indeed. She didn't think people could get away with saying such things these days.

It turns out her collapse was stress related, which is ridiculous. She has three grown-up children she may as well have raised single-handedly. There's no way that becoming involved with some local charity work would be the cause of her collapse. Pam untangles a length of blue wool.

Pam blames Will. She's made sure everyone on the ward knows it. Made sure he knew it when he visited. She feels no guilt. It's his fault for behaving the way he does. In one ear, out the other.

As she sits and waits, Pam realises she has come to hate and love her husband in equal measure. It should make her sad, but it doesn't. Her knitting needles start to clack rhythmically.

Will has recently retired, altering the equilibrium of their forty-year marriage. He was a long distance lorry driver, you see. Used to the freedom of the open road. To the hotel living. To being away from home half his life. He is also used to the fast food, which now hits his slowing metabolism. He has the fat body he swore he never would. He can't adapt to the fact their house is a home, not a hotel, or motel or whatever he chooses to refer to it, saying, 'I'm only joking, love. You shouldn't take everything so seriously'.

The main problem with Will is that he doesn't listen. Most of her friends laugh when she says this. He's a man, what does she expect? But it isn't funny. Will really doesn't listen. She spent two days in the wrong nightdress, rereading an old book, before he finally got it right.

She sees the way people look at her. Knows they think she is harsh and unfair to the old sod. They should try living with him. They would soon change their tune.

Here he comes. Ambling along like he's on time. Pam can actually feel her blood pressure rise. Luckily, the doctors have already signed her release paperwork. If one of them saw her now they would have her tucked back in before she could say, 'Have you met my husband?'

Will kisses her on the cheek.

'You're late.'

'Sorry, love.' He doesn't even bother to come up with an excuse. Again, she shouldn't be surprised. 'I picked up a menu from that little Chinese on the corner for tonight, though you might like a night off.' He smiles, small teeth in his fat, round head. Is she supposed to be grateful? They both know he hasn't picked it up. It's been delivered along with the greasy feasts he'll have been stuffing into his obese form for the past three nights.

'My bag's down there,' is all she cares to muster.

'Hop on then.' Will gestures to the wheelchair. Removes the knitting from her hands. Slings her bag over his ample shoulder.

'I'm fine, I'll walk.' Her voice is cool but she doesn't care. He won't notice either way.

'The nurses insist, said if they see you walk past you'll be straight back up here.' He takes hold of the handles. 'Honestly, love, I'm not lying. It's because you need rest, something like that.' He patronises her with a smile. Anger does a little somersault in her stomach.

'I would be well rested if you'd been on time and I was at home right now.'

'I said I'm sorry. Not something I've ever done before, pick someone up from the hospital.' Pam closes her eyes and breathes in deeply through her nose. It's a loud sound. Her favourite nurse recommended it for combating stress. Pam thinks of her own house. Her own kitchen. Her own chair. It softens and comforts her. She wants to get home. She opens her eyes and eases herself into the wheelchair.

'That's my girl.' If she had the energy she would climb straight back out and punch him in the face.

19.

Rhys and Quinn arrive back at the station after brunch.

Brunch consists of Quinn stuffing down the hugest all day breakfast Rhys has ever seen. 'They don't call it the belly buster for nothing.'

Rhys can only stomach coffee. Milk. Plenty of sugar. He focuses on Quinn's words. Blocks the stark images of the creature in the hospital from him mind. The voice in his head mocks, *do you think if you ignore me I'll go away?*

Quinn talks while he eats. He spits as much food back across the table as he swallows. His subject matter, loud and off-putting to other diners. He informs the café about the escalation in the killer's rage. Discounting the hands, Eddie has over twenty-two broken bones. Quinn points his knife at Rhys,

'No wonder the poor bastard doesn't want to regain consciousness. I know I wouldn't.'

The first male victim had only a few defensive wounds. His name was Ron. His wife was Jess. Rhys remembers. Andrews told him about Jess. The mirage in the summer heat. One half of the first couple to die. The husband of the second couple seems to have put up more of a fight. That's what they had assumed, however, some of his bones had been deliberately broken.

'Now there's Eddie.' Quinn shakes his head and refills his mouth. More greasy meat to spit onto the tabletop.

A mother at the next table tuts – moves her little girls to a table across the room. She shoots Quinn a look of sheer disgust he's oblivious to.

'Why has Eddie been left alive?' Quinn's loud words continue. 'A mistake, surely?' He soaks up some of the bacon grease with a piece of white bread. 'Mistakes are good. It's a thread in the intricate pattern of the killer's crazy mind and if we pick at it hard enough the whole thing will unravel.' Quinn sits back, looks proud of his analogy. His eyes drop to his tie. 'For fucks sake.' Quinn dabs off the red sauce, takes a final loud slurp of tea.

Quinn's chair legs scrape on the floor. It's time to go. Quinn smiles and waves at the little girl on the way out. She bursts into tears.

Box after box after box. All squeezed neatly into the Couples Killer operation room. The smell of damp that permeated everything in Andrews's house has transferred too. The air is thick, heavy to breathe.

The coffee kicks in. Rhys feels grounded. In control. The solution will be simple. It will come to him. It always does. Hold onto the fact he must know the man from somewhere. Embarrassment at his behaviour at St James' flares in his stomach, push it aside, focus on the case.

One thing at a time.

There's no visible desk space. Boxes still arrive. In the far corner Davies is setting up more noticeboards.

The mind map on the wall is growing. It spews out information on Eddie and Cathy's attack. Crime scene photos are juxtaposed with recent holiday snaps. Rhys recognises them, the ones from the yellow kitchen wall. Spider-like lines scurry out to a map of Eddie and Cathy's street. Pictures of neighbours with reference numbers relating to their statements. Potential evidence collected at the scene.

'It's old school but I like it,' says Quinn nodding to the mind map. 'Helps me think visually, far easier than everything on printouts and spreadsheets.'

People and activity are everywhere. The Constables from Eddie and Cathy's house are here. The Constable that found Eddie. Constable Johnstone. Slim and tall and jittery. He jumps every time a box drops. He can't look at the photos of Eddie. Constable Chantelle Watts is here too. Davies still ignores her; she doesn't look much like she gives a shit.

A system has been established. There's an area of the room for each couple murdered. Andrews would be sad to see Claudia Rose is still alone. There's an additional area for unrelated information. Demons and the dark arts. It will all need to be sifted through. No stone left unturned. Just in case.

'Good morning,' Quinn's voice brings the room to silence. 'I am sure I don't need to tell you how much work we have to do. You can all thank Detective Inspector Andrews for that later. Not only do we need to sift through this lot,' a hand gesture to the piles of boxes, 'we also need to revisit witness statements from the previous victims' families and friends, ensure all the details are correct and in order.' A collective groan from the room. Quinn raises his voice,

'Please people; remember this is nothing personal. I have no doubt you all did your jobs thoroughly at the time. This is about crossing the i's and dotting the t's for those upstairs. The quicker we get it done, the quicker we can get on with nailing this bastard. We'll start top end, the families of the victims, and work backwards.'

'I've already made some calls, sir,' says Davies. Quinn nods.

'Until then let's start sorting this shit. It's pretty self-explanatory boys and girls, open a box, see what's inside. There's an area for each victim and a special area at the back for all the ghoulish dark arts shit. Myself, Davies and Rhys Morgan here will work through the detail. Clear?' A round of nods. 'Excellent. Morgan, you can start with the dark arts, after this morning's performance you could do with something to lighten your mood.'

A telephone starts to ring. Quinn grabs it from its cradle.

'Quinn speaking. Yes. Okay. Someone will be right down.' Quinn hangs up the phone, turns to Rhys, a smile playing on his lips. 'Change of plan.'

Martin Cullen was the boyfriend of Claudia Rose, the first victim, DI Andrews's green-eyed girl. Now Martin's a pale young man in baggy clothes, waiting in reception. Checking the accuracy of his statement is not Rhys's job, far from it. He's doing it for Quinn's amusement, for him to assert a little power.

'Mr Cullen?' A nod. 'Detective Sergeant Rhys Morgan. Thanks for coming in.'

'What is this about?'

'Please come through.'

'Have you caught someone, is that it? Have you caught the person that killed Claudia?'

'I'm afraid not.' Martin follows Rhys through to a side office that's little more than a cupboard with a window and a desk.

'Then what is this about?'

'We're reviewing the details of the case.'

'Why?'

'To ensure all the information we have is accurate.'

'Has someone fucked up? I've seen the papers?'

'No, sir, they haven't.' Rhys sits, opens the folder. Is this better or worse than sifting through the piles of stuff from Andrews's house? He can't be sure.

'If you could run through your movements of the night Claudia disappeared–'

'Was murdered. You can say it.'

'If you could run through the details for me it would be much appreciated.'

Rhys removes the statement.

'I was cleared; you know that right, of being a suspect?'

'Mr Cullen, no one is accusing you of anything, like I said, we need to check the details we have are correct.'

'And like I said back then, I worked all day then headed to my mums.'

'And what time did you work until?'

'Four o'clock as per usual.'

'And what time did you arrive at your mum's?'

'About eight...' Rhys looks up from the paper. Martin's cheeks visibly drain of colour.

'Could you repeat that please?'

'I arrived about eight.'

'And you finished work at?'

'Six o'clock.' Rhys places the paper on the table.

'That's what it says here. But that's not what you just said.'

'Isn't it?' Rhys looks at him, raises an eyebrow. This just got interesting. Martin laughs, a big fake sound. 'My mistake, it's difficult to remember, sometimes I worked until six, sometimes four. It's a long time ago.' Rhys sits back.

'I think I would remember quite clearly every detail of what happened the day my girlfriend was murdered. So I'll ask you again, what time did you finish work? And before you answer bear in mind this is a murder investigation and lying to the police is an offence. If you do lie, I will find out.'

Martin fidgets in his seat, chews at the inside of his cheek. At the time Martin's boss hadn't been contacted. Martin and his mum were in the cinema a hundred miles away at the time of Claudia's murder. But still...

'Okay, okay.' Martin sits forward, places his hands on the table. 'I finished work at four, okay. I went for a pint with a mate, Gary, before I hit the road.'

'Why didn't you say that at the time?' Martin chews the inside of his cheek some more, shrugs. 'How many pints did you have, Martin?'

'Two, possibly three...'

'Are you aware what the legal drink-driving limit is?' The last of the colour drains from Martin's face as he shrugs and slowly nods.

'Why do you think I said I was working 'til six?'

Gary White wears overalls covered in paint and smells slightly of white spirit. He taps his foot on the floor in time with the chew of the gum in his mouth.

'Tell me please, Mr White, how do you know Martin Cullen?'

'Why, what's he said?'

'How do you know him?'

'I used to push a little work his way, you know?'

'Not really.'

'The lad's handy with a paintbrush. He was a bit strapped for cash, you know, back then, what with having just moved in with... I needed an extra pair of hands on a big job at the hospital, one of my guys fell off a ladder and broke his arm, daft bastard. It was, as they say, a mutually beneficial relationship.' Rhys flicks through the papers on the table.

'You're not listed as an employer of Mr Cullen?'

'I paid him cash in hand.' Gary's eyes widen. 'Is this about tax? Because if it is I can assure you all of my work is above board, what Martin chooses to do–' Rhys holds up a hand.

'No, it's not about tax, it's about verifying Martin's whereabouts the night his girlfriend was murdered.' Gary eyes Rhys wearily.

'Shame that was, eh? What happened to Claudia. She was a little sweetie, one of the bonuses to having Martin on the job, she used to make the best bacon butties and drop them off mid shift.' Gary smiles.

'The day she disappeared, Mr White?'

'Yeah, sorry. We finished up at the hospital early, went for a couple of pints before Martin headed to his mum.' Rhys sighs.

'Are you aware of the drink-driving limits, Mr White?'

'Me? Nah, I always get the bus.'

'What a waste of time,' Rhys speaks to no one in particular. 'Couple of amendments to the alibi.' Rhys hands the paperwork to the fraught looking Constable. 'Nothing of note, other than Martin Cullen is now fully aware of both the dangers of drink-driving and stretching the truth when speaking to the police.' The Constable gestures to the stack of paper next to her.

'Add it to the pile.' Rhys places it on top. The Constable smiles, moves it to the bottom.

Rhys tries and fails to dig significant workspace out of his desk, his desk that has become the dark arts corner. His desk that now looks far more like the table in Andrews's front room than Rhys is comfortable with.

Andrews. Andrews with his absolute non-wavering, soul-crushing, life-ruining belief that his theory is correct. That the rest of the world is wrong. Andrews who has lost everything, everyone he loves, because of his belief. Andrews, who has slipped into the abyss. Rhys moves a pile of books onto the floor. Perhaps Andrews's loss is a reflection on the people he has chosen to love. Love is 'no matter what', isn't it? The thought needles Rhys as he pulls up a chair.

Rhys knows they will not catch the killer based on him flicking through gothic fiction, but it has to be done. He sighs heavily. There are hundreds of books. Small town myths. Big city nightmares. Origins of demons. Circles of hell. Nosferatu, ghouls, torture, incarceration. Any book imaginable that seeks to absolve man of his actions. Page after page after page of horrors Rhys doesn't want to see.

Outside the daylight begins to fade.

Each book is scattered with bits of paper. Handwritten notes in Andrews's scrawling font. There are things written in the margins. Pencil sketches of human sacrifice inside front covers. Andrews has revisited scenes, observing, scribbling. He grows further and further removed from reality.

Killers revisit scenes. Could they have been noted as one of Andrews's delusions? Rhys doubts it. None of the creatures that claw their way across the centrefolds are responsible. They have not leapt off the pages to commit some deadly sin. Even if the images say they would have been more than happy to.

Several of the books are centuries old. They give the impression they could hold great power. They don't, of course. They are just words ordered on a page. Rhys remembers a news article about a book in America that was discovered to have been bound in human skin. Apparently the practice wasn't as rare as they would have us believe.

Dusk turns the sky dark blue to black.

Andrews has submerged himself in so much fantasy he has become blind to any other possibility. Rhys's sigh is loud. He needs to stretch. One more book. He selects it from the ever-increasing mound in front of him.

The book appears to be bound in leather. Rhys sniffs it. It has no smell.

The taste of must on the back of his tongue.

The pages yellow with age. The text handwritten. It speaks in an angry flourish. A rush of panic. The words form detail of Nosferatu survival. Of creatures hiding and killing for centuries, disguised as aristocrats. Passing themselves off as their own children. Protected by great family wealth. The pages are full of wrath that no one is listening.

The pages crinkle. An image catches Rhys's eye. A man. A Nosferatu. It is said he plagued rural areas of Ireland for centuries. Rhys stares at the ink sketch. Something starts to move in his mind. The temperature in the room drops. Wind rushes through the damp air. He can smell orchids.

The creature in the sketch furrows its brow. On the page. In the dream. Slowly it turns its head. Lips open to speak. Rhys can't breathe. Can't tear his eyes away. It is not the hard edge of the eyes, the dark lips that make his heart stop. It's the sharp white teeth. Glistening incisors. In the book. In the dream? The creature holds him tight and they plummet into darkness.

Rhys stands sharply. Nausea rises. The world tips. He slams the book shut. Throws it across the table. He hears the back of his chair hit the windowsill behind.

Not possible. Not at all possible. He needs coffee. He needs fresh air. He needs to go home and see his kids. Coat on and heading for the door. No one will question him. All too busy. Take a box home. Any box. That one there will do. Work at home. Is Quinn muttering something to Constable Watts? Are they sniggering at him? They can go fuck themselves. He needs air. Tie too tight. Can't breathe. Just walk. Focus on the pace. Get out. Get home. Get the hell home.

20.

This time it's a dead vole under his pillow. Anna is shouting and hitting and crying. She wants to beat the desire out of him. Erase what she can't understand. Anna thinks Harry likes dead things. Terror has formed her judgment and she doesn't know what else to do.

Round and round in circles they go. She has tried shaking Harry and shouting at him. They've sat quietly and talked... she talked, thought he listened. She's ignored it, hoped it would go away. The smell in the back of her nostrils feels like it will never go away. She's looked on the internet, didn't like what she saw. They've run full circle again and are back to shaking and shouting.

Louise screams he is a freak, and leaves. Anna shouts for her to come back. She doesn't.

Harry only cries when Rhys gets home from work and puts the vole in the bin. Anna shakes her head and leaves. Doors slam.

Harry and Rhys sit in silence.

'Why?' Rhys looks down at him. He seems tiny. He shrugs, kicks his trainer on the edge of the bed. Sniffs. Wipes a trail of snot on the back of his hand.

'He was my friend and then he died.' There's no eye contact. Harry picks at the edge of his sleeve.

'Why really?'

'I don't know.' Still no eye contact. The small tear-stained face. He shuffles across the bed. They cuddle in silence until long after it is dark. The room is grey shadows.

'Dad?'

'Yes.'

'Why did you have to put him in the bin?'

21.

He lays awake, stares at Anna's back. He lays awake and wonders if every creak is Harry off to find new friends. New dead friends.

When Anna returned, she said they needed to talk. Rhys agreed.

But she doesn't want to talk now, says she can't. Of course not. She will want to talk when he can't. When she can scream that he's a poor father. Now she wants to sleep. Or says she does. He knows she's wide awake.

He lays awake and wonders how a picture in a book can move. He lays and stares into the dark, at least it's better than the dream.

The front page of the morning newspaper is cruel. Spits jibes at the police. Demands to know why people are still dying. There's a photo of the street outside Eddie and Cathy's house. Hundreds of bunches of flowers. Shame people didn't care more while they were alive. Didn't notice their absence. There's a sensationalised interview with the concerned neighbour. Rhys doesn't read it.

Rhys can still feel the soft fur of the dead vole in his palm.

He doesn't sit at his desk. That is where the book is. He makes sure he sits were he can see it. Keeps it on the edge of his vision the way arachnophobes do with house spiders they can't catch or kill. It's stupid and sensible all at once. No one will know. No one can tell.

Davies sidles over. Shoves a piece of paper in his face. Rhys has no idea what he's looking at. A load of jumbled letters on a page. He rubs his eyes. The letters refuse to take order. Rhys wants to ask Davies what the fuck he's doing? Wants to scream that they are not friends, not anymore. It doesn't matter how much time passes, Davies cannot make up for what he did. Ignoring it won't make it go away.

The operations room is hot. Too many bodies. Too many artefacts fighting for space. The radiator belches out heat. The dial that turns it down knocked off somewhere in the past. Rhys's palms start to sweat.

'Stop staring, man. Tell me what you think?' Davies shakes the page. The letters swirl. 'Will she like it or what?'

'Ladies and gentlemen, if I could have your attention please.' Quinn is ready to begin. Davies sighs and sits. All focus to the front. 'Today will be much the same as yesterday. We have contacted the colleagues of Jess Simmons, they should be in later to run through their statements.' Jess, half of the first couple to die. 'They don't have long, apparently they've been asked to work double shifts up at the hospital.'

Rhys head snaps up, 'Sorry what?'

'Wakey wakey Detective Sergeant.' Quinn's stare is cold. 'Keep up.'

'What did you just say?' Quinn shakes his head.

'Jess Simmons' colleagues will be in later to run through their statements. Well volunteered.'

'After that? Sorry, I mean where did you say they worked?'

'They are cleaners at the hospital. Why? If you like I could arrange for you to chase them round the corridors?'

'Martin Cullen, Claudia Rose's boyfriend worked there too.' The air in the room shifts slightly. 'Yesterday, when I was checking his statement, he'd done cash in hand work for a mate, painting up there.'

'When?' Rhys rises, digs the statement out of the pile. A low mutter of excitement breaks free at the back of the room.

'At the time Claudia was murdered.'

Quinn picks up a marker, spits the lid onto the floor, draws on a whiteboard as he speaks,

'Martin Cullen worked as a painter in St James' Hospital in February, correct?' Rhys nods.

'Claudia used to take food up there for them apparently.'

'Fast forward five months, that's to July for the slower ones of you in the room. We have our first couple murdered. Jess and her husband Ron. Jess worked in the hospital to earn extra cash. She started at Christmas and never quite got round to leaving.' The pen squeaks as Quinn draws a crude timeline. 'Finally, thank god, a connection between two of our sets of victims. Same hospital. Overlapping time periods. It's not much but it's better than anything we've got so far.'

'About bloody time,' says a Constable at the back of the room.

'What about Claire and Phil, our second couple murdered?' Quinn looks around the room. Heads shake.

'No link to the hospital that I'm aware of, sir,' says Davies. Quinn draws a large question mark. It reminds Rhys of the one on the wall in Andrews's front room.

'Until yesterday we weren't aware of this one, Detective Constable. This takes top priority,' say Quinn.

'Sir,' Davies speaks again. 'Eddie and Cathy's son, Tony. Wasn't the reason he moved up north to go to university to study medicine?' A murmur ripples around the room like an inappropriate Mexican wave. More paperwork shifting. A nod of confirmation.

'Okay, quieten down.' Quinn raises his hands. 'Morgan, you head over to the hospital with... actually on second thoughts, hospitals aren't really your thing are they?'

'Davies, you and a couple of Constables get over to St James' I want as much information as possible on all of these people.' A wave to the wall behind him. 'What are their connections to the hospital? There must be a common denominator here. Really dig around for something on Claire and Phil. They are the only ones we have nothing hospital- or medical-related on. Yet.

'Morgan. You call Tony. Get him back in here. Did he do work experience at St James, or even—'

The phone rings. Constable Robertson answers.

'It's for you, sir.'

'Tell whoever it is I'm busy.' Robertson shakes her head. Her skin has gone a mint green colour. Quinn takes the phone.

'Hello? Yes... Bloody hell.' Silent listening. Quinn hangs up. The room is airless. All eyes on Quinn. 'Scratch that, Morgan. You're with me.' Heads swivel to Rhys. 'They've found another pair of bodies, just as I thought it couldn't get any worse. It bastard well does.'

22.

The remote country cottage is miles out of town. Isolated. Bleak. Rotting back into the landscape. It sits in several acres of land. Overgrown and unloved for what could easily be decades, dark and cruel, it growls out into the cold winter sun that has finally managed to force its way through the clouds.

A pothole-ridden dirt track fights its way through tumbledown drystone walls. There is no birdsong. No sense of life. Quinn crunches the gears and over revs into a clearing in front of the cottage. The oldest man in uniform Rhys has ever seen emerges from the gaggle of confusion at the front door. He comes towards them.

'Bloody hell, it's Egg.' Quinn's mouth drops open. 'Thought they had retired that poor sod years ago.' Quinn strides to the elderly man. Slams him hard on the back. The two men laugh, shake hands.

The remains of a rusty pickup truck stand to the left of the cottage, tangled in vines, fingers pulling it back into the land. Four windows run along the ground floor of the cottage. Black with grime and cobwebs. Several panes of glass are broken, one crack crudely fixed with parcel tape. Dead flies collect in piles having bounced their last, trapped behind the panes. Upstairs hang dirty nets.

The once-white paint of the cottage is stained and peeling. A brown streak seems to split the facade in half, a groove worn by rainwater pouring from broken guttering. The roof of the cottage is dipped and rotten. Sinking back into the walls that sink back into the ground. The cottage must once have been beautiful, fairy tale. Now it is a thing of children's nightmares. Specifically of the two boys Rhys sees huddled with a Constable next to the ambulance.

'Morgan!' Quinn bellows. Rhys joins him. 'This is Egg.' The old man extends his hand. Up close he's younger than expected. Life has not been kind. Rhys nods an acknowledgment. 'Egg here was first on the scene after one of the kids called it in.' Egg is solemn and grey. Grown out of the landscape around them.

'Local kids don't come up here much.' Egg speaks in

monotone. 'The couple who live, lived, up here were seen as, to use the kids turn of phrase, "mad freaks".' Egg looks at Quinn. 'Mind you, who could blame them after what happened?' Egg and Quinn nod.

No one offers an explanation.

'The ginger one...' Egg nods towards the boys. '...is new in town. For a laugh his new mates decided he should be the one to take the plunge and break in.'

'Good mates.' Rhys looks to the boys.

'I was thinking the word "bastards" is a better fit,' says Quinn.

'So Ginger there breaks in,' Egg continues. 'Not a hard task when you realise the front door is rotten. Him and his mate start to have a sniff around. Normally sniff would be a keyword but not in this case.' Rhys glances at Quinn, 'because all they found were bones.'

'Bones? How does this link to our case?' Is this a waste of time? Rhys thinks of the crammed operations room. Should someone else have come here? Movement in the bushes to the left catches Rhys's eye. He stares hard at the dense mass of green leaves. Nothing. Probably a bird. Or a cat.

'Morgan?' Quinn bellows next to Rhys's ear. Rhys jumps slightly 'Sorry to bother you, but if we could have your attention that would be much appreciated.' Rhys blinks rapidly.

Egg continues,

'From what little information has been released to us through the official channels, the formation and condition of the bones seems to link to the other bodies you've found.'

'In what way?'

'The way the bones in the bathtub are... piled... have fallen...' Egg shrugs. 'It looks like they were once suspended there. That and the fact there's a meathook in the ceiling.' Rhys grimaces. Bones in a bathtub, not the kitchen. 'We also found a skeleton under the stairs. I'm no expert but this one looks like it's been broken.'

'Broken? What does broken mean?'

'Several of the bones look like they have been broken.' Egg makes a snapping gesture. 'And there appear to be no hands.'

'Shit.' The three of them stand in silence.

The movement is there in the bushes again. This time Rhys

doesn't turn. It's just birds, birds and cats. No one else looks either.

'Winters and his CSI lads and lassies are on their way,' says Egg.

'Oh, good. I'm glad.' Quinn's tone says otherwise. He turns to the cottage.

'When he gets here we should find out more.' On cue, a police car pulls into the clearing. Quinn heads for the cottage, shakes his head.

Rhys opens the car door for the large man.

'Rhys Morgan, right?' Rhys nods. 'Hello, again.' This time there is no handshake. Winters looks towards the cottage, towards Quinn who pulls on a white paper boiler suit. Winters sags. 'Oh good, always a pleasure to work with the delightful Detective Inspector.'

'You don't get on?'

'It's a long story.' Winters doesn't elaborate. The Crime Scene Investigator's van pulls into the clearing.

'Morgan,' Quinn's voice bellows across the clearing. 'You stay out here and talk to the kids.' Quinn pulls up the boiler suit's hood and disappears into the cottage.

'Look, we didn't do nothing wrong.' The one in the cap is older. Cocky. Predictable.

'You broke into someone's house.'

'Yeah well, kind of, but not really. Not like they give a shit, is it?' The boy stares up at Rhys from under the peak. It is okay to be confident now. Daylight is still with them. Soon it will be dark. The shadows will start to dance.

'Tell me what happened.' Rhys's eyes itch. The headache is staring across his forehead. The boy in the cap shrugs.

'Best ask him, innit.' He thumbs over his shoulder to his mate. 'Like I told that old guy, I waited outside till I heard him screaming like some girl, then we called you.'

'Did you go inside the house?'

'Yeah, but only to the doorway, like, to see why he was screaming. When I saw them bones, I was like, no way, shit, I ain't stupid, I seen police stuff on telly, didn't want to contaminate no crime scene.' His smile is smug.

Sitting by the ambulance, the ginger-haired boy stares vacantly ahead. He shivers even though he is wrapped in the bright foil blanket.

'So, is it true?' The boy in the cap pulls Rhys's attention. 'That there are more bones upstairs?' He tilts his head. Rhys sees his soft baby face, a few rouge hairs trying to sprout through his chin. The small, dark eyes stare at him. 'You can tell me, innit, like coz I'm involved. I'm like a key witness. Were they...' he pauses, lowers his voice, '... like, murdered?'

The sun sets as Rhys speaks briefly to the other boy. The boy looks at him with dead eyes. His voice is flat. The trace of an accent. Somewhere southern. Rhys can't place it.

'It was his idea. I went along with it. Said the couple that lived here were right freaks. No one had seen them for ages. We should investigate. I should investigate if I wanted to fit in round here.' His eyes fix on Rhys but he doesn't see him. 'We get here. The house is quiet. I knew it was wrong but...' He lets the sentence hang. Shrugs. 'So we look around. Nothing moves. Nothing. He says it's time. I have to go in. So I did.'

'Do you always do what other people tell you?' Rhys is not sure why he asks such an obvious question.

'No. But you know what it's like, to have moved, you know? It's best to just do what's needed to fit in.' The kid looks at the ground, scuffs the dirt with his trainers.

'How did you get into the house?'

'Through the front door. It's all rotten so it only took one little shove.'

'Tell me exactly where you went inside the house.'

'Through to the back. To the kitchen. Then back round to the living room.'

'What made you open the cupboard under the stairs?'

'Dunno.' His shrug seems genuine.

'What happened when you opened the door to the cupboard under the stairs?'

'I saw the bones.' The kid starts to shake.

'Did you touch the bones?'

'No.'

'Did you go upstairs?'

'No.'

'Do you have any idea how much trouble you're in?'

'Yes.' The ginger-haired boy sniffs. Tears are in his eyes. 'I didn't touch them, I promise.' His eyes plead. 'The... the head, it rolled out. The teeth kind of chattered like it was laughing.' The tear rolls down his cheek. He rubs it quickly away with a grubby hand. Rhys knows this is not possible. The night dance has already started.

Car headlights illuminate the clearing. An old Volvo crunches to a halt. A woman in leopard print leggings climbs out. Heads for the Constable stationed near the cottage door.

'I got a call about my son.' The ginger-haired boy looks up. 'What the bloody hell has he been up to this time?' She takes out a cigarette.

'I'm afraid you can't smoke here, Miss.'

'Little shit. Probably on the rob, was he? Wait until I get my hands on the little bastard.'

'You can't smoke here.' The woman looks from the cigarette to the Constable with distain, pushes the cigarette back into its packet.

'Mum.' The ginger-haired boy comes alive. He throws the foil wrap to the floor and runs to her. She allows herself to be embraced.

'What the bloody hell have you been doing?' She holds him at arm's length. Rhys crunches across the gravel.

'Hello. I'm Detective Sergeant Rhys Morgan.'

'And?' She stares up at him.

'And your son has been involved in an incident.'

'You best not have been talking to him without a lawyer. I knows about this stuff you know. I've seen it on the telly. Frighten a false confession out of him before a respectable adult arrives.' The woman looks about twenty, which of course is not possible.

'Mrs...?'

'Miss. Miss Elaine Rowe.'

'Miss Rowe, your son is not in trouble. He has discovered something relevant to an ongoing investigation.'

'I don't care what he's discovered. You ain't talking to him without a lawyer. We done? I need to get my son home. He's obviously traumatised.' Rhys sighs.

'Miss Rowe. As I said, your son is not in any trouble. There's no need for a solicitor.' She doesn't know whether to trust him. 'What does need to happen is for you to go with your son to King's Mill station where a formal statement will be taken.'

'What, now?' Her stare is cold.

'Yes please. This is an ongoing murder investigation.' Elaine's eyes widen. Murder always peaks their voyeuristic curiosity. 'Detective Constable Dan Davies will be waiting for you. Ask for him when you get to reception. Do you need a lift?' Elaine looks at him like he is stupid. She turns and pulls the ginger haired boy toward the car.

'We best get this over with then. You'd better not be involved in anything here, Jamie. I'm fed up to the back teeth of having to move you around.'

'I'm not involved with anything.'

'And I had to borrow Uncle Bob's car to get here. You best remember to show him you're grateful.'

'He's not my uncle.'

'He is now.' The car door slams. Gravel sprays. They're gone. Rhys watches until the tail-lights disappear from view.

The old cottage behind Rhys grumbles, then vomits Detective Inspector Pat Quinn out of its putrid mouth. He looks smug. The paper hood is pulled tight around his red face.

'So, I think we've found something.' Quinn shoves a greasy photo frame in a large evidence bag under Rhys's nose. In the frame is a photo of a smiling boy and girl. The boy looks about six. The girl younger. The style of kids' clothes tells Rhys the photo is at least a decade old. 'We know what happened to one of them.'

Rhys does not.

'Now all we need to do is find out what happened to the other.'

23.

Rhys doesn't believe he's ever met a man who can drink a pint as quickly as Pat Quinn.

The boy serving behind the bar doesn't look old enough to drink beer let alone sell it. This near a police station it's more likely to be an issue of Rhys's age than the boys.

The Travellers' Rest is underground. A concrete staircase leads down from the street into the square basement. Booths run around the edge walls. An even lower sunken dance floor sits in the centre. It's late. The music's loud. The clientele less than salubrious.

Quinn's talking. Quinn is always talking. He tells his tale like a campfire horror story. His audience sit, eager to hear. All that's missing are the marshmallows.

'From what Winters said,' a round of boos and hisses from the King's Mill collective, 'the bones have been there for a very long time and by bones that's exactly what I mean. Just Bones. No clothes. No flesh.' Quinn pauses for effect. Takes a long drink of beer.

'How come no one noticed sooner, that these people were missing, if they've been there that long?' Constable Robertson asks the question to no one in particular. Some around the table study their drinks, some shift slightly in their chairs.

'The cottage is miles out in the country, not the kind of place you'd go unless you were invited.' The words are weak, and slurred. Rhys looks at his own empty glass, how much has he had to drink?

'I thought the local kids played up there?'

'There's a difference between playing inside and going out.' No, hang on. 'I mean there's a difference between playing outside and going in.' Rhys pushes the empty glass across the table, tilts his head towards Robertson. It's odd seeing people in their normal clothes, the ones they wear when not in uniform. Constable Robertson suits pink, he wonders if he should tell her?

'Wouldn't there have been a smell?' asks Constable Chantelle Watts.

'Yeah, but....' Davies finishes the sentence with a shrug.

'They'll get the teeth matched against dental records, see if these poor souls are the cottage owners.' Quinn drains the dregs of his pint. 'I think we should be in no doubt. This is the same killer. These are his first victims.' It is a bold statement. More than likely true.

'How do you know that, Inspector?' Watts twists to face Quinn as she speaks. 'There is no doubt for several reasons.' Quinn goes to jab the table with his heavily strapped forefinger. After a moment's contemplation he uses the other hand. 'Firstly, we have two sets of bones, one male, one female.' A jab of the finger, or was that two fingers? Rhys closes one eye to try and get a better focus. 'Secondly, the male set shows signs of the kind of torture we are currently finding inflicted on our male victims. Less torture so we can look at this poor bugger as bridging the gap from cats to humans in our killer's development.' Quinn clatters his empty glass onto the table. Watts grimaces. Quinn's finger jabs the table, Rhys thinks of the vole lying in the top of his rubbish bin.

'Thirdly, the position on the female body, in this case, remains. And of course, the meathook.'

The sound of drinks being gulped.

'I wonder where he's been all this time?' Watts winds a finger in her hair as she speaks. 'Could he have been killing all of these years?

'Or she,' says Davies. 'Let's not be sexist about it.' Robertson shakes her head.

'These bones give us more questions than answers. Questions are good. Questions start to create a bridge that will stretch across the gap to the answers.' Quinn is proud of this analogy. The gin makes Rhys think it isn't all that bad either.

Has anyone mentioned the kids in the photograph? He can't ask. He'll look like a dick if they have. Come on brain. Focus. Shit. Too much gin...

'Your round, Morgan.' Quinn's voice. One more, for the road. One more won't do any harm. It's good to get to know the team, more than good, it's important. Rhys levers himself out of the booth. Funny, he's never noticed the way the floor tilts slightly before.

One more leads to one more. Rhys has had way too many to

drive. He calls Anna. She doesn't say much other that she'll be there in ten minutes. Rhys knows the conversation in the car will start with how angry Anna is. Angry at having to leave Louise looking after Harry. Angry at him for being drunk. Angry at the whole goddamn world.

Rhys hiccups. His mind swims. Swims in gin and images and words on the hundreds of pieces of paper he has had to organise and file. Claudia Rose's twisted face. Eddie no hands. Ancient demon carvings. Cathy's naked body. Street maps, not enough blood, books covered in human skin. Meathooks, no witnesses, the smell of blood, tear-stained faces, a pile of bones, Quinn's sweat, Andrews's screams, the smell of orchids, the sky alive with lightning strobes and the creature with the fire-blond hair.

The world spins in a carousel of colour as Rhys climbs the stairs from the basement.

The cool night air calms the prickle on his skin. He takes deep breaths, waits for Anna. Steadies himself on the wall. Suddenly he becomes aware of how tired he is. How much his body aches. He yawns loudly.

Car headlights flash up the wall. Anna draws up.

'You know how much I hate leaving Louise at this time...' And so on and on... Then the descent into silence. Goddamn deafening silence. Rhys knows it's a bad idea to speak but the words tumble out before he can stop them. Anything is better than the silence.

'I'm sorry. Tough day. Quinn offered...' He says the words slowly, they don't sound slurred.

'Oh, and you couldn't say no?'

'You know how it is.' Shit.

'No actually, I don't.' Her jaw tenses. She drifts a little further away. Their relationship has become a strange tug of war. Rope at full stretch. Neither of them want to win, or let go. Not yet. He yawns. Not something to start thinking about after a long day and a lot of gin. He should have called a taxi. Calling Anna was a bad idea. Anna tuts. It appears the yawn was a bad idea too.

They approach the house. Anna slows. A car travels the other way. It crosses a speed bump Rhys doesn't remember being there. Its headlights flash in his eyes. Straight away there is another car. Blinding him, distorting his vision. Black. Then white. Then black again.

He brings his arm up to shield his eyes.

'What's going on?' Where is all the traffic coming from? He turns his head away from the lights. Looks past Anna, out across the cul-de-sac.

And there he is.

The world slows once more. Rhys's heart freezes, his blood turns to ice. The creature is unmistakable. His clothes are the same as at the hospital. The creature turns. Holds Rhys's eyes with his piercing blue gaze. He's smiling.

'Jesus Christ.' Rhys's voice is loud in the confined space.

'What?' Anna turns the car onto their drive.

'That's him.' Rhys points past Anna's confused expression to the old witch's house. 'From the hospital?' Her face is blank. 'Forget it.' No time for this. Has he told her about the man in the hospital? He can't remember. Has he even told her about the dreams? Rhys is out of the car and hammering across the cul-de-sac to his new neighbour's door before Anna pulls on the handbrake.

No escape this time, you bastard.

Anna sighs heavily. She watches Rhys in the rear view mirror. He darts across the road – steady on his feet considering how much he's drunk, how much the car stinks of booze. She sits, not sure what she's watching. He heads straight for what the kids refer to as the old witch's house. The house of their new neighbours. What on earth's going on? She saw no one. Has no idea what he's babbling about. Why has he been at the hospital? Has someone been hurt?

He tears up the front path. Starts fiercely banging on the front door. She should go over, she should stop him. Her hands grip the steering wheel so tight her knuckles go white. She wants to swear. Or scream. Or both.

A very handsome, but very old, gentleman answers the door. Rhys shouts in his face. For god's sake, he's trying to barge into his home. He's patting his pockets the way he always does when he's looking for his police identification to prove a useless point. Anna sighs heavily, closes her eyes and counts to ten. She gets out of the car, slams the door hard enough to wake the dead.

'Don't treat me like I'm an idiot.' Rhys's words reach her. 'I saw him come in here with my own eyes. Why the hell are you lying?'

'I am sorry, sir, but as I have said, no one has entered the house in the last few hours, never mind the last few minutes.' Anna reaches them. Looks up at the elderly gentleman's defined features. Still there to admire after decades. She's impressed at his strength. He barricades the doorway. Strong against Rhys's onslaught.

'And as I have said, this is important police business. Either go and get him or let me in.'

'I am afraid neither of those things are going to happen.'

'I can come back with a warrant.'

'Rhys!' Her words are strong. This is more than enough. Rhys ignores her.

'I'll arrest you for police obstruction.'

'Then so be it.' The gentleman holds Rhys's stare. He is calm, cool, collected. He turns slowly to Anna. 'Does he belong to you?' There's no malice. A straightforward question. His arm still across the doorway. Access denied. Rhys turns and paces on the loose gravel path.

'Yes. I'm afraid so.' Anna hears the footsteps stop. Feels his eyes bore into her. She doesn't take her gaze from the elderly gentleman. She doesn't want to. 'Hello. I'm Anna, this is my husband Rhys. We live across the street.' She turns to gesture towards their house. Rhys stares at her open mouthed.

'Arthur.' The gentleman outstretches his hand. Anna shakes it. Surprised again by his strength. Arthur extends his hand to Rhys. Rhys doesn't move.

'I can only apologise for my husband. He has had an incredibly stressful day and a few too many gin and tonics.' She laughs. A nervous sound. 'So anyway, we'll head home now and leave you in peace. Won't we, Rhys? We don't want to make a scene.' She reaches out for Rhys. Expects him to protest but he is strangely calm. 'And when he has had some rest, if he still feels the need, Rhys can come back and talk to you rationally.' She smiles. A light across the street comes on. A curtain twitches. 'Or perhaps apologise?' Anna realises her voice is pleading. To Rhys. To Arthur.

'That will be fine, but my answer will still be the same.'

'Don't think I won't come back.' Rhys's voice slurs. Anna looks at the floor. 'So you can tell your mate, whoever he is, that hiding in there won't do him any good because I will find him. I don't know what his game is but it won't work.' Anna smiles weakly.

'Goodnight then.' Arthur shuts the carved oak door. Several bolts slide. Rhys sways slightly, turns his full attention on Anna.

'Thanks for that. For making me look like a right dick.'

'I think you managed to do that all by yourself. What the hell is wrong with you? These are our neighbours. We have to live here.'

'I'm not a child. Stop speaking to me like one.'

'Then stop acting like one.'

'Screw you. You're supposed to be on my side.' He shoots her a look she has never seen before, not in him. Her heart freezes. Her stomach drops. Is that hatred in his eyes? Something is different, something is very different. Chalk it up next to the other things that are just not quite the same. He shakes his head in disgust. Turns and weaves away across the street.

She stands there alone on a stranger's lawn. Swallows the hard lump in her throat. Slowly follows Rhys back across the street.

Behind her, deep within the house, she could swear she hears someone laugh.

24.

The creature's eyes stare down at him. Once again they fall. He feels the creature's hands clasp him. They pirouette into nothing.

'Ask.' The creature whispers, again and again and again. The man has no idea what to ask for. His head spins. Which way is up? Which way is down? The creature's breath is cold against his cheek. He is near and he is far. The man is afraid and at peace. He wants to laugh, to clap his hands like a child, but this may madden the creature and he doesn't want to be left alone in the dark.

'Ask.' The creature's brow furrows then straightens. Light eyebrows. Dark lashes. Crystal-blue eyes. The image crashes from close to far. Intimate to reaching. Soft focus to startling clarity. He is the creature, the man from the hospital, the man from across the street, all rolled into one. One and the same in every detail.

The man tries to speak but has no words. He stretches out his hand towards the creature's face. He is just out of reach even though the creature holds the man's arms tight as they spiral into nothing. The man's words stick in his throat. His mind has already forgotten them. He feels the laughter rising. The creature's eyes suppress it. He hears the questions whisper again. Then they are lost.

'Ask!' The creature is angry now. 'Or be prepared to die.' Its voice rises. The man still has no idea what to ask for. He does not want the creature to be mad. So many questions. Questions that dance physically in the space between them, then disappear into the darkness.

What is the question again?

The man shakes his head. Once. Involuntary, almost a jerk. He is not sure it is. A no? A negative? A refusal to ask for something unknown.

Rage explodes from the creature like nothing the man has ever seen before. A physical ripple from its heart to its fingertips. Up its neck and across its face. The creature lets out a deafening roar that shifts the nothingness around them. Vibrates in the confined yet endless space.

In this moment its mouth is torn wide. The man stops breathing. It is the picture from the book? The glistening incisors from somewhere far away. Another time. Another life. The man feels the ice enamel slice his skin, although the creature is nowhere near.

Instantly the creature is gone. It propels backwards into the black. Its white skin becomes a distant pinprick. Then nothing.

Now the man really is afraid. The wind rushes louder than ever before. He has no idea which way is up or down, just that he is falling in the pitch blackness.

There is an almighty crash. It takes a second for the man to realise it is the sound of his body impacting with a hard flat surface. Or maybe there was no sound at all? In panic, he tries to draw back in the breath that has been punched from his body but cannot. He is warm and cold. His eyes move from side to side.

Is this surface wet?

Like punching shatterproof glass, the cracks pause for a moment then gradually start to crackle out to the extremities. Bone after bone, and now he is too late to try and move his fingertips. Through all of this, he knows the pain will come with burning glory and it does not disappoint. If he could he would screw his eyes up tight, he would open his mouth and scream. Instead he lies and waits for an even darker pitch of black to come.

25.

The house stinks of crispy beef. Pam doesn't care. It's nice to have a break from cooking. Shame she had to knock on death's door to get it. Plus it's not like it's a total break. Not like she is getting the complete and utter rest the doctor ordered as she left the hospital. She was still the one who had to call the takeaway order through. She'll be the one who puts all the containers in the bin. She'll cook tomorrow. Not that Will would be bothered if they ate takeaways every night of the week.

Pam is enjoying being home. Possibly even enjoying the sound of Will snoring in his chair across the room. It amuses her that a few days away seem to make home all the more bearable. Is that how Will has found it all these years? Being away from her made being with her bearable?

What an odd concept.

Maybe she'll start planning little trips away, just for her. The local library advertises coach trips on their noticeboard. Or there's bound to be something on the internet. Something to the coast would be nice, for a night or two. She's never been away on her own. Could it be as liberating as she imagines or lonely and frightening? She looks at Will. A thin line of dribble snakes its way down his chin. She settles on liberating.

Her stomach groans but she reaches for another prawn cracker anyway. They are so moreish. They must put something in them so you keep picking even when you're full. She wipes the grease off her fingers. Now, where is the iPad? Upstairs on the bedside table no doubt. Will would have left it there. He spends all night watching reruns of game shows. She considers waking him to go and fetch it, but after the amount of food she's eaten, she could probably do with the exercise.

He watches her move around the front room. The image is clear as day. Plenty of background light. Why do people never shut their curtains when they turn the lights on? Don't they ever wonder who might be outside watching?

She shuffles towards the window. Sucks something off her fingers. Desire and repulsion fill him in equal measure. He wants to move closer, press his face against the glass. Touch her. Smell her. Taste her. It is nearly time.

She pulls one of the curtains closed. The husband can still be seen, for a moment longer. Bloated and asleep. Same chair night after night. His fat fingers twitch even as he sleeps. Ready to do her bidding when she calls. Pathetic and wonderful wrapped up in one.

The fat on her upper arm wobbles as she pulls the curtain tight.

Slowly he licks his lips.

She's right. There on the bedside table is the iPad, its battery completely flat. Will's grubby fingerprints all over the expensive leather case. What will be quicker? To plug it in and wait for it to charge or try to get the main computer working? If she plugs in the iPad can she still use it while it is charging? She's never tried that. She always plugs it in overnight to ensure it is fully charged. Plug it in and see is probably the best option. Their computer is about twenty years old and can take any time between two minutes and two hours to boot up and connect to the internet. There's no rush. She's just excited to get looking at trips. She can feel change in the air.

He checks his watch. It's time.

The blood pounds through his veins. Demands his attention. Demands to be heard. It chatters away. Always. It gets angrier and angrier until he can't bear it. It demands appeasement. It must have his full attention or it will burst out through his skin.

'You have my full attention,' he mutters, soothing.

He's on fire. All the juices in his body start to boil. The boil will become the rage and the rage cannot be contained. The rage is always just beyond control. He wants to scream but that can wait. Soon the chatter will be less, will be appeased. Peace again. Comfort again. Love again.

He smiles. The smile becomes a giggle.

He swings open the gate.

The doorbell rings. Pam looks at her watch. It's late. They aren't expecting anyone. Her mind runs back through the takeaway order: one crispy beef, one sweet and sour pork, egg fried rice, chips, prawn crackers and some of those deep fried chicken balls Will likes. The bread they added themselves once Will got back from the Spar. They had had everything. Had she given the delivery boy the right money? Had he given her the right change?

The bell rings again.

Could it be one of their girls? Doubtful. The eldest, Sally, has been over and won't be back until tomorrow evening.

'Will, can you get that?' No answer. She didn't expect one. Will is already deep asleep.

Pam heads to the top of the stairs, iPad held tight. The charger is beside the sofa ready and waiting. It has taken so many discussions to get Will to leave it plugged in there. That way she'll know where it is. They'll both know where it is without having to search the place. Simple logic escapes that man.

The shadow behind the bubbled glass in the front door looks a little like the takeaway delivery boy. The change on the small tabletop beside the door is correct. Odd.

Her hand flicks the catch open.

'Hello,' says the young man. He is not the delivery boy although his cap is the same colour blue. 'Really sorry to disturb you but you'll never believe what's happened.' There's something off about him. Something she can't place. He continues. 'Not only have I been stupid enough to leave the interior light on in my car and run the battery flat, but my phone is dead too.' He waves a mobile at her, its face black. He laughs. Something not quite right about the laugh. She can't see a car over his shoulder. Does she know him from somewhere? He looks familiar. 'I couldn't be cheeky and ask to use your phone, could I?' He has a backpack on. Odd. Why hasn't he left it in the car?

'Of course.' Pam turns towards the handset, in its cradle, next to the takeaway change.

It is the sound more than anything that stands out. The crack of the catch against the wall as he pushes himself into the hall behind her. He is so fast. So very fast. The door is shut. His arm around her throat before she's even drawn breath. Before her hand is even halfway to the phone.

'Shhhhhh,' he whispers, his breath warm on her ear. He needn't worry. All the words, all the sounds, are jammed in her throat buried deep within the crook of his elbow. 'As it turns out I'm not that stupid, but you are.'

Then she feels it. The pressure as he tightens his arm around her throat. She gags, tries to wriggle free, brings her hands up to pull at the arm that feels like it's made of stone. Her nails scrabble against his skin. He uses his other hand to pull one of her arms down. He leans back, lifts her body until her toes are the only things left touching the carpet. Oh my god. Oh my god. Panic and adrenaline surge through her body. She tries to call to Will. Tell him to wake up. To move. All that comes out is a gurgling croaking sound. She feels her eyes start to roll. What did they teach her in that self-defence class, why is her mind so blank? Oh god. Oh Will. Oh...

They really are that stupid. It's the classic line from all the films. They must watch enough telly. He likes the line for that reason. He picked it for that reason. The psycho behind the shower curtain. The classic 'Let the bad man into your home' line. They fall for it time after time after time. If they said no, he would just walk away. Possibly walk away. Possibly not. Actually no, definitely not. As soon as they open the door they are, as they say in the trade, fucked.

He enjoys how their eyes try to place him. Wonder why he is at their door. Where they know him from. They really should pay more attention.

He looks down at her lifeless body. She'll be heavy to lift. He should have made her walk herself to the kitchen before he knocked her out. Damn it. He could wait for her to come round? Move herself. Knock her out again.

No.

Too much waiting. The chatter can't wait. Luckily there's a fat sod asleep in a chair in the front room, a fat sod that looks like he could do with a workout.

He closes his eyes. Breathes deeply. Their words taunt in his head.

'You poor little vile boy. Look, you've gone and done it all wrong. Can't even get this right.' He bites his tongue to stop himself screaming 'shut up.'

'Why would anyone love you?' The voice starts to shriek. 'Why the hell would anyone even like you? You're pathetic. I can't even bear to look at you. You disgust me. You make my sick.'

'Pardon?' he turns his head towards the front room.

'You really are a vile little boy,' the fat man shrieks from the chair. His eyes are black beads in his pasty face. 'You repulse me, you really do.'

Eyes ablaze, the young man yanks the hammer from his backpack.

The iPad crunches under foot as he steps towards the front room.

He'll show the fat man the meaning of the word repulsion.

He watches her for a long time. She stops moving quicker than the others. Her body pulsed like a fish out of water. It was mesmerising. It didn't last long.

The beautiful Pam. Beauty in its loosest sense of course. They are all beautiful in their own special ways. Will thought she was beautiful right up to the end. He really begged for her life. Touching, after all those years. He wonders: if she had been able, would Pam have done the same for Will? Love is always a little one sided, isn't it? She had all the power. That's why he picked her. Picked them.

He would say it is a shame, but it really isn't.

The blood is appeased, for now. Quiet in his veins. She's calmed him. Loved him. The chatter is quiet. The silence is golden.

He watches her for a long time, even now she is still. Makes sure he logs every detail. The dimples of her skin. The colour of her hair. Her perfect, varnished nails. He doesn't take trinkets, items of clothing. There is no drawer stuffed with knickers back at his place. No. He takes what he needs another way.

It is time. It is over.

He blows her a tender kiss, turns off the light and leaves her alone in the dark.

26.

Rhys is tired and drunk. Sleep is unavoidable.

The dreams tear him awake. Haunted. Terrified. Sweating and alone in the dark. The coffee is hot and bitter. Not enough sugar. Painkillers for the dull ache in his head as the gin wears off.

Anna's face is burnt onto his brain. That look of complete distain, horror, as they stood on the damp grass hours earlier. She thinks he's making it up. The nightmares. The creature. She couldn't make her lack of support any clearer. Isn't she supposed to be there for him no matter what? She made him look like a fool.

That needle once again deep in his skin.

There's no doubt in his mind. He saw the creature, the man, he's only a man, go into that house. Anna helped him elude Rhys once again. They should get together, have a good laugh.

He wills her to wake up, to come through and see what he's doing. He dares her to ask why he's not asleep. He'll whisper cruelly in her face that it's all her fault. If she'd helped him speak to the man, get an explanation; he could be sleeping soundly now.

Instead he paces. Paces around like… like this… too afraid to go back to sleep. Going without sleep makes you crazy. He'll whisper this too. He's seen that on the telly. He'll go crazy and it'll be her fault.

Except she doesn't come.

He pushes the button of the laptop harder than needed. Eases the bedroom door closed. He pulls over his sister's comfy wicker chair. Flicks on the soft lamp.

It's not the case that brings him to this point. He wants to make sure that is understood. Is on record.

It's the nightmare. The nightmare and the man at the hospital – the man across the street. Anna can rant on about the stress of work causing the nightmares until hell freezes over. Blame the alcohol. Drop all the not-so subtle hints she likes. There is more to it. He knows it. He can't quite place it. Not yet.

How does a person from your dreams end up being real?

He laughs. It's ridiculous.

How does a person from your waking life travel through your subconscious to your dreams?

Equally obscure.

Yet here he is. At three a.m. with a cold cup of coffee. In a room his sister was last seen in twenty-two years ago.

Tears prickle at the edge of his eyes. The mocking laugh becomes fire in his throat.

His fingers move quickly. The internet gives nothing up easily. 'How to make your dreams come true, twenty steps to happiness.' Not what he is looking for. He changes his search title. His eyes move quickly, but carefully.

The Middle Ages. Dreams are seen as evil. Images of temptation sent to man from the Devil. As man sleeps the Devil fills his mind with harmful ideas.

Rhys swallows. Could the creature be the Devil? Are these his first steps towards being a minion for the damned?

'Jesus Christ, Morgan.' He chastises out loud. Talk about melodrama.

Is there an echo in the room?

The Greeks and Romans. They believed dreams were direct messages from the gods. Good, that's more like it. Or the dead. Shit. That dreams could predict the future.

Rhys is cold. The heating is on high. He's never had cause to think of gods or devils. His parents were far from religious. As for messages from the dead? He glances up at the faded Polaroid of his sister and her friends and waits for that sick feeling in the base of his stomach to come. It doesn't disappoint.

His fingers slide across the keys. His eyeballs scratch like they are full of sand. He needs to make more coffee. Find more sugar. Lots more sugar.

Lucid dreaming. Interesting. This theory is that the dreamer controls their dreams through imagination.

This could be possible? The night before they visited the hospital he hadn't slept well. Could he have drifted off and had in fact been in a dream state when he saw the creature in the corridor?

His heartbeat quickens.

And in the car. He was tired. Drunk. Is his imagination capable of playing such tricks? Is he putting himself inside some kind of perpetual cycle that will result in some kind of continuous lucid dream?

Shit.

He's too hot now. The room is too hot. He rises. Goes to the window. Stares at his reflection in the black glass. He chased the creature in the hospital. You can't run and still be asleep, can you? He saw him again through the swing doors. That was real. The conversation with the nurses was real. He was awake. He was in a goddamn hospital. If he were asleep they would have been able to tell. Would have said something.

The relief cools his skin.

The questions are still unanswered. At least he's not losing his mind.

People from dreams entering reality. This leads only to dozens of nutcase sites. Teenagers believing they are being stalked by spirits. People hiding in rooms, afraid and running out of food. He hopes they are pranksters. Knows enough of the world to fear otherwise.

The search has shown nothing. It's embarrassing.

But it's more than the dream leaking into reality.

It's the image in his head. The image in the book. It's the teeth. The creature's teeth.

The Nosferatu. Except they don't exist? Right?

For fuck's sake. Rhys slams shut the laptop lid.

This is Andrews's fault. His words have bled into Rhys's subconscious. Messed with the confusion that is already there. He shouldn't have let him talk in the cells. He should have walked away. It would have been insignificant in the scheme of things. It really is that simple. He shouldn't have brought that box of books home from the station. Rhys looks at it now, hunched in the corner of the room. It stares straight back, goading.

Cold metal needles sear into Rhys's throat. He gasps. Fingers to neck. He rubs until the pain passes. Sweat prickles on his skin.

Something in the house creaks. He jumps. This is ridiculous. He's either going to swear or shower. He settles on both.

His feet pad along the landing. The word 'devil' playing heavily on his mind.

27.

Anna is furious. Too much time lying awake in the dark. Too much time to think.

Why is Rhys so damn selfish? Does he ever think about anyone else? By anyone else she means her... their children. He has plenty of time to think about people he'll never know. Bad people. Dead people. Imaginary people.

Anna is up and dusts furiously. The physical task does little to help. She throws the duster to the floor. Stomps to the kitchen.

Selfish. Selfish. Selfish.

She would love to stay out late, drink gin and tonic. Not worry about the children. Know some mug will pick her up. She would love to drunkenly charge around the neighbourhood, shout the odds. Know nothing truly awful will happen. A sensible do-gooder will be there to smooth things over.

But she can't, can she. She is always the sensible one. He gets to be out there, take risks. Have fun. Do whatever the hell he pleases.

What about her?

Does he spare a thought for her at home? Her desire for sensible, adult conversation? There are only so many times she can bear Louise telling her she 'doesn't get it' and Harry asking if he can make magic potions, before she wants to scream.

Harry.

They need to talk about Harry. If Rhys can bother to slip it into his busy social schedule.

Why are other people so much more important to her husband than his own family? Why are their needs more important than hers? Good old Anna. She'll be here when the case closes. Pick up the pieces. Always has.

Always will?

Anna sighs. Is she being irrational? Unfair? No she bloody isn't. Rhys upset her last night. Hurt her. Go Rhys. Well done. Mission accomplished. It was the way he looked at her, cut her to the bone. So cold. So much hate. He won't have realised he was doing it. It was the booze. The late hour.

It doesn't hurt any less.

She fills the kitchen sink with bleach. Snaps on rubber gloves. Digs around for the scrubbing brush. The bristles move back and forth across the draining board. Back and forth. Back and forth.

Anna made a fuss about Rhys's move to murder. It's beyond his control but so what? She wanted to matter. Wanted him to pick her. She is lonely, fed up of being lonely. Things should be so different.

Anna shouts at Rhys more than she should. Her feelings of neglect turning to anger. She behaves like a petulant child. Throws things back in his face. Bins his dinner. Deadlocks the door. She doesn't feel guilty. If it's his right to choose this career path, it's hers to be true to her reactions. There are hundreds of routes he could take within the police force, why choose the one he has to travel alone?

Anna sighs. These thoughts are pointless. It will make no difference.

Is she the issue? She has too much time on her hands. The kids need her less and less. Her mind turns over the idea of work. A job after all these years. A paid job. She isn't sure what she fancies. Or more truthfully what she can do. Who will want her? It's a conversation to have with Rhys. A conversation that slips further away by the minute. She's this upset already. He's only been on the case for hours. There's a long way to go yet. Mind you, the sink looks good as new.

'What are you doing?' Rhys's flat voice breaks her thoughts.

'What does it look like?'

'It's seven a.m.'

'So?' No mention of last night. No apology. Unbelievable. She wants to scream. Shout. Punch. She doesn't. She looks at him. Swallows hard. He can apologise first this time.

'I have to go.' He leans forward to kiss her. She pulls back. He smells of soap and the aftershave she bought him for his birthday. She knows he hasn't slept because she hasn't. He was up with his 'other woman'. Jenny. Into the shower not long before she rose. As if she wouldn't know he's been up all night with her, rather than in bed with his wife. His skin is scrubbed and pink.

'I have to get the kids up.' She turns away. Stares at her

reflection in the sink. Does not turn around until she hears the front door close behind him.

28.

'So what do we actually know so far?'

'Not a lot.'

'That's a bit unfair.'

'Well it's true, considering how many of them are dead.'

'But we know a hell of a lot more than we knew yesterday.'

'Sure. But tell me this, does any of that point to anybody, I mean a physical person, that could actually be responsible?'

'Well no, but – '

'Ladies and Gentlemen, please, this is not a social club. Quinn draws them to order. 'As you will all be aware, there are many strands starting to emerge within this investigation. They need to be looked into.

'First, we have the possible link to the hospital,' a nod in Rhys's direction, 'which Davies has been following up.' Davies sticks his hand in the air. Waves. Heads turn to see where he is.

'Second, we have yesterday's discovery of the bones.' Mutters rise. 'Third, we need to finish sorting through this lot,' a point to the towers of boxes, 'to check for... How shall I put this? Indiscretions.' A lot of uncomfortable nods.

'Let's start at the top. Davies. What have we learnt from the hospital?'

'Not much, I'm afraid.' Quinn's neck starts to redden. 'Yet, not much yet. The HR guy is pulling all the paperwork together for me. He's going to see if there's any correlation between the dates Jess worked, the dates Martin worked, staff and patients at that time. It's a bit of a nightmare, staff turnover is high, it's a training hospital. It's busy. We'll keep at it. If there's anything to find, we will.' Quinn's nod is slow. Measured. He gestures to someone at the back of the room.

'I followed up the university lead... Tony and the university...?' Rhys turns to look at Spenser. 'I hope you don't mind.' These words to Rhys. 'I thought you guys would be pretty tied up yesterday.'

'Initiative. Good. I like it.' Quinn speaks, flicks a smirk at Rhys.

'It's a dead end, so to speak. Eddie and Cathy's son, Tony, he's never been in St James' Hospital, other than to visit his dad, obviously, and that's recently, not at the times we are looking. He's, Tony that is, specialising in dermatology.' Someone says 'yuck'. 'Not something they cover at St James'... ' Spenser shrugs.

'Okay.' Quinn is dismissive. 'We're still waiting for any news on the formal identification of the bones discovered up at the cottage yesterday. Rather than waste time on idle speculation, we'll focus on following up the leads we already have.'

'Morgan.' Quinn catches his attention. Flicks through the sheets in front of him. 'The first couple that were killed, Jess and Ron. They have a daughter. Go and see her. We need to know as much as we can about the time her mother worked at the hospital. The link has to be there, we just need to find it.' Rhys nods. Happy to be anywhere but here. Quinn addresses the room.

'There are very few of us and a lot of this.' The boxes of Andrews's possessions tower around them. 'If you are a Constable lucky enough to be in this room, you can take an educated guess as to what you will be doing. Let's not have this stuff lingering around any longer than is needed. It doesn't reflect well on any of us. Any questions?'

'How's Eddie?' Constable Bayne speaks softly from the back of the room.

'Eddie's condition at the hospital is unchanged. If there's any news, you'll be the first to know.' No news will be good news. No mention of the hands. 'Anything else?'

'Why is he taking the blood, from the crime scenes?' A female Constable. The hairs on the back of Rhys's neck rise.

'To drink according to Andrews.' A male voice. A murmur of awkward laughter somewhere in the room. 'That's why we never find any isn't it, sir? He sticks in a straw and off he goes...'

'Enough!' A voice booms from the doorway. Everything stops. The room becomes a tight vacuum. Detective Chief Inspector Alec Jenkins stands, hands on hips. 'Quinn, my office. NOW!'

'Nice one, dickhead.' Quinn mutters. He shoves the male Constable a little too hard as he exits.

'What? I was only saying what you were all thinking.' The group disperses. Ashamed. Eyes to the floor. 'Tell me it wasn't,

122

go on, tell me...' The Constable's voice is lost in the scrape of chair legs, the beep of mobiles being turned on. Davies sidles over, like a dog that just won't get the hint.

'You look like you've had about as much sleep as I have.' Davies rubs a fist into his eye. Yawns. 'I was at the hospital all night trying to find reasons to question nurses.' He has the audacity to wink. 'What's your excuse?'

'Couldn't sleep, that's all.' The answer bores Davies.

'So what does she look like, this daughter you have to go and see?' Davies tries to intercept the file as Watts passes it over.

'It's a fair question though isn't it?' says Rhys.

'What? Whether she's a hottie? You dark horse.'

'Why is the blood being removed?'

The question is tentative. Peppered with embarrassment. Davies fails to notice. He sucks his teeth, more interested in seeing if there's a photo in the file.

Rhys turns to the mind map. The floor falters slightly beneath his feet. The cold metal needles sear into his neck once more. He grabs the tendons. Lets out a small sound.

'You okay?' Davies is behind him, not overly concerned.

'Cramp.' Lies. Rhys rubs his neck, focuses his attention on the wall. It shifts slightly. 'The human body can hold, what, an average of eight to ten pints of blood depending on size?' Davies nods. 'How much is being found at the scenes?' Rhys traces his finger down the statistics.

First, Claudia Rose. Roughly six pints believed to be at the scene. Over half. Then Jess Simmons. Just over four pints. Followed by Claire Abbot. Roughly the same. Now Catherine. Cathy Reynolds. According to the newly added lab figures little more than three pints of blood left at the scene.

It seemed like so much more. Up the kitchen units. On the yellow carpet tiles. Rhys feels Davies's eyes follow his finger down the wall. How do they even work these things out?

'He's getting better,' says Davies.

'Or greedier.' Rhys's voice is a whisper.

'How the hell does he get the blood out of the houses? Five pints of blood isn't something you can conceal. How much does one of those big things of milk hold? Four pints aren't they? Not exactly conspicuous. As for getting it from the body, catching it,'

Davies pulls a face of disgust, 'whatever the term is. You've got to be some sick fuck to lurk around, with what, a bucket...?' Davies's voice fades away.

All Rhys sees is the image of himself. He stands in the kitchen. Drinks milk straight from the four-pint bottle, fingers crossed Anna won't come in and see.

29.

It is the thirty-first of October. All Hallows' Eve.

It makes sense now, Harry wittering on about witches. How the hell has she missed it?

Anna hates Halloween. Some mothers at school really buy into it. The whole family in fancy dress out trick or treating. Houses decorated with pumpkins. It is her mother's influence, Anna knows that. Her mother thinks trick or treating is glorified begging. Begging and scaring the shit out of each other.

The kids like to carve pumpkins. That will guarantee only the little rotten ones will be left. Although these days, Louise probably thinks carving pumpkins is for babies.

Anna takes a deep breath. The air is crisp. She's glad she walked the children to school. The blood pumps through her veins. On top of which the house is spotless.

Lack of sleep, that's Rhys's problem. That's what's making him behave like this. She's been telling him to see a doctor for weeks. He refuses. Well tough luck. She'll pop into the surgery when she goes to get the sodding pumpkins.

She rounds the corner. The weak winter sun glistens. She read somewhere that lack of sleep leads to a drop in your IQ? That would certainly explain a lot.

Anna twists her mobile inside her pocket. Why hasn't Rhys called to apologise? He has more important things to do, the demon on her shoulder jibes. Shake it off; enjoy the feel of the sun of your face.

She turns into the cul-de-sac. There it is. The old witch's house. New occupants. Less than a week old and Rhys has ruined relations. A tree surgeon measures the thick trees around the property.

Do children live there? They'll hardly want to be friends with her two now.

Arthur did seem quite old. An elderly couple. Great. Even better. Her husband can be known for terrorising the elderly. Her cheeks flush with embarrassment.

A deep, cold breath. Shoulders pulled back. This is the day for action. What is done is done. Time to make it better. Bold, confident strides. Up the gravel path. Knock on the door. All done before she can lose her nerve.

Instantly the door swings open. Arthur stands before her. Grey, three-piece suit. Crisp white shirt. He smiles down at her.

'Hello.'

'Hi.' Shit. She should have though this through. He looks over her shoulder. 'He's, Rhys, he's in work.' Her face burns with shame. 'Actually that's why I, erm… look, I wanted to come over and apologise for my husband's behaviour last night. I have no idea what came over him…' The words tumble out.

'Arthur.' A strong voice inside the house stops her dead. 'Don't be so rude. Invite the young lady in.' Arthur hesitates for a fraction of a second. Anna catches his eye, it tells her nothing. Poor man. He's terrified she's like her husband. Will kick off inside and they'll be stuck with her. She smiles reassuringly. Arthur steps back, allows her in.

The hallway is cold and dark. The walls are hung with heavy, worn wallpaper. Arthur shows her to the front room. It's gloomy and cool. Rich curtains drawn tight. It could easily be the middle of the night, not morning.

'It's to protect the furniture.' The strong voice speaks from across the room. Velvet smooth. Reassuring. 'A lot of it is antique and would perish in the sunlight. Until I decide where it's going, it's better to be safe than sorry. Wouldn't you agree?'

Then he is in front of her. The most beautiful man she's ever seen. Later she'll ponder this as he drifts in and out of her thoughts. What about her husband for one? Shame will blush her cheeks. Surely she didn't mean ever seen?

He is tall, over six feet. Slim, yet muscular. His blond hair is swept back off his face – a natural wave fights to break free. Anna knows nothing about him but is drawn to him. He smiles. Her heart melts.

'Hello.' His hand reaches towards her. 'Kier Finnegan. I am hoping you are one of the people I now have the pleasure of living near.' A smile spreads across her face.

'Erm, yes, hello.' A firm shake, yet tender. 'Anna. I live across the street.' She smiles again. Why hadn't she spent longer on her hair? Goddamn her 'around the house' jeans. Kier smiles back. His eyes never leave her face. 'I came over to apologise for my husband's behaviour last night.' A dark shadow flits behind his eyes. She's never felt regret mentioning Rhys before.

'There is no need to apologise, Arthur has told me all.' Anna still holds his hand.

'I think it's work. It can get a bit much sometimes. You know how it is? Stress...' Her voice trails. How to defend? Kier turns away. Did he stoke her hand gently with his thumb as he dropped it? She shivers slightly.

'Of course, but he really should be careful. Arthur is an old man, vulnerable. A less compassionate friend than I could take offence at the elderly being accosted in their own homes at that hour.' The shame rises again. 'However, let us not start wrong footed. Your apology is accepted.' He flashes her a half-curled smile. 'I must say I am very glad you came over.' Her joy opens in a way it has not for a very long time.

The house is quiet. Anna can smell freshly cut flowers. They stand and study each other in the gloom.

'Erm, I was wondering...' Anna's mind darts. His eyes never leave her. His chest drops and rises with each breath. Her mouth is dry. 'Erm, if you would like to come over for a drink one evening?' Shit. That sounds like a pathetic come on. 'You ... and Arthur of course... to see Rhys and me, as an apology, for the other night, and a kind of get-to-know-your-new-neighbours kind of thing?' She hardly recognises her own voice. It is pathetic and hopeful. Does he have a wife? Why does that matter? 'And anyone else that lives here of course.' Now she sounds like a nosy neighbour. God, what's wrong with her. She's behaving like a teenager. She's a fully-grown, married woman. Get a grip.

'Arthur is busy but I would love to.' She didn't specify a date. He is near her once again. The sound of blood rushes through her ears. Fills the silence. He touches her again. A gentle hand on her shoulder. A touch full of something else. It's time to leave.

'And there is no one else that lives here.' His breath is soft on her face.

'Great. I shall look forward to it.' Barely a whisper. She smiles again. A stupid smiling clown.

'You should consider working with children.' He holds her gaze. 'You have a kind demeanour and it is what you know best.' The words are out of place but perfect all the same.

Then instantly she finds herself emerging from the dark building. In the moments it takes for her eyes to readjust to the light, Kier is gone. Arthur stands once more in the doorway. A watchman at his post. Children. It is obvious. Why hadn't she thought of that? Her head spins. Her mouth hangs open.

'Goodbye, Anna.' Arthur's body blocks her view back into the house. She quashes the urge to jump up, try and see over his shoulder. Catch a glimpse of Kier. There is sadness to the old man now. She hadn't noticed it before.

'Goodbye, Arthur. Lovely to meet you again, after, you know.' She motions towards her house. An embarrassed laugh escapes her lips. Arthur steps back into the dark. 'I hope you can make the drinks too.' He smiles a sad smile at her, closes the door. She hears the bolts slide into place.

30.

His feet pound along with the rhythm of the machine.

Beat, beat, beat.

He likes to run fast. What's the point otherwise? He likes to count the beats of his feet as they hit out the rhythm. He likes to feel his lungs pull for breath. Feel life as it pulsates through his body.

Disrespect your body, it will disrespect you. Obesity offends him. Pam had offended him a little. It upsets him to admit that after all they've shared.

He flicks the machine up a gear.

The sweat runs down his scalp. Down his back. Down his legs. It feels hot and red. Hot like her life. Her life he has taken and made his own.

Beat, beat, beat.

He should be sweating blood. His blood. Her blood. Their blood. He shakes sweat from his head.

Around him, machines hum. Ready to be filled by the post nine-to-five crowd. A woman on the end of the row keeps trying to catch his eye in the mirrors. Trying to catch his eye and smile. He ignores her. She is trying desperately to look good and run at the same time.

Of course, he could smile back.

They would share a coffee. He would go back to her place. They would enjoy another kind of workout. He giggles to himself. Starts to relax. That's good. Better. How it should be. He looks at the woman. She is okay. Not his type, but okay. Any other day and things could be so different. For her. But not today.

He runs the machine to a stop. It is important to cool down properly.

He smiles back at the woman on the end of the row then disappears into the changing room. It never hurts to keep your options open.

In the showers. Steam rises all around him. Gyms are always empty at this time of day. Only ever a few overweight, middle-aged women trying to keep hold of their men. A few unemployed men thinking getting fit will get them back into employment.

He likes the gym. Likes to visit many different gyms at many different times. Pay to use the equipment. No hidden costs. No lengthy forms. Moving around keeps it fresh. Keeps his interest. Keeps his mind moving and alert. He likes the way his muscles feel after a workout. Hot and toned. Sore but full of strength. Relaxed but ready to go. He smiles to himself as he lathers up the soap.

There's a small bar attached to the foyer of the gym. On the bar is a small plastic witch on a broom. She's next to a large bowl of mints. The barman is dressed as a vampire. For a moment, the man stares.

'Good costume, eh?' The barman does a twirl.

'Orange juice, no ice.' The barman doesn't look impressed. People are very, very odd.

The man knows he will make his orange juice last. He likes to watch the world pass by, watch the people pass by. Especially at this time. When he is most relaxed. While their bodies are still one, him and Pam. Him and any of the ones that came before her. There is no pressure. No need to look other than for pleasure. It is company after so long alone in the dark, their company, running through his veins.

The bar is quiet. He almost cries with joy when he sees that the front window faces the busy high street. It is a huge viewing room. A massive glass television designed just for him.

A man in a business suit paces past the window, lost deep in a telephone conversation. Oblivious to the world around him. Two young girls, probably from the local sixth form, amble the other way, giggling. One of them looks at her reflection, adjusts her hair slide. The other pulls her away, laughs. Both of them lick toffee apples in a way a lesser man would find arousing. A mother with a pram passes, an old fashioned pram you don't see so often these days. The undercarriage is packed with fresh fruit and vegetables. The mother's hand-knitted hat is pulled tight over her ears. One hand darts down to fuss whatever is in the pram every other second. A baby the man assumes.

This feeling will pass. It passes quicker each time. This makes him sad and happy all at once. Soon the need will grow within him once again. He'll have to look properly. To observe. To pay attention and select. It doesn't bother him. There are always plenty to choose from, but it's a different kind of fun to this.

Then something beautiful catches his eye.

Someone beautiful.

Through his own reflection he sees her, nearly lost out there on the busy street. She's so perfect she takes his breath away. The way she walks. The way she looks. Then she turns. Turns towards the window and smiles. Smiles right at him, right through the reflection of himself. Her smile overlaid with his face. She's already inside him.

It's meant to be.

His heart jumps into his mouth. It's very soon, all things considered. It is... it has to be a... a... he can't think of the word. Not a sign but... right? He really hopes everything else fits as perfectly. He can't let this one get away.

Quickly, he drains the glass. Heads out into the street.

31.

Rhys looks up as the phone starts to ring.

The day shift are packing up. They lick their lips; taste that well-earned pint. There's talk of cosy meals with husbands. Plans to visit a nightclub. Of a hot bath to try and relax, get some peace laid down in their minds. No one mentions what day of the year it is. No fancy dress. No tricks to make each other jump. All they want is a few hours away from the madness. To hold something normal. One or two of them will call the night shift with a thought or idea that can't wait until morning. Something tiny that will seem massive in the dead of night. Something that will lead to nothing other than divorce.

Amongst the goodbyes, the phone starts to ring. Nothing out of the ordinary. Someone shouts to leave it. They all know they can't.

Quinn sighs as he replaces the receiver.

He nods to Rhys as the colour drains from his face. The pint will wait. The room looks to Quinn in silence. They know without him saying. There is no smiling. No comments. No crass jokes. There are no words at all as Rhys follows Quinn to the car.

Earlier that day, Detective Chief Inspector Alec Jenkins made a few things very clear. He has reached the end of his patience. Should there be any more bodies, the press, the Divisional Superintendent, the whole of the known universe, will be down on them like a sack of shit. A sack of shit he won't stink of alone. The Detective Inspector and his goddamn team best work every second they have to catch this sick bastard before anyone else dies. Do they all understand? Do they understand their shift patterns and what 'until further notice' means? Do they need him to come and supervise the investigation more closely? All the press needs is one sniff of Andrews's misdemeanours, one sniff there has been a potential mess up, and none of them, he emphasises these words, none of them, will work so much as issuing a speeding ticket in this town again.

The street is full of kids. It's that kind of street. Full of kids on bikes with dirty faces that shout dirty words at the police. They dress in sheets with eyeholes. Vampire capes. Plastic axes come out of the top of their heads. Buckets for sweets and money dangle from handlebars. Someone shouts 'a penny for the guy'. Someone shouts something ruder.

It is a terrace house. Red brick. Victorian. A front door with a bubbled glass panel. A small concrete rectangle masquerades as a front garden. A mirror image of the neighbour, and the neighbour after that. Street after street of these houses. Lined up next to the park. A park full of dog shit and flashers. Teenagers drinking cider and starting fires. Little wonder the kids are on the streets. It's cheap housing. Inhabited by generations of families all born, living and dying a few streets from each other.

Crude pumpkin faces leer out of windows at Quinn and Rhys as they arrive. Laughing at the joke they are.

The couple in question are Will and Pam Jones. They live at number one hundred and seven. Female wailing fills the air.

No one's thought to move the pumpkin. It stares toothlessly up from behind the boot of the Constable positioned at the front gate.

'What the hell's that noise?' Quinn snaps.

'Crying, sir. It's the daughter, Sally, sir. I think she's a little upset.' The Constable looks down at his highly polished boots. Knows he sounds ridiculous. The pumpkin catches his eye. 'She's waiting for you, sir. She's the one who found the deceased. The paramedics wanted to check her over, give her somewhere to calm down, the neighbour offered. I thought it would be okay.'

Another wail emanates from one hundred and nine. The front door is open. Rhys sees the outline of a Constable in the gloomy hall. 'It's all a bit busy out here, sir.' The Constable nods to the gathering crowd. Quinn's neck is bright red.

'Move this bloody cordon back then!' The blue and white tape is only metres behind. 'Tell the vultures they can wait and see this on the news, like the rest of the world. Get back!' The last words barked to the gathering crowd. The man closest to the tape steps back. 'Show some bloody respect.' The front gate squeaks in approval as Rhys and Quinn pass.

The hall smells flowery. Fragrance from a wall adapter plugged in across from the dark mouth of the understairs cupboard. A cupboard that swallowed Will Jones whole. Nearly whole. As whole as can be expected. No need for the paramedics. Will is going nowhere in a hurry.

'Jesus.' Quinn peers into the darkness. 'Where are the CSI guys? They usually beat us here? I always got the impression they slept in the van, fully kitted up and ready to go. You would think that, the amount of bitching that goes on.' He takes a step closer. 'There's a lot of blood in there. A hell of a lot of blood.' His face is a grimace. He turns. 'There's never been this much blood before. Mind you, I can't really see fuck all without the lads and their lights.' He sticks his head closer. Double checks there's no light source.

'Why do people keep so much shit under the stairs anyway? Bet they haven't looked at half of it for years.' Had Will thought the same as he lay there in the gloom? 'Bet that would really piss him off, the killer, if he came to shove someone in and it was too full of crap. Police safety warning: keep those understair cupboards full, folks. It will stop the bogie man getting in.' Quinn doesn't even bother to laugh. He rises. Joins Rhys. They stare into the lounge.

'There's a lot of blood in here too,' says Rhys. He looks at a pool that floats like oil on the white leather sofa. Quinn sniffs. The air is stale. The smell of old Chinese food. Open containers are stacked next to wiped-clean plates. A bag of prawn crackers has been knocked to the floor. One of them is soaked crimson.

'So, it's the lesser of two evils really. May as well go next door and speak to the daughter while we wait for CSI to arrive.' Rhys nods. He picks the living over the dead any day.

'Wait for CSI so we can see everything clearly?' It's not a question that needs to be answered. Quinn steps back. Looks into the kitchen.

'I think I can see what's in here clearly enough. Let's talk to the daughter first, then she can get out of here.'

32.

Time grinds to a halt. It always does when he talks to the lost. More so with those catapulted into loss when all they expected was a cup of tea, a cake, a moan at something crap on telly. Sally is a large woman. She looks tiny as she sits, trying to control her shakes.

'Husband's on his way.' The paramedic rises. Sally grabs his arm, pleading. Funny the attachments people make. He looks from Quinn to Rhys. 'Is it okay if I stay?'

'Sure.' Quinn perches on the arm of a second floral couch, crammed in at ninety degrees to where Sally shivers. Rhys walks to the window.

Sally picks at a lose thread on the arm of her large brown cardigan. She opens her mouth to speak. Shuts it again. Lost for words. No, not lost, there are no words. Nowhere to begin where she can guarantee ever being able to stop.

'Sally.' Rhys turns to face her. 'Do you mind if I call you Sally?' A headshake. 'I understand how hard this is, I really do, but if you could talk us through what happened from when you arrived at your parents' house that would be great.' Sally nods.

They continue to sit in silence.

'What time did you arrive, Sally?' Quinn this time. Sally looks pointlessly at her watch for guidance.

'About half an hour ago, I think. Yes, no, longer, it was about half-seven. I had to wait until the kids had had their tea and got ready for trick or treating, you know with it being... It's not fair on Barry otherwise. He doesn't get in from work until seven you see, so yes, about half-seven.'

Just over an hour ago. Sally is sixty-five minutes into her new life.

'Oh god what if I'd brought the kids with me? They wanted to come, they really did, to show nanny their costumes, but I said no, said it was too late, took pictures to show her...' Sally's voice starts to shard.

'How did you get into the house?' She focuses on Quinn.

'I have a key. It's for emergencies. That's what Mum says.' The tense catches in her throat, 'said? Saved her having to get up to answer the door all the time, Dad is, was... oh god.' Her eyes on Quinn start to plead. 'He was a lazy sod. And I'm always over here.' She points towards her parents' house. 'There.'

'You're doing really well, Sally, just a few more questions and we can leave the rest until tomorrow.' Sally clenches her teeth. Does she hope it'll hold the pieces together? 'So what happened after you let yourself in?'

'There was no sound. I thought it was odd: there's always sound, usually from the television, but there was nothing, so I called out. I wondered if they'd gone out but Mum would have said yesterday, told me to come later.' Her head drops. She picks at the thread. If she pulls too hard she'll unravel. 'Oh god why didn't I come earlier...'

'It wouldn't have made any difference,' says Quinn. Blunt. To the point. 'No difference at all. Please...'

'Really?' A tiny drop of relief in this dark storm. The briefest moment. Swept away as the horror of reality returns. Quinn says nothing. Lets the silence settle.

'So I called out, no one answered and that's when I saw all the blood.' Sally starts to shake violently. The paramedic looks at them with concern. 'So much blood in the lounge. I started to panic, ran into the kitchen. At first I thought, you know, she had done something stupid, the way she was hanging there.' Sally laughs suddenly. Eyes wide. 'Then I realised she was upside down... and naked... and so pale... and her face...' The twisted scream hammers into Rhys's mind. Shake it off. His hands are in his pockets. He balls them into fists.

'I didn't touch her, I couldn't. I think I screamed. Yes, I screamed. That's what she must have heard, next door... here.' The thought forms physically in front of her. 'Why didn't they hear anything here? Why didn't they hear anything when she could hear me screaming? Maybe they did. You'll have to ask them. You will ask them, won't you?' The paramedic rests a hand on her arm. Signals to Quinn it is time to stop.

'And Dad, I didn't even know Dad was there. Why didn't I know Dad was there?' Her eyes dart back and forth. Questioning. Self-accusing. 'Why didn't I see the blood coming from under the cupboard door?' She gags. Snot pours from her nose. 'It was the first thing the policeman noticed when he got here, the blood on the carpet: at the door. What if I had noticed? Would he still be...?'

'No.' Quinn stands. 'There is no way that could have been the case.' He goes as if to carry on but stops himself. 'No.' Quinn nods to Rhys; they rise to leave. Quinn reaches the door. Hand on the knob.

'I mean Mum's only just got home.' Sally takes big rasps of air. 'Home from the hospital.' That stops Quinn, stops them both.

'Which hospital?' Quinn pivots slowly.

'St James'.'

Quinn nods to Rhys. Rhys excuses himself.

'When was she admitted...?'

Rhys calls Davies, gives him all the relevant information, then paces the hall. The homeowner twitches in the kitchen. She is poised to flick the switch of the kettle, open a new packet of biscuits. Keen to help. A voyeur to someone else's nightmare.

The reality of what happened through the thin brick wall has not set in. Yet. Was she sat at her table while through the wall the killer sat at Pam Jones's and watched her blood drain? Rhys considers mentioning it. Extinguish that twinkle in her eye.

Quinn exits the living room to a crescendo of Sally's sobs. Rhys half expects him to take a bow. He strides past Rhys and out onto the street. It's time to go back next door.

33.

Quinn's phone rings at the front door. He looks at the caller ID.

'I need to take this.' Quinn steps away.

Winters and his team have arrived. Winters passes Rhys in the hall. Rhys nods. Winters doesn't notice. He mutters something about evidence bags.

Rhys steps into the kitchen.

Pam fills the space. They're alone. Strangers on a first date.

Her face is twisted. The silent scream of terror.

The room is ice cold. Is it coming from her skin?

Rhys couches down low. His face near Pam's. Her eyes are open. Stare directly at him through their thin, red veil. He resists the urge to close them.

Pam's flesh is covered in cellulite. Does that make it harder to get the blood out? Harder for it to fight its way through the fat? Or did her massive heart pump her life out all the faster? Rhys feels the warm liquid at the back of his throat.

He rises, takes a steps back. His blue shoe covers make him silent. Through the front door, he can see Quinn on the telephone.

Rhys moves around Pam. Careful to stay on the foot boards. Careful not to contaminate the scene.

Did the killer do this? View her from every angle. Rhys tilts his head. What does he think about as he watches her die? Does he sit or stand? Rhys circles her slowly. Does he hold them close at that final moment? Feel their heartbeat slowly fade next to his?

Rhys feels a second heartbeat next to his. The breeze rustles his hair. The ground shifts slightly under foot. Someone should push the front door shut. They'll all be blown away, not that it's all that windy. He completes his circle. Looks back to the front door. It is pulled tight shut. Rhys frowns. Rhys's paper boiler suit suddenly seems too tight, more his tie is too tight underneath. He can't draw breath properly; he can't undo the zip with these goddamn gloves on. He pulls one glove off, yanks the zip, loosens his tie. Inhales deeply even though the air is rank.

The colours of the kitchen start to swirl. To merge. He blinks rapidly. Is he having a panic attack? The room feels like it's swaying, tipping from one side to the other. He staggers slightly to the left. In the hall, the lights flash. Black. Then white. Then black again.

'Ask.' The voice whispers in his ear. Just an out breath but enough. Cold. Hard. Full of purpose. Rhys whips his head round. Nothing. His heart stops. Adrenalin explodes through his veins.

'What for?' he shouts. He reaches out to steady himself on the worktop.

'Talking to yourself in here, Morgan?' Quinn steps into the room. All movement stops. The wind lulls. Everything is still. All bar the adrenaline buzzing through Rhys's veins, his heart as it hammers in his chest. He can't move.

'You know what that is? The first sign of madness.' Quinn's laugh is distant. He finishes fiddling with his phone. 'Actually that's probably not appropriate, all things considered.' Quinn looks up. Stops dead. 'What the hell are you doing?' He stares at Rhys's fingers that cling to the wood.

'Rhys!' The sound of his name clicks the final edges of the kitchen back into focus. For the first time he is aware of the smooth wood beneath his fingers.

'Sorry. Shit.' What on earth is he doing? Where is he? He jerks his hand back. Tries to use the sleeve of his paper boiler suit to wipe the worktop. Why the hell hasn't he got gloves on? He always put gloves on. 'It was a mistake. I didn't mean to. I just... it was a mistake.' He can hardly speak. He looks from his one gloved hand to the other gloveless one. His tie, he took it off to loosen his tie.

'You're a fucking mistake, Morgan.'

'It was my tie, I was—'

'I don't want to hear it.' Quinn steps close. Rhys is definitely awake. 'You know they haven't finished in here, right? You best not give that fat bastard reason to have one up on me. Fuck me.' Quinn's head shakes. He glances over his shoulder. Checks the hall is still empty. 'Hands in pockets. Now.' Rhys complies. 'Shit, if you're going to act like a dick, I'll treat you like one. Let's go. Now.'

Rhys isn't sure his legs will work. Will he fall? Crash headlong into Quinn. Into the voice. The voice. The one simple word seems to resonate around his body. Shake his bones until they hurt.

'*Ask.*'

The reverb on his eardrum. The echo in his head. The sound of waves crashing all around him. Quinn is talking. Focus on the words. Use them to pull yourself back towards the light. A pinprick on the horizon zooming into focus. Rhys feels sweat break out all over his body.

Quinn moves down the hall. Opens the door to a flash of press photograph bulbs. His voice is far away.

'Not sure about you, but I really fancy a Chinese for dinner now, once you've given your details to Winters so he can eliminate you from the crime scene.'

34.

'Clean it.' Mother's voice shrieks above him. 'Clean it faster, you vile little thing.' Tears stream down his face, land on the stone floor. Snot pours from his nose but he daren't stop. Instead he breathes through his mouth. The fumes burn his throat – make him cough. This makes her laugh louder, harder. His hands are red raw. They feel like they're on fire. They burn and itch in equal measure. He pulls and pushes the heavy wooden scrubbing brush back and forth. He's down on all fours like the disgusting animal he is. He wants so badly to make it shiny. To make her happy. Why can't she see how hard he tries to please her?

The flagstones beneath his knees are cold. Pain shoots up his thighs as his bones push down. Back and forth in the slippery bubbles. Soaked and sore and vile. He looks up at her. From this angle she looks like the light fitting is going straight into the back of her neck. She is suspended in the gloom like a grotesque theatre puppet.

'Don't you look at me. Not like that. Not at all, you vile creature.' She kicks him then. Hard. Violent. He sprawls across the wet floor. She grabs the bottle of bleach. Pours it all over him. All over him and the floor. She screeches that he isn't fast enough. Doesn't scrub hard enough. He is vile and if she wants a job doing properly she'll be as well doing it herself. She spits down on him. Screams her wish that he was dead. That he was dead and his sister was still alive. He screws up his eyes and almost wished the same thing.

In the dark, he finds her there, little Elizabeth. In the corner of his mind. In the corner of his room.

He doesn't think about her, his little sister. It's as if the memory of her has almost been erased over time. Time has changed so much. Things have changed so much. There is no room for her. He likes to kid himself it's because things are so horrible now that he refuses to think of her. Doesn't want to taint her with the stink. That's a lie. He just doesn't think of her. It's as simple as that.

Elizabeth has a round, fat face and soft smile. She seems to smile all the time. Life is one big happy event from the moment she wakes until the moment she sleeps. Such a pleasant, well-mannered little girl. That's what he hears the grown-ups say. Not like her brother. They all agree he is, well, a little bit odd. She's always been so keen to help, his little sister. Follows Mother around. Does whatever is asked.

Mother was nicer then. No, don't laugh. Now it seems that's impossible. That his mind has made it up to give her some kind of redeeming feature she doesn't deserve. But it's true.

No, if Mother didn't keep reminding him, he could quite easily forget all about her. About what happened in the previous chapter of his life. Life with smiling little Elizabeth. It could be that everything before this is a dream.

Mother always wanted a girl, she said she hadn't realised it until she had one. A little girl to dress in pink with bows in her hair and frills on her socks. A little girl to teach how to bake and play tea sets with. To knit and sew for. To paint pretty pictures. He was the most important, then he was replaced by something better. Completely ignored with his bullish toys and close-cropped hair. That's a lie. Not completely ignored, not if Elizabeth needed something.

She tried so hard to please, did little Elizabeth, to be liked, even then it made him feel sick.

Father left not long after Elizabeth was born. He obviously hated pink as much as the silent little boy, only he was big enough to leave. The boy never remembered his parents arguing. His father was there one day and gone the next. He became the shadowy outline seen leaving through the door, nothing more. Nothing more, nothing less. A nothing black shape. He never questioned why his father didn't take him too. Father had made it clear he never really liked his son all that much. It was fine. The silent boy didn't like him all that much either.

In the silent boy's mind, his sister is so very small. That's how he last saw her. Small and clean and pink, tucked under a silk sheet, surrounded by a cheap mahogany veneer. Everyone's crying, saying his sister is gone. He shrugs then. He can clearly see her lying in the centre of the room. Mother starts to cry that day. Cry and shriek. She has done ever since.

He can tell by the look in Mother's eyes that she blames him entirely. At first she doesn't say it, but he can tell. It takes time to start bleeding out. The hatred is like a scab she isn't able to stop picking. A sore that will only weep and never heal. She snaps one day when he drops a glass of milk. A putrid wash of hate floods over him. Elizabeth was always so good and he was always so naughty. He should have been watching her. He should have known better. He was the responsible one. And finally, how she wishes it had been him, wished he was dead. Silence hangs heavy in the air after the final words. Mother slaps her hand over her mouth involuntarily to mimic the wish that she had never said the words. Her eyes tell a different story. They dance with the liberation of speaking the truth. Now she is liberated there is no going back.

The silent boy and his sister were playing out one day when they were far too young to have been left alone. He suggests an adventure. She's unsure, little Elizabeth. Unsure of anything without Mother there to hold her hand. He tells her not to be such a baby. Keen to please, to gain the respect and love she so seeks from her big brother, she follows him tentatively through the broken fence at the back of the garden. The silent boy knows exactly where they're going. He's been there before. He's too young to be out alone but Mother doesn't care or notice.

She'll care now.

Through the small pocket of trees at the back of their house is a field. At the back of the field is an old dairy farm. It's been shut for years. Closed when the final son of the family rejected two hundred years of family sweat and tears in exchange for a dream in the city. The For Sale sign has fallen down. Teenagers use the barns to drink and smoke and try to touch each other.

Through one of the barns full of rusty metal equipment, is a smaller room with a heavy metal door. At the back of this room is an even smaller room, not much bigger than a cupboard. The room has no windows. Floor to ceiling shelves. There are crates of glass milk bottles. Most of them are broken. He tells Elizabeth to be careful. Not to cut herself. He says they're going to play a game. Hide and seek. She's to stay in the little room and count to one hundred. He'll go and hide. He knows she likes hide and seek. He has watched her play it with Mother. She nods, shivers slightly in the gloomy room. He can see she's afraid, wants to ask if she can count somewhere else. She also wants to please him. To seem brave and grown up. The boy knows she can't count to one hundred. Hasn't learnt that far.

Her small voice starts. Cut off instantly as he steps out and slams the door of the little room. He just wants a bit of peace. A bit of peace and quiet to think. A bit of peace to spend some time with Mother, without his sister getting in the way. She'll be okay in the little room for an hour or two. Maybe a little frightened, but it will be good for her. Perhaps she wouldn't even notice. It could take her that long to try and count to one hundred. She starts knocking then. Calls out his name. Cries. Asks him to open the door. Cries that she's frightened. Can he let her out? Cries that she wants Mother. He turns and walks away.

How was he supposed to know there wouldn't be enough air? He was too young to possibly know these kinds of things, wasn't he? He swallows the tiny smile and lets a tear roll down his cheek.

It didn't take Mother long to call the police. She didn't want to play with him. She wanted to pace and wring her hands and call Elizabeth's name. It doesn't take the police long to arrive and start asking questions. He thinks it best to say they were out playing. That Elizabeth said they should sneak off and explore. That he wanted to go back but she wanted to play hide and seek but never come to find him. Mother is shouting. Shouting why didn't he say something sooner? He really cries then. Says he's frightened. A policeman places a massive hand on his shoulder. Tells him to calm down. It isn't his fault.

In the end, it doesn't take them long to find her. The same way it didn't take her long to run out of air.

The police rule it as an accidental death and really it is. An accidental death brought on by her own stupidity. She would have been panicking and flapping and wasting all the air. All she had to do was count to one hundred and by that time he would have been back. He would have gone back sooner too if Mother had just wanted to play one game with him. But he had to keep waiting. Hoping she would change her mind. Elizabeth was still the focus even when she wasn't there.

He isn't sad she's dead. Not for one moment.

Builders come to the farm very soon after Elizabeth dies. Spurred into action that is long overdue. Very quickly they pull the place down and throw it in the bin. This is when Mother meets Strong Hands. He moves in not long after, and everything starts to change. So slowly the boy hardly notices his new existence until it takes shape and has him by the throat.

Now he is here, wet and cold and alone in the dark.

Somewhere far away, equally as dark but not quite as alone, he wakes up drenched in sweat and finally screams.

35.

Quinn stuffs food into his face. Rhys watches in silence. Quinn's lips move. They flap and spit food. He's trying to find a motive. Pull information together. Create, as he calls it, a 'crime line'. He speaks behind a wall of water.

Rhys needs to speak, input. His lips won't move. They feel glued together. Unlike his ears. They tingle. Pinprick sharp.

The voice at the crime scene was real. Not a dream. A fully formed sound, whispered from nowhere. It clings like a hand around his brain.

Is Anna right? Does he need to see a doctor? What if he's told he can't work? Or worse? He remembers what they did to his mother. Doctors are not an option. Too many questions in his head. The words fight to be heard.

Speak, Morgan. He chastises himself. Redeem yourself. Be needed.

Quinn doesn't notice Rhys's silence. He's too busy trying to impress Chantelle Watts who appears from nowhere. Mind you, Quinn is cleverer than he looks. He probably is noticing. Storing away notes to tell the boss. Get him kicked off the case. Take all the glory. Is that why she's here? Sitting with her extra dark make-up and cobweb stuff in her hair? Maybe she's a spy? She seems too clever, for how she comes across. Come on. Think of something. Say something that will add weight, aid the investigation.

Where does the blood go?

Stupid question.

How does he remove the blood from the scene?

Stupider question.

Why is the blood being removed from the scene? Why? Why? Why? His lips part. There is no sound. Watts looks at him. His mouth closes.

Quinn pays the bill. Says they should go for a drink. He angles for Rhys to go home. Makes a comment about the kids. Rhys ignores him. He really needs a gin and tonic.

The Travellers' Rest is decorated in the theme of a cave, which is a cop out – it pretty much looks like a cave the rest of the year too. Someone has half-heartedly strung fake cobwebs across the walls. Watts screams as she walks into a rubber spider outside the cloakroom. Quinn leaps to her rescue. He pretends to kill the spider to cries of 'my hero'.

The boy behind the bar has made no effort on his costume. He's bought one of those fake knives that look like you have been stabbed through the neck. He hasn't bothered to try and hide the clips. He's sprinkled a little fake blood onto his ripped white uniform. A lot more passion and effort has gone into the ripping than anything else. Rhys and Watts select a booth halfway up one side of the dance floor. Quinn gets the drinks in.

'Pretty quiet in here tonight.' It's the first time Rhys has spoken since Watts joined them. It's better than the silence.

'A bit like you,' Watts replies. She really could be a spy. 'Everything okay?' They both ponder the idiocy of the question until Quinn joins them.

'Over eleven pounds for that round. I mean, it's not like we are paying for the ambience is it? That's your fault, Morgan, for drinking poncy girls' drinks. No offence Chan.' She smiles. 'Why can't you drink a pint like the rest of us?' He takes a loud slurp. 'So, I was thinking, a quick one here then the two of us could head on somewhere else?'

Their voices fade. Rhys watches a lone teenager dressed as The Crow, dance to the melancholy music. That hadn't worked out so well for Brandon Lee now, had it? The gin is perfect. A little weak. He knew Quinn would be too tight to buy a double. Rhys's eyelids start to droop. He's so very tired. He could sink into the dirty booth and sleep forever. Except he doesn't want to sleep. Is too afraid. Too afraid of the night-time visits and the creature that stalks him there. Here. Everywhere.

Shit.

He rubs his eyes. Must stay awake.

'You look tired. We'll leave you to it.' Quinn is out of the booth before Rhys can speak. 'See you tomorrow. Ciao for now.' Rhys drains the last of the gin.

'Mind if I join you?' Two wide tumblers of ice and gin clink onto the table. 'They call it mother's ruin, you know.' The voice laughs. 'I hope me saying that doesn't offend you.'

Rhys is tired. He should be at home. He needs to be at home. He needs to see his kids. Make amends with his wife. Get his head round everything that has happened. The last thing he wants is company, polite small talk.

'Actually I was just...' Rhys looks up. His heart freezes. He is looking straight into the piercing blue eyes of the man, the creature from his dream. The hospital. His street. His neighbour.

The creature smiles. Razor sharp incisors catch the light. Rhys's mouth drops open.

'As I suspected,' says the creature, 'time for another.'

36.

'Who? What?...' Rhys can't find coherent words.

'Why, where, when?' The creature laughs, mocks. It slides into the booth opposite him. Pushes a glass of gin across the table. The glass leaves a watery trail of condensation. 'Kier Finnegan.' It extends a long, well-manicured hand.

This must be a dream. It's what he read about, isn't it? Lucid dreaming. That's what's happening. Right here, right now. A live feed of his life projecting straight out of his brain. Kier's handshake is firm, cool. Very much real. Not asleep then? The other dreams all felt physically real, why should this be any different?

'Stop torturing yourself. You're awake. See.' Kier's hand darts across the table and pinches his arm. By the time Rhys flinches, it's as if Kier never moved.

Kier takes a sip of his drink.

'Close your mouth. People will start to stare.' Rhys closes his mouth.

Kier tilts his head to one side. 'It is good to finally meet you, Rhys Morgan. Up close, you are much more than I ever imagined. Unlike your choice of drinking establishment.' Kier looks around in distain. 'We shall have to work on that.'

'Do I know you?'

'No. Not really.'

'Have we ever met?'

'Again, not really. At least not properly.'

'Did I see you at the hospital?'

'Do you think you saw me at the hospital?'

'What? Yes of course.'

'Then you saw me at the hospital.' Kier smiles. Looks at Rhys with intrigue. 'I work there. I am a surgeon.' He was at the hospital. That's good, right?

'And in the street, my street, last night?' Rhys already knows the answer.

'Of course. I live there. You didn't seem... How can I put this politely? Capable of rational conversation?'

'And whose fault is that?'

'Hardly mine, Rhys. That really isn't fair.'

Is this even real? How on earth can this be real? There's no way this can be real. He should leave. Get up and go. But what if this is the only chance he ever gets for answers? They must have met somewhere before the hospital. Their paths must have crossed regardless of what this creature says.

'Hardly likely, Rhys. I've only just moved back to town.'

Has he lost his mind? Is he actually sitting having a conversation with himself? Rhys has seen films like this. Could this creature be a character from his own mind? Can this character answer his questions? Answers only his subconscious knows? Shit. It's complicated. Rhys takes a sip of gin.

Kier looks at him and sighs, shakes his head. Does Rhys detect pity? Rhys rubs his eyes.

In reality he feels fine. A little tired, but otherwise fine. If you were losing your mind, by the very definition, you would feel the opposite of fine. Sure, there have been a couple of moments of 'not so fine' but hardly anything life-changing. Not now, he knows he's right. He has seen this Kier both times.

'You are not losing your mind, Rhys.' Kier's voice breaks into his thoughts, bored. 'Can you save the self-analysis until you get home? You humans are all so predictably boring.' Kier looks at his nails. 'Maybe I should have picked someone dumber, a little less self-conscious? But then where would be the fun in that?'

'Sorry?' Focus, focus, focus.

'So you should be. I do have other things on tonight you know.' Kier laughs loudly. 'Which is odd as I usually hate Halloween. It's all so contrived and well, wrong, don't you think? So stereotypically predictable?'

'I meant, sorry what did you say?'

'When?'

'Just then.'

'What?' Kier laughs, teases. 'I know, I know.' He lifts his palms. 'I said you are all predictable, and a little boring. In the nicest possible way of course.'

'You said "you humans".'

'Yes.'

'Why would you say that? Are you taking the piss because it's Halloween? Has someone put you up to this because I'm a copper?' The words sound lame. He doesn't care.

'No.' One simple word.

'Who are you then?'

'I've told you.' Kier sits back.

'What? No you haven't. You've told me your name.' Kier raises an eyebrow, listens. 'Why are you in my dreams?' The words are out before Rhys can stop them.

'Oh Rhys, you do flatter me.' Rhys stares at him. Hard and blank. The smile fades from his lips. 'Who do you think I am? Actually the more pertinent question would be, what do you think I am?'

'I don't know. That's why I'm asking.' Is this conversation even real?

'Yes you do, of course you do. I have seen you up at night tucked away in that pretty little shrine of yours, internet surfing, as I am told it's called. Always preferred books myself.' Kier holds Rhys's eye. Rhys feels his throat tighten.

'I don't know.'

'Yes you do.'

'No, I don't.'

This is crazy. Get up and leave. This man is mad. Delusional. Possibly dangerous. He is saying ridiculous things. Making Rhys say ridiculous things.

Rhys wracks his brain. How are you supposed to deal with delusional people? Why hadn't he paid more attention at the training session? Too close to home?

'Rhys.' Kier pulls his attention, a razor edge to his voice. 'This is getting more than a little tedious. Go on, say it?' Rhys can't. 'Yes, you can.'

Rhys takes a deep breath. This is crazy.

The other option is of course that this is some kind of surreal experience. Has he somehow ingested some drugs? Has Quinn slipped something in his gin?

It comes to him then. A flash of remembered inspiration. You are supposed to play along. It stops the delusional person turning nasty.

He looks Kier dead in the eye.

'You want me to say I think you're some kind of demon. A Nosferatu.' Kier claps slowly. 'Except you can't be can you, not really. They don't exist. Only crazy people, kids and depressed teenagers think that. Which does that make me?' Kier pretends to ponder the question.

'Let's not go getting all philosophical here, Rhys.' Kier yawns theatrically. 'It is again all rather boring. Have you noticed how many things bore me, Rhys? It's such a shame, isn't it?' Kier leans across the table. 'You want to be more accepting, like that lovely little boy of yours.' Rhys feels his face harden. Something like glee dances behind Kier's eyes.

'What's Harry got to do with this?'

'Harry. Nice name. Kids always respond so much better once you know their names.' Kier sits back, takes a long slow drink of his gin. A rage starts to open in the pit of Rhys's stomach. 'Harry, Louise... Jenny.' Rhys feels something crush his windpipe. 'Too much? Okay, a different tack, perhaps. Want to touch my fangs?' Kier grimaces, exposes long, razor sharp incisors. Only for a moment but it is enough. 'Will that convince you? I can assure you they are very real.'

Instantly he is next to Rhys, the cool rush of his skin everywhere. Incisors glinting as the disco globe pulsates above the dance floor. Cramp surges up Rhys's neck.

'Get the fuck away from me.' He is gone. Back round his side of the table. As if he never moved.

'As you wish.' Kier straightens his collar. Rhys pushes thoughts of Jenny, his family, far from his mind. Kier is playing with him, looking for a rise he won't get, for a reason Rhys can't yet understand. The rage is bitter as he swallows it back down.

Kier Finnegan. Rhys has a name. He can run it through the database at work. Has Rhys arrested him before?

'Feel free. You will be wasting your time and taxpayers money.'

He'll go to the hospital, demand to see their records; tell them what kind of nutjob they've employed.

'Oh please, yes they employ me; I can assure you my record is impeccable. What do you think they will tell you, other than to go home and have a nice long rest? Hospitals are dangerous places to talk crazy, Rhys.'

Who is this creature... no, this man, he is just that, a man. A man with expensive dental work and mind trick movement. It is okay. Rhys is okay. It'll all be okay?

Kier knows the names of his family. That is not okay.

If he is just a man, what does that mean for the dreams? They are not okay.

'What is this?' Rhys tries a different tack. 'What do the dreams mean?' Kier looks at him, intrigue on his face.

'You mean you don't know?' Rhys shakes his head. This seems to anger Kier. He drops his gaze. When he looks back, something has changed within his eyes. He is the creature from the nightmares. There is something cold and hard. Something has shifted. Rhys feels ice start to weave its way into his blood.

'What do you want from me?' An edge of panic in his voice.

'It's not hard to figure out, Rhys.'

'If I asked, would you leave me alone?' Is this the kind of thing a crazy person asks? The kind of thing a crazy person asks another crazy person who has just told the first crazy person he is a Nosferatu?

'Only in exchange,' says Kier.

'For what?'

'You know.' Rhys does. It turns his stomach.

'My family? Are you crazy, are you threatening them in some way?'

'Not all of them, no. Please, you make it sound so crude. It's not my fault that I find that wife of yours almost as enchanting as you.' A distant look passes behind Kier's eyes. 'She would do, yes, she would definitely do... If I'm honest, which I feel I should be if this is to work, I am more than a little lonely.' Kier dabs a mock tear. Chuckles. 'You try living with Arthur for fifty years,' Kier can't be older than thirty. 'He can't half be a drag. Especially since we moved back here and he's taken a shine to some old crone across the street. You would really think he'd have learnt better by now.' Kier sighs, shakes his head. 'There really is no telling some people.

'Then I saw you. More than saw you, I felt you, the night that we came to view the house.' Kier's face looks far away. 'A wave of utter sadness that, for a moment I thought might overwhelm me. Then I realised where it was coming from. It was coming from you, Rhys.'

'I'm fine.'

'Really?'

'Please stay away from me and my family. This conversation is over.' Fuck this. Lonely? Whatever. It is clear. This Kier is crazy. Dangerous. Delusional. There is nothing to be gained by this. He can sort everything out himself. Perhaps the dreams will stop now. Now he's put a name to a face. Now there is a physical, if crazy, man to attach it to.

'I have overstepped the mark mentioning your family. Good. That makes it easier for me. Now please sit down. This conversation is not over.' Rhys looks over his shoulder, a big mock gesture.

'I'm sorry. For a moment then I thought you were telling me what to do. Who do you think you are?' Rhys presses his palms onto the table. Leans across to Kier. 'You are not right in the head. I should arrest you for...' Kier cocks his head. Looks at him. Where are the right words?

'Speaking some home truths?'

'Screw you.' Kier raises an eyebrow. Pouts.

'If you will let me finish, as I fear you have reached the end of your attention span. I will cut straight to the point, it's quite simple. Join me.'

37.

'I beg your pardon?' Rhys laughs out loud.

'You aren't deaf, Rhys, any more than you are stupid. Join me.'

'Join you? As in become another nutter at large in the community.'

'No.'

'Oh what, as in become a demon of the night and we can creep around in the shadows sucking the blood of virgins and princesses?' Kier flinches. Rhys laughs. He can't help it. People turn and stare. The laugh is a loud, crazy, desperate sound that echoes round the bar.

'I'll tell you what, that's great, brilliant, ten out of ten.' Rhys steps from the booth. 'You can go back and tell your mates you really had me fucking going.' He ducks in close to Kier's face. 'But mention my wife or family again, come near me again and I swear to god, it'll be the last thing you do.'

The move happens before Rhys sees it. Kier grabs hold of his wrist in a hard, icy ring.

Rhys can no longer breathe.

His knees buckle. The wind rushes through his hair. The light swivels into a tiny pinprick and disappears.

And there she is.

She takes the remainder of his breath away.

He may have cried out loud, he can't be sure. Fire burns through his body as she stands before him. So real he could reach out and touch her.

So he does.

He reaches out and touches the brown ringlets of her hair, soft, so soft. He touches her cheek. Warm and fresh like that final day. The day she let him kiss her goodbye.

He can smell her soap. Her hairspray. The cheap perfume their mum gave her on the promise she didn't tell their dad. He can really feel it. Her skin. The beat of her heart. She smiles the cheeky smile she always smiles. There is a twinkle in her eye. She is here for him. She always will be. She knows he'll always be here for her.

Her forehead creases suddenly.

He can't hold her. She slips through his fingers.

'Rhys, don't leave me, Rhys. Don't leave me on my own in the dark.'

Now he is falling.

The arms catch him, hold him close. He feels safe for the first time. Safe and whole. There is no pain. There is no unknown.

Rhys jerks backwards. Gasps. A deep rasp. Air rushes back into his body. He pulls away from Kier whose face curves back into focus. Rhys convulses, every muscle in his body spasms. His eyes are wide, do not leave Kier. He falls back into the seat. His wrist burns where the creature held it. A thin line of angry blisters rise.

'What the...?' No more words will come. Rhys pants. A thin film of sweat breaks out all over his body. He can't move. He can't even remember why he wants to.

'I must say I am a little disappointed in you, Rhys. I thought you would have been more fun, more perceptive.' The creature spits the last word. 'You are going to have to lighten up. You are lucky you interest me enough to hold my attention. You make it all such a challenge and I like a good challenge. It can all be too predictable otherwise.' Rhys tries to shake the water from his head.

'Jenny...' Is all he can whisper.

'Jenny,' Kier mimics in disgust. 'My offer of course is not a decision you need to rush into.' He looks at his watch, 'I can give you... say, a week?' Playful eyes back on Rhys. 'After all, I have all the time in the world.'

Rhys is numb. He opens his mouth. No sound comes. Kier is inches from him. 'Of course you don't want to take too long.' The sound tickles across Rhys's skin. 'Or I might get really bored, and you wouldn't like me when I'm really bored.'

Kier steps back, straightens his jacket.

'It really is all rather straightforward. You come with me, your family are safe and so are you. Your entire family.' Rhys stares at him. Kier sighs. 'You really are no fun today.' He turns to leave, throws a parting shot over his shoulder. 'He's not a very nice man, is he?'

'What?' Rhys's mind can't keep up.

'It's pardon, not what. That fat idiot you have the misfortune of working with.'

'Quinn?' What? Pardon? What?

'Are there more? I can sort him out for you if you like? As a good-will gesture, soften up his edges, so to speak.' Kier laughs. 'Anyway I must dash. I have a pressing dinner engagement.'

And he is gone. Just like that. One moment he is at the end of the booth, then he just disappears.

Rhys's mind races. Has a man just come up to him, claimed to be a demon of the night and threatened his family? And Jenny... how did he...?

Rhys rubs his thumb and forefinger together. Feels the silk of her hair.

He's going to be sick.

Take long deep breaths.

He had seen her, touched her. She was real. Needles prickle up his body.

He slides quickly from the booth and runs to the boy behind the bar.

'Did you see him?' There is an edge of hysteria to his voice. He doesn't care. His spit showers the bar. 'Tell me, did you see him?'

'See who?' The bored boy with the knife through his neck dries a glass.

'The man I was having a drink with. Did you see him?' Rhys points to the table. One empty glass stares back.

'Look mate, whoever you want to have a drink with is your business.' The boy drops his eyes to Rhys's wedding ring. 'Me, I'm just here to pour the drinks and see as much, or as little as is needed.' Rhys growls. 'But seeing as you ask so nicely, no, I don't think so.'

'Then think bloody harder. This is important. I'm a police officer.' Rhys fumbles through his pockets. Where's his bloody badge? Shit. He fights down the urge to scream. Or cry.

'You and everyone else who comes here,' the boy chuckles, sends vibrations up the knife in his neck. He wipes the bar. 'As far as I know, you've been sat over there on your own ever since that fat bloke and fit bird left. But if you want me to say there was some guy with you. I can... if it means that much.' He chuckles again. Rhys fights the urge to smack his smug face into the bar top.

Instead he turns. Runs up the steps and out onto the street.

'I know you're out here, you fuck!' A bloke stares while his girlfriend looks away like nothing is happening. 'Come on, where are you?' Rhys kicks one of the large bins that line the street.

'Are you hiding somewhere, watching me? Are you? Is that what you get off on?' More people start to look. 'You sick bastard.' Rhys strides up the street. Turns. Heads back. Looks behind the bins. Up a side street.

'How did you know about my sister? Who the hell told you about my sister? How did you make her so...?' His voice cracks. How had he made her so real? Her perfume lingers in his nostrils. More real than any memory, any photograph. It was her – exactly as she was. Does Kier know something about her disappearance? He doesn't look much older than Rhys, but then if what he says is true, he could be any age...

'What the fuck!' Rhys berates himself out loud. The guy is obviously crazy. With crazy comes dangerous and here Rhys is looking like the madman. He needs to be at home. He really needs to be at home.

'I'm watching you.' He shouts to nowhere in particular.

He turns his back on the pub's dark mouth.

He walks away from the bar. He can't walk away from the tiny prickles of doubt as they start to pick away at his brain.

38.

Anna didn't expect Rhys home early, but now it was getting ridiculous.

Harry refuses to sleep until Dad's home. He's afraid. Anna told him this would happen if he read ghost stories after dark on Halloween.

The doorbell rang non-stop from dinnertime until after eight.

Children laughed. Parents complained. Buckets of sweets rattled. Older kids made everyone angry throwing eggs. Harry spent a happy hour carving a pumpkin. Louise said it was gross. Harry cried. Louise said it proved he was a baby. They all made friends over toffee apples.

Harry isn't the only one who doesn't want to go to bed before Rhys is home. Anna wants talk, is fed up of feeling this way. She hates it when they fall out. She hates feeling this angry all the time. She will apologise first, even though he's the one in the wrong. Just this one last time. Rhys needs to sort himself out. Anna sighs. She needs to create an opportunity to drop into conversation the doctor's appointment. Possibly mention her meeting with the new neighbours.

Kier pops into her head. Not for the first time. Those beautiful blue eyes… She pushes the thought away. Throws aside the magazine she can't concentrate on. Rhys's key sounds in the front door.

'Anna?' He shouts. His voice shakes.

'I'm here... Jesus.' The words are out before she can stop them. A knee-jerk reaction. Rhys looks awful. His skin is pale and clammy. Grey. Dark purple circles under his eyes. Did he look like that this morning? He stops in front of her. Twitches on the spot. Agitated or alert? He doesn't register what she's said.

'You will never guess what just happened.' His eyes dart around the room. She rises in concern.

'Rhys?' She goes to lay a hand on his shoulder. He steps back, winces.

Is he still that mad at her?

'Rhys, do you feel okay? What on earth has happened?' His

brow furrows. Has he heard her? Has he been drugged? Is he having some kind of seizure?

'No, I do not feel okay. I feel very far from okay and not in the sick in the mind way you keep inferring, oh no.' He starts to pace the room. 'I feel like everything has become clearer. Well kind of.' He runs his hands through his hair. Drops to the sofa. Rises again. 'At the same time, not clearer at all.'

He goes to the window. Pulls back the curtains.

'Do these windows lock?' He tugs at the handle. It doesn't budge. 'Good. Good. Don't unlock them. They need to stay locked.'

'Rhys.' Anna's concern rises. What's he doing?

'Have you seen him today?' His finger leaves a greasy smudge on the window as he points across the street.

'Sorry?'

'Him. Kier Finnegan. Have you seen him today?'

'No.' Why is she lying? Rhys pulls the curtains tight. 'How do you know his name?'

'A very good question.' Rhys paces out of the room. Into the kitchen. Anna follows and finds Harry at the bottom of the stairs.

'Harry, go to bed please.'

'But, Mum...'

'Now!' It's not up for discussion.

Rhys is pouring himself a large glass of wine as she enters the kitchen.

'How do I know his name?' Rhys turns as he speaks. Leans back on the worktop, 'I know his name because I've just met him in a bar.'

'Good, that's good right?' It is good. As long as Rhys apologised. Did not behave like a lunatic. Again.

Shit.

Has Kier mentioned he saw her earlier? Is that why Rhys is behaving like this? Why on earth did she lie?

'No, that is not good.' Rhys takes a long drink. 'It is very far from good,' he looks her dead in the eye. 'Do you want to know why? Go on ask me?' She braces herself. She's done nothing wrong. Rhys continues.

'The man is insane. I use the term "man" in the loosest sense of the word.' Rhys takes another long drink. 'Do you know what he told me?' Rhys starts to laugh. A manic laugh that causes little butterflies to dance in the base of her stomach.

'He told me he is a Nosferatu. A demon. Can you believe that? One grown man to another. There we were, sat in the bar having a drink, and that's what he said. It wasn't even a Halloween prank, before you ask, because I sure as hell did.' Rhys's eyes are wide. Anna's mouth opens. She realises she has no idea what to say.

'Rhys, are you...? Is this...? Why are you doing this?' Anna has met Kier. He is most definitely a man and not a mad one. She is a good judge of character. What has Rhys said to him? What has he done?

'And do you know what else the madman said?' Rhys stares into the space above her head. 'He'll refrain from... he will do me the massive favour of, not hurting my family, you, if I join him. If I join him and became a creature of the night.' Rhys raises his wine glass in a mock toast.

'That makes him crazy, right? Cuckoo, gone in the head. Him, not me, him.' He taps his temple violently. 'A crazy man who knows where we live, thanks to you. Hi my name's Anna, we live across the street.' Rhys comes close to her face. 'A crazy man who thinks he's a Nosferatu and knows exactly where we live. Where we sleep.' His face twists.

'And guess what else. It was him all along. In the dreams. He admitted that.' A finger jabs at Anna. 'I told you that, Anna. I told you and you didn't believe me. I told you, him, there, all of those times in my head, everywhere. So real.' His laughter stops abruptly. 'And then there was her.' Rhys rubs his fingers together softly, thoughtfully. 'How did he know about her? How did he make her so...' His face crumbles.

Anna shakes as his tirade crashes over her. Is it fear or anger or both that's causing her heart to hammer in her chest. Something close to panic starts. What is going on? She hardly recognises the man that stands before her. Who does he think he is taking whatever issues he has out on her when all she ever does is support him?

What is really the cause of this change in behaviour? Should she call her mother? His final words linger – 'How did he know about her?'

'Who?' Anna snaps. 'Who did he know about?' Another woman? That would make sense. An affair would cause the guilt, the lack of sleep, the strange behaviour. Perhaps it's someone at work. That's why he's been moved so suddenly. Has this Kier somehow found out? That would make sense. Explain why he plagues Rhys's dreams. Taunts from his subconscious. It is almost a relief. She doesn't want to hear him say the words. She holds her breath. A hand squeezes round her heart. She is ready. She can deal with it.

'Jenny. How did he know about Jenny?' Something inside Anna crumbles. Not *that* other woman. Not that ghost that lurks in the shadows. Her who is always around the corner, just out of sight, just out of reach. Why does it always come back to bloody Jenny?

'I told you he was a bad man,' says Harry. He peers round the doorframe. Anna doesn't know whether to laugh or cry.

'And I told you to get to bed.' Why does he never listen? He can't see Rhys like this. 'You can't lurk around listening to other people's conversations.' Her words are harsher than intended. Harry's bottom lip quivers.

'Dad was shouting.' He blinks away the tears. Rhys turns his back.

'I don't care. I told you to go to bed.' Anna bombards her tiny target. She knows the anger should be aimed at Rhys. She can't stop herself.

'You'll get them though, won't you Dad?' Harry runs towards Rhys. Anna intercepts. 'Won't you, Dad?' Rhys's shoulders shudder. 'You won't let them get us, will you?' Rhys raises his head. His shoulders rise as he takes a deep breath.

'No son, I won't.' Rhys doesn't turn around.

'Rhys!' He knows fine well Harry needs little encouragement. 'For God's sake, why would you say that?' To Harry: 'Bed. Now.'

She half drags, half carries Harry out of the room.

'They're Nosferatu, Mum, aren't they? Those two men across the street. That's what I heard Dad say,' says Harry.

'There is no such thing as Nosferatu.'

'They can't get in though, Mum, can they?' He looks up at her with big questioning eyes. Full of fear and tears. They search for comfort. God, if Rhys is looking to push someone into doing him some serious harm, he's going the right way about it. What on earth is she supposed to say now? It's late. She's tired. Rhys is having some kind of breakdown. So much for the united parenting front they swore they would always uphold.

'No honey, they can't get you. I've told you, your dad and I will never let anything bad happen to you. That's a promise. Now get into bed.' He wipes his nose on the back of his hand, climbs under the covers. Anna hands him a tissue. Alleviate his fears. Get him to sleep. Deal with realty in the morning.

'Why can't they get us, Mum? What will stop them?' Genuine fear. It breaks her heart.

'I will.' She tousles his hair. 'And your dad.' She leans forward. Kisses his head.

'Mum,' he says as she rises, 'could you stay for a little bit?' He smiles weakly. 'Just because, you know...' She sits on the side of the bed. Cuddles him. Strokes his hair. Murmurs words of comfort. Rhys has to stop this right now. She can't allow Harry to get upset. Can't allow the flames of his fantasies to be fanned. Not Harry. Not now.

Downstairs, she hears Rhys crash about. The sound of furniture scraping the floor. Harry's breathing deepens as he finally slips into a deep, exhausted sleep.

Rhys's footsteps sound on the stairs. Anna lifts here head. Waits for the door to open. Waits for the apology.

His shadow passes.

The sound of the unmentioned bedroom door as it opens and closes. Anna wants to run in there. To scream in Rhys's face that Jenny isn't coming back. It's time he accepts that. It's time he focuses on her and his kids because they are here and love him. They aren't going to walk away without explanation. She wonders if she would be able to hold his eye and say the words. She wants to tear the room to shreds and scream and scream and scream. She doesn't. She strokes Harry's hair until he's soundly asleep. Slides from the edge of the bed. Heads back downstairs, a silent 'fuck you' aimed at the door Rhys has closed behind him.

Rhys has moved the sodding furniture. The solid oak coat rack is pushed across the front door. The Welsh dresser in the kitchen over the back door. The kitchen table pushed up against it. The blinds have been knocked out of place as he checked the window locks. They are well and truly barricaded in.

What if there's a fire? She wants to shout. How will we get out? 'Burnt to death by husband's stupidity', the headlines would read. 'Oh but why?' the neighbours would ask. Because Rhys thought you were all demons after his soul. Or at the very least mad men pretending to be. No, you didn't mishear me. Yes that's Detective Sergeant Rhys Morgan. Yes, the one working the highest profile serial killer case the city has seen. That's him there. The one entrusted with the search for truth and justice. The one sitting upstairs in his dead, sorry, missing presumed dead, sister's room. Yes, you're right. She disappeared twenty-two years ago, the room? Bit of a sore spot actually.

Anna slumps onto a chair at the table in its new position. Pours herself the last of the wine. She's not going to cry, she's not going to goddamn cry. The glass leaves a red ring on the pine surface. Sitting here she notices for the first time she's missed a spot when she painted one of the kitchen walls.

Interesting what you can see, when you look at things from a different perspective.

39.

The look on Anna's face is clear. She fails to hide it. He's not sure she even tries. Disbelief. Despair. Then anger.

She believes he's stupid. That he says these things to hide his own mental failings. He knows what she will say. He is a detective after all. She will say he needs medical help. Patronise him with a doctor's appointment that will be all wet handshakes and 'unpacking mental boxes'. Anna will say he's the one with the issue. Sleep deprivation. Blah blah blah. Why is it so hard for her to understand? He's not the one with the problem. Not that kind of problem. He does have a problem. Kier Finnegan. As with all other problems he just needs a way to resolve it.

Rhys paces.

Kier said he worked at the hospital. Simple then, he'll call the hospital. Rhys pats at his pockets for his mobile phone. Call them up and ask them... what? The look in Doctor Curtis' eye was already judging. Ask if Kier Finnegan is the man he chased through endless corridors? Rhys taps the corner of his phone on his chin. Doctors, doctors, doctors. He takes a deep breath, dials Davies's number.

'It's me... No, nothing like that. Are you still at St James'?' Davies sounds like he's eating something crunchy. 'Can you look into the name Kier Finnegan for me?... Someone I met... Not sure yet.' Davies carries on eating and talking. Rhys takes that as a yes. He listens for a few moments more before hanging up and turning off his phone.

He needs to know more about the man.

Is he even a man?

Why does Rhys even ask himself that question?

Rhys paces.

The dreams that contain Kier are so real. Kier made Jenny real.

How?

Rhys peaks through the gap in the pink floral curtains. Looks across at Kier's house. The upstairs windows are all he can see. The lights are on. Something inside moves. He should go over there. Demand an explanation.

A shiver scuttles up his spine.

So many questions, his head may explode. He's not going out there. Not tonight. Not while it is dark. Better to go in the morning. When it's light. Purely so he will have digested the information. No other reason. Don't look like that.

He could go to the station? Type Kier's name into every available database. But that would involve leaving Anna and the kids alone and at the very least Kier is a madman who threatened his family. Should he call the police? He is the police. Rhys stares at Kier's house. He'd have to explain his actions to the night shift. It can wait. He'll do it in the morning. First thing. What can he do now?

Rhys paces.

Rubs at the tiny blisters around his wrist. A physical reminder. A physical reminder! Rhys strides across the landing to Harry's bedroom door. He'll bloody go in there and show her, he'll... Harry's blotchy distressed face flashes in his mind as he raises his fist to thump on the door. Rhys blinks. His fingers rest on the wood. Behind the door he hears Anna's soft murmur of comfort. He'll wait. He'll wait until she comes out, then show her. Then she'll be sorry, for that look, for the words she didn't have to say. So many things to do, that he should do. All these reasons to have to wait crowding into this mind. He strides back into Jenny's room. Sits on the cool bed. Unplugs the laptop.

He stares at the blank screen for a while, then slowly types *Kier Finnegan* in to the search engine. His heartbeat quickens as he waits for the results to appear.

The first pages show little. Pages teenagers have set up about themselves. Links to amateur music videos. Drunken photographs. Rhys refines the search. This time something of interest appears. It's the title 'After two centuries local farm to close, Finnegan family set for life' that catches his eye. It's a small article. A local community magazine. A surprise they even put it online.

The Finnegan family have over two hundred years of dairy farming experience with many families in the local area still enjoying fresh milk delivered to their door daily. Sadly this is all about to end. Following the death of his father last spring, Simon Finnegan has decided to wind up the family business to pursue 'other interests' in the city. This is a blow to the local community as the farm currently employs over twenty local men and women. Moira Finnegan, Simon's mother and widow of the late Kier Finnegan did not wish to comment. Friends of the family have said she is understandably devastated by the decision but respects her son's wishes. She will not be moving with him to the city. Finnegan Dairies will be a much-missed part of our everyday lives and we wish the family all the best for the future. The property will go on sale at the end of the season and is believed to be worth millions, a drop in the ocean of the Finnegan family wealth. To celebrate the role this family has played in the local community, we look back over the generations that have helped us enjoy our cereal and coffee every morning for the last two hundred years.

And there they are. A small handful of posed photographs of family and employees throughout the decades.

Rhys moves to the desk. Twists the lamp. Shines it onto the laptop.

All the photos are titled *Finnegan's Dairy Annual Family Photograph*. The first is the then-current family and a few local workers. A dower-looking Moira Finnegan, dressed in black. Her son, Simon, to her left looks like the weight of the world has been lifted from his shoulders. No one else in the photo smiles.

The next image is forty years earlier. Eoghan Finnegan is listed as head of the family. To his right is a man who looks a lot like Kier. Could it be him? He wears a large brimmed hat, is turned slightly to the side. Zooming in only makes the pixellation poor. Rhys prints the picture. Saves it to the desktop in a folder named 'Truth'.

There's nothing of interest in the next three images.

Then there it is.

The last image. The photograph shades of sepia. He stands slap bang in the middle. Taller than the men on either side of him.

Kier Finnegan. Nausea rises in the back of Rhys's throat. It can't be him though, can it? His name is there in black and white, 'Dairy owner Kier Finnegan (centre) with his younger sister Bronagh and fellow employees Emmet, Joseph and Henry.' But what does that mean? Families often pass names down. The date printed next to the article is 1920. Rhys's head feels light, like it doesn't really belong to him anymore. He zooms into the picture. There is no pixellation. No doubt, not really, not in that place in his stomach that points out the truth even when his brain doesn't want to listen. That casual crooked smile to camera. Hands resting on the men's shoulders. It could be a relative though; couldn't it that does happen, people looking exactly like their distant descendants?

Rhys prints the picture. The printer is loud in the now-silent house. He returns to the bed where he sits and stares at the image for a very long time.

40.

Now the man really is afraid. The wind roars. He has no idea which way is up or down, just that he falls in the pitch black. Then there is an almighty crash. It takes a second for the man to realise it is the sound of his body as it impacts with a hard, flat surface. He is warm and cold. His eyes move from side to side, peer into the blackness. Searching. Waiting for the pain to pass.

Endless time ticks.

He opens his eyes. Can see nothing in the dark. He draws in a deep breath, tries to stop the shakes that wrack his body.

His eyes close.

It's the stench that wakes him. The stench of rotten vegetables. Of bins long forgotten. It makes him gag. Worse, it makes him retch. He rolls onto his side and heaves bile onto the cold flat surface.

Then it comes. The tiny pinprick of light. It grows brighter and larger until it is a massive orb in the sky that illuminates everything. He has to raise his hand to his eyes to see as if it were a brilliant summer's day.

It is not.

Everything around him is dead. Rotten. Black.

Tendrils of light shoot from the orb. Great electric fingers. The light pulsates and glows like a heartbeat.

The landscape around him is charred, as if by a great fire. The once-lush fields now charcoal mounds. The once-lush flowers, piles of ash. The rip in the landscape has spawned towering black masses. A dark, cold cityscape against the stark white orb.

Slowly the man rises. He has no idea which way to turn. The rot spreads in every direction. Never ending.

Did someone call his name?

A whisper on the wind.

He realises he is at the white fence. The one that contained paradise within paradise. It is no longer white. It is black and broken. Splinters of wood crack beneath his feet. The great apple tree at the centre of the paradise is a dark impression of its former glory. A tree struck by lightning, over and over again. Angrily beaten until it can no longer remember what it once was. Again he hears the voice whisper on the wind.

It takes a while for him to notice her. She is camouflaged against the base of the tree. Her charred skin blending with its roots. It is only when she opens an eye he can identify her at all. He sees her momentarily in his mind's eye. She runs through the lush garden, happy and in love. A pain twists like a knife in his chest. She opens her mouth. A tiny dark hole against her leather skin. He has to lean in close to hear her. Close enough to feel the heat that radiates from her body.

'Run,' she whispers. So much fear. So much pain. He holds her eye for a moment, as he cannot identify her hand. His forehead creases. There is nowhere to run. Nowhere to go. Everything is broken. Everything is rotten.

41.

Anna's angry because she's tired. Tired and hungry and dragging the kids round the supermarket when they should be at home thinking about what to cook for dinner. Angry at being angry all the time.

She taps the redial button on her phone harder than necessary. The phone she's calling rings and rings and rings. Clicks to answerphone, again.

'Rhys. Where on earth are you, you've been gone all day? Work have called and said you haven't shown up. I told them you're ill. Why? I don't know.' Anna stops. Scratches her head. 'Maybe because you are?' The phone continues to record the silence. 'I'm worried about you. Will you please call me back?' A sigh. 'Will you be home for dinner?' The sound of Harry and Louise as they fight further down the aisle. 'The kids are fine by the way. Don't worry about us, we're fine.' The anger rises. She hangs up before she says more.

It's Rhys's fault. Anna thought he was there. Tucked up in his little shrine. But he wasn't. He'd disappeared by the time she got up in the morning, ready to go in there and shout, shout at him for upsetting Harry. Gone, just a dent on the bed next to the laptop. No goodbye. No call. No nothing. All bloody day.

Argue is all Anna feels she does these days. One argument after the other. Harry's still adamant there are Nosferatu living across the street. Not helped by his father who seems to believe the same. It should be laughable, but it isn't. Rhys has hung garlic above all their barricaded doors. Anna had to squeeze out of the house around a coat stand that's too heavy to move. God, what is he out there doing? Maybe she should've told DI Quinn the truth when he called? Whatever that is?

Anna argued with Louise. Her cheeks flush as the words replay in her head.

'I'm not saying it again. You're not old enough to be left looking after Harry. We're all going to the supermarket together, that's the end of it.' Louise stamps her foot.

'I'm old enough when it suits you.'

'I beg your pardon?'

'When Dad's too drunk to drive home from work. It's okay to ask me to look after Harry then, while you go and pick him up.'

'That's completely different.' Anna knows it isn't.

'And where is Dad anyway?' Louise stares at Anna defiantly. 'Is it true that he's finally lost his mind? I'm not surprised if it is, he's been acting all weird lately.'

'That's enough.'

'All I can say is I hope no one at school finds out or we'll have to move.' Tears appear at the corners of Louise's eyes. 'Except we can't, can we?' Louise's voice is loud. 'Dad won't leave that creepy room he keeps for his sister who's obviously dead!'

Anna shouts a lot then. About Louise being disrespectful and rude all the while feeling like the hypocrite she is. Harry cries. They all cry. Then hug. Apologise. She can tell Louise doesn't mean it. Anna wishes Rhys was there. Could see what his behaviour does to the kids.

But he isn't.

Anna has no idea where he is.

That's why she insists they all go to the supermarket. She doesn't want the children to be home alone if Rhys comes back. The thought makes her sick with shame. He's their father. He will never harm them... would he? Since when did everything get so complicated?

Her mobile starts to ring. Bloody typical, just as she's dropped it back into the depths of her bag. She juggles it back out, alongside the basket of shopping, the extra items on offer that will be perfect for Sunday lunch and a plastic dinosaur she's sure she asked to be left in the car. Harry tugs at her coat. Louise stands there, texting. Number withheld. Could be the police station, they always withhold their number. She sighs, yet again, not sure she can tell anymore lies... Perhaps it's time to ask for help?

'Hello, Anna speaking.'

'Oh hello, is that Anna Morgan?'

'Yes. Who is this?'

'It's Elsie, Elsie from down the street.' Anna feels her face harden. Another shadow from Rhys's past Anna can't quite shake off. Elsie. The woman who behaves like a mum to Rhys, but a stranger to his wife. Anna's tone is cold.

'How can I help?'

'It's to let you know Rhys is here.'

'Sorry?'

'Rhys. Rhys Morgan, your husband,' like she doesn't know who her own husband is, 'he's here.'

'Where?'

'At my house.'

'Why is he at your house? Is everything okay?'

'Oh yes dear, it's fine. There's no need to worry, it's just to put your mind at rest. He was in rather a state when he arrived, I wasn't sure if you knew –'

'Of course I knew.' Who the hell does she think she is? 'Can you ask him to head home, please?'

'Well the thing is, dear, he's fast asleep and I'd really rather not wake him, but when he does awake I shall be sure to send him on his way.'

'Sorry, asleep? It's the middle of the afternoon? Look, I'd really rather you just...' Dial tone.

What the...? For a brief second, Anna is a blank canvas, unsure what her reaction should be. Offended by the dial tone? Who actually hangs up the phone halfway through a conversation? Relieved Rhys is okay? Smug and hopeful that he could be wreaking the same kind of disaster in that old cow's home? Jealous he's with Elsie when he should be with them? Angry that she was worried, is worried? Angry that she is stood in the middle of the supermarket while he is warm and fed and asleep? She would love to be asleep on some old dear's couch, being looked after. Yep, angry is going to win. Rhys isn't here to take it out on so she shamefully does the next best thing. Harry rams another dinosaur's head through the holes in the side of the basket.

'Harry, for god's sake, will you please stop doing that. You can be so bloody naughty sometimes.'

Further up the freezers, he already watches. Has been watching for some time. Long brown hair. Big brown eyes.

'You can be so bloody naughty sometimes'. A naughty, vile little boy. He feels his flesh start to goosebump. She taps something into her phone.

'Rhys,' she's saying, 'will you please come home.' She is angry. Her brow furrows. 'I do not appreciate that... woman calling me to tell me where my husband is, all smug and self-righteous... for god's sake... please.' She hangs up. The little boy pulls on her coat. Naughty little boy, naughty little vile boy. There is a girl, the girl doesn't notice anything. She is a younger, smaller copy of her mother. She is perfect too.

Rhys, that's his name. She wants Rhys to come home. She tells Rhys to come home. She's angry with Rhys. Rhys is weak and will do what she says. They always do. Rhys will try and stop him like the others did. He giggles to himself. He likes it when they try to stop him.

Everything is coming together this time. It really could work. She must have been sent to him, to appear like that.

Anna.

He turns her name over in his head. He likes it. He likes it a lot.

Anna demanded his attention through that window. She pretended not to. Pretended not to see him as she crossed the road in front of the gym, entered the supermarket, came out again with pumpkins.

He knew she would be back. Would not be able to stay away from him. All he had to do was wait. Pam waits with him of course. A little put out at the interruption.

He sniffs the air. Her perfume is sweet. He turns slowly, she comes clearly into focus. Her mouth opens, sound high pitched. She hasn't seen him. Hasn't noticed he's here. She's too busy screeching at the boy, the vile little boy with the perfect fingernails. Naughty vile little boy – never does what he's told. Watching, he runs his own broken fingernail across his lip.

Anna backs up along the row of freezers, heads straight towards his basket. His basket he has left on the floor in front of the freezers. Have you done that on purpose? And then she's turning, moments too late, as she's already falling. The bloody beef joint she carries hits the floor with a thud similar to her own. Meat on meat. One packaged, one fresh. Quickly he is above her. Reaches out his hand. Her skin is soft to his touch. It takes his breath away. He helps her to her feet.

'I am so sorry. Here, let me help you.' Like words he is

observing, knows he should say. 'Totally my fault for leaving my basket there. Are you okay?' She smiles up at him. Apologises. It is her fault. She was not looking where she was going. It's true but he doesn't say so. The smile lights up her face. A smile she has been saving especially for him. Her basket is full of meat. Meat for the naughty little boy if he has been good enough to deserve it. He realises she has noticed he is starring at her basket and laughs again, a sound that is light, like a bird. He smiles too.

The bird is punched from the air.

'Just stocking up on the deals while they are available.' She nods at her basket. He has no idea what she's talking about. Her skin looks as soft as it feels. Go on, touch her again you know you want to. He shakes his head. She seems to be waiting for him to speak. He's clenching his teeth so turns it into a smile. A smile for her. Teeth knocking teeth. Metal on bone. A line drawn in biro on her long, pale throat.

'Anyway, best be going.' She turns, half nods to the children she's with. Introducing them to him with the tiniest of movements. 'You know how it is.' No, he really doesn't. But he would very much like to.

Slowly, he licks his lips.

One minute Anna is trying to wrestle a dinosaur head out of the slats of her basket and the next she is flat on the floor, the wind knocked from her. Serves you right, she thinks to herself. That's karma for you. The man is above her instantly. Reaches down. His complexion white as milk. His skin clammy against hers. He looks down at her and speaks.

'I am so sorry. Here let me help you.' His mouth opens and a thousand insects seem to scurry out and run all over his body. She contains a shudder. 'Totally my fault for leaving my basket there. Are you okay?' She nods. Still winded. Her hand is damp from his touch. Something indescribable emanates from him, makes her skin crawl. His eyes roam over her. Pause on the shopping in her basket, then dart off to Harry. To Louise. He grimaces at her. Not physically near, but far too close. Anna smiles back. Her mouth on polite autopilot, ending this... meeting as quickly as possible.

'Anyway, best be going.' Her eyes dart, make sure the children are close. 'You know how it is.' Whatever else they need they can do without. There's always something in the freezer. She needs to get out, be as far away from this man as possible. She sweats under her heavy winter coat. Louise is paying attention. Keeping up.

'Mum, who's that man?' asks Harry as they round the corner to the checkouts.

'I have no idea, honey.'

'Why did you fall over his basket?'

'Harry, don't ask stupid questions.'

'I didn't like him. I don't think we should be his friend.' Anna couldn't agree more. Neither can she shake off the feeling of the man's eyes following her all the way home.

42.

Panic had woken Rhys at three a.m. The smell of her charred skin lingered in his nostrils the way bonfire smoke lingers in clothes. He sat and looked at Kier's house for a long time. Nothing moved. No sign of life. His eyes moved to Elsie's house. A thought flitted like a shadow through his mind, just out of reach.

He sat and thought about the photographs for a long time too. It could be a distant family relation. These things happened. But that exact? Was that possible? Don't genes get watered down as generations pass? Different families making different children. Does Kier come from a family of inbreeding? That would make a lot of sense. More sense than the alternative. He tried to shake the ridiculousness from his head.

Night-time creaks and groans of the house made Rhys jump and jitter. By six a.m. he could bear it no longer. Couldn't bear to look at Kier's still house, couldn't bear the pressure of Anna's distain seeping through the wall. The look of crazy in her eyes, a look she'd aimed right at him.

Is anything Kier said true?

Rhys needed someone to talk to. Someone who wouldn't judge him, laugh in his face. He needed someone to tell him everything would be okay. There was only one person. Someone who promised never to judge or question him. Who promised to always tell him the truth. He needed to see her so much it hurt.

'Son?' says Elsie as she opens the door to Rhys. He isn't her son of course. She has no children. Rhys is as near as it gets. She loves him without question. Rhys is twitchy, panicked. His eyes dart around the street. Is there something wrong with his children? Please god don't let there be anything wrong with the children. Why else would he call so early? Rhys pushes into the hall, deadlocks the door, slides the chain across.

'Rhys?' He blinks away tears as he turns to her. 'Is it the children?' He shakes his head, he nods his head, he shrugs. His face crumbles in on itself.

'Oh Elsie,' is all he says. She takes him in her arms and holds him tight, feels her shoulder grow damp with his tears.

She gives him sweet tea when he asks for coffee. He eats chocolate digestives even though he says he's not hungry. He sits in silence. Shivers under the thick blanket. She rubs his hands. They listen to the tick of the mantelpiece clock.

'It's all going wrong and I don't know how to stop it, and that's my job, I should know, shouldn't I?' Rhys looks at his fingers. 'It's like everything is slipping slightly out of reach. There are too many things I can't work out, can't understand. Things that sound unreal, stupid, crazy.'

'Tell me.' Rhys shakes his head.

'Their faces, you should see their faces, these poor women.' His eyes dart up. 'Of course you shouldn't see them, no one should see them. No one should suffer like... And the man who was in charge, Detective Inspector Andrews, everyone thinks he's mad, I thought he was mad, but now....'

They sit in silence. Rhys stares at nothing.

Elsie always knew this day would come.

'And what does that mean, really, what does it mean? What does it say about me? He was definitely real, so very real...' Rhys looks at his fingertips again, suddenly pulls at his sleeve. 'He did this.' Rhys looks at his wrist like he's never seen it before. 'But how...? He held me here, Elsie. Like this.' Rhys takes her wrist between his thumb and forefinger. 'And when he let go, there were blisters, a burn, kind of.' They both look at his unmarked wrist. 'The dreams, that's where he came from.'

'Dreams?' Elsie's blood runs cold. Rhys laughs.

'Nightmares now I guess. It was all so beautiful when it started...' Elsie shivers. Rhys doesn't notice, his eyes appear to be looking at something faraway. He wouldn't notice if the devil himself walked into the room. Which of course, he already has.

Rhys's words bleed with words Elsie has heard before. For a moment the hand she holds becomes someone else's. A hand held under her smooth young skin as she struggles to give comfort. She blinks. Her hand is wrinkled once more.

'Anna thinks I'm losing my mind, of course. She hasn't said the words. She doesn't need to. I'm not thought, am I?'

Elsie shakes her head. Rhys smiles sadly.

'And it all comes back to him... He's there in the dreams, but is also real. He did this, remember?' A shake of his wrist. 'They were there, honestly they were.' He pulls his sleeve back down.

The stone hand starts to squeeze Elsie's heart.

'This man, I have met him, you know... But I've already said that, haven't I? Do you know what he said? Of course you don't how would you? He said he isn't a man at all.' Rhys laughs again, a joyless sound. 'And Jenny, he made Jenny real, so real...' Rhys's eyes shine wet, then his jaw tightens. 'Then he threatened them, my wife, my children. Propositioned me in exchange for their lives. He is everywhere and nowhere. He is real, but can't possibly be. A man who seems to have lived within his family for decades. Centuries. The same man, it has to be the same man.

Look.' Rhys pulls a piece of paper from his pocket. Unfolds it. Pushes it into Elsie's hand. Her throat constricts. She can't be sure she didn't gasp.

Then he says the word. It hangs like mist in the air. Settles like poison on her skin. Violates her senses. The word is so loud it rings in her eardrums. Spoken after being buried for so long.

Nosferatu.

Rhys is laughing. A hysterical laugh, cut with sobs. She has waited so long for this moment, her whole life. Why does it have to be him? She can feel his eyes on her. They sit in silence. She knows he is building up to the question and lets him.

'Elsie. What happened to Fredrick?'

In spite of everything Elsie smiles at the mention of his name. The beautiful man she had loved with all her soul. Elsie was a young woman when she last saw him. They were not long married; living in the house she now shares with a cat and memories.

The years peel away around Elsie to reveal her broken heart.

'It isn't long after dark when the knock on the front door comes. I'm upstairs getting your mother ready for bed. She is only a child. Her parents, your grandparents, have gone out for the night. She's sleeping over.

'The sound of the knock stops us singing, stops us brushing each other's hair. There's such shouting coming from downstairs. I tell her to stay in the room, not to leave under any circumstance.

179

'He's in the front room. The creature. He casts great shadows on the walls. Fills every speck of space.' Elsie stops. Has time distorted the memory? That's not possible, right? Yet every movement, every word that's to come, is burnt into her brain.

'The creature is exactly as Fredrick described him when he woke night after night screaming and terrified.' Elsie feels Rhys's body stiffen next to her. She can't look at him — instead she stares at the front room, seeing it as it was then, all those years ago. Seeing herself as the young woman she was.

'What on earth is going on here?' Elsie's younger self demands.

'Be quiet, please.' Fredrick pleads. 'Go back upstairs, this doesn't need to concern you.' Fredrick turns to the creature. 'This doesn't need to concern her.'

The creature laughs. A wheezing cackle that shakes the room. It extends its hand to Fredrick.

'Then let's go.' The creature's voice scrapes along Elsie's bones.

Fredrick steps towards the creature. The creature turns and smiles at Elsie. A hideous smile that stretches its whole face. Exposes glistening white incisors.

Elsie screams. The creature moves to silence her before the sound is even fully out of her throat. Its hand burns ice cold across her throat.

'Leave her!' Fredrick shouts. 'You touch one hair on her head and the deal is off!' This stops the creature. It lets Elsie drop, nods a half apology. Fredrick turns to her and speaks.

'Elsie, I love you more than you will ever know. More than the moon and the stars. I love you to heaven and back.'

'I know that.' Elsie goes to take a step towards Fredrick. A growl from the creature stops her in her tracks.

'I'm so sorry.'

'But, why?'

'I hope that one day you will understand. One day you will be able to forgive me.' Elsie realises she is crying. Her body shakes with a fear she can't place.

'Fredrick, I don't understand.' Fredrick smiles. He smiles the same way he smiled the first time she met him, a smile that always wins and melts her heart. Fredrick steps to her. Touches her cheek.

'Enough!' The creature shouts. Anger ripples beneath the milk white of his skin. 'We leave. Now.'

Fredrick's fingers linger against her skin, then he and the creature step out into the dark. Fredrick looks back only once. Tears stream down his face. By the time Elsie reaches the door, they are gone. She touches the line of blisters where the creature held her throat.

Tears stream down Elsie's face as she tells the tale. Words she has not spoken for fifty years. Rhys presses a tissue against her cheek.

'I hear them whisper,' Elsie continues. 'Everyone that comes. From the neighbour who answers my screams, to the police, to my parents. They say I'm in shock, after all who wouldn't be if their husband walked out with another man? They whisper for years. The crueller ones laugh at the accounts I give to the police.' Elsie sniffs. 'They mock me. For a while I was questioned as a suspect. Did I fight with Fredrick? Did I kill him?' Elsie laughs. 'That shows how little they knew me. They shouted it was time to confess, tell them where the body was.

'Then they tried another tack. Did I have a lover? Had Fredrick found out? On and on, they went, round and round. I learnt it was better to say nothing. Keep my opinions to myself. They never found a body. After all he wasn't dead. Not in the sense they meant.' Elsie holds Rhys's eye.

'Fredrick worked for the police. He raised a fear with them. A man, some kind of creature was stalking him. The force laughed it off. After he vanished they wondered if he'd been paving the way to leave with another man. Hiding his own failings by pretending they were theirs.'

'Nosferatu?' Rhys barely whispers the word. She knows he feels stupid, crazy, saying the word out loud. She has felt stupid and crazy and alone all these years. Now she doesn't have to. She nods.

Why did it have to be Rhys?

'The same one?' Elsie hardly hears his words. She doesn't know. She shrugs. 'How is that even possible?' She has no answer but there's a hole in her life to prove it is. 'I'm not crazy?'

'I wish you were.'

'How...? But...? I...?' He turns to her. His skin pale, eyes dark and sunken. 'I'm not crazy?' She reaches up and pulls him into her arms.

'No, son. You're not.' He slumps against her as he had when he was a boy. Rests his head on her lap. A calm seems to settle over him. He sighs deeply. Elsie strokes his head. His breathing calms. He drifts into a deep, dark sleep.

43.

To say Quinn is angry is an understatement. He's incandescent with rage.

'Where, the fuck, have you been?' A hush falls over the operations room. 'I was under the impression we were in the middle of working the highest profile murder case anyone can remember?' Quinn pauses for effect. 'Therefore, unless you're dead, no pun intended, deciding you can't be arsed to get out of bed and turn up is unacceptable. Or am I wrong?'

'No, sir. Sorry. I was ill. Stomach bug. Twenty-four hour thi…'

'Morgan. You're confusing me with someone who gives a fuck. Your inability to turn up will be discussed once the case closes. As will following sickness protocol, part of which does not include pussying out and getting your wife to answer your calls.' Quinn goes on for longer, lists the ways he intends to ensure Rhys never works on his team again. Quinn's instructions come back into focus.

'As you've finally decided to join us this afternoon you'd best get your arse over to Linda Simmons's house. Linda being the daughter of Jess and Ron, the first couple murdered.' Quinn speaks to Rhys very slowly, emphasising each word. 'Just in case you have forgotten that with being absent for so long. Find out everything about her mother's Christmas job at the hospital. Detail, detail, detail. I want to know everything from where she liked to shop on her break to what perfume she liked to wear and who may have smelt it.' Quinn uses big, slow lip movements, jabbing his broken finger into Rhys's chest.

Rhys slept the undisturbed sleep of kings. Deep, dark sleep. No thoughts. No dreams. No disturbance. He awoke with no idea where he was, allowed Elsie's front room to slowly pull into focus. Elsie sat, watching the world go by through the window. Rhys stretched, yawned. He felt regenerated. Renewed, pulled back from the brink. Better than all of that, he was not alone.

'You need to go home, Rhys. Speak with Anna.' Elsie let the net curtain drop, turned to face him. Elsie looked older, smaller somehow.

'I need to stay with you, I need your help.' Elsie shook her head.

'What you need to do is protect your family. You can't do that here. We can talk later. I need to think.' Outside children shout and chase. Children outside.

'What time is it?' Rhys looks to the clock. It's afternoon. Shit. Shit. Shit. What he needed to do was get to work, about seven hours ago. He kissed Elsie on the cheek and headed towards the operations room.

There's a police car outside the small semi-detached. Trim lawn. Brightly coloured pots waiting for flowers in summer. The car door opens. Davies steps out. Davies. The phone call. The hospital. Kier Finnegan.

'How did you get on at the hospital?'

'Hi Dan, how are you? I'm good thanks, Rhys, are you feeling better?' Rhys has no idea what he is talking about. How does Davies know about the dreams? Shit. 'You still look a bit peaky.'

'I'm fine.' The words are sharp. 'Thank you.' The two men face the house. 'So how did you get on at the hospital?'

'Yeah, fine.'

'What about the name I gave you?'

'Before you hung up on me? Then didn't show up for work?'

'My battery died.' Davies runs his tongue along his teeth. Pulls out his notebook.

'Kier Finnegan works at the hospital, a cardiothoracic surgeon no less, that's heart surgery to you and me.' Davies eyes Rhys as he speaks. 'He only transferred to St James' three days ago. How does this link to our case?'

'Has he had any contact with any of the victims?'

'He's only been at the hospital for three days, Rhys.' Davies snaps the pocket book shut. 'What's this about?'

'I don't know yet.' Davies shakes his head, knocks on the front door.

Linda Simmons is a tall, thin woman. Her file says she is in her mid twenties. Bereavement has aged her about twenty years. Her skin is grey. Her smile fake. The heating in her house is up high to compensate for the lack of warmth her own body offers. She perches on the edge of her chair. Keen to hang on to their every word.

Davies establishes they have no news. No answers. She deflates slightly. She does not ask if the rumours are true. That the killer has struck again. Rhys can see the case on the front page of a national newspaper that lies at her feet.

Davies says they are there to talk about the time her mother spent working. Specifically the time she had spent working at St James' Hospital.

'Do you know exactly where your mother worked in the hospital?'

'All over I think, wherever they needed her that night.' Davies pretends to think. Rhys knows he will have standard questions well prepared.

'It would really help us if you could remember anywhere specific.' He pauses again. 'We need to try and narrow down a list of people she may have come into contact with during her time there.' A slow realisation dawns across Linda's face.

'Oh god, do you think it was one of them? Someone she met?' Her bony hands rise to her face. 'I persuaded her to get a job there, pretty much forced her. Her and Dad got into so much debt the year before, buying things for my little one, silly things, precious now.' She swallows hard. Breathes heavily through her nose. Davies waits.

'We're not ruling out that possibility, but it's only one of the many lines of enquiry we're following.' The mantelpiece is crammed with photos of a little boy, about six years old. A timeline of his life in frames. Mainly on his own. Occasionally with Linda or one of her parents. In the last photo the little boy is in a shiny new school uniform, chest pushed out, baby face all smiles.

'It's important you think as hard as you can. See if you can remember anything your mother might have mentioned.' There's a clock somewhere on the mantelpiece. Behind the photos. They all sit and listen to it tick.

'She seemed to work on the chemotherapy ward the most.' Rhys's eyes flick to her. 'I remember that because Dad had a scare. Turned out to be nothing but I know Mum was thinking that's where he could've ended up.'

'Did your mother ever mention any men who visited that ward, hung around there?' Rhys can't hold the words in. Davies glares.

'No, I don't think so.'

'You don't think so or you know so?' Rhys sits forward in his chair. 'Did your mother ever mention any blue-eyed, blond-haired men?'

Jesus Christ. Has Andrews been right all along?

'No.' Linda shakes her head.

'Think really hard.' Rhys rises. 'About so tall, quite well built, pale.'

'Rhys!' Davies's voice is hard.

'No, really I don't think so.' More head shaking.

'Then think harder.' Rhys's head spins. He takes a step towards her. Could it be him? Is Kier Finnegan the link they look for? But he's only been there for three days? How does that work?

Shit.

'Rhys.' Davies rises. Steps towards him. Gestures to the door. 'If you could give the station a call and let them know we won't be much longer with Miss Simmons.'

'But...' Davies's stare is chilling, says there's no alternative.

Rhys steps out into the hall. Into the garden. He pulls out his phone. Stares blankly at the screen. He has no idea what he is supposed to do. His head pounds. He needs to go back to the hospital, speak to them himself. Find out if someone is lying, covering up. Does Davies have actual records? A paper trail? Why has he got his phone out again?

It's him. It has to be him. He looks the type she would go for. Until she realises the error of her ways. Until he makes her realise the error of her ways. He's tall and dark haired. In far better physical condition than the others had been. Not as good as himself, but still more of a challenge than he necessarily wants to take on. He's a police officer. More than that he's a police officer looking into the work he's responsible for. He has to be. Why else would they be here talking to the beautiful Linda?

He has seen Linda before. Months ago when he followed her mum here. There was no shrieking then, just ice cream, laughing and bikinis. He started to wonder if he'd got it wrong. Got Jess wrong. Oh that nagging doubt that always plagues him as the time grows near. Then Ron arrived with some other men and the shrieking started.

He giggles as he watches the police officer pace back and forth up the garden path. A beautiful irony.

What it must be like for this police officer to go home to the beautiful Anna every night? To do her bidding? The thought darkens his mood somewhat. The man will do her bidding, he's sure of it. There's the same weakness in him as all the others. As there was in Strong Hands. It's a weakness the young man cannot and will not abide. A weakness this officer will pay for, as the others have. The blood starts to pump faster in his veins.

The police officer will need to pay in a different way. It makes it all that little bit more complicated. More exciting? At first he is scared, scared by the idea of change. Then slowly it dawns on him. This change signals that she is different. That things will be different. This changes the fear to excitement.

He giggles again.

The women never appreciate what he does for them.

The problem is the violence. Not his problem. Yet. But it quite easily could be. The violence seems to explode out of him these days. That will not do. He will have to satisfy the rage another way. This time it will be different. Anna will be left free to realise they can satisfy each other. Or at the very least she can satisfy him. This officer will have to live with that? Yes, he likes that idea. He will have to realise it is his fault for being weak. For not paying enough attention. For blindly doing what he is told. Yes, that is far more damage than any hammer can ever do. Why has he never thought of that before?

He's pleased with himself for being so clever.

'What the hell was all that?' Davies's voice reaches him as he strides out of the house. Rhys turns. He says nothing. Davies stares at him. 'Well? You getting all in her face about a blond-haired, blue-eyed man?'

Davies steps in close.

'Believe it or not I like you, Rhys. We go back a long way, but that doesn't mean you can start behaving like a lunatic. Not with me.' Davies's voice drops. 'I heard what happened at the hospital. Hell, Quinn was there. Everyone's heard what happened.' Rhys does not register the words. 'That one thing you can fob off, stress, new job whatever, but not more. One time, that's it. You know the Chief is keeping an extra close eye on this one. Don't give him a reason to get rid of you.' He nods for them to leave.

Rhys clenches his teeth. Balls his fists. Anything to stop himself running back into the house. He wants to hammer on the front door until she answers. Shake her until she tells him what he needs to know. Shake her until she understands how important it is.

'As it happens she did remember someone.' Rhys stops dead.

'What? Who?'

'And it was a man,' Davies continues. Rhys's throat dries.

'Kier Finnegan?' The words are a croak. Davies's brow furrows.

'No,' Davies shakes his head. Turns away. 'Man, you need some serious help. A guy she thinks was called Jonas, Jonas Jones.' Davies is at the car. 'Jonas was, possibly still is, a porter.' He smiles. 'Apparently he was a bit creepy. We like creepy. And who gets everywhere in a hospital, access all areas kind of thing? Exactly. This could be the break we've been waiting for.'

Rhys gets into the car. He doesn't take his eyes off the house, he doesn't un-ball his fists until it disappears from sight.

44.

What's left of the shift is long and hard. Hard not to run back to Linda Simmons house and shake the truth out of her. Hard to pretend he finds her words useful. Hard to swallow his anger and pride. Hard to laugh with the others as they congratulate Davies, as excitement grows about the hospital porter. Rhys wonders if his colleagues can see through the fake smile he has plastered to his face.

He calls Anna. At first she's cool. By the end of the call, they're on speaking terms. Just. Rhys apologises. Lies. Says he knows she's right. Pretends to be happy when she mentions some doctor's appointment. In hindsight, Elsie's right. How can he protect Anna if he pushes her away? He tells her what she needs to hear without a shred of guilt. She asks him to ensure he's home on time. She has a surprise. Something to help him. He promises he will be. He means it.

Quinn calls the team together as the shift is finishing. His face is red with excitement. The news bursts out of him.

'People, people, people.' He bangs his fist on the table. Brings them to order. 'I have some excellent news. After all these months, we may finally have the bastard in our sights.' No one cares about the melodrama. They're too tired. Too hopeful. Quinn holds up the photograph of the two piles of bones from the cottage.

'We have confirmation. This is Mr and Mrs Jonas Jones.' Rhys sees Davies eyes grow wide. 'To be exact this is Mrs Jones.' The pile of bones in the bottom of the bath. 'And this is her long-term lover, Kevin.' Quinn places the photographs back on the table. 'This... ' He holds up the image of the little boy and girl. The photo from the cottage. Removed from its frame and placed in a smaller evidence bag. '... is a picture of little Elizabeth, and her brother, Jonas Jones Junior.'

'No fucking way,' says Davies. Quinn ignores him.

'Little Elizabeth here never got to be any bigger than this. She became trapped in the old cold store of the disused dairy farm behind the cottage. About fifteen years ago. Made headline news.' A couple of heads nod sadly around the room.

Rhys's ears prick. Alert. Did Quinn say dairy farm? He feels the picture of Kier in his back pocket burn into his flesh.

'Trapped in this cold store, poor little Elizabeth ran out of air and suffocated. She'd been playing hide and seek with her big brother, Jonas, who stated he hadn't realised she was trapped. We... to be more precise, our fellow officers, ruled it as an accidental death.'

Quinn looks at them all speculatively.

'It was Kevin and his mates who were entrusted with pulling down the farm. We assume this is how he met Mrs Jones.' Quinn shrugs. 'I guess she must have gone in for that kind of thing. The perceived hero destroying what killed her daughter. Considering what has come to light, we may eventually choose to reassess the accidental death theory.' He places the photo down. Picks up another. 'Earlier today Davies and Morgan, thanks for deciding to finally join us this afternoon, Morgan...'

'He's not a very nice man, is he?' The voice tickles in Rhys's ear. He jumps. Jerks around. Chair legs scrape the floor. Davies shakes his head. Looks at the floor.

'Morgan? Problem?' Quinn glares.

'Yes. No. Yes.' Come on, pull it together. 'The dairy farm, who owned it?' What is he saying?

'Sorry?'

'The dairy farm Elizabeth was trapped in, who owned it?' Rhys's heart hammers in his chest.

'Erm...' Quinn shuffles the papers. Swears under his breath. 'A Simon Finnegan.'

Davies's eyes dart to Rhys. A warning.

'Not that it has any relevance...' Quinn's words fade around him.

Rhys does not believe in coincidence.

The killer just happens to commit his first crime in a farm owned by 'Simon' Finnegan? Rhys needs to speak to Elsie. Shit. What does this mean?

'... Bloody Irish seem to own everything these days.' Quinn's words twist back to full volume. An uncomfortable laugh from somewhere in the room. Focus on something. Anchor your mind. Quickly. Rhys wants to get up and run from the room. He holds onto the edge of the desk.

'As I was saying,' Quinn continues. Focus on his words. Rhys watches Quinn's thick lips move. 'Morgan and Davies went to interview Linda Simmons with regards to the hospital connection. Linda mentioned a hospital porter. Would you believe it if I told you his name was, drum roll please... ' Quinn holds up a large mug shot. 'Jonas Jones.'

A collective gasp scurries round the room.

'We have reason to believe he is one and the same Jonas Jones as the little boy in this photo.' The two smiling children wave in the air. Rhys focuses on the large photo of the young man. Focus on the photo. Don't think about the dairy farm. Not here. Not now.

Jonas Jones has close shaved hair. Cold blue eyes. Pointed cheekbones. He looks strong. Calm. Calculating. Did he really trap his little sister in an abandoned fridge and leave her there to die?

'Bit of background on the Jones family, coz I know you'll all be keen to hear.' Quinn continues. 'They lived in the cottage. Were reported to be loners who made it clear they wanted to be left alone even after Mr Jones left.

'There's some documentation from a social worker who visited the family a few times following Elizabeth's death, offered grief counselling and such, but eventually the support was withdrawn. Child services visited a couple of subsequent times but that's all we know.' Support just fades away. That's how it is. Resources at full stretch. New, more needy families. What happened to little Jonas Jones?

'The family made it quite clear they wanted to be left alone and that's exactly what happened. For the truth of what went on up there we'll have to wait and ask Mr Jones Junior when we eventually catch up with him, which we will. There is no record of him appearing anywhere and the initial reports seem to suggest the bones have been in the cottage for anything between ten to fifteen years.

'For now, we shall assume Mummy and Daddy are the first victims. This is often how these things start. After all, who hasn't wanted to kill their folks at one time or another?' No one laughs.

Rhys feels the soft fur of the dead vole in his palm.

His head may explode. Too many thoughts. Too much information.

'So the question is, where has little Jonas been for all this time? He could have been living up there with Mummy and Daddy's remains but I very much doubt it. He's not an enigma. He must have lived somewhere. He must still live somewhere. We just need to find him.' A hand shoots up. Quinn's eyebrow rises. An acknowledgment.

'What about the biological father?' asks Constable Bayne.

'Good question, Bayne. Nice to know someone's awake. He's currently serving twenty years at Her Majesty's pleasure for armed robbery. His wife, second wife that is, has nothing to do with him. She was surprised to learn he has a son, pleased her old man could get more years for bigamy, then concerned this son could get dumped on her. Nice sort. Prison records have no mention of anyone remotely fitting Jonas Jones Junior visiting, no record in fact of anyone visiting at all. One to follow up though, if you could please, Spenser.' The young detective nods. Makes notes. Quinn continues.

'I've spoken with Davies's HR contact at the hospital; he said Jonas hasn't turned up for work yesterday or today. They called the number he gave them to find it not in use. His contact address does not exist. Up to this point he's been the model employee. On time. Never absent. Clean. Well presented, the works. They were actually all rather worried about him, glad we were there to help but unable to work out how we had been called in so soon to a missing persons case. I didn't put them right. If Jonas is our man I don't want him getting wind we're on to him.' Quinn sits.

'We don't want this creepy little bastard slipping through our fingers.' He has a point. Jonas does look creepy. 'This could be massive. As you all know, I don't believe in coincidence. This boy lived where three people have been murdered, his immediate family no less. Two of them were murdered in the same style as all of our recent victims. He now works in a place that is fast becoming the intersection of all our victims. He's our number one suspect until we have reason to believe different. The number one priority is to find him. We have no address and no family we can speak to, so we go back over every inch of that cottage and every inch of that hospital. We speak to everyone who ever so much as heard him fart until we find out where the creepy little fuck is.'

Tasks are handed out for tomorrow morning's early start. People clap. Someone cheers. It's suggested they celebrate this victory. It's small, but a victory nonetheless. Someone shouts,

'It's the first proper breakthrough since the discovery that Andrews is mad'.

Rhys excuses himself.

The more he thinks about it, the more he's certain, they're wrong. Whoever this Jonas is, however he's connected, Kier is more so. Rhys feels it. He doesn't believe in coincidence either. The more he turns it over in his mind, the more it makes sense. Kier has access to patients, staff and casual workers. People who are weak, defenceless. But why the display? Why attract attention to himself? Why not just kill them? And why has the creature picked him? Is it a taunt? Is he laughing at them all?

Rhys feels sick. He calls the hospital, asks to speak to the HR manager. The HR manager has finished for the day. Rhys could kick off. Demand his home number, demand his home address. Across the room he sees Davies look in his direction. On the desk his phone vibrates. Anna. The HR manager will be back in tomorrow. Rhys leaves his number, says it's urgent. Then finally, he heads home.

45.

The key slides into the front door. The smell of homemade lasagne greets him. He drops his keys into the bowl beside the front door. Anna has moved the coat rack back.

Rhys is so damn tired. The hours of sleep stolen on Elsie's knee feel a lifetime ago. He's glad Anna and he are at least pretending to be friends. No more fighting, at least not tonight. His mind has raced all day. Now he's exhausted. So many things to think about. All he wants to do is sleep, sleep the undisturbed sleep of last night. He'll speak to the hospital first thing – no he'll see Elsie first thing. He'll have had time to get all these new facts straight in his mind.

Then he hears the laughter.

Anna's laughter floats out of the living room. It's strange and beautiful. He hasn't heard her laugh like that for a very long time.

Slowly Rhys pushes the door to the living room open. There he is.

Kier Finnegan.

Kier Finnegan sits in the middle of the sofa. Arm outstretched along the back. Glass of red wine in one hand. Anna sits to his left. She is side on so she can better see him. Louise is to his right. Both of them laugh. Play with their hair. Harry is stood next to the door. His back is against the wall. His eyes are fixed on Kier. Fear freezes him rigid.

Everything moves in slow motion.

Kier's head turns towards Rhys. Eye to eye. Smile dark on his lips. The creature is in his home. He is sitting there on the sofa, beating like a black heart.

'What the fuck are you doing in my house?' The words out before they even notice he's here.

'Rhys.' Anna rises. Her face drops from pleasure to anger in a second. Kier doesn't move. He slowly raises an eyebrow. 'Don't be so rude. Kier is our guest. I invited him.'

'Dad!' Louise and Harry say the word in unison, their meanings poles apart. Harry is at Rhys's side. Clings to his leg.

'What the fuck are you doing in my house?' Rhys's eyes don't leave the creature. Kier rises, one fluid movement. He smiles apologetically at Anna. His presence is huge. It pushes against Rhys from across the room.

'As your good wife said, she invited me over for a drink. A welcome to the neighbourhood as it were.'

'You are not welcome in this house or this neighbourhood.'

'I'm so sorry.' Anna says the words, Kier hands her his wine glass.

'Thank you so much for the hospitality, I can see I am causing distress to your husband. This is the last thing I want so I shall leave.'

'You can't be fucking serious? The last thing you want to do is cause distress?' Rhys takes a step towards him. 'I won't say it again. Get out of my house!'

'Rhys, please.' Anna's voice is strained. Rhys doesn't care.

'You know damn well why I don't want him in the house and so does he,' Rhys points from one to the other.

'Rhys, you're embarrassing yourself and me. Why are you doing this?' Her teeth clench. Tears glisten at the edges of her eyes.

'Please.' The creature holds up its hands. 'I do not want this. I shall leave.' He leans in close to Anna. Kisses her on the cheek. He doesn't break eye contact with Rhys. 'Thank you, Anna. I hope to see you again.' Just before he pulls back, he licks his lips.

Rhys is across the room in seconds. He lunges for Kier's chest. Sends him crashing back into the fireplace. Anna shouts for him to stop. Louise screams. Harry could have cheered. The bastard goes down. Throws his hands up to defend himself. Feigns shock. Pretends to be weak. The impact sends the candlesticks and family photos flying.

'Don't you go near her, you hear me!' Kier cowers beneath him, his face a shroud of lies. Is he smirking? Anna shoves Rhys aside. Helps Kier to his feet. Apologises over and over again. She shakes her head. Shouts at the children to get to their rooms. Shouts at Rhys that she doesn't know what's wrong with him. That he seriously needs help.

'Get out!' Rhys knows his voice is loud. The children will be afraid. He ignores Anna. Shoves her aside to get to the creature. Kier has the audacity to stand there, looking like he's the victim.

Rhys pushes Kier towards the door. Kier again holds up his hands in apology.

'Get out!'

They're in the hall. They're through the door. They're in the front porch. Rhys hears Harry's screams for him punctuated by the sound of Louise's bedroom door slamming.

Kier turns slowly. Fixes Rhys with a cold hard stare. He sniffs. Looks up at the garlic clove that dangles above their heads. He barely conceals a smirk as he rips it down. Tosses it into Rhys's face. He hisses. Pulls back his lips to reveal long white incisors.

'Don't believe everything you read,' he growls into Rhys's ear. 'Nice moves in there. Shame your wife doesn't agree. You could have really hurt... yourself... and remember, the clock is ticking. Tick tock. Tick tock.' Then instantly his face is of innocent hurt. He flinches as if Rhys may hit him again. Rhys is aware of Anna at his shoulder.

Rhys turns. Shouts in her face. 'Did you see that?' She must have seen that. She ignores him.

'I'm sorry.' Her voice cracks. 'I'm just so sorry.'

'It's not your fault.' Kier's voice is smooth. 'I understand honestly. I should never have come.' To Rhys, 'I'm sorry if somehow I've offended you.'

'Get the fuck away from my house!' Rhys screams again. He does not care. What the hell's going on? How can this be happening? What has Anna done? Why has she done it?

Kier shakes his head and crosses the street.

Rhys slams the front door so hard the frame rattles. He turns on Anna.

'Why did you do that? Didn't you see him just then?'

'Why did *I* do that?' Her mouth hangs open.

'Yes, why did you do that? Why the hell did you invite that creature into our home? Don't you know anything? We're not safe here now and that's because of you.' A tear rolls down her cheek. Good, well she should cry after the danger she's put herself and the children in. 'Didn't you see him in there? The way he behaved? He was mocking me, mocking us. Pretending to be all weak and helpless, as if he's weak and helpless. Does he look weak and helpless? I told you what he said to me, his threats.'

'Jesus Christ, Rhys. Have you heard yourself? Really, have you? All I saw in there was you acting like a lunatic. I was having a really nice time. I was doing something I was enjoying, something to try and help you feel better, help you see he's a normal, everyday man. But oh no, you bowl in and ruin it. All I saw in there was you terrorising some poor man, some poor man who was only here because I invited him. Who do you think you are, behaving like that in our home?' Rhys can only stare. How can she be so wrong? So naive? 'In fact, you get out.'

'What?'

'Dad don't leave us. He might come back, Dad.' Harry trembles.

'You heard, get out!' Anna opens the front door. Gives him a hard shove into the night. 'That...' She points back into the house. '... is your doing. He's eight years old and doesn't need this. I don't need this, but don't worry I'll tidy up after you, again. Right now I don't want to look at you. I don't even want to think about you, so you get out, go away and come back when you can behave like a rational human being.'

She slams the door in his face. Simple as that.

46.

For a police station, it's a lot easier to gain access to the back areas than he imagined. That is the problem with the law these days. It makes it far too easy for criminals.

Not that he's complaining. Not at all.

It takes him no time to find what it is he is looking for. Carelessly discarded, as he'd expected it would be.

There are dozens of photographs on the wall.

He leaves as he arrived, in the shadows.

In the shadows, where he likes to be.

47.

It's cold outside. He can see his breath. The streets are empty. It's long past kicking out time. Long past bedtime. Only those up to no good are left. He likes it outside. It's easier to breathe. The buzz in his blood seems quieter when he's outside.

The stone of the wall is cool beneath his fingers as he watches her. She's young, too young to be out alone at this hour. Her thick auburn hair flows down her back. Her cheap patent heels clip. Her hips in her short silver skirt swing. She's drunk and lost. Has spent her taxi money on cheap drinks. She picks her friends badly, to be left alone, trying to make her way home long after dark.

Not quite alone. Not ever going to get home.

She really should have listened to her mother, really should have left when her father offered to pick her up. Sometimes these lessons are learnt just a little too late. Fate has just dealt her a very poor hand indeed.

It would be a lie to say he isn't excited as he watches her. It's been a very long time since he's been this spontaneous. At first he isn't sure if it is for him, but needs must, as they say.

She's so perfect. How can a place be so right for one person yet so wrong for another?

A discarded can clatters as he kicks it in the shadows. She turns, the auburn-haired girl, a look of panic in her eye. He feels himself come alive.

The hammer is in his pocket. His fingers wrap around it.

He knew he should have left the hammer at home.

Naughty little hammer. Naughty little boy. Naughty little vile boy.

48.

Rhys doesn't mean to cry. But once he starts, he can't stop.

Anna pushes him out of the house. Anna forbids his return. He shouts and bangs. Lights across the street come on.

Then he's in his car and moving, fast. He drives aimlessly. Drives out the anger. Lights and houses fly past. Through the window everything blurs. He realises it isn't the speed, but the tears. He pulls onto a small grass clearing. He isn't sure where he is, doesn't care. Thick hedges line the roadside so he must be outside the city. Tears drip off the bottom of his chin.

'I'm not mad.' He speaks out loud. 'I'm not mad.' Over and over, a reassuring mantra.

Kier was in his house, sitting on his sofa, laughing with his family. Kier who is in his dreams and now his waking moments. Kier who is very real, can make Jenny real.

Kier... the Nosferatu?

Rhys cries harder. He realises he believes but has no idea what that means, he just knows what he has seen, has no doubt. Andrews believes too and it cost him everything.

Rhys needs to see Elsie. Why hasn't he gone straight to her? That was the plan? No, wait, go to the hospital, not that he's sure what would achieve, not now. Go to Elsie then?

But what about Andrews? Rhys sniffs hard, wipes his nose on the back of his hand.

He'll go and see Andrews. That makes sense. Andrews seeks the creature. Rhys needs to find out more about Andrews's theory, the one that a Nosferatu is responsible for the murders.

A Nosferatu or Kier?

How much does Andrews believe? How much does he know? Is Kier responsible for the killings? Is that possible? Does the grieving daughter, Linda, confuse the image of Jonas Jones with Kier? Rhys should have shown her the printed image, held her face, fingers pressing into the flesh, until she was sure. Davies would not have let that happen.

'I'm not mad.' The car is full of the words. Rhys could reach out and touch them. 'I'm not mad.' He wants to laugh. 'I'm not mad.'

A rush of cold air as the passenger door opens. The seat creaks. A large ornate handkerchief is held out in a long white hand.

'If you continue to sit in the car crying and talking to yourself, people will think you are. Please stop, it's not becoming.' Kier stares at him with those hard, blue eyes. His hand and the handkerchief fall to his lap when Rhys doesn't take it.

'What the hell are you doing?' The snot bubbles in Rhys's throat. He swallows hard.

'I thought we had a little unfinished business following your altogether abhorrent behaviour earlier.' Kier tilts his head, looks at him. Rhys opens his mouth. Realises he has no idea what to say. Kier shakes his head sadly.

'How did you sleep the other night at the old crone's? Like a baby, I'll bet. No need to thank me, I was otherwise engaged. Bet you missed me though, in the silence?' Rhys turns his face, stares straight ahead. Teeth clenched. Forbidding the realisation to show on his face. 'She really does love you, doesn't she? Mad old thing. Do you know what she asked me? To leave you alone, she said I could have everything she owned, even her,' Kier winces, 'if I would just leave you alone. She ran, well shuffled right across the street to beg.'

Kier's laugh is cruel. Rhys's heart sinks lower.

'Bless her cotton socks eh?' Kier leans in close. 'Doesn't she realise I took everything I wanted from her a long time ago? I have no interest in her if she has so little interest in herself.' Kier looks nonchalantly down at his nails. Rhys stares at his own reflection in the windshield. On the edge of his peripheral vision, Kier's reflection burns like a bright white orb.

'Leave her alone.' Rhys's voice cracks. Kier shakes his head. 'Why are you doing this? Why me?' Rhys is drained. The sensation hits him suddenly. He can hardly keep his eyes open.

'Let me tell you a story.' Kier sits back in the seat.

'I don't want to listen to stories. I want you to explain and get out of my car.'

'The story is the explanation.' The ice in the voice. 'You really must learn to be more patient. Are you sitting comfortably? Then I'll begin.

'Once upon a time, in a not so very far away land, there lived a woman. This woman was the most beautiful in all the land. Okay, so I'm being indulgent, she was the most beautiful woman that the man, the Nosferatu, I, had ever seen.' Kier's face becomes flat, expressionless, smooth as marble.

'This is back when people were more open-minded, believed things people these days do not.' Kier opens an eye, looks at Rhys. 'We could argue the pros versus the cons for this all night but we shall not.' He closes his eye again.

'The concept of Nosferatu was not unusual at this time, although it did not make people less afraid. The Nosferatu central to this tale, me, fell in love, not lust, with the woman the first time he saw her. Her raven black hair, her pink, full skin.

'This creature knew the woman would not love him were she to know who he truly was, so he hid his true nature and over time the woman fell in love with him too. They were so happy.' Kier's eyes flick back and forth behind his eyelids.

'The creature however was sad. He knew the day would come when the woman would learn what he really was and then he would lose her. He was, after all, a creature of the night, to be feared and hated, not loved. However, as it turned out the creature underestimated the woman and her love for him regardless of who, or what, he was. On the night she discovered the truth, she did not run, she did not leave him, but embraced him and said her love had not changed.

'Years passed and inevitably the woman grew older. The creature could not bear the thought that one day he would lose her. He would beg and beg her to join him but she would always refuse, for this woman was deeply religious and however deep her love was for this creature, it was not deeper than her love for her God. She would not give up her seat in paradise for him. This angered the creature for he had seen enough to know God would easily give up His love for her. She would not be persuaded. He soon realised he did not want to waste the time they had together with anger and instead vowed to treasure every moment.

'There was one thing this man, I, had never considered, had never entered my head, and that was the possibility of procreation. Nosferatu are not living, we create through the exchange of blood, so when my love told me she was pregnant I was floored. Not for one moment did it enter my mind she had been unfaithful, for I knew she had not, would not, could not, be.

'We went into hiding, afraid and curious as to what would happen and, after nowhere near nine months, our daughter was born.' Kier pauses, swallows hard. Something like pain ripples across his face.

'I use the word daughter in the loosest sense of the word. She was a collection of all that was wrong, all the bad in both of us, condemned to us in a tiny bundle and we called her Kate. She was God's cruellest trick played on his most devoted pilgrim. She tried, my love, oh how she tried to love this little creature who screamed and fought and found no comfort. Kate aged at an alarming rate, had no tolerance of sunshine and an unstoppable bloodlust. She was both human and Nosferatu, unable to speak or communicate, and so very angry at the world, and who could blame her?

'My love could find no solace. She no longer believed in a God that loved her and at the same time had seen what I was at its most basic level. I could do nothing to comfort her, nothing to comfort either of them.

'Over time, my love slowly lost her mind.

'It was me who found her when I rose one evening, hanging from the beams in the old barn we had tried to make home. All her note said was "sorry" for which there was no need.

'The pain, Rhys, oh the pain. I have never felt anything like it. It tore me in two. I wished I were dead. I wished the helpless creature we had created were dead. I wished she had never been born.' Outside the rain starts. Kier stops. Lets his words settle. His chest rises sharply.

Rhys listens, but he sees a different image. Something similar but not the same. An image inside him – usually locked away. It isn't an old barn Rhys sees but an old bedsit. Rented out by the council to those they should be looking after. To those who are beyond help, just needing somewhere to pass away the final few moments of their wretched lives.

It is a rope and she is swinging, so in that way it is the same.

Rhys is the one who finds her. It is not a case. He is not called there by a distressed neighbour. He's just dropping in to see how she is. He tries to do that as often as he can, not often enough.

Not enough for his mum.

She is never good. Some days she is bad. Some days she is worse. The doctors are supposed to help. They haven't, couldn't. The creak of the rope sticks in his mind the most. There is no note, there is no need. Just one of Jenny's dresses on the dirty single bed.

Rhys calls his dad. His dad is drunk, pretends he doesn't care, pretends it isn't his problem. In many ways it isn't, hasn't been for years. Dad is angry. Dad is always angry.

'She's still alive. Kate.' Kier's words pull him sharply to the present. 'After all these years, she is grown now and aged beyond anything comprehensible. She must remain in the dark and has no comprehension of what the sunshine will do to her. Oh how many times I have wondered would it not be fairer just to let her meet her fiery maker. That's why we chose this house you know, because there is a wonderful network of caverns beneath it.'

Kier lets out one dry laugh. A single blood-red tear rolls down his cheek. He dabs it with the handkerchief. Rhys watches the spot spread on the cloth, like a flower opening its petals.

'I no longer chose a companion based on love. Why would I do that again? Nor indeed do I allow a choice to be made. You are a safe choice, Rhys, and an interesting one. Many things have changed since that day I found her hanging in that barn.'

'Get out of my car,' is all Rhys can say. His voice cracks.

Kier looks at him and nods. He leaves without fuss or comment. The cold air caresses the wet lines on Rhys's face as the car door opens, then closes.

He is left with the single blood-red teardrop on the handkerchief beside him.

49.

Anna doesn't want to call him. She really doesn't. Rhys has left her no choice. She's furious. More than that, she's scared. Out of her depth. No idea which way to turn. Needs someone who knows Rhys, her, them. Or used to. Someone who will understand.

Louise jams something under her door. Refuses to come out or let Anna in. Anna walks away. Goes back downstairs, leaves her to it. She shouldn't, she should persist. Say she will kick the door down. She doesn't have the energy to fight anymore.

Harry still shouts. Pulls at the front door. He cannot reach the top bolt she's thrown across. He wants her to let him out. He wants to be with his dad. Dad understands. Dad can see the man is bad. A realisation dawns. He needs her to open the door, let Dad back in. The bad man will get him if he's out there. Harry has missed the sound of the tyres screeching off the drive. Harry cries. Pulls and kicks at the door until he's retching. Then stops, comes to her for comfort. Falls asleep exhausted. Again.

The house is strangely quiet then. Anna picks up the photos and candles that were knocked from the fireplace. There's a crack in the glass of their wedding photo. She takes her guest's half finished wine through to the kitchen.

Rhys was so furious, so angry. He has so much hate for this man. She watches the red swirl against the white sink until all that is left is an oily stain. It scares her to see that anger in him. Watch him flit from anger to tears. Listen to him talk with more passion than she's ever seen. Talk such nonsense. She can appease Harry. He's eight. He knows no better. It breaks her heart to hear a grown man talk about demons as if they are real. To believe they're after him. That they will kill his family.

That makes her truly afraid. Are they safe? Safe from him? Is this what the families of those slaughtered by their husbands while they slept would have asked were they able? Rhys will have access to guns and knives. She's cold suddenly. Turns up the thermostat.

Then the phone is in her hand and she's calling. The phone rings for a long time. He answers just as she's about to hang up.

'Hey.' His voice is soft, gentle. It doesn't sound as if she's woken him.

'Hi.' She feels stupid. Stupid for calling. Stupid. Vulnerable. Afraid. He waits. Says nothing. Gives her the time she needs. 'Can you come over?'

'Sure, give me half an hour.' The line goes dead.

Detective Constable Dan Davies. They used to all be friends, Rhys and Anna, Dan and his wife, Sandy, although Sandy wasn't his wife then, just his on-off girlfriend. Rhys and Dan trained together, hit it off. They used to all go for meals, laugh and drink. Tell secrets. Share fears. They even had a holiday together.

Rhys was always the better pupil, more studious, more committed. It was more important to him. Dan had that cheeky smile, and could look at you in a way that made you feel like you were the only girl in the world. He would also listen, Dan, really listen and pay attention, make you believe he gave a shit. Anna saw him do it dozens of times, with dozens of women, but still believed it was different when he listened to her.

It was one night, one time, one stupid mistake the best part of a decade ago. Anna was stuck at home with Louise, felt like she was going out of her mind. Rhys was all over the place, having a daughter making him think more sharply about his sister. He'd been offered a job working missing persons. Dan had not. Longer working hours, more time away from home. Then one night, only one night, Dan came over and smiled at her like she was the only girl in the world.

Anna turns on the coffee machine. She feels sick thinking about it even now. She'd told Rhys about Dan, as soon as it happened. And he forgave her. The one proviso was neither of them had anything to do with Dan ever again. And it worked, for ten years it worked. Then Rhys was transferred to King's Mill.

Anna had only seen Dan once in that time. Recently. They'd bumped into each other in the street, if you'd believe that. Anna knew Rhys wouldn't.

'It's good to see you, Anna.' Dan had said. And smiled that smile. Who else can she turn to? Really, who else would understand?

The knock is soft when it comes. Dan looks tired, ruffled. His shirt isn't buttoned correctly. This is how they always look in the middle of a case, any case. Something else is priority. That's why he'll understand. Wouldn't judge. Will he?

Fingers of doubt start to tickle the back of her neck.

'Hello.' His voice is soft. She smiles – lets him in. He accepts a coffee.

Now he's here, stood in her kitchen, with the furniture all the wrong way round, she isn't sure where to start. It suddenly all seems silly. Is she overreacting? The words will sound ridiculous. He doesn't pressure her. Doesn't even ask why she called. He just takes his coffee and waits for her to speak.

They stand and drink in silence.

In an instant, the coffee is half drunk. The words form, but stick in her throat.

'Rhys?' Dan prompts. The sound of his name, said in the soft male voice starts the avalanche.

'I don't really know where to begin. It'll sound so stupid, but it isn't, far from it. Thanks for coming by the way.' Anna places her cup on the worktop. Turns to stare at the black window. The bright kitchen is reflected behind her. It'll be easier if she doesn't look at him. She stares at her own reflection, eye to eye.

'You know I'll never think what you say is stupid, Anna.'

'Okay. Shit. Okay.' Start speaking. Start anywhere, just start. 'Since he started on this case they've been getting worse, the nightmares. I guess that's where it all started.' She stares hard at her reflection.

'For weeks, he's being having these horrendous nightmares, not just bad dreams but terrors. Waking up drenched in sweat, too afraid to go back to sleep, becoming too afraid to sleep. Have you ever had that kind of nightmare? I never have, thank God.' Her eyes flick to the left. Dan's reflection shakes his head.

'Then he started the case. As with every case he tells me nothing, says he can't.' A look left. A nod from Dan. 'But he goes into Jenny's room a lot and I know that means it's bad, really bad. I read the papers so I have an idea. I'm not stupid. You remember Jenny's room, right?'

'Of course.' Davies's eyes drop. Anna turns to face him. Takes a deep breath.

'Then the dreams seem to be seeping into reality. During the day he thinks he sees the man, the creature that plagues him in the night. He thinks he sees him in the pub, in the street, while he's in work.' Dan draws breath to speak. Anna holds up a hand. 'Please, let me finish. Rhys says the man, the creature, he sees in his nightmares is real. That he lives across the street.' What would Rhys say if he could hear her now, another betrayal, another betrayal with Dan?

'And he's on the internet, all through the night, tucked up there in Jenny's room, researching, cramming more information into his full, tired brain. A brain that should be resting after the things he's seen while awake. Then one day he comes out with it.' Anna pauses. Takes a deep breath. Screws her eyes up tight.

'He says the creature across the street is a demon. A Nosferatu to be precise. A Nosferatu after his soul in exchange for our safety.' She should hear Dan laugh. Laugh like she has done. But he does not.

She opens her eyes slowly. He has the saddest look on his face. She tries to smile. It's lost before it meets her lips. They stand in silence. She can see Dan digest the information. Tiny flickers on his brow. What has she done? Will he think she's the mad one, call the men in white coats? Who will look after the children then? What has she done? She could beg Dan to leave. Forget everything she's said. Walk away and forget it. She was only joking, hilarious eh? But the words are out, come what may.

'Shit,' is what Dan eventually says. The laugh bursts out before she can stop it. His brow furrows.

'I'm sorry. I was just expecting a little more.' Dan smiles too.

'Sorry, wow, that's...'

'Ridiculous, crazy, unreal...'

'Sad. Serious.'

Anna's smile fades. She nods. Tears prickle in her eyes.

'Do you think it's happening to him?' A genuine question asked to the wrong person. A question that has been building in her mind for days, weeks. One that finally has to be voiced or she will explode. 'What happened to his mother. Do you think it's happening to him?'

Rhys's mother is mentioned less than his sister. She, however, is not an enigma. She is, was, very real. Dan shrugs. Looks at his feet. He was the one Rhys called, when he found his Mother's body. Dan finally meets her eyes.

'I hope not, I really do, for all of you.' He reaches out. She shakes her head, hesitates. But she so wants someone else to be in charge, to make everything okay. She steps into his strong embrace. 'Look I'm no doctor but maybe he needs to see one?' He speaks into her hair. She relaxes against him. He smells of apples, feels like he can make everything right. 'What you're saying, it's serious, for him. You do realise that?' She nods against his shoulder. 'You want me to have a word with the boss?'

Anna shrugs. 'I don't want him to get into trouble.'

'It sounds to me like he's already in trouble.'

'Thank you... for coming over,' says Anna.

'It's no problem.' Anna stands and lets Dan hug her for a long time, lets someone else take charge, just for a little while.

50.

The rain beats mercilessly on the car roof. Rhys wakes just after seven. Stiff and sore. His reflection in the rear view mirror makes him wince. He needs a shave. He needs a wash. He needs not to be wearing the same clothes as yesterday. More than all of these things he needs to see suspended Detective Inspector Andrews. Kier must be the creature Andrews seeks. Must be. Andrews said he was searching for a Nosferatu? Rhys has one. It's too much of a coincidence for there to be more than one, isn't it?

Rhys picks up Kier's handkerchief.

The blood tear. The blood tear Kier cried.

Rhys smiles.

'Gotcha.' He doesn't have an evidence bag in the car. He scrabbles, under the seats, in the glovebox. Nothing that would do. He folds the handkerchief so the blood is on the inside, careful not to touch the blood. The DNA. Far from ideal but it will have to do, should be enough.

What was that last night? A display of power? An attempt to give humanity to something inhuman? Rhys doesn't understand. He's not sure he wants to.

It's early. He can get to Andrews's house, still be on time for work. He turns the car's cold air blowers on full blast, shivers.

Rhys is outside the city. Hidden within the intricate system of lanes that existed when the city was just a town. How on earth had Kier found him? He turns the radio up loud. The sound shoves out any thoughts before they can take shape. Only the image of Anna, the pain on her face, slips through. He turns the radio up a notch.

Andrews's street is still. As is the house. The heavy curtains still drawn across the windows. Rhys pulls his raincoat off the back seat. Turns the collar up against the rain.

He bangs on the front door. Waits. Bangs. Waits. He steps back. Stares up at the windows. Shields his eyes from the downpour.

'What the hell's all the racket?' A voice from next door. A large man in a dirty white dressing gown stands on the step. 'You trying to wake the whole bleedin' street or what?'

'Sorry,' Rhys knows better than to extend his hand. 'I'm looking for Mr Andrews. Any idea if he's in?'

'You the filth too?'

'Do you know if he's in?' Rhys stares at the large man. The man scratches his belly. Shrugs.

'What's that mad bastard been up to?'

'Is he in?'

'I'm not his bleedin' mother.' The large man takes a deep snort. Spits out onto the step. Rhys starts to hammer on the door again.

'Guess I'll just keep doing this until I find out then.' A female voice inside the house shouts something obscene about the noise, followed by the general sentiment that if the fat slob doesn't do something to sort it out, he can deal with tired kids and a pissed-off wife for the rest of the day.

'Look.' The fat slob pulls his dressing gown tighter. 'He was alright.' He thumbs towards Andrews's house. 'All things considered.' The phlegm rattles behind his face. He sniffs deeply. 'But lately, since what's her name left him – never did like her much, skinny young bitch – he's been obsessed, obsessed with, well, what do you call them? Vampires? Nosferatu.'

The fat slob laughs.

'Not in a teenage romantic way either, in a creepy, intense, obsessed kind of way. Would tell anyone who'd listen he was looking for a killer Nosferatu. That he was going to save mankind, then seek his revenge on those who deserved it. Surprised it took you lot so long to kick him out... actually nah, I'm not... more surprised it took her so long to leave him. Mind you, she had it pretty good.' The fat slob has obviously never been in Andrews's house. More female bellowing from deep inside. Does she have to come down there because if she does there'll be trouble.

'Look, truth be told, I haven't seen him for a day or two, maybe more. Not since before your lot came and cleared his place out. Hang on.' The fat slob disappears inside. Returns with something in his hand. 'Andrews gave me a key, for emergencies.' Rhys wonders how long the fat slob would wait without seeing Andrews before it would class as an emergency.

'You want to see any kind of identification before you go handing out a vulnerable neighbour's key?' Rhys reaches for his pocket.

'There's nothing vulnerable about that mad bastard.' The fat slob laughs.

The door slams shut.

The key turns easily. Rhys is back inside the tunnel of magazines and newspapers. Some of the piles have been kicked aside then badly restacked. The team were not kind when they came to remove what they believed was theirs.

A towering archway of print still leads to the living room. How different the room is. It's had its heart torn out. There are dark patches where the photographs prevented the wallpaper fading. Rhys can still see the image of Claudia Rose. Her eyes as green and dark as the wallpaper. The carpet is also green. Covered in coffee stains so black they look like blood. A bald patch worn in front of the sofa. There's a coffee table. A side table. A couple of lamps. The room is otherwise empty. They'd cleared it back to King's Mill. Taken a piece of Andrews with it. Rhys can see that now.

The smell of damp is heavy. Rhys moves cautiously through the house. There is a small, squalid kitchen. A fridge full of rot. An even smaller bathroom containing a selection of dust-covered hand soaps. Upstairs is the master bedroom. An empty wardrobe. A bed with dirty, greasy sheets.

Rhys pauses outside the daughter's bedroom. Will Andrews be in here? Does he too feel solace in loss? Will he be crying? Will he be poised ready to pounce? He need not have worried. Andrew's wife removed every trace of herself and the baby the day she left. The room contains a couple of sticks of furniture, all too small even in this tiny space. All Andrews was left with was the case, and they had taken that from him.

All he had been left with was Kier?

Rhys can't tell when Andrews was last in the property. It doesn't look like it has been fit for human habitation for some time. Had they brought him back here and left him to fester? His colleagues. His friends. After everything he's done, everything he's sacrificed. Why hasn't the neighbour seen Andrews? Where is he?

Rhys's mobile rings. He jumps and swears.

'Where are you?' says the voice.

'I'm not late.'

'Get your arse down to Queen Street pronto. Someone somewhere has decided we haven't got enough to do. There's another bastard body.'

'What number Queen Street?' Rhys fumbles for his pad. Isn't the centre of the city all businesses and clubs? How can the killer have managed to get to another couple there? The voice laughs.

'No number, just the street. All over the bastard street.'

51.

Blue and white tape is strung wide to try and keep her from the prying eyes of the early morning commuters. Already their cappuccinos and croissants line the end of the street. Mobile phones ready so as not to miss a moment. Her body, or what is left of it, is down an alley just off the main road. Dumped on a pile of rubbish bags. All very television drama, except the girl is not an actress. She won't get up and walk away.

The rain pours down, gutters overflow. Drains, like the Constables, work overtime. The alley is sheltered by several large awnings. Awnings put up for disgruntled employees to break more rules smoking in fire escapes. The awnings sag under the weight of the rain. Plastic sheets have been put up where necessary. The water pours off the edges in torrents. Everyone below the rank of detective is soaked. Preserving the evidence is key. Protect what is left. Ironic really, if you think about it.

Quinn is at the cordon as Rhys arrives. Too self-absorbed to question why Rhys is already soaked. He waves Rhys through to the flash of press camera bulbs.

'They think it's the same one.' Quinn points to the press as he speaks. He slurps at the coffee he's managed to get his hands on. 'Stupid bastards.'

They walk towards the alley.

'Kid there called it in.' A pale-looking teenager huddles under blankets in the back of an ambulance. 'They were starting early as they had a wedding on. If this doesn't put them off marriage nothing will.' Rhys looks at the expensive cocktail bar. It fronts onto the main road. One of the fluorescent strip lights inside the window flashes.

'Kid wanted to get ahead. Whoever worked last night was kind enough to leave all the rubbish inside. In fairness, it was pissing down. The kid popped out to the bins...' They reach the mouth of the alley. '... which are situated here.' This time the camera flash comes from down the alley. From deep inside the evidence tent. A tent erected to try and keep her safe. Hours too late.

'What if they had put the bins out?' says Rhys.

'I doubt it, but we'll never really know. They can't give us that tight a window of death.' Quinn shrugs. 'He spent a while with her though, so...?'

They step towards the tent.

'Best keep your hands in your pockets, eh.' Quinn is close behind him. 'Don't want to go potentially fucking up any more crime scenes.' Rhys ignores him. 'This is not our guy. Not at all. Just another bastard adding to the shit storm.'

To the sides of the alley are several Constables. They work inch by inch along a grid pattern. Check every single square. They work quickly and efficiently. Know every minute counts as the downpour continues. The killer has been thoughtful enough to leave them with pockets of shelter. There's no guarantee he will have left a vital piece of evidence in a place of such luck. Rhys treads carefully towards the evidence tent. Do two of the younger Constables at the end of the alley turn and giggle to each other as they see him?

Are those deep, dark stains along the wall? Stains from someone being dragged? Someone fighting and screaming? Someone frozen ridged with fear? He overhears a snippet of conversation as he passes Constable Bayne.

'I feel sick. I walked this way about eleven last night. You can cut along the river from the station and be here in half the time.' Rhys knows it well. Has walked that way himself. They all walk this way at one time or another.

Rhys stoops, enters the small white tent. The man taking photographs isn't someone he knows. They nod to each other.

She's on her back. Arched over a pile of rubbish bags. Thrown there like a rag doll a child has tired of playing with. Her tiny silver skirt still manages to give her some kind of dignity. It would be the last thing on her mind. Her hair is thick. Auburn. It reminds Rhys of the first girl he dated at school. The hair covers the left side of her face. Not that it makes much difference. The right side of her face no longer exists. Beaten and bloody beyond recognition. All over her naked flesh, her neck, arms, midriff, legs are deep, brutal bruises. The skin broken in deep black holes. Her ribs look to have broken through her skin leaving a blood trail to the floor. A giant claw dug into her. She still wears one pink patent heel. It twists at an odd angle where her ankle is broken.

'Doesn't look like she got the chance to put up much of a fight, poor kid.' The man taking the photographs rises. His colleagues wait outside to do their jobs. To swab and sample in the tiny space. 'Hopefully that was because it was over quickly. For her anyway.'

The space inside the tent is as tight as a second skin. Rhys feels he's suffocating. The smell of the rubbish is overwhelming. The smell hits the back of his throat. The floor starts to shift. Everything starts to burn and char. The smell of rot mixes with the smell of burning.

'Run,' her voice whispers in his ear. 'Run.' But he can't. He turns. The wet entrance flaps of the tent wrap around him. Holding him in. He's trapped and terrified. Smothered in wet plastic, he cries out. The panic rises. Then he's free.

'Hey mate, are you alright?' The photographer's voice is distant.

Outside everything is burning. The alley is charred and black. There's a great rip in the landscape. Huge pillars of dense black matter have torn up through the earth. Everyone's laughing. He turns his head from side to side. A few feet away, Quinn turns.

'Ask,' says Quinn. The flesh from the side of his face falls away. His skull is exposed. His face contorts into an almighty grimace. 'Ask.' His voice is louder than humanly possible. Rhys screws up his eyes. Brings his hands to his ears. Gasps. He staggers back. The outside of the tent is wet against the back of his neck. He can feel the heat from the flames burn his skin.

And then it's gone.

Slowly he opens his eyes.

Everything is normal.

'... ask me, then stupid people will believe anything you tell them.' Quinn speaks to the bored-looking Constable that guards the entrance to the alley. 'That's the problem with the world today. We can use it to our advantage, but it can also be used to disadvantage us.' Rhys fights for breath.

'Sir.' Constable Bayne holds up something on the end of a lanyard. 'I've found something, sir.' She looks awkward, unsure.

'Give it to Morgan there. He looks like he could do with something to focus on. He's gone a bit green around the gills. Again.'

'No, sir, I really think this is one you need to look at.' Quinn sighs. Stalks over. Peers at the object. Shoves it into an evidence bag. Mutters to Bayne. Stuffs the evidence bag into his pocket. Bayne doesn't take her eyes off Rhys.

Rhys struggles to catch his breath. Looks like a rookie who has never seen a dead body before. No wonder Bayne looks at him strangely. The air is damp on his face. The cold rain cools his skin.

What the hell just happened?

He fights the urge to vomit. He needs to sit down. He needs something solid to lean on. The tent is flimsy. It could collapse and send him backwards into the rotten embrace of the bloody corpse. He's watching everything through water. A third person perspective on himself as he stands in the filth.

Quinn stands for a long moment. He comes silently to Rhys. Nods for him to follow.

Something is wrong.

It takes all of Rhys's energy to get his legs to move. The ground gets firmer beneath his feet the further they get from the tent. The end of the alley is like a looking glass. Rhys steps through it, back to reality. He feels like he has awoken from a dream.

On the main road, Quinn signals them into his car. As the doors shut Quinn pulls the evidence bag out of his pocket. Holds it close to Rhys's face.

'You are in some serious shit.'

Staring back at Rhys is Rhys. At least his police photo identification. Covered in blood and apparently found wrapped around a second pink patent heel.

52.

'As I keep saying, there is no way my identification could've been there. It's just not possible.'

'You were there, with Detective Inspector Quinn, when the discovery was made?'

'Yes, I know that. It's just not possible. I have it here, look.' Rhys fumbles into his pocket. Shit. Where's his identification? The other pocket? No. Why is there so much stuff in his pockets anyway? He starts to empty them onto the desk. Tissues, coins, keys, a piece of Lego? His heart skips as he throws the picture of Kier down. It smiles up at him.

There is no identification. Harry must have it.

'Harry must have it, must have moved it. He does that all the time.' Rhys laughs weakly. Harry does move his identification all the time. He loves to play cops and robbers. He's always the cop. Rhys tells him countless times how important it is not to touch Daddy's identification. He needs it for work. He will get into trouble without it. They even spent a rainy Sunday afternoon mocking Harry up his own card, complete with photograph and realistic hologram. Obviously the message hasn't got through. 'Let me call Anna. I'll ask her to look.'

'Rhys, is this your identification?' Detective Chief Inspector Alec Jenkins pushes the clear plastic evidence bag across the table towards him. Inside the blood congeals in bubbles.

'It looks like it, yes, but as I keep saying that is not possible.' Rhys stares at the photo of himself. 'It must be a fake or something. Can't you get it analysed?'

'We should get you analysed.' Quinn speaks under his breath. Jenkins frowns.

'Yes, thank you, Detective Inspector. Rhys, this is really important.'

'I know that. Do you think I don't know that? Like I said, call Anna.' Rhys drums his fingers on the desk. 'No, wait – don't call Anna. It's in my desk. In my desk. I remember now.' It is in his desk. Of course. The relief is like a weight being lifted. 'When I moved all my stuff in, it was in the box. It'll be in my desk. Shall I go and get it?' He rises. Of course that's where it is. He just needs to calm down. To think clearly.

The Detective Chief Inspector signals for Rhys to sit. He nods once to Quinn who leaves the room. The Constable at the door shuffles. Rhys sits. Fidgets. Jenkins's eyes bore into him.

'Rhys, this is not a question I like to ask but hope you understand I have to. Where were you between eleven p.m. last night and seven a.m. this morning?'

'What? Are you serious?' He is of course. 'Is this an interview? Am I a suspect? Shouldn't we be heading down to the interview suites to do this? Do I need a solicitor?' He really needs to clear his head.

'Rhys.' Jenkins's voice is calm, firm. 'You're here voluntarily, helping us with our investigation.' Rhys looks down at the tabletop. 'I'm trying to help you here. Your police identification has just been found next to a young girl's body. A young girl who was violently beaten to death at some point between eleven p.m. and seven a.m. this morning. You're saying that's not possible. I want to hear why. Help me out here. Help me find the right answer.' Rhys sighs. Rubs his itchy eyes. Why are his eyes always so itchy?

'I was at home.'

'Don't lie to me, Rhys.' Rhys looks up. 'I've already spoken to Anna.'

'Anna and I had a fight. I went out. I drove around. I fell asleep.' No lie.

'What did you fight about?'

'Our neighbour came over for drinks. We don't get on. I didn't want him in my house, Anna did. We fought, I left.'

'How did your neighbour feel about this?'
'What? I don't give a shit how he felt about it. He knew he wasn't welcome in my house. He was there taking the piss.' Rhys feels his anger rising. Control it. The thought of the creature sitting there with his wife. His children.

'Was there any violence?' says Jenkins.

'A little bit of shoving, that's all,' Rhys shakes the image of Kier's sly smile from his mind. 'You've spoken to Anna. She must have said the same?'

'And what's the name of your neighbour?' Jenkins looks at his notes. Are they real notes? Notes about him. Or just blank sheets of paper in a file, there to make Rhys feel uncomfortable?

'Kier Finnegan, not that I am sure how that's relevant.' Kier's picture smiles up at him from the table. Jenkins makes a note. Rhys wants to stand up and scream, instead he says, 'I wouldn't bother going during the day.' Jenkins raises an eyebrow.

'So, you left around what time?' says Jenkins.

'Seven p.m.'

'And then what?'

'I drove.'

'Where did you drive?'

'Here. There. Everywhere. I couldn't say, I was just so angry,' Jenkins makes another note. 'Do I need a solicitor?'

'Not at this stage.' Shit. 'How angry were you exactly?'

'I was very angry, but driving calmed me down. I wasn't "get out of my car and beat some poor teenager to death" angry, if that is what you are asking.' Being smart will get him nowhere but this is ridiculous. Quinn will be back any minute with his identification. They'll all have to apologise. He needs to get out of here. He has bigger problems on his hands.

'And where did you end up after all this driving?' says Jenkins.

'Out of town. In the old lanes.'

'Can anyone vouch for your whereabouts?' Rhys pauses.

Interesting.

'Yes actually, my neighbour, Kier Finnegan.' Let's see how Kier likes the police knocking on his door. Bringing the net closer.

'Kier Finnegan? The neighbour you say you had a fight with earlier that night?'

'Yes.'

'But you said you were driving "here, there and everywhere" How would your neighbour have found you? Why would he want to find you after there had been some "shoving" earlier in the evening?'

'I have no idea. You could ask him for me when you confirm my alibi, not that you will need to as this is all a big mistake.' Jenkins stares at him. Rhys does not break eye contact.

'Do you keep any tools in your car?' says Jenkins.

'No. Like what?' A hammer?

'A hammer?'

Rhys shakes his head. Slowly he reaches across the table. Pulls his belongings towards him. Slips them back into his pockets.

'It's been brought to my attention,' Jenkins continues, clears his throat, 'that your behaviour has been, how can I put this, a little erratic lately.' What is that look in his eyes?

'Who told you that? Quinn? Well he's a lying bastard.'

'The issue at St James' Hospital? The need to eliminate your fingerprints from an active crime scene?'

'I....' Right on cue Quinn comes back into the room.

'There's nothing there, sir,' says Quinn.

'You lying bastard.' Rhys shoots out of his seat. 'See, what did I just say, he's a lying bastard.' Rhys turns to the door. 'Let me go and look myself.' The Constable steps in front of the door. 'It's there. It has to be there. How can it not be there?' How can it not be there?

'It isn't. Both myself and DC Dan Davies were present,' says Quinn. Davies was there too? Fucking brilliant.

'There has to be some kind of mistake,' says Rhys. 'Look on the CCTV. Someone must have taken it.' A slow reality dawns. He sits back down. 'He must have taken it.'

'Who must have taken it Rhys?' says Jenkins. He leans across the desk.

'Kier Finnegan,' says Rhys. The words are out before he can stop them. His mind races. A light comes on in his brain. It is Kier. Kier setting him up. It's perfect if you think about it. A way to discredit him, ensure no one will believe a word he says. If they believe he's capable of this, he'll lose everything. Have nothing to protect. It makes perfect sense.

'Is this the same Kier Finnegan that you had the fight with? The same Kier Finnegan who managed to find you out in the back of beyond?' says Jenkins.

'Yes.' Rhys is hardly aware he speaks. Is Kier trying to get the finger of blame pointed at him for other reasons too? To cover his own tracks, cover the fact he's the one responsible? 'Don't bother to look on the CCTV you won't see him.'

'Is that because he wasn't here, Rhys? But then he couldn't have been here if he was with you could he? Where were you really, Rhys?'

This is some kind of interview. Do they think he's stupid?

Rhys snaps back into the here and now. He'll figure out how the bastard has done it later. Now he needs to focus on proving he hasn't beaten some poor thing to death with a hammer.

It springs into his head.

'Look, here, look at this.'

The handkerchief.

This time he digs in his jacket pockets.

'He gave me this. Kier gave me this. This is his, see.' He waves the handkerchief in Jenkins's face. 'Run the DNA on this handkerchief. His will be all over it. You'll have to get a sample off him too of course. I bet he's too clever to be on any database. I know where he lives. I have told you where he lives. You'll see, you'll see I'm telling the truth.' Quinn's eyes have dropped. 'What? Why can't you look at me? It's because you know I'm right, isn't it? You know I'm right, ha!' Rhys throws the handkerchief onto the desk top in triumph. The wilting flower of blood folds in half; it looks like the petals are falling off. There's the proof he didn't kill the girl, that he was with Kier. They can get off his back and let him get back to figuring out how to stop all this. Kier has scuppered himself. Ruined his own set up. It's funny in a way. Kier shows Rhys emotional attachment is a weakness. It's proven to be just that.

'That's your handkerchief, Rhys.' Quinn's eyes seem sad.

'Well it is now, yes, but he gave it to me. Last night. In my car. You can get forensic evidence off it.' Rhys sits back, folds his arms across his chest.

'No, it's always been yours. You offered it to Tony when he came in after his parents were attacked. Remember?'

'What? No!' Rhys's mind rewinds. The big rasping sobs. The sharp teeth of the tissue box. The handkerchief... 'That's... not that handkerchief.'

'Yes it is,' say Quinn.

'No it isn't.'

'It still smells of that bloody awful vapour rub.' Rhys snatches it up. Sniffs.

'Well of course it does. They've been in the same pocket.' Where's that other hanky? Shit. Not that pocket. Where the hell is it? He always keeps his hanky in the same pocket. Always. He starts to empty his pockets.

'Please,' Jenkins holds up a hand, 'I don't need to waste anymore time watching you empty your pockets all over my desk... again. This is ridiculous.'

'Shall we run the DNA test on the hanky before or after we run the authenticity test on your identification?' Quinn's voice is taught. 'Or, how about I spend my time running tests that will actually solve the cases I have piling up on my desk?' The redness from his neck has reached his face.

Jenkins stares at the tiny blood flower on the handkerchief.

'Whose blood is that on the handkerchief, Rhys?' Jenkins looks at him as he speaks. 'It that her blood? Is that your blood?'

'No! It's his blood.'

'His blood? Your neighbour, Kier Finnegan? The one you had a fight with, who then somehow managed to find you in the middle of nowhere?'

'Yes.'

'Why are you so obsessed with this man, Rhys?'

'I'm not.'

'How did his blood get on your handkerchief?'

'It's a teardrop.'

'I beg your pardon?'

'It's a teardrop. He was crying.'

'He was crying blood?'

'Yes.' Jenkins rubs his temples.

'I was hoping it wouldn't come to this Rhys I really was.'

'What?' says Rhys.

'There is obviously something going on here that neither myself nor Detective Inspector Quinn are qualified to help you with –'

'What? Why would you say that? Interview Kier Finnegan, speak to Anna. You'll see I didn't do this thing you think I did.' Jenkins pauses for a long time. He takes a deep breath.

'Rhys, is this the same Kier Finnegan you think is a Nosferatu after your soul?'

'No fucking way,' says Quinn. His mouth drops open.

Rhys's world grinds to a halt.

Anna's betrayed him.

She's the only one he's told, her and Elsie. Anna's run to his boss, not even had the decency to tell him. It would've been last night, after they fought. She'd told tales to the teacher. Rhys would have told the boss himself, when the time was right. When he had enough evidence. But not yet. Not fucking yet.

Now he looks like a nutter. A nutter without the support of his wife. Is that why they've all been laughing at him? Does everybody know?

'I... we... what I think is... who would say that?' says Rhys.

'That's not relevant. What's relevant is do you believe it to be true?'

'Run,' her voice whispers in his ear. Everything starts to tilt.

'I can't,' says Rhys. There's a Constable in front of the door.

'I'm sorry?' says Jenkins. 'You can't what?'

'I can't... I don't...' The tilt rocks the room back the other way. Rhys holds onto the edge of the desk. 'I do... I do.' His voice cracks. He clenches his teeth tight. Drops his head. Breathes deeply.

'Just to confirm.' Jenkins's voice is distant. 'You do think there is a Nosferatu, sorry, hypothetical Nosferatu, after your soul?' Rhys nods. The movement in the room subsides.

'Jesus,' says Quinn. 'What the fuck are they putting in the water round here? First Andrews, now you?'

'In that case I have no option other than to refer you to Occupational Health as a matter of urgency...' Jenkins's voice slips far away Rhys can hardly hear. Jenkins explains it'll be best if Rhys takes a few days leave, stays at home until his appointment comes through. Thinks clearly about what he's saying. Rhys hears someone laugh.

'There really is no need.' Rhys manages to say. 'There is nothing wrong with me, I wish everyone would stop saying there was.'

'Oh, I think there is.' Jenkins's tone is flat and cold. 'And with regards to the other matter, your identification being found at a murder scene, I do expect your full and ongoing cooperation.'

Rhys nods. Jenkins shuffles the papers. 'We'll be in touch again very soon.' Rhys rises slowly. It's as if he is watching himself from a distance as he leaves the room. As the door starts to swing shut behind him, he hears Jenkins voice, 'Quinn, call the Divisional Superintendent, I want a full psych report of every single copper in this station before we become a bloody laughing stock.'

Someone's laughing alright, but in a way they are yet to hear.

53.

Rhys, Rhys, Rhys. Why is Rhys everywhere he turns?

Here Rhys is, walking down the cul-de-sac, heading home as if nothing has happened. How can that be? He went to so much effort. He kicks at a stone.

'Don't kick the stones you vile little boy.'

He's cold. Wet. Stiff from standing in the same position hour after hour. Do they not realise what he's done? What he's done for them?

'Done for them? Done for you more like. You disgust me. I told you this wouldn't work, but then you are so stupid you don't listen.'

'Shut up,' he mutters.

They've let Rhys go. Interesting. Could it be they've not found his identification? It wasn't well hidden.

Could someone else have found it? Stolen it? Was he too impulsive?

She made a terrible mess, his fiery princess. He's sorry for that. Sorry they had so little time together. Sorry the time was spent in a dirty street surrounded by rubbish. The blood caked her hair, matted it together. Made it chewy when he placed a strand between his teeth. He shouldn't have done that. He couldn't help himself, couldn't resist. A naughty kid in a sweet shop. He giggles. He'd giggled then too.

'A naughty boy, a naughty vile little boy.'

The giggle stops abruptly. He can feel it now, that strand of hair. He plays with it in his pocket. It's not a trophy. Trophies are for the weak, remember? It's a necessity, after she distracted him so.

She made him so angry. Refused to play, to fight. On reflection, the first blow was a bit hard. He was excited. Got carried away at the thought of his plans coming together.

But here he is, Rhys. Large as life. He strolls down the cul-de-sac without a care in the world. Don't they realise what his auburn-haired girl has sacrificed for them? Could they be any more ungrateful? Disrespectful? The anger starts to bubble. That will not do.

There will be an explanation. Give it time. Wait. Be patient. That's something he's very good at.

He snuggles further back into the thick foliage. The owner of this house doesn't care about the front garden. The trees are massive, overgrown. Branches bend down to the ground behind the low stone wall. The bushes that wind around them knot together – their branches create a thatching. It was easy for him to push inside. The perfect spot to watch for her. His Anna. The perfect spot to ensure Rhys is out of the way. The perfect spot to wait and watch. There's even an old for sale sign abandoned just behind the wall. He flattens it to stand on, to stop his feet getting wet.

54.

Usually Elsie loves it when the children come to stay. It makes her feel alive, gives her purpose. Today it fills her with a deep foreboding. A dark feeling in the pit of her stomach. Not for the first time since the children arrived she goes to look out of the window.

'What are you looking for, Nana?' asks Harry. Louise rolls her eyes. It irritates Louise that Harry calls Elsie Nana. She states only babies refer to non-family members as things like Aunty or Nana. Elsie isn't related to them so she should be called Elsie. Harry is adamant she's his nana, says it doesn't matter that she didn't give birth to Mummy or Daddy. It's what he'll call her. Louise says only babies used the term Mummy and Daddy. Harry looks close to tears.

'Nothing darling.' Elsie turns. The nets drop. She shuffles back to her chair. Pats the top of Harry's head. He smiles up at her.

'Were you checking for the Nosferatu?'

'More likely checking Dad isn't freaking out again.' Louise doesn't look up from her mobile as she speaks. 'Having another crazy turn and embarrassing us all.'

'Don't say such things about your father.' Elsie is a little too quick. A little too defensive.

'There's nothing wrong with Dad,' says Harry. Louise looks up.

'Is there something wrong with Dad?' She looks at Elsie. 'Is that why we're here, because there's something wrong with Dad?' Concern fleets across her face. Then she remembers concern is not cool, especially for your parents.

'There's nothing wrong with your dad.' Elsie wills her face to stay expressionless. 'Nothing a quiet, relaxing night in with your mum won't solve.'

Elsie told Rhys he needed Anna's help. Needed to make her understand, to believe. She told him that they, he, could not deal with Kier alone. She could see Rhys's mind race. Race for ways to convince Anna. Race with more unanswered questions.

'They, he, did not take Jenny.' Elsie said it several times.

Grabbed hold of his wrists, made him look at her until she was sure he's taken it in. 'It's mind tricks, that's all. Jenny's gone. Focus on the children you still have with you, on keeping them safe. If there's a way to beat him, you'll need Anna's help.' She was lying. Cursed herself for it but did it nonetheless.

'There's nothing wrong with Dad. Nana's right. We're here because he's going to kill the Nosferatu.'

'You're such a baby believing in all that, isn't he, Na… Elsie?' Louise laughs uncertainly. 'There's no such thing as Nosferatu, isn't that right?' They both look to Elsie. Slowly she rises, goes back to the window. 'I mean, I know what Dad was saying last night, but Mum said he's just tired from work and confused. Isn't that right?' The eyes bore into Elsie. Search for reassurance. 'Only babies believe in Nosferatu.'

'I wouldn't like to say,' says Elsie quietly.

'See,' says Harry.

'Just because you can't comprehend something doesn't mean it isn't real,' Elsie continues, forgetting herself for a moment. The street is still.

'I'm worried about Dad,' says Harry.

'Me too,' says Louise. Cool forgotten, she moves to sit close to Harry, takes his small hand in hers. Elsie does not turn from the window.

'And perhaps you should be.' The truth escapes on an out breath. She's distracted – sure she's seen something move in the bushes in front of Kier Finnegan's house.

55.

Rhys has asked Elsie to look after the kids. Anna prays this is a good sign. That she hasn't made things worse blabbing to Dan, but then she wasn't blabbing, not really, she was asking for help, right?

Rhys comes home from work early. Says he has something to tell her. Her mind fleets once more to the notion of another woman. An internal laugh as she remembers Rhys's issues are nothing as simple as that.

They stand in the kitchen. Rhys's words rain down on her. He's been referred to Occupational Health. Instructed to take a few days off. Why could this be? Because someone has told the Chief Inspector he believes he's being chased by a Nosferatu. Anna feels her cheeks burn with shame.

Dan has done what she hoped he would. She sent out a distress flare and he answered it. Now Rhys can get professional help. Talk to people who can figure out what's wrong and make him better.

She draws breath to say as much but he cuts her off.

He tells her the person that informed the Chief Inspector will think they've done him a favour. She will think she's done him a favour, but she hasn't. He tells her he spent the night in his car in the old lanes. Kier found him there. How is that possible if he's just a man? He will leave that with her. She can come back to him when she has an answer.

At this time, a young girl was beaten to death in the city, his police identification placed at the scene. Kier is his alibi. Kier, the same one his boss has just been told Rhys believes is a Nosferatu after his soul. Doesn't do much for his chances, does it? He feels it's obvious; Kier is framing him. How can he prove that now? Kier's trying to take his whole life, make it so he has no choice but to join him. Anna has helped him along. He stares hard at her for a long time.

'How could Kier have framed you if he was with you?' The words he has said are ridiculous. The alternative is far worse.

'What? I don't know. I haven't had time to figure it out fully yet with all this other shit going on, but I will, if you give me a moment.' Rhys paces as he speaks, back and forth, back and forth.

'Maybe he followed you?'

'What?'

'Maybe he followed you when you left here and that's how he found you?'

'Why would he want to do that? He doesn't need to do that. He can always find me, that's the point.'

'I don't know, I don't understand. I don't understand you anymore.' Anna pours herself a glass of wine.

'And drinking won't help, you need to stay alert.' He leaves the room. He's full of shit. He drinks several large gins every night. Just because the bottle is in Jenny's room doesn't mean she doesn't know.

One thing from his tirade stands out above all else. His police identification found at a murder scene? She follows him into the hall.

'How was your police identification found at a murder scene, Rhys?' The words echo up the stairs. Her only answer is the slamming of a door.

He must have dropped it, right? Or someone else must have dropped it. The wine sloshes as she refills her glass. Yeah, that will be it. Someone else must have picked it up in all the chaos of leaving the station, then they must have dropped it... The words are lame.

This is serious. Not actually accused of murder though or he would be being held in the station? They don't let people wander off home if they really believe they have committed a heinous crime, do they? What's the name for it, circumstantial something? She runs her hands through her hair. What the fuck is going on? Her fingers twitch. She could text Dan? Just one small text. Just to find out what is really going on. There's nothing wrong with that.

Anna sits at the table.

Rhys's father served a five-year prison sentence for grievous bodily harm just after Jenny disappeared. Another nail in the coffin of both his marriage and his relationship with his son. His temper is still wild.

It's there, in the genes.

Rhys has never been a violent man. Anna knows it isn't possible. You can't live with someone for all these years and for them to suddenly kill another human being and you not to have seen it coming.

There would have been a change in his behaviour...

Dan has tried to help. Maybe it's not enough. She should call his boss. What's his name again? Has Rhys even told her? She still has Chief Inspector Wallace's number somewhere. She could call him, he'd know what to do.

Above her the floorboards creak.

What the hell is Rhys doing up there?

56.

He came home to make her understand, to make her see but she wasn't even prepared to listen, his own wife. Rhys is so angry, so betrayed. The look in her eyes says she will never be on his side. Will not even try to understand.

He's alone. Anna makes that quite clear.

He'll have to be careful what he says to her now, what he lets her see. She's working against him. Everything he does is to keep her safe yet she still refuses to understand. He has told her that over and over again. Still she refuses to see it. He's so angry he could scream.

He has to let the anger go for now. He can deal with the betrayal, the lack of trust and belief later. When they're safe. He's not sure he can forgive her but will always love her.

The laptop whirls to life. He digs around in the papers on the floor. The answer has to be here somewhere.

What a fucking unbelievable day.

Did they really sit there and as good as accuse him of murder? Do they really think he's capable of that? It's like a punch to the stomach. The disbelief on Quinn's face. The cold stare from Jenkins. Rhys has never so much as raised his hand to a woman. The very suggestion is insane. And they have the gall to insinuate he's the mad one. It will be all round the station by now. Pigeonholed with Andrews.

Andrews.

Where the hell is Andrews? Why didn't he remember to ask? Isn't the station supposed to be keeping an eye on him? You would think so, all things considered.

Rhys stops. Sits on the edge of the bed. This is very serious indeed. He could be arrested. Go on trial. End up in jail. What will happen to his family if he isn't here? Would Kier take second best?

Rhys gets up, paces.

Will Kier give him an alibi? Unlikely. Who will they believe? A discredited police officer or a lying hotshot surgeon? Rhys will be branded a murderer. His head is about to explode. An irony indeed that being questioned about involvement in a murder is the least of his worries.

Murder.

The word sits in his stomach like a rock. A copy of Kier's photo stares up at him from the floor.

Murder.

The thought opens up in front of him. Why hasn't he had it before? It's so obvious. He could laugh, except it isn't funny. If he's going to be accused it may as well be for a murder he's actually committed.

So simple.

'For fuck's sake.' Why didn't he think of it sooner? A stake through the heart. Isn't that what he read? All he needs do is ram a stake through Kier Finnegan's black heart. He can make a stake. Easy. No, wait. Too cumbersome, too hard to conceal. What he really needs is a knife. A nice, big, sharp knife. He knows exactly where there is one. Where there are many.

The attic ladder slides down easily. His hand is on the box in minutes. Anna's father collected knives from all over the world. Rhys was surprised at the size and scale you could walk into a shop and buy without question. Anna's parents downsized, her father passed them on to Anna and Rhys, something for Harry when he grows up. They are kept in the attic for safety, of both the knives and Harry. Rhys's hands are sweating. He wipes them on his shirt.

Look at all the knives. A dozen or more. Looking at them makes him feel strong and safe. He settles on a six-inch flick-knife. It feels solid in his hand. Easy to carry in his pocket, poised for when the moment comes. Kier will be so surprised as he feels the cold steel push into his heart. Rhys will stare into his eyes the whole time. Rhys looks at the knives some more, selects a second one, a large hunting knife. Two knives. Better to be safe than sorry.

Kier will burst into flames or dissolve into a pile of dust. If that doesn't happen, Rhys will gladly walk into the police station and confess. It won't take them long to figure out who Kier really is, once they have his corpse in the morgue. It won't take long for them to realise the killings have stopped and Rhys was right, Andrews was right and they really should have listened.

They really should've bloody listened.

57.

Anna watches Rhys for a long time before he realises she's there. He's left the door to Jenny's room open. He sits at the desk, intently studies whatever it is he's looking at on the laptop. The wine has helped calm Anna down – at least she thought it had. The room is a tip. When did he bring all this stuff home? Where did it even come from? Books on dark arts. Books on things she doesn't want to see, doesn't want to know are here. She'd come upstairs intent on telling him this was his last chance, last chance to listen, to hear sense. Has that chance long sailed? She needs to be strong, take control. For Rhys. For herself. She steps into the room.

'You know I don't like anyone else in this room.' Rhys's fingers scurry across the laptop keys.

'And you know I don't like it when I fall out with my husband.' She perches on the edge of the bed, why does she always have to be the appeaser? When did they slide into these roles? 'Please, Rhys, can we talk without falling out. I want to help you. I want you to see that all of this is madness.' He turns and looks at her. Shakes his head sadly. Something like a knowing smile tugs at the corner of his mouth.

'Did you know that in most European countries blue eyes are the sign of the Devil?' Anna can't bear to look at him 'And that most Nosferatu survive hidden for centuries within families of extreme wealth and power.' He stands. Flaps some sheets of paper in her face. They move too fast for her to see. 'That's how they–'

He freezes. Spins to look out of the window. Sees something she can't.

'He's there! He's fucking out there! This is it! Now is the time!' His voice is loud, frantic. Then he's gone. Feet pound the stairs. The front door slams.

Anna looks out of the window. The street is silent. Nothing.

She runs down the stairs. What the hell is he doing now? She can't cope, has no idea what to do. She should've made the call. Why hadn't she made the call? Why has the station allowed him to come home?

Her hand reaches the front door knob and pulls. The front door doesn't budge. She pulls and strains at the handle. Kicks the door the same way she had chastised Harry for. Rhys has bloody locked it from the outside. She turns to the table, empties the key bowl. Nothing other than loose change and a key for the shed.

'Where are my fucking keys?'

She runs through to the kitchen, the back door. Locked. Key removed. She runs back to the front door, pulls at it some more, like somehow something will be different, somehow it will open.

He's left her no choice.

'This is your own fault, Rhys Morgan!' she bellows into the wood. 'Your fault, not mine.'

58.

Rhys can see his breath – it races ahead of him in a little cloud. His eyes dart, look for the movement he saw. Behind him Anna thumps the door. She'll understand in time. It's for her own safety. She'll try and stop him. Refuse to understand.

There! The movement is further down the street. Away from his house. Away from Kier's house. Behind one of the trees planted to give ambience to the street. Trees that crack the road and burrow into house foundations.

Rhys approaches slowly. His fingers come away from the flick knife in his pocket. It won't be Kier creeping down the street looking back at his own house in the darkness. Disappointing, he was ready for the moment. Now it'll have to wait. He's a police officer, however. It's his duty to discover who scuttled from outside Kier's house. Who pulled his attention, brought him out. The figure tries to blend into the shadow of the tree, tries, but not hard enough.

'Andrews?' The narrow face stares out at him from under the thick hood.

'You.'

'What are you doing here?' Rhys's mind races. This is a good thing. No, this is a great thing. Andrews has come to his street. He's heard what's happened. Sought Rhys out. Come to form an alliance. This is very good indeed. They can combine information, discuss a plan of action. A wave of relief washes over Rhys. Andrews can back him up with Anna. Two of them saying the same thing will prove what Rhys says is true. Two of them can't be mad together. Rhys smiles.

'What am I doing here?' says Andrews. 'What am I doing here? A more pertinent question would be what are you doing here?'

'Sorry? I live here, over there.' Rhys points down the street. His house glows in the dark.

'How very convenient for you.' Andrews's spit lands on Rhys. 'How very bloody convenient.' Rhys's smile fades. Rhys follows Andrews's eye line right to Kier's front door.

'That's him,' says Rhys. 'Kier Finnegan. He's the one you talked about isn't he? He's the one responsible.'

'I know that,' says Andrews. Pain fleets across his face. 'I know and I told you. I told you and this is how you repay me.' Rhys's brow furrows.

'That's why you are here, isn't it? So we can join forces? So we can prove what he is, what he's done? So we can beat him?'

'"Join forces", have you heard yourself? What do you think this is, some kind of playground game? I'm sure you've read the books, think you have all the answers in your clever little academic head, think you are better than me.'

'What? No I don't... Look... what...?'

'You aren't, not for one moment. You think you can destroy him, don't you? I can see it in your eyes. You think he will let you do that.' Andrews laughs. 'Why would you want to do that, Rhys? Why would you want to destroy him when he offers you so much?' Andrews's laugh morphs into a cough. A hard sound. He spits blood onto the pavement. His eyes turn on Rhys, bore into him, full of fury.

'He was mine. I told you that. I made it very clear. I was the one who cracked the case. I was the one who discovered the truth behind the murders, me. Not you. Me.' Rhys nods, dumbstruck. 'All I had to do was locate him then you come along, meddling, taking everything away.'

'I'm sorry.' Rhys is. But not for that reason.

'Not sorry enough. In spite of you, I've tracked him down. And here you are again, getting in the way.' Andrews's face is flat. 'Destroy him.' Andrews's head shakes. 'I don't want to destroy him. I want to join him.'

'What? That's... I don't understand.'

'I find that odd. You of all people should understand clearly. You've read the books, but more than that, you believe.' Andrews is short of breath. 'You believe in the innate power they have, he has, that they can offer us.' Andrews's gaze turns back to Kier's house. 'I am ready, so ready and yes I will admit, in need. Dying. Petrified.

'Do you know what he did, Kier? He laughed. He laughed at me. He came this far from my face.' Andrews gestures with his fingers, 'And laughed. He said I was pathetic. I didn't deserve the gift he has to offer. I begged him then. I told him I truly believed. That I would serve him without question for the rest of time. That I needed him to help me. That I was afraid. This angered him. He told me he had found someone better than I could ever hope to be. He told me he found you.' Andrews turns back to Rhys. His eyes blaze. 'You. You who has mocked me. You who refused to believe. You who deny him. You are the one he chose.'

The floor falters beneath Rhys's feet. How has Andrews got it so wrong?

'But I do, I believe now, this, what he has said to you is proof of what he is, what he has done. Come with me, help me, together we can beat him.'

'You. With your happy family and friends, your youth. Why do you need anything from him? How can you take that from me?'

'I don't want any of this. He won't listen.'

'If it wasn't for you, I would have everything I ever wanted.' His eyes fix on Rhys. 'If you were out of the way, things would be different.' Rhys's mind whirls.

'Is it you?' Rhys shouts, then lowers his voice, doesn't want to wake the whole street, 'is it you trying to set me up?' Andrews looks confused, but recovers quickly.

'Don't flatter yourself any more than you already have.'

Rhys sees the glint of the knife blade in Andrews's hand. Rhys's head turns. He's too close to the tree, can't move fast enough. He thinks of his own weapon. Knows he won't reach it in time. Which pocket is it in again? He screws shut his eyes, wonders if anyone will believe him after he's dead and how many people will come to his funeral. He wonders how long Anna will grieve and who she will eventually re-marry. He hopes Kier will leave them all alone if he's dead. He hopes Anna wouldn't move in case Jenny comes home but knows she will and that makes him sad. He draws a breath, anticipates the knife's cold blade.

It never comes.

Cautiously, Rhys opens one eye. A thin line of blood runs from the corner of Andrews's mouth, like dribble but far too dark. The knife drops from Andrews's fingers, lands with a dull thud on the grass. Andrews's eyes bulge. His lips part. His eyes drop down. Rhys follows his gaze. They both stare at the tip of the large hunting knife sticking from Andrews's chest, a knife jammed in his back, straight through his heart. The blade's tip is so close to Rhys it's nicked the front of his shirt. Andrews opens his mouth to speak. Shuts it again. The solid tree trunk is tight against Rhys's back. Andrews's fingers slowly rise and touch the tip of the knife blade.

'I have to look after my investment.' Kier's voice is loud in the night. His face appears over Andrews's shoulder. The other man's body slumps back against him with a grunt.

'Fuck,' says Rhys. Kier blanches.

'As eloquent as ever. A "thank you" will suffice.' Kier turns his face to Andrews, sniffs his skin. 'Looks like you owe me.' He turns back to Rhys.

'What have you done?' Rhys whispers.

'He would have killed you, Rhys. I've saved your life. You could at least pretend to be grateful.'

'He was only here because of you, because of what you are. We were both only here because of you. You didn't need to... there was no need to do – '

'Because of what you are.' Kier mimics. 'Because you are a nasty old Nosferatu.' He turns on Rhys. 'You were both here because of yourselves but flattery will get you everywhere. Never underestimate the human ego, Rhys.' Kier is too close. Andrews's body is wedged between them. 'Now, if you will excuse me.' Kier nods towards Andrews. 'He's already colder than I'd like.'

Kier throws back his head, reveals his incisors. The movement contorts his face beyond human recognition. He tilts Andrews's neck away from him and lunges, turning them both away from Rhys. They are still too close. The image of the twisted face is too close. Rhys hears the piercing of the skin, the suck of blood.

He screams and runs as hard and fast as he can.

From the bushes someone watches the men fight. Did the word Nosferatu catch the air? He hears one of the men scream so loud he could awake Satan himself. The man in the bushes giggles until his eyes water. Suddenly he doesn't feel so crazy after all.

59.

The front door slams. Anna jumps, stands. Angry. Ready for confrontation. Rhys is wild, sweating. He rants at full pelt, shakes and paces in front of her.

'He was out there. He did it. He killed Andrews. He killed him right there in front of me. He killed Andrews, right in front of me, with a hunting knife straight through his heart. It was at the tree, over at the tree. Andrews was going to kill me, lock the doors, phone the police, quickly phone the police, phone the army, phone anyone, get them out there now.'

'What have you done?'

'What have I done? What have I fucking done? Jesus. Phone Elsie tell her to lock the door, tell her not to answer it under any circumstances, it's not safe. God I wish they were all here, we were all here together, that way I would know we were all safe. Pass me the phone, I need to call her, them. Why are you just standing looking at me like that? He's out there. Call the police.' He's ashen, green around the edges. He paces the hallway, points wildly, goes to the front door. 'I'll go and get them, the kids, Elsie, except he's still out there.'

'Here.' She offers him a large gin. 'Have this. It'll calm you down.' He downs it.

'Did you hear what I said? Where's the phone? Andrews, Kier killed him, stabbed him through the heart.' Rhys brings his hands up to his chest. 'He was this close to me.' He steps in close to Anna. 'They both were. I could smell it. I could smell the death. I could see it, the life leaving his body.' Anna notices the tremble in his fingers. 'Stop standing staring at me. Call the police. Where's the phone? I'll do it myself.' He turns wildly on the spot, head jerking from side to side, not seeming to notice the phone. She picks it up. He paces the hall.

'Hello? Police please...' She walks into the kitchen. Easier to lie to the dial tone if she doesn't have to look at him.

'Tell them there's been a murder.' Rhys shouts from the hall. Anna hears the sound of him sliding the chain across the front door. 'And I know who did it, oh yes, I know.'

Anna mutters instructions into the handset. Rhys paces and

shouts.

Anna concludes the call, stands in the hall and waits.

Rhys paces. Stands. Paces. Rants. Paces. Stands. Shouts about how the police are taking too long.

'You'll have to believe me now.' Eventually he turns his words on her. 'When the police get here. You'll have to believe me when you see his body.' Rhys is close once more. 'When you see what the monster has done.'

Rhys steps back.

'Shit. When you see what he's, what did he... oh god... what the...' He staggers against the banisters.

Finally.

'I don't feel... shit.' Everything from the shelf in the hallway tumbles to the floor as he stumbles into it. 'What have you done?' He looks at her then. The saddest look she's ever seen. The shelf comes away from the wall as he crashes to the floor. Anna winces, hopes he hasn't hurt himself, hopes he'll understand when he wakes up.

The sleep will do him good. He looks pathetic, crumpled on the floor. How is she going to move him? She hadn't really thought it through, just panicked at the authority in Divisional Superintendent Wallace's voice. She feels sad it was so easy. A handful of sleeping tablets in the gin.

What has he done out there?

She shivers.

There's a tiny hole in the front of his shirt. Why would she notice that now? Funny how your brain homes in on the oddest things. She'll have to add mothballs to the shopping list.

A noise in the silence makes her jump. Three firm knocks on the front door.

Knock. Knock. Knock.

Divisional Superintendent Wallace was not surprised to receive a call from Rhys Morgan's wife.

He'd dined with Alec Jenkins and their respective partners, was fully up to speed. Mrs Wallace and he were getting out of their taxi home as his phone started to ring. Mrs Morgan was frantic. Her type often were by the time they filtered through to him.

'Mrs Morgan, please, just take a deep breath and tell me exactly what's happened.' Wallace stood on the driveway as she filled him in. His own wife stood and waited for him to finish, a look of concern on her face. He nodded for her to head inside. She did not.

'First, we need to ensure your husband's safe, Mrs Morgan. Running round the streets in the middle of the night will do him no good. I need you to get him back inside the house and keep him there until the morning... Yes, I understand it's difficult... You do whatever you feel is needed.' Wallace missed the next few words as Mrs Morgan was shouting. 'Would you like me to send someone over, Mrs Morgan?... I understand. Good, good.'

Wallace really couldn't have one of his detectives running about the streets in the middle of the night. It would only take one rogue journalist and the whole force would be in disrepute, and there were plenty sniffing around with this crackpot on the loose. No, he's worked too hard, sacrificed too much to allow that to happen.

'We all need to work together here, Mrs Morgan. You ensure your husband gets settled for the night and I'll arrange a meeting for Rhys with Alec Jenkins and myself first thing tomorrow morning... of course, we will only ever have his best interests at heart... Please, don't cry...' He really did wish she would stop crying. He needed to get off the phone and reschedule his day, luckily the golf club were very understanding. Finally the call ended. Mrs Wallace had gone ahead and unlocked the front door, turned off the alarm.

Mrs Wallace asked if he was okay, he said of course. She asked if the lady on the phone was okay, he said yes. Mrs Wallace asked if he should send someone to support the lady on the phone, he thought about it. Said no. She'd be fine, he had, after all, told her to call back if there were any problems.

60.

'Run,' she whispers, so much fear and pain in one single word. He holds her eye, as he cannot identify her hand in the charred form that was once her body. Her eyes plead with him; beg him to go, to save himself. He does not want to leave her here like this. He wants to do something to help her, but knows she is beyond help. Pain comes off her in waves, mingles with the heat from her cooked flesh.

He stares into her eyes and sees a reflection of himself. He sees who she truly is, was, and it breaks what is left of his heart. He sees her in his bedroom, hugging a bright red cushion. He sees her running down the path to meet her new-found friends. He sees her freckles in summer, little sun kisses across her cheeks, cheeks that dimple when she smiles. He sees the dark shadow left when she is no longer there. He feels her soft hair between his fingers. The love he feels for her will overwhelm him. It clings to his skin and seeps into his soul.

He can see her running through the summer garden, happy and in love.

He feels the presence behind him, pulsating under the neon orb that lights up the sky. He does not turn; he can't take his eyes from the woman. Her lips move as she tries to speak but cannot. Her mouth seizes, her lips and throat too dry. The creature moves silently to his side, places a cool hand on his shoulder. The creature tilts its head towards the woman, smiles, turns to the man.

Kier leans in close to Rhys. The cold emanates from him. As he speaks his breath brushes his skin.

'Ask,' Kier whispers, 'just ask and I can stop all of this.' His forefinger taps Rhys's chest.

At the base of the tree, the woman convulses as another wave of pain beats through her body. Slowly Rhys twists his face towards Kier. Kier shrugs light-heartedly.

The words stick in Rhys's throat but he knows they are there. They fill him with icy fear. He swallows them back down, over and over again. They are hard and sharp, cut his throat. Swallowing razorblades, but he cannot let them escape.

'Ask,' Kier whispers and suddenly Rhys knows...

Rhys throws back his head and screams.

Under the blanket on the sofa, Rhys's eyes twitch back and forth but his lips stay pressed tight.

He needs to wake up but he can't.

Kier's icy hand is on his chest, pushing him towards the darkness.

He needs to wake up but he can't.

Down the corridor in the kitchen, someone laughs.

61.

The house is quiet. Rhys pulls himself awake. Nausea fresh in the back of his throat.

It's just before dawn. He pads out onto the street in bare feet. Everything is various shades of grey, waiting for the winter sun to add its colour pallet. Nothing is out of place. There's no blood around the tree. The grass is not squashed. There's no sign a man lost his life there. No police tape. No commotion. No one doing door to door.

A bird starts to sing as Rhys walks back across the tarmac.

Rhys has a missed call from the station. The message asks him to come in for more voluntary questioning. There are details they need his help with.

He has to step over the fallen shelf in the hallway to get upstairs. A reminder of Anna's betrayal. How weak her love for him is. She trapped him, physically and mentally. He's exhausted from spending the whole night fighting.

Upstairs their bedroom door is shut tight. Fine by him. He has no desire to see her face.

The shower is hot, but not hot enough. The towel rough against his skin. He should shave, he should put on a suit, he does neither, nor does he shout goodbye as he leaves.

It's like a firing squad, except they don't put a bag over his head. He's told repeatedly he's here voluntarily and is free to leave at any time. They've moved to the interview suites. The light bulb still needs replacing. There's no air. The cheap plastic chair digs into his back. There are no tissues. No cups of coffee. He asks repeatedly if he needs a solicitor, is told repeatedly not yet. Not yet. Not yet.

Rhys can't see him but knows Divisional Superintendent Wallace is through the two-way glass. Is there a doctor there too? Rhys fights the urge to wave.

'I'd like to report a murder,' says Rhys.

'Is this a confession?' asks Jenkins. His eyes widen.

'What? No, why would I want to kill Detective Inspector Andrews?' Quinn's eyes drop to the floor.

'We are not here to discuss Detective Inspector Andrews.' A firm, flat tone. 'We are aware of your thoughts with regards to Detective Inspector Andrews and they are being looked into.'

'My thoughts?' says Rhys. 'He was murdered right in front of me. I saw it with my own eyes.' Rhys looks from Jenkins to Quinn. 'I saw it. He was murdered by Kier Finnegan.'

'Why would Kier Finnegan want to kill Andrews?' says Quinn. He clicks his pen as he speaks.

'To protect me, Andrews was... Andrews was going to kill me. He misunderstood. We should have been working together.'

'As I said, we're not here to discuss Detective Inspector Andrews,' says Jenkins, his tone rising. 'If you would like, someone can take a formal statement from you when we're finished?'

What's wrong with them? Don't they hear his words? A man – one of their own – has been murdered and he's a witness. They need to get a team out there, gather evidence. Why are they wasting time?

'What's wrong with you? I've just told you a man was murdered right in front of me. I saw who did it. Why aren't you doing anything? Why aren't you taking me seriously?' The final words shot at Quinn. Jenkins sighs deeply.

'Okay then, so you say Kier Finnegan murdered Detective Inspector Andrews?'

'Yes.'

'The same Kier Finnegan you say is your alibi the night of Alison Fleece's murder?'

'Alison Fleece?' As Rhys says the words, Jenkins slides a picture of the auburn-haired girl across the table. She was so very young. 'Yes.'

'The same Kier Finnegan that you say is also a Nosferatu after your soul?'

'Yes.' Quinn snorts. Rhys wants to reach across the table and smash his fat face into the desk.

'He's a bit of a multi-tasker, this Kier Finnegan,' says Quinn.

'You see we have a bit of a problem here, Rhys,' says Jenkins. He leans back in his chair. 'We have spoken to Mr Finnegan and he says he was at your house until around seven p.m. on the night in question, the night of Alison Fleece's murder. You arrived home and took issue with him being there, at which point he returned to his home where he was for the rest of the evening.'

'He's lying,' says Rhys.

'His lodger backs up his statement.'

'Of course he does. He's lying too, obviously.'

'Why would he lie?'

'To set me up.'

'And why would he want to set you up?'

'So I'm left with nothing. So I have no choice.'

'No choice?' says Jenkins.

'No choice but to join him.'

'Join him?'

'As a Nosferatu,' says Rhys. Quinn's eyes drop to the floor.

'I was hoping that we may have moved away from this by now, Rhys, once you'd had time to sleep on it,' says Jenkins. He straightens the brown manila file in front of him.

'Move away from what? The truth? Andrews knew, Andrews knew the truth, that's why Kier killed him.'

'I thought you said Kier killed Andrews to protect you?' Quinn goes to interject. Jenkins holds up a hand to stop him.

'He did,' says Rhys.

'Why would he protect you if he wants to kill you himself?'

'He doesn't want to kill me. Why aren't you listening?' Why aren't they listening?'

'What does he want to do then Rhys?' asks Jenkins.

'He wants to turn me into a Nosferatu, like him.' It's amazingly easy to say now, now he has accepted it. Knows it to be the truth. They can think he is crazy, he doesn't care. They just need to understand.

'So did Kier kill Andrews to protect you or to prevent the truth coming out?' says Jenkins.

'Both.'

'Two birds with one stone, eh? A lucky night for Mr Finnegan,' says Quinn. He doesn't bother to try to hide his contempt.

'If you can't take me seriously then why don't you fuck off?' says Rhys. He doesn't mean to shout but why won't they listen? Why are they all sitting laughing?

'Enough.' Jenkins raises his hands. Quinn stares hard at Rhys.

'Where were you on the second of November between eleven p.m. and seven a.m.?' A change of tack, still the same answer.

'I've already told you. I was in my car in the old lanes with Kier Finnegan,' says Rhys.

'And as I have said, he denies this,' says Jenkins.

'And as I have said, he's lying.'

'How did your police identification badge end up covered in Alison Fleece's blood in the same location as her body?' says Jenkins, swerving once more.

'I don't know.'

'You know how this works, Rhys. You'll have to do better than that.'

'I think I'm being framed,' says Rhys. Quinn shakes his head.

'By Kier Finnegan?' says Jenkins.

'Yes.'

'The Nosferatu?'

'Yes. Either him, or Anna, or Andrews, or you?' Rhys points at Quinn.

'Me? Why the hell would I want to frame you?' Jenkins ignores Quinn, continues.

'So you're saying there are several people who would want to frame you for murder?'

'Yes.'

'One of them being Detective Inspector Andrews, who you since say you have seen being murdered by one of the other people you think may be setting you up? This is all very confusing, Rhys. Then you say one of these people trying to set you up could be your wife?'

'Look, I know it seems complicated but really it isn't, and yes, I do,' says Rhys.

'The problem here, Rhys, is in order to frame you, the person responsible would either have to be very lucky and happen upon a body that had been beaten to death or... ' Jenkins tilts his head. '... beat them to death themselves. Are you saying you think your wife is capable of murder?'

'No, of course not.' That's not what he is saying at all.

'Then what?' asks Jenkins.

'I don't know. She's just not the same. Things aren't the same.'

'This isn't a marriage counselling session, Rhys. Just because you aren't getting on with your wife doesn't mean she's setting you up for murder.'

'That's not what I mean.'

'Is what you really mean that she doesn't believe what you are saying about Kier Finnegan?' Rhys is silent. 'Rhys?'

'That's correct.' The admission jams in Rhys's throat. For a moment he's back in the dream. Back in the charred landscape feeling Kier's breath on his face.

'And why do you think that could be Rhys?' says Jenkins.

'Because he hides it well. You've met him.'

'Nice bloke,' says Quinn.

'Or, could it be because what you're saying isn't true?' asks Jenkins.

'Do you think I'm capable of murder?' Jenkins does not answer. He lets the question hang.

And so it goes on, back and forth. Rhys knows how it works. They look for inconsistency in his account. Wait for him to trip himself up. He won't. What he's saying is the truth. He doesn't know how his identification was present at a murder scene but he could make a very good guess. He didn't kill Alison Fleece because he was with Kier Finnegan. Why the fuck don't they believe him? They're more than content to keep kicking him in the balls. How had his identification got there? Why would Kier Finnegan lie? What's really going on? And so on and on and on...

Finally the stalemate ends. Constable Robertson knocks on the door, whispers in Jenkins's ear. He nods.

'We'll leave it there for now, Rhys.' Jenkins rises. He does not extend his hand. 'Thank you for your help.' Liar, liar pants on fire. Jenkins is sweating, red faced, frustrated. If he would just listen, truly listen to what Rhys says he would feel so much better. 'If you could go and take a seat in the canteen, Doctor Flynn will be along shortly.'

'That'll be fucking right,' is what Rhys wants to shout, but he doesn't. He smiles.

'He's clinically insane, you know.' Rhys pushes past Quinn, out down the corridor. 'Andrews, mad as a bag of badgers, mind you, it takes one to know one...' The heavy double doors cut the sound of Quinn's voice.

Constable Robertson has been instructed to escort Rhys to the canteen. It reminds him of being a naughty boy sent to see the headmaster. Doctor? Fucking doctor. No way, no how. A doctor is the last thing he needs.

'Do you mind?' He nods to the gents as they pass. Constable Robertson shrugs, uncomfortable.

In the gents Rhys splashes cold water onto his face, looks at a reflection he doesn't recognise in the mirror. What's he going to do? He'll have to make a run for it, there's no other way. He presses his palm against the mirror. Are there any security doors between here and outside? Why can't he remember? How fast does Constable Robertson look? Can he run faster? He peeks out into the corridor.

Constable Robertson isn't there.

Rhys pushes the door a fraction more. There she is, a few feet down the corridor, bent over to retrieve something out of the bottom of the vending machine. No time to think, Rhys slips from behind the door and starts to run.

The air outside is cold on Rhys's face.

Images explode in his mind.

Andrews with the knife sticking out of his chest. Kier's contorted face. Ice cubes in a glass of gin, Jenny's soft brown hair. Harry screaming, Anna screaming, everybody screaming. Jonas Jones baby sister locked in a chiller, Cathy's swinging body. Andrews's green-eyed girl, Quinn smirking, lights flashing, Elsie crying, old photos, blood splatter, dark cupboards, floors shifting, rotten corpses, wet plastic, doors slamming, and Kier bursting into a ball of flames as Rhys twists a knife into his heart.

Don't stop. Don't stop. Don't stop. One foot in front of the other, fingers trailing the wall to keep him upright. Round a corner, round a corner. Faster, faster. Lungs bursting.

Focus, focus, focus.

He thinks of Harry's smiling face. The images settle. The road pounds beneath his feet.

He needs a place to wait. A place where he knows Kier will come. A place where he can pick his moment and strike. Kier will come for him, he's sure of that.

He needs his raincoat too, there's a second knife, the large hunting one, tucked into the pocket. He stops running, gets his bearings. He can double back to his car, that's where his raincoat is. He'll have to be fast, before they find his car. The others. Quinn's bound to send them to look for him. He needs that knife. He must have left the flick knife in his other trousers. He ignores the niggle in his brain. The one that tells him he's wearing the same trousers as yesterday.

62.

Drip. Drip. Drip.

The noise pulls Anna into consciousness. In that moment between sleep and awake, everything is okay. The drip sounds again.

She wishes Rhys would fix the tap in the en suite.

Her feet drop to the carpet. Reality twists in her stomach.

She drugged her husband.

In the fresh light of day, she's not sure that can be justified. She'd called the Divisional Superintendent, interpreted his words to mean 'drug your husband'. How would that stand up in court? Rhys will be furious.

Her head pounds. It's too hot. At the top of the stairs she stops. Afraid to go down. Afraid of what Rhys will say.

'You deserve to be afraid,' she tells herself. Slow, quiet steps. Past the pieces of shelf in the hallway, the shelf that fell under the weight of her drugged husband.

She peeks cautiously into the living room. The sofa is empty. The blanket she placed over Rhys lies crumpled on the floor. Her heartbeat quietens as she realises Rhys is not in the house. Has he gone into work already? When did Wallace call?

She heads to the kitchen. What time is it? Rhys could be with the boss right now. Yes, that boss, the one she grassed him up to. What else was she supposed to do?

The clock in the kitchen says it's well after eight. Anna reaches for her mobile. The battery is flat. Using the house phone, she calls Elsie who is more than happy for the children to stay. The pleasure in her voice grates. The coffee machine bubbles to life. The previous night's events dance in Anna's head.

Dan answered her call within minutes and arrived like Batman out of the night. She apologised until he said he'd leave if she didn't stop. He helped her move Rhys to the sofa without judgment. She told him what Rhys had said.

Dan made some quiet phone calls, muttered out of earshot. She hadn't told him the children were with Elsie.

He said he'd go and take a look around, something about procedure. She watched him through the living room window.

Behind her Rhys twitched on the sofa. She hoped he wasn't allergic to what she'd given him. His mother wasn't, it was her prescription. Dan crossed to Kier's house. The door opened. He stepped inside. He was gone a long time. Anna was on her second coffee by the time the three soft taps on the door signalled he was back.

'Nothing,' he said.

'Nothing?'

'Nope. No blood, no corpses, no sign of a struggle of any kind. I even knocked on his door, Kier Finnegan, wasn't too pleased to see me truth be told.' Anna sat a coffee on the table. 'He said our lot have already been round disturbing him first thing, for an... erm... ' He looked shifty. 'For an alibi for another case.'

'It's okay, he's told me.' Anna ran her fingers through her hair.

'Kier was even less pleased when I asked him if he'd been sneaking around the street stabbing police officers.'

'You didn't?' They both smiled.

'No. Not in so many words, but Kier said he'd been in all evening. That old guy was there, backed him up.' Dan shrugged, sipped his coffee.

'Arthur?'

'Yeah, that's the one.' Dan looked up at her, eyes lingering a fraction too long. 'It's a bit of an odd set up over there, isn't it?' He waved in the direction of Kier's house.

'What do you mean?'

'Well, an older man living with a younger one. Said he was his lodger, if you'll believe that?'

'Well as my mother always says, there's nowt so queer as folk.' They laughed as she realised what she'd said.

'From what I hear, Andrews has been moved to a hospital down south to be near his sister,' said Dan, 'which is fine. Will be a while before we can get to him, you know, carry out a full investigation into what he did. It'll probably do him good, to be with his family.' Anna nodded. She had no idea what Dan was talking about, didn't care.

They talked for hours, about nothing and everything. Dan made her smile and laugh with only a tinge of guilt.

Dan left in the small hours. He didn't want to go but said he must, had work, would have an extra report to write up now. She apologised again for phoning. He smiled, said it didn't matter. He asked if she'd like to meet him for dinner that evening? If she thought she could get away. He said it would do her good. She said yes even though she knew she shouldn't. It wouldn't mean anything, they're just old friends meeting for some food, and a laugh. God, how she needed a laugh. Plus everything would be sorted by tomorrow, Superintendent Wallace promised.

'Excellent.' He hugged her goodbye, kissed her on the forehead.

Anna watched him all the way up the street while her drugged husband lay on the sofa behind her.

63.

'A gin and tonic? Really, Rhys I'm disappointed. I thought you would have learnt by now.' Kier's voice is smooth. He slips into the seat opposite Rhys. Rhys smiles. The knife is comforting in his pocket. 'Firstly, I feel I should say I'm sorry for the other night, on reflection it was rather crude.' Kier clinks the ice cubes around in his glass. 'That does not however excuse the fact that I'm still waiting for you to say thank you.' He looks at Rhys. He'll be waiting until Hell freezes over.

Bad analogy.

Kier shrugs. 'A little petty all things considered.' Rhys studies Kier in the dim light. His skin as smooth as marble, not a blemish or line, and so pale. How does no one else see this? How can Anna not see this? How could his colleagues not see this?

'People only see what they want to see. Talking of which, that friend of yours was sniffing around your wife again last night. I use the term friend in its loosest sense.' What friend? 'Although in fairness I think she called him.' Kier smiles. 'Go on, it's killing you, ask me and I'll tell you more.' The hairs rise on the back of Rhys's neck.

'I was in all night. No one called.'

'Oh Rhys, please. She drugged you. Now why would she do that?' There's no answer to that question Rhys likes. Kier leans forward.

'She drugged you because she doesn't believe you, because she thinks you're crazy, because she wants you out of the way. Out of the way so she can play cops and robbers with that new boy, nice teeth but not much else going for him.'

Kier's lying. Anna wouldn't do that... not again. Rhys clenches his teeth. Kier's messing with his head.

'Dan Davies, that's his name.' Fuck. What the fuck? Why would Davies be at his house? Acid bites in the base of Rhys's stomach. Rhys stares hard at Kier. Only Kier's eyes smile.

He's lying. Nice try. Rhys shifts in his seat.

'Dan,' Kier rolls the word around his mouth, 'was at your house until god knows when this morning, and there you were, fast asleep. Who knows what they were getting up to right under your nose?' Kier takes a sip of his drink. Breathe deeply, let it wash over you.

'Maybe Anna would like my lifestyle, what I have to offer, seems like she would be up for any offer, other than one from you.'

In his mind, Rhys lunges across the table, stabs Kier in the heart. Stabs him in his smug face over and over again. Instead he looks away. The young boy serving behind the bar catches his eye, no knife through his neck today.

'There,' Rhys bellows across the room, 'you see him now?' Rhys points at Kier. The boy behind the bar looks away, embarrassed. He should be. Kier winces, shakes his head. He draws breath but Rhys cuts him off.

'Why are you setting me up?'

'I'm sorry?' Kier has the front to look bemused.

'Don't play all innocent. My identification at the murder scene?'

'I genuinely have no idea what you're talking about.' Is he lying again? His face is so smooth. 'Someone's setting you up for murder? Are you sure, sure you weren't out having a little practice?' He winks.

'You disgust me.'

'You can be so cruel. No wonder I felt I couldn't give you an alibi...'

'Lying to the police is a criminal offence.'

'... Couldn't say I was with you when bad things were happening, couldn't give a nice little alibi to that nice young policewoman when she called.' Rhys stares at him, hard. 'I could change my mind if it would make you happy?' Rhys waits. 'I could walk over there and tell them I was confused, that you were with me?'

'Really?'

'No. Where would be the fun in that? It really doesn't matter anyway.' Kier looks at his watch. 'Your time is almost up.'

Outside something bangs.

'Remember, remember, the fifth of November, well as good as,' says Kier. 'You certainly will.' He pushes away his glass. 'Now I know I said I'd give you a week but what's a couple of days between friends? I'm bored with this so I will have to press you for an answer.' Kier looks at Rhys. Rhys leans across the table.

'There's no way on God's green earth that I will ever say yes to what you ask.' Kier looks perplexed, crosses his arms.

'How did I know you were going to say that? I must say I'm disappointed. I credited you with more intelligence.' He sighs. 'I'm going to have to do what I hate to have to do, resort to violence.' He drops his shoulders. 'Just so we're clear, everything that happens from this moment forward, everything, is entirely your fault.'

The air around them shifts. Rhys is very cold. The knife in his pocket insignificant, like the little boy who tries to stand up to the school bully and gets his head kicked in. Real life is not like the movies.

'All you had to do was ask me and I would have taken you away from all this. Prevented what is now going to have to happen. All you ever had to do was ask.' Kier shakes his head, almost sad, if Rhys was still stupid enough to believe him capable of sorrow. 'Now we're going to have to play a game. It won't take long and I have to admit I've never lost, which doesn't bode well for you.' Kier rises. 'It's quite simple. Your refusal has deeply offended me, so I am going to slaughter your family. This will help change your mind and make me happy.' Rhys stares up at him. 'You can try and save them,' Kier leans in close, 'that's the game bit by the way. Usually when they, you, see your family in, how shall I put it, mild discomfort, you change your mind. Not only will you ask but also you will beg me to take you and not hurt them. That's the bit I like the most. The bit that makes me really happy.'

Rhys's heart pounds.

'Now, I like you, Rhys. It appears you've had a hard week so I will give you a clue. I won't start with your wife. Sound fair? The disadvantage is you have no idea where your children are, but I do. Good luck.'

And he is gone. Simple as that.

64.

Elsie sits and stares straight ahead. Sitting next to her on the small, worn sofa, Arthur takes her hand. Elsie turns and looks at him. Usually when she's with Arthur she giggles. Today she can't even smile.

Arthur had come round the day after he, they, moved in. He takes her breath away. He visits often. Makes her giggle until tears of joy run down her cheeks. But not today.

The children are upstairs, unable to hide their distress as to why Mummy asked if they could stay another night. Elsie says it's so Daddy can rest.

She knows Rhys isn't home.

She has no idea where he is.

Elsie saw the man Rhys works with pick Anna up. He wasn't in a police car. If something bad had happened they would've sent a police car.

Arthur was hesitant to stay, once he knew the children were here. He loitered on the doorstep, looked back towards his house. Elsie persuaded him in with the tale of cake Harry and she spent the afternoon making. They sit now, the two of them. The electric fire is high. Empty cake plates and teacups sit on the table in front of them. They are warmed by the image of Harry's proud face. Elsie will drift off soon. Upstairs the children play. She starts to relax...

A thump on the front door wakes her instantly. A thump held in her memories for fifty years. Her heart pounds. Arthur's face shows only fear as he rises. His hand on the latch, he turns to her.

'I'm sorry.' He need say no more.

Kier stands on the step. His face furrows with rage.

'We really don't have time for this, Arthur,' he says. Elsie rises, curses her lack of speed. Kier turns his attention to her, studies her as a scientist would an experiment. With curiosity, he waits for her to reach Arthur's side.

'You're not welcome here.' Her hand reaches for Arthur's arm. Does he step deliberately out of reach? 'You are not welcome in my home. I will not invite you in.'

'Ooops,' says Kier. He steps over the threshold. 'Too late.'

His shadow cast by the fire fills the whole room. The exact same shadow as was cast all those years ago.

'Not the exact same shadow surely. That would be boring.' Kier's distain is clear as he inspects the room. 'This...' He waggles a finger at Arthur and Elsie. '... is all very touching but it's over.' He extends a hand to Arthur. 'We need to leave. We have urgent business to attend to.' He leans in close. 'As the great detective himself would say, "the game's afoot".' The colour drains from Arthur's face. His skin ages, wrinkles before Elsie's eyes. Kier turns to her. 'This bit always makes him sad. He's not a massive fan of the game.' Elsie has no idea what he's talking about. She needs him out of her home. Away from all of them. It's him, she's never been more sure. She knows it's him. Her palms sweat.

'I know who you are.' Is she shouting? 'I know what you are,' she repeats, shuffling to the coffee table. Arthur hasn't moved a muscle since Kier entered the room. He stares straight ahead, unblinking. Elsie lifts the newspaper. Where the hell is it? The photograph Rhys showed her? 'I have it here, the proof. I'll find it, take it to the police. They'll believe me.'

'Oh please.' Kier holds up his hand. 'This is too pathetic to watch. The police will believe what?' He bends down. They are face to face. 'Oh look, detective. This is a picture from nineteen blah blah blah that shows a nasty Nosferatu? Oh no wait, hang on, I can't even find it.' He laughs. The power blows the hair back off her face. 'They won't, of course, just think you are some mad, old bitch,' emphasis heavy on the last word, 'there to defend your crazy neighbour because you think of him like the son you were never able to produce?' It's as if he's physically slapped her. His eyes dance. 'They will think you're as crazy as they think he is, and they won't be far wrong now, will they?' He straightens up, adjusts his cuff. 'What is it with you and the type of men you attract?' He glances over his shoulder at Arthur. 'No offence. Now sit down.' He taps Elsie on the shoulder. She falls. Winded. Gasps on the sofa. Arthur comes to life as Kier touches her.

'No,' says Arthur. He turns towards them. 'No.' Kier's face contorts as he ponders for a moment. Arthur reaches out towards him.

Kier's face explodes with rage. He turns and slams his fist into the old man's chest. The force sends Arthur sprawling back across the room. He hits the small bookcase. Books crash down and scatter around him. The sound of the wind being knocked from him is loud. He's too still. Elsie can't move. Can't get up to him to help.

'He struggles to know his place, what with all these twenty-first century new man ideals kicking about.' Kier smiles. 'But then we all knew this... ' His finger flicks again from Elsie to Arthur. '...would never end well.' He sits down next to her on the sofa. They both look at the motionless body of Arthur. 'He'll be fine.' Kier twists to look at her. 'Now, give me the children.'

'They aren't here.' Somehow Elsie manages to keep the tremble from her voice.

'Oh please.' He sighs. 'Okay, I'll play along. Where are they?' He's mocking her – they both know it. Where is Rhys? Where is Anna? Where is anyone? How can she get to the phone? How can she get him out of the house, buy some time? Thought upon thought compound, her brain will explode. She reaches for a thread and pulls.

'They're with friends. You know Anna. She doesn't like me, never has. She doesn't trust me with them.'

'Let's suppose I believe you, which I don't, how do I persuade you to tell me where they are?'

Something bumps upstairs.

Air is sucked from the room.

A smile slowly spreads across Kier's face. 'See,' he says, 'that's the trouble with kids these days, they struggle so much to be quiet. They really should learn it's best to be seen and not heard.'

'You leave them be,' Elsie reaches out, takes hold of his sleeve. She can't, won't let him near the children. Anything but the children. Anything. Kier snarls.

'What's it worth?' He's playing with her the way a cat plays with a mouse; she knows it but doesn't care, anything but the children. He crushes her without even moving.

In her head, she urges the children to run. To climb out of the window and scurry into the night, find safety. She can't move, not one muscle. She's paralysed but fully aware. Kier's shadow dances around the room.

'The problem with you, Elsie...' His words are far away. '... Is that you've always been so much more trouble than you're actually worth.' His shadow casts huge shapes all over the walls.

Time stands still.

It is the day Fredrick disappeared. There has been nothing in between. Nothing since his final goodbye. Kier's shadow looms over her, then comes down close, wraps her in its arms. Elsie feels his lips against her thin skin. She looks over his shoulder. Through the shadows, she sees Arthur. He anchors her in the here and now. Anchors her in all the wonderful, yet untimely, insignificant things she's done as Kier let her dance in the sunlight between his shadows.

She wills Arthur to wake up, help the children. He does not move.

There is no pain, which is strange. A fuzzy black circle starts at the edge of her vision and slowly pulls inwards, turns everything dark. There's the sensation of an ice-cold hand on the side of her face. No pain. No nothing.

Then Arthur's eyes open. In the last moment, they open and lock with hers. It is beautiful and perfect and final.

As everything turns black, she swears she hears him say, "I love you".

65.

Where the hell is Anna? Rhys rings her phone all the way home. She doesn't pick up. Why?

What did Kier mean, he won't start with Anna? They'll all be together, Anna and the children. Anna will fight. Rhys is sure of that. He wonders when the reality will hit her, when she'll realise he was right all along. He wishes he felt smug, but he doesn't he feels angry. And afraid.

Why hadn't he stabbed Kier there and then, while he had the chance? Why hadn't he done that? He hits his forehead with his palm. Kier is right, if anything happens to the kids he'll blame himself. Blame himself for not pushing the steel blade through flesh.

Rhys stops outside his front door. The house is dark and silent. The house is never dark and silent.

Across the street Kier's house is dark. The whole street is dark. Too dark. Too silent.

Rhys opens the front door. The only sound is his heart as it hammers in his chest. He reaches for the switch; the hall is flooded with light. The only thing out of place is the shelf that fell the night before. It's propped on its side waiting to be fixed.

Still there's no sound.

He turns to the living room. The door's closed. He slides the knife out of his pocket. He can feel his heartbeat pulse in his throat as he pushes the door slowly open. The image of the charred woman's body flashes through his mind. Eddie Reynolds twitches, beaten with a hammer. Cathy slowly swings. Alison, the girl without a face. He shakes his head. Screws his eyes up tight. He opens them slowly, flicks the light switch. He wants to scream with terror as he sees... nothing.

The room is empty.

He repeats the process. Grows more confident with each room. He quickly covers downstairs, turns on every lamp and light as he goes. Illuminates the house. Upstairs, he does the same. Light after light goes on as he looks in every corner. His heartbeat grows faster every time he pushes a door open, every time he checks inside a wardrobe. His mind races ahead to the horror he could face, yet blocks it out. He needs to concentrate, needs to think. He moves faster as he finds nothing after nothing.

His mobile shrills in the silence. He jumps, swears.

'Where are you, you bastard?... Hello?... Anna, where the hell are you?... What? Why? With whom?... Stop, no I don't need to know that... I can tell you later. Where are the kids?... Okay... Listen, I need you to come back here straight away... Back home, of course.' He heads down the stairs. 'It's the kids. He said he's going to hurt the kids.'

Anna feels the colour drain from her face as she hangs up. Dan, fork of steak suspended mid air, looks at her.

'He answered. He's at home,' she says.

'That's a good thing, right?' Dan lowers the fork back to his plate, food untouched.

'I don't know.' She doesn't know.

Rhys hasn't called her all day. DCI Jenkins called, said Rhys had left the station 'prior to the resolution of their session', whatever the hell that meant. She was to call him as soon as Rhys got in touch. She should've stayed at home. DCI Jenkins told her to stay at home.

'I think we should leave.' Anna reaches for her coat as she speaks. 'We shouldn't have come here. I shouldn't have come here.' She holds Dan's eye. 'Rhys said something about someone being after the kids.' Dan rises, signals for the bill.

'Not this Kier Finnegan stuff again?' Anna shrugs.

'I don't think it's fair for Elsie to have to deal with it, that's all.' Dan nods. 'I need to be there.'

'Shall I come with you?'

'No. Yes. I'll need a lift.'

It's suddenly hard to breathe. What the hell is she going to find when she gets home? A nasty feeling sits in the base of her stomach. 'If something bad happens Anna Morgan,' she tells herself as they head to the car, 'it will be your fault, you should have been there for them all, not here doing this.'

66.

Rhys hammers on the front door, then waits. Paces. He knows it'll take Elsie a while to answer. This is too long. He bangs again.

'Elsie. Harry. Louise?' No answer.

Elsie will send one of the kids. They should've opened the door by now.

Is she being cautious, afraid? He cups his hands, presses his face against the front window. Bloody net curtains. All he sees is the glow of the electric fire, a fuzzy orange orb. No movement. He would pick up on that. He steps back, looks at the upstairs windows. A light is on, faint, but there. A lamp, perhaps a nightlight? He hammers on the door again. There's no time for this. He needs to be in there now. Anna won't phone Elsie, won't have told her about Andrews, what happened. Elsie will still be cautious. She knows what lurks out here.

Rhys studies the front door. Could he kick it in? It's a lot harder to do than it looks, especially with external doors. This one is new, bought by a lady who likes to feel secure. Rhys heads round the back.

The side gate is locked but easy to climb as adrenaline hammers through his veins. The garden is neat, completely paved, a few easy to manage flowerpots. Harry earns pocket money pulling the weeds from the cracks in the patio during summer. The kitchen is dark. The light from the fire in the front room seeps through. He tries the back door handle. To his amazement it opens.

'Harry?' No answer. 'Louise?' Rhys steps into the small, warm kitchen. Half a Victoria sponge sits on the work surface. Its top slopes, one side significantly lower than the other. Through the doorway, he sees into the front room. There are books all over the floor. The bookcase looks like something has hit it hard, the books like someone has kicked them as they passed through to the kitchen. He steps over them into the room.

That's when he sees her, slumped forward on the sofa, her head nearly on her knees.

'Elsie!' Rhys runs, lifts her upright. Her eyes are wide open, staring, her mouth set in a silent scream. He shakes her hard, shouts her name. Tears choke their way up and out of his eyes. Her skin is cold and grey. She looks different, not like herself at all. Her head lolls back and he sees them. Two small puncture wounds on the side of her neck.

'I'll kill you,' Rhys screams. 'I will kill you.' Elsie's head drops forward again, heavy on his shoulder, her hair soft against his cheek. The sob escapes before he can stop it.

Gently, he lays her down on the sofa. He desperately wants to shut her eyes but knows it will further contaminate a crime scene he's already destroyed.

Where are the children?

Where the fuck are the children?

He does not think. If he does the fear will paralyse him. Rhys runs up the stairs, shouts their names.

Elsie's house is one of the smallest on the street. They have often discussed how every house is different, all thrown together to make a ramshackle kind of place. Rhys likes that, likes that no one else has a house the same as his. No one can sit and wonder where he has placed his furniture in a mirror image of their own home. There are two bedrooms. Both doors are wide open. The smaller back room is where Harry sleeps. A dinosaur battle is well underway, but abandoned. The front bedroom was Elsie's. Now Louise's overnight bag lies open on the bed, a magazine showing some boy band open at its side. There's no sign of them in either room. Rhys pulls out his mobile, dials.

'Hello, ambulance please...' As he starts to give the address he looks up and out of the window. He can clearly see his own home from up here. It glows in all the light he's turned on. Something moves in an upstairs window. The phone drops from his hand. The tiny voice still speaks to him from the carpet.

'Harry?' Rhys steps close to the window. It is Harry. His small face terrified as he stares across at Rhys, his hands press against the glass. It's not possible. Rhys has just been there, the house was empty. A shadow moves behind Harry. A twisted, smiling face rushes forward, presses its grimace against the glass. The speed of the movement makes Harry cry out. He jumps. The twisted face steps back, straightens himself, waves at Rhys.

The face of Kier Finnegan.

67.

In reality it takes two minutes for Rhys to get from the window in Elsie's house to his own bedroom door. It feels like hours. Each second drags out, each second his children are alone with the creature. Rhys's legs pump fast. Not fast enough. His heart feels like it will tear through his chest. The front door to his house is open. Rhys crashes in. The man in the front room catches his eye. Arthur looks up from the sofa. A long, sad look.

'You bastard.' Rhys breathes as he takes the stairs two at a time.

Rhys is in his bedroom doorway, gasping for breath, hands deep in the pockets of his raincoat. Kier stands in the middle of the bed, a stance wide and sure.

'I know what you're thinking, all a little melodramatic,' says Kier, shrugging. 'What can I say?' Rhys doesn't look at him. He can't. He can't take his eyes off Harry. Kier holds Harry tight around the throat, suspending him off the ground at arm's length. The knife in Kier's other hand catches the light. Rhys's eyes flick to it. Kier sneers. 'Nice isn't it?' he nods towards the knife. Rhys chances another look. It's his flick knife. How's that possible? 'That's the problem with carrying a weapon, Rhys. It can so easily be turned against you. Or those you love.'

'Let him go,' says Rhys. Kier laughs. Harry pulls futilely against Kier's fingers, fights to find a way to let oxygen in.

'Oh okay,' says Kier. Harry's eyes start to roll as the pressure around his throat becomes too much.

'Please.' There's desperation in Rhys's voice but he doesn't care. 'Please, I'm begging you, let him go.' Rhys steps towards them. Kier does not move, just tightens his grip around Harry's throat.

'Then ask,' says Kier and for a moment Rhys is in the dream. His stomach drops. He feels like he is falling. The dream and reality spliced hurriedly together like a bad piece of film. 'Ask to join me and all of this will be over.' Kier's voice sounds in his ear and miles away. Rhys looks at Harry. His face is turning a shade of purple. What choice does he have? Is it really going to end like this?

'Can I join you?' It's barely a whisper. No ceremony. No grand gesture. It's enough. Kier's eyes lock with his. Rhys steps towards them. This time Kier's move is to begin to lower Harry. Rhys steps up onto the bed. The ground falls away around them. The edges of colour start to fade. Rhys is inches away now. Not for one second does he break eye contact with Kier. He feels the creature drop Harry. Feels Harry's small hands as they grasp his leg. Kier face starts to change, to ripple as a thousand tiny creatures scurry under his skin. He pulls back his top lip to reveal his long white incisors. The grimace grows from within. Kier closes his eyes, throws back his head ready to strike. It's a split second but it's all Rhys needs. All he's been waiting for. He pulls the hunting knife out of his pocket, lifts it to strike.

Something somewhere crashes.

Kier's eyes fly open.

They pull up outside the house. Anna didn't want Dan here, but had no other way to get home. Arthur limps out of the front door, the look on his face tells her she will be glad Dan is with her.

'Please come quickly,' says Arthur. He's not the calm, composed man she has previously met. Every step seems to cause him great pain. 'I was with Elsie. She felt unwell so I said I would bring the children home. We were in the front room playing when he crashes in ranting like a madman and drags them upstairs. I can't get up there you see.' He gestures to his foot. 'But there was banging and shouting and now it's gone terribly quiet.'

'Who?' asks Dan. They both know the answer.

'Rhys,' says Arthur. Dan pulls out his phone. Anna runs up the stairs.

She reaches the bedroom door, shoves it open – the handle hits the wall with a loud crack. Her heart freezes, drops through the floor.

Rhys stands in the middle of the bed, a hunting knife held fist down in a plunging motion. Rhys's words from the previous night ring in her mind – 'He killed Andrews, right in front of me, with a hunting knife straight through his heart'. The sound of the bedroom door hitting the wall pulls Rhys's attention to her. He snaps out of a trance. Blinks his eyes rapidly. Searches the room. His head flicks back to look for something that he thinks is in front of him.

What glues her to the spot is Harry. He clings to his father's leg in the direct line of where the plunging motion would've ended had she been a second later and Rhys had begun.

'No!' Rhys roars, primal, animal. He swerves from the bed to the window and back again. The blade of the knife jabs and waves in the air. Harry flows behind him like a piece of ribbon blown loose at the fair.

'Harry, come to me!' Anna cries. She crouches down, arms wide. Harry shakes his head, clings tight to his father's legs. His father, motionless once more in the centre of the bed.

'No!' Rhys roars again. Drives the knife down to his side and back again. Swift, sharp movements, each time the blade inches from Harry's face.

'Please!' Anna is screaming too. 'Harry, please come to me!' Harry shakes his head again, buries his face in his father's leg.

'You.' Rhys turns his wrath on her. 'What have you done?' His eyes are cold and hard. Nothing there of the man she knows. 'I was this close.' He lifts his empty hand, gestures millilitres. 'This close and it would all have been over. What have you done?'

He screams then. Loud and wild, Anna brings her hands up to her ears. She watches as Rhys falls to his knees, hugs Harry, his small body behind the fisted knife. He clings to his father just as tight.

Then Rhys starts to cry. And laugh.

'You think you've won?' Rhys screams. 'No chance. Never. I will kill you.' To her over Harry's shoulder. 'What have you done?' Distant sirens sound. This makes Rhys laugh harder, between his wretched sobs. 'Too late!' He screams. 'Far too late.'

Anna is frozen in the doorway. She flicks her eyes left, sees Louise. Louise stands with her back pressed flat against the wall, a small pool of urine at her feet. Anna gestures urgently for her to come over. Anna doesn't take her eyes from Rhys. From the knife so near her baby. Louise doesn't move a muscle, doesn't make a sound.

The sirens grow louder. Anna holds her breath, prays a silent mantra, wills them to hurry.

'Too late!' Rhys shouts again and again and again. A single tear rolls down Anna's cheek. He is right. They are far too late.

68.

The woman is still there somewhere, under the piles of ash that blow gently on the breeze. More than that, he can still feel the love for her, the love that she represents. There is nothing here now. Nothing more than black dust that dances on the wind. Light, almost magical around the base of the great tree.

He's alone. He knows he won't be for long.

He stands high up on what he suspects is a hillside, looks down at the land below. There's a strange feeling of calm in him today, a quiet resignation of what's to come. Resignation and sadness. Not acceptance. There will never be acceptance.

He appears from nowhere, the creature with his fiery blond hair and pale complexion. He's untouched by the dark, burnt surroundings. The dust that settles on everything doesn't touch him, would not dare. Rhys knew he would come as soon as the sky started to darken, deep grey swirls, like a black and white photocopy of a Van Gogh masterpiece. The temperature drops. The lightning strobes begin. Rhys blinks and holds up his arm as a shield. Black, white, then black again.

The creature is silent as he steps towards Rhys, his hand outstretched. Rhys knows this is how it has to be. The creature's hand is cold as he takes it, but the embrace is strong. Everything around them starts to shake, violent and angry. The vast black pillars that have torn through the once-beautiful landscape vibrate in rage. Are they trying to shake off this creature, this thing?

Rhys closes his eyes tight but he can still see their faces, Anna, Louise, Harry, Elsie, Jenny. They overlap, distort. They mould together and become the woman in the garden. The woman who's suffered because of him and is now at peace. They will all be at peace. It doesn't matter what happens to him as long as they are at peace.

The creature is amused by this. It silently mocks him, laughs deep down.

Rhys is cold to his core. Has he made a terrible mistake? Perhaps they are not safe at all only he's no longer able to protect them.

Rhys realises then that they're moving. They shoot upward through the sky, scream towards the intense bright light. Rhys screws his eyes tight shut. Pain explodes in his head. Pain of the situation. Pain of the speed of movement. The creature's laughter vibrates through them both.

Rhys dares a glance down. The land beneath them is black. How green and luscious it used to be catches in his mind's eye for just a moment. Then it's gone. Was it ever there?

The landscape starts to burn. Intense fire destroying everything that is left. Rhys cannot remember if the fire has just started or has always been there. He cannot remember their faces or whose faces it is he's trying to remember. He can't remember ever feeling afraid. Rhys is laughing before he realises it. He looks up into the creature's bright blue eyes.

They laugh together and Rhys feels complete.

69.

He really is a naughty little boy.

It's easy to move amongst them with all the commotion. It doesn't take the crowds long to gather. Voyeurs of someone else's misery. Blue flashing lights pull them out into the night. Too many people too close together. But he needs to get near, needs to see. He pulls his cap down low, sneaks as close as he dares.

What's happening in the house? What she's done to him? Mother. Anna. Mother? He giggles. Someone looks. He pushes the naughty little thought away. They're not the same. Anna is much better than Mother could hope to be. Yet they are the same. They are exactly the same.

He sees Anna through the open front door, a brief glimpse of her in the hallway. She talks with a policewoman, tries to push her way past. Mustn't let the policewoman see him. He takes a step back, knocks into a fat man in a tracksuit.

Inside the house someone is screaming. Rhys is screaming.

He giggles. The fat man looks.

'What?' he says without thinking. The anger. It's always the anger. Too many people. Naughty little boy. He should leave. He wants to look at her for a moment longer. The policewoman's looking. Time to leave.

Further down the street an old lady is brought out of her house. She's very still and pale. She's rushed away in an ambulance. The crowd move like a wave in her direction. He steps back. People, people everywhere. Too many people. He retreats back to his hiding place.

70.

The ambulance felt like it took forever to arrive. Rhys's screaming feels like it could last a lifetime.

The police arrived first. Anna was removed from the bedroom. The authority of the police in their uniforms gave her something to hold onto.

'Please Mrs Morgan, your son will be fine. Please go downstairs, let us do our jobs.'

Anna sat on the couch and hugged Louise, Louise who was ridged with fear. Louise who didn't hug her back. They listened to the thumps and screams above. Anna hadn't realised there was a Constable at the door to the front room, until Harry started to scream too, and she tried to leave to get back upstairs, to get to her baby.

'Please, Mrs Morgan, if you could stay in the front room.'

'But that's my son?' It was non-negotiable.

More police arrived.

Harry was bought to the door of the front room, but he wouldn't come in. His neck was purple and swollen. He croaked for his dad. He croaked at Anna for not believing them, for scaring the Nosferatu away. He croaked that he hated her, would never forgive her. A large female Constable took Harry into another room.

Then the ambulances start to arrive.

'Anna. Anna, please!' Rhys begs as they bring him downstairs, hands cuffed behind his back. He struggles against the paramedics, against the police. He writhes and throws himself against the wall. Someone shouts to call ahead to the hospital.

'Anna, please don't do this. Don't do this to me.' Rhys cries now. Snot and tears pour down his face. 'Anna please.' Harry breaks through from somewhere. Clings to Rhys. He croaks he loves him, joins in the words to Anna that she's wrong. What she's doing is wrong. She has to stop them taking Rhys away. The large female Constable comes and lifts Harry, who kicks and screams all the way back to the kitchen.

'Louise!' Rhys shouts. Anna hadn't noticed Louise come to the door of the front room. Rhys tries to lunge towards her. The policemen hold him firm. 'Louise, it will be okay.' Rhys fights for eye contact. There is a small movement in the veneer of Louise's face. 'I promise it will all be okay. You don't need to be afraid.' Anna wants to shout that they are all afraid, petrified and it's Rhys's fault.

The sight of an ambulance through the open front door makes Rhys shout louder.

'Elsie. Where's Elsie?' He swivels his head back and forth. It's the only part of him left free to move.

'She didn't make it Rhys,' says Anna. The words sound like someone else is saying them. They had taken Elsie in the first ambulance, her body at least.

'Of course she didn't make it. He killed her!' Rhys shouts. 'Like he was going to kill you, the children. Like he will kill you, like he will kill the children if you don't listen to me, if you don't let me stop him.' From the dark street dozens of pairs of eyes peer at them.

'Enough,' says a Constable Anna doesn't recognise.

'She had a massive heart attack, Rhys,' says Anna. Anna doesn't know how she knows this. Someone must have told her. Everything feels like a dream.

'No. No she didn't. Check her neck, check her neck. He killed her I'm telling you, he killed her. Kier Finnegan killed her and no one is listening.' Rhys twists to look through the open front door at Kier's house, desperate. His words muddle as they dash out. 'Look under his house, go on. It's where he keeps his daughter. He told me, he told me that that night...' Anna turns away. She can take no more. Where does Rhys get these things from?

Across the road, Anna sees Arthur stand in his front doorway. She raises a hand. He smiles sadly back.

As they lift him towards the ambulance, Rhys starts to scream.

Slowly, Anna shuts the front door, the sound of Rhys's screaming still ringing in her ears. She pads back to the kitchen. Harry gets up as she enters, says,

'I hate you.' He pushes past her and stomps upstairs.

71.

He didn't think he nodded off but he must have because the noise causes him to wake. He isn't surprised. Leaning against a tree in the cold is more comfortable than many of the places he has slept over the years. The foliage keeps the frost out.

The street is deathly quiet. How long has he been asleep? No sounds, no police lights, no commotion. Anna's house is dark. He giggles.

But there is the sound. There's the sound of footsteps on gravel. Footsteps that crunch up the path past his hiding place towards the front door behind him. He can only see a pair of smart polished shoes. He twists round, ducks into the bushes. The shoes stop at the front door. An orange pool of light spills out as it's opened.

In the bushes he doesn't hold his breath for fear of being caught. He's not afraid of being caught hiding in a bush. He isn't sure if he's afraid of anything anymore. Nothing is more frightening than what he's already endured and he put an end to that. He giggles, remembers the sensation of the hammer against Strong Hands's bones.

'Perhaps you should be afraid.' The voice is so close at first he thinks he imagines it. The feeling of breath continues next to his ear. 'Because I really don't like finding people lurking in my garden, especially people like you.' He turns slowly, looks into the most piercing blue eyes he has ever seen. They are set in a pale white face, haloed with fire-blond hair. The creature tilts its head to one side, shakes it slowly. 'You really have been a very naughty little boy.'

The vile young man may have screamed he can't be sure. A silent scream that lasts a very long time.

72.

It was definitely a date. Quinn was sure of it. He'd left no room for misunderstanding. No two ways to interpret it, but obviously she had. Constable Chantelle Watts had lost interest the second her friends walked into the pub, the second they mentioned a firework display.

'You don't mind if I go do you?' A flutter of those eyelashes. No offer for him to go too. No offer to pay for half of dinner.

Quinn kicks at a can of beer left upright on the curb. Why the hell can't people use bins? Somewhere in his pocket, *God Save the Queen* begins to play.

'What?' It's late. He's pissed off.

'Detective Inspector.'

'Sir?'

There's another body.

Only one.

Quinn notes the location even though it's somewhere he's already been. He alters his route, wonders if soon there'll be anyone left alive in this town.

Detective Chief Inspector Alec Jenkins is waiting as Quinn arrives. Quinn is glad. Everything feels like it's spiralling out of control.

'Get a grip, Quinn,' he says as he tramples across the gravel. They're back at the old cottage, the 'elephant's graveyard' as it has been nicknamed. What the fuck is a body doing here? For one horrible second Quinn wonders if they missed something, the first time round. Not possible, surely?

'Pat.' Jenkins extends a clammy hand. His face is red, sweaty. 'You're not going to believe this.' Jenkins shakes his red face within the white boiler suit hood.

Winters appears in the doorway behind Jenkins. He walks away from the house. Takes deep gasps of air. Leans against a nearby tree. Quinn should be glad, Winters looks traumatised. Instead Quinn's stomach sinks even lower.

Around them the CSI team is already in place. Someone jokes it was hardly worth them taking down the lights, falls silent as the Detective Chief Inspector catches his eye. Above them, the ramshackle cottage's dark, dead eyes stare down, unblinking and cruel.

'You sent a team back to the cottage, right?' Quinn nods. That feels like a lifetime ago.

'Yes, sir. Once we identified Jonas Jones Junior as the son of the woman murdered here. He's our number one suspect. We wanted to cover all bases.' Jenkins nods for Quinn to follow him inside.

'Brace yourself,' says Jenkins. He isn't joking.

There's a smell in the air as they step into the hallway, Quinn sniffs a couple of times, until he realises what it is. The tang found in a butchers shop. His feet slow down as he approaches the door to the living room. He stops. Stands side by side with Jenkins. Closes his eyes and turns, opens then to look into the room.

'Holy shit,' says Quinn. His hand rises to his mouth involuntarily as it fills with warm bile. Something in his stomach convulses in a way it hasn't for a very long time.

A man sits in a chair in the centre of the room. A young man. His head lolls back on the chair edge. His throat gapes open. A deep black slash grins at them in a way his mouth no longer can. His wide eyes stare blankly at a spot on the ceiling. Sandy blond hair, close shaven. His once white T-shirt is soaked a deep crimson. So is the top of his jeans. And the padding of the chair he sits on. His right hand rests in his lap, fingers loose around the handle of the long sharp knife, its blade dulled with thick, congealing blood. His other arm flops outwards. His open hand has dropped what looks to be a lock of hair. A lock of hair stuck in the pool of blood at his feet.

There are glass jars broken all over the floor. They look thrown rather than dropped. Blood red on the inside and out. Some of the larger glass fragments hold bloody pools. Some have dried, look like they have been painted and left in the sun.

The walls are soaked in blood. There are circular stains on the walls, a pattern not on sale in any shop. The only way Quinn can described them, and he will many times in the pub for weeks to come, is as if water bombs of blood have been thrown at the walls. The whole room is various shades of deep red. Colours that all bow down to their King who sits frozen in the centre.

The metal tang settles in the back of Quinn's throat.

Quinn is no blood splatter expert, far from it. He once attended a road traffic accident where a mother of two was pierced through the jugular on impact. Blood sprayed ten metres down the road as her own body pumped her life away. All she could do was watch in horror and betrayal.

The man before them knew exactly where to strike.

They can go no further until CSI have finished. Quinn pulls on his professional face.

'Jonas? It's got to be, hasn't it?' says Quinn. Jenkins nods slowly. They've all seen the A4 photograph.

'First impressions seem to suggest that. He's the right age.' Young. 'The right build.' Muscular. 'He seems to match the description from the hospital. Plus we know this is where he grew up, probably where it all began. Still waiting for a positive ID.'

'But what... how?' Quinn runs a finger across his own throat. 'Did he do that to himself?' He looks at Jenkins who shrugs. 'Bollocks. I don't believe it.'

'Winters' initial thoughts are yes.'

'What the fuck? How does someone slit their own throat? Why does someone slit their own throat?' This doesn't make sense. Nothing quite makes sense. This is something he's never heard of, let alone seen.

'With a very sharp knife and a lot of loose screws apparently,' says Jenkins. 'Again we don't want to speculate. But look, look at the scene. No footprints. No sign of anyone else being here when...' Both men scan the room.

'Bollocks,' say Quinn again. There must be. He can see there isn't. 'What about all this other... stuff?' Quinn points to the carpet of smashed glass and blood. So much blood.

'I don't know,' say Jenkins, unable to fully hide his frustration. Quinn knows they are alike in many ways. Need instant answers. Don't like being kept out. Don't like it when science and analysis have to help produce the answers. Have to go first. 'Looks like it could have been thrown, but, well you can see as much as I've been able to.'

'Why now?' says Quinn.

'Maybe he got wind we were getting close, that he was about to have to spend his life behind bars.' Jenkins shrugs again. 'Maybe something finally snapped in that dark mind of his. That's one for the head people.'

'Once they've finished with Rhys,' says Quinn. Jenkins almost smiles. They stand for a moment, both looking into a black hole of humanity. A kind of conclusion but with none of the answers.

'There's a lot of blood,' says Quinn, 'a heck of a lot of blood.' Jenkins just nods.

Two women who look as fragile as birds pick their way inch by inch through the carnage. They bag and swab in silence. Chosen, Quinn imagines, for their tiny feet and delicate nature as much as the strength of their stomachs. Quinn turns away from the room. His skin is sticky. Jenkins gestures for them to head out. Breathe some air not heavy with blood.

Outside it's cool. The night even darker. Quinn lights a cigarette. No one complains. It annoys him if this is how it's going to end. Which it probably is. No glory, although Jenkins will dress it up as such. Great police work leads to villain taking his own life as the net closes in. Smiling faces in pressed uniforms on the front page of the local paper, maybe even the nationals. He grinds the cigarette end into the dirt. Someone slitting their own throat though, Quinn has never heard anything quite as dark. It makes him feel very uncomfortable. Like everything he believes and knows has shifted slightly out of kilter.

He calls Chantelle Watts.

She doesn't answer.

73.

Rhys's eyes are glued shut. Someone has taken sand paper to his throat. Weights have been tied to his limbs.

The world is dark for a long, long time.

Is he dead?

He sees himself standing in a cold, empty space. Why is his mind so empty, so blank?

A pinprick of light appears. His body is thawing out. The weight starts to lift. The throbbing pain begins. He can feel something soft beneath his back. He manages to peel an eye open. A room he doesn't recognise, a room in shadow. He blinks. Everything is still blurred. Where is he? Is this his shroud?

Endless time crawls past.

His body is stiff and slow. Shadows form memories. He was so close. So close he could taste the dust of Kier's skin. One second more, that was all he needed, one second more.

He moves his fingers and his toes. The feeling comes back slowly. Faces from before, faces from the house seep back into his mind. He remembers hugging Harry close, refusing to let him go. Then they all arrived. Penned him into a corner like an animal. Rhys had shouted for a long time.

They took him from his house, heads shaking, still refusing to listen.

They took him from his house! That means they're alone, unprotected. He wants to scream but his lips won't move. His mouth's too dry.

Rhys understands with clarity. There's no point trying to explain. No point trying to make them understand. They've made their position clear. All of them. Anna. Quinn. Davies. Jenkins. The only answer is to get out of here, wherever here is. He needs to get to Kier, finish what has started. Kier will be asleep now – it's daytime, right? It's hard to tell in this gloomy room. All Rhys has to do is get into Kier's house. Breaking and entering will be frowned upon, but as part of the overall picture it isn't so bad. Kier is vulnerable now. Once dark falls that will not be so. He will be strong. He will be angry. A dog someone has spent all day poking. A wasp released after a day trapped under a glass.

Rhys shoves off the heavy blanket. The effort of forcing his weighted limbs into an upright position makes him want to cry out. His head is submerged. Liquid sloshes between his ears. It's hard to catch his breath. He uses all his willpower to push himself off the bed. He moves too quickly. His legs buckle. He crashes to the floor.

The light in the room is dazzling as they all rush in.

74.

'Your husband's very sick Mrs Morgan. It's never an easy thing to deal with.' Anna can't decide if the words make her want to cry with relief or despair. She watches her own life from inside a bubble.

She's not slept, not one wink. She sat in the living room, stared at the blank wall. She was so angry for most of the time. So angry she wanted to charge to the police station, or the hospital or wherever Rhys was and shake him by the throat until his neck was bruised and torn. Make him so afraid he'd wet himself.

She remembers someone, one of the policewomen, saying Rhys was being taken somewhere he could be helped. She remembers one of the policemen saying he was being taken somewhere he couldn't hurt them.

They wanted to take Harry to the hospital but he screamed and screamed until he was sick. The police called a doctor to come to the house, at least that's who Anna thinks it was. She was nice. Calmed Harry down. Looked at his throat, told them all everything would be okay. Harry eventually cried himself to sleep. Anna carried him to bed. Hot and heavy, and damp with tears. Anna cried herself as she stroked his bruised neck. What the hell happened in there? What had Rhys done? When will everyone stop screaming for long enough to tell her?

Everyone apart from Louise. Louise hadn't spoken a single word. Hadn't cried a single tear. She sat. Unresponsive until she was told to go to bed. She did. She lay and stared at the ceiling. The doctor said that's normal.

Anna doesn't know what's normal is anymore.

By dawn, Anna feels a great sense of sorrow for Rhys. For herself. Most of all for her children.

'Your husband is very sick. Mrs Morgan. It's never an easy thing for anyone to have to deal with.' The head of psychiatry, or someone like that's words repeat from far away. They all sit at the kitchen table.

'But why, how, why him?' says Anna. She knows she gabbles, tries to pull herself together. The children both sit silently at the kitchen table. 'What I mean is, why has this happened now?'

'Is there any family history?' asks the possible head of psychiatry. Anna shrugs. Rhys's mum hanged from the banisters in a cheap council house? His father smashing someone's face into the pavement over and over again? His sister walking out and never coming back? The list is too long. Anna shrugs again. 'We will need you to come in and give us as much of a medical history as you can.' Anna blanches. 'Not right away of course, but the sooner the better, so we can best assess his care. We appreciate this is all a lot to take in.'

There is an awkward cough from the doorway. An overweight detective stands there. He looks like he's slept in his clothes. He extends a hand.

'Detective Inspector Pat Quinn,' he says. 'I am here to have a chat with the children.' He seems to notice the way she stares at his crumpled clothes, unwashed hair. 'Busy night.' He smiles then sees she could misunderstand. 'On another job, got some extra guys coming in to help, might get back to my flat before I completely forget what it looks like.' He laughs. A sound that's loud in the silence of the kitchen. Anna says she wants to stay while Detective Inspector Pat Quinn speaks to her children. He says this is fine. He needs to speak with them separately. Eventually Anna allows the possible head of psychiatry to take Louise upstairs. Louise doesn't seem to hear her, doesn't seem to care.

Quinn sits opposite Harry and smiles. Harry looks up at him.

'Who hurt your neck Harry?' says Quinn. Straight to the point.

'The Nosferatu,' says Harry. Anna sees Quinn's shoulders sag. She wants to get up and make him a cup of coffee. She should have offered him a cup of coffee before they began. He's on her side. He's come here to speak to Harry rather than drag them to the station. For now.

'The Nosferatu?' Quinn repeats. Harry nods. 'And who do you think the Nosferatu is Harry?'

'The man across the road. He's not a man, he's a Nosferatu.' Harry twists, points to the front door.

'And he was here yesterday? It was him that hurt you?'

'Yes.' Harry's head bobs up and down. Quinn sits back slowly.

'Do you remember your mum arriving home, Harry?' Harry

nods, gives Anna a weak smile. 'The thing is Harry, when your mum arrived home, there was only you, your sister and your dad here.' Harry's brow furrows.

'That's because he heard a noise and flew away,' says Harry.

'Flew away?' says Quinn. No malice in his voice. Harry nods. 'Or,' Quinn speaks slowly, softly, 'is it because, really, there was no one else here?'

'He was here,' says Harry. He starts to look distressed. 'He was here, but it's okay, my dad is brave, my dad is going to kill him and then we will all be safe.' Anna looks away.

'The thing is I've spoken to the man across the street Harry. Mr Kier Finnegan, and he said he wasn't here, he was at work.'

'He can't have been.'

'Harry, did someone else do this to you?' Quinn gestures to the angry finger prints on Harry's throat. Harry keeps shaking his head. His breath gets shorter, 'Harry, did your dad do this to you?'

'No!' Harry shouts. 'No, no, no.'

'Did your dad do this to you and say not to tell anyone, to say it was the man across the street?'

'No!' Harry shouts again, runs from the room. Anna and Quinn both rise. How has she let it get this far?

'I'm so sorry,' says Anna.

'Not at all,' says Quinn. 'He's a kid. He's in shock. Give him a bit of time to calm down and we'll try again.' He places a hand on her shoulder. 'It's okay. Honestly.' They both know it isn't okay. It's very far from okay.

It's a few days later that Detective Inspector Pat Quinn calls her from a withheld number. They've already been to the station, given their official statements. Harry said over and over again it was the Nosferatu. Anna looks at the child psychologist's business card tacked onto the fridge.

Quinn calls to tell her the line of questioning involving Rhys and the murder of a young girl is being closed. Not because Rhys is mental, he laughs then, ignorant to the offence caused, but because Rhys is innocent. They've found a body in an old cottage, a young man who killed himself. There was a blood-covered strand of the murdered girl's hair at the scene. Quinn explains how they analysed it. Anna doesn't understand or care. They found the young man's DNA on the girl's body. Open and shut really, according to Detective Inspector Quinn. There's no joy in his voice. There's no explanation of how Rhys's identification was found with the girl. No apology.

Quinn also tells her they've cracked the serial killer case Rhys was working on. It turns out it was the same young man. The cottage his body was found in contained jars of all of his female victim's blood. Looks like he was removing it from the scene and keeping it. Anna is numb. Quinn says more about DNA but Anna doesn't hear the words, not really. The post-mortem of the young man's body found traces of the most recent victims' blood in his stomach. Quinn laughs without humour. Says when she next sees Rhys she will have to tell him.

'A Nosferatu of sorts, eh?' Quinn says. 'As near as sane people think we'll get.'

Anna hangs up the phone.

She has no idea when she will see Rhys. It won't be for a very long time.

She cries then, cries until she has no tears left.

75.

The bright strip lights flash overhead in time with his heartbeat. Rhys doesn't understand why they feel the need to strap him to the bed. Possibly because he fights them when they try to give him drugs. He doesn't need drugs. He will go as far as to say drugs are the very last thing he needs. They freeze his mind. Slow everything down. How is he supposed to think, come up with a plan, if they keep on freezing his mind?

The small white room floats in and out of focus. One of the overhead strip lights flickers, the way they do when a bulb needs changing. Nurses come in and out. They prod and poke him. He finds it harder and harder to stay awake. They ask him if he would like any dinner. He says he isn't hungry. That's okay for now, but he will have to eat tomorrow if he wants to keep strong and get well. They speak to him like he is a child or has mental health issues.

The sound of the door as it opens again pulls his attention. The figures are just fuzzy outlines. The nurse laughs, says,

'Thank you, doctor.' The door closes and they are alone.

'Rhys. Rhys. Rhys.' The face is fuzzy but the clear, sharp voice stops Rhys's heart. He tries to pull his senses together. Too difficult. He is drowning. 'That was a very mean trick you tried to pull back there at the house. Very mean indeed.'

How is this even possible? He can't breathe.

Rhys blinks rapidly. Tries to clear his vision. Kier's face looms above him.

'I like to believe it's what will keep our friendship exciting, a little bit of tussle here and there.'

Rhys tries to call out. There are no words. The drugs have trapped them deep inside. Has he even moved his lips?

'However,' Kier's fuzzy outline raises its hands in an upward gesture, 'if my memory serves me right you did definitely ask.'

Rhys tries to move. Come on arms. Goddamn it!

Move! Move! Move!

His muscles should be tense. They've not moved at all.

'And once you have said it, I'm afraid you can't take it back, and this,' Kier spins, pirouettes in glee, 'just makes it all so very easy.'

Shit.

No.

Focus Rhys.

Do something.

Think of something.

Kier leans in close. Rhys knows he should feel the cold rush from Kier's skin but feels nothing. 'So very, very easy.' Kier's voice is barely a whisper.

In his mind's eye, Rhys throws back his head and screams.

He feels the skin of his throat puncture with two rods of ice-cold steel.

Electricity shoots through his body.

The edges of his vision start to blur.

The ground falls away beneath him. The wind roars all around.

The flickering light flashes. Black to white to black.

A brilliant white beam sears into the back of his eyeball.

Then everything goes black.